Whiteness and Trauma

Whiteness and Trauma

The Mother–Daughter Knot in the Fiction of Jean Rhys, Jamaica Kincaid and Toni Morrison

Victoria Burrows

First published 2004 by
PALGRAVE MACMILLAN
Houndmills, Basingstoke, Hampshire RG21 6XS and
175 Fifth Avenue, New York, N.Y. 10010
Companies and representatives throughout the world

PALGRAVE MACMILLAN is the global academic imprint of the Palgrave Macmillan division of St. Martin's Press, LLC and of Palgrave Macmillan Ltd. Macmillan® is a registered trademark in the United States, United Kingdom and other countries. Palgrave is a registered trademark in the European Union and other countries.

ISBN 1–4039–2198–9 (HB)

This book is printed on paper suitable for recycling and made from fully managed and sustained forest sources.

A catalogue record for this book is available from the British Library.

Library of Congress Cataloging-in-Publication Data

Burrows, Victoria, 1951–
   Whiteness and trauma : the mother–daughter knot in the fiction of Jean Rhys, Jamaica Kincaid, and Toni Morrison / Victoria Burrows.
      p.   cm.
   Includes bibliographical references (p.) and index.
   ISBN 1-4039-2198-9
   1. Caribbean fiction (English) – Women authors – History and criticism.   2. Women and literature – Caribbean Area – History – 20th century.   3. Women and literature – United States – History – 20th century.   4. Mothers and daughters in literature.   5. Rhys, Jean. Wide Sargasso Sea.   6. Human skin color in literature.   7. Psychic trauma in literature.   8. Kincaid, Jamaica, Lucy.   9. Morrison, Toni. Sula.   10. Whites in literature.   11. Race in literature.   I. Title.

PR9205.4.B87 2004
813'.540935252 – dc22   2003060958

10   9   8   7   6   5   4
13   12   11   10   09   08   07   06

Printed and bound in Great Britain by
Antony Rowe Ltd, Chippenham and Eastbourne

For my mother, Fan;
for my children, Lucia, Tansy and Joshua;
and for Gail, who made this possible

Contents

Acknowledgements

I wish to thank my colleagues in the Department of English, Communication and Cultural Studies at the University of Western Australia for their great support during the long gestation of this book, which grew out of my doctoral thesis undertaken in the department. In particular, I want to acknowledge with deep-felt gratitude the inestimable intellectual mentoring and personal affirmation that Gail Jones provided during this time, and also the wonderful help that Judy Skene so willingly gifted with her eagle-eyed proofreading.

I would also like to express appreciation to Professor Cheryl Wall, Professor Linda Anderson and Dr Sara Ahmed who marked my thesis. Despite their heavy commitments, each provided detailed close readings of my work and these were very important to the reshaping of the text for publication. In relation to the book's publication, I thank Emily Rosser and Paula Kennedy of Palgrave Macmillan who have both been exceptionally helpful, friendly and supportive, and Sally Daniell for her immaculate copy-editing.

I am lucky enough to have a group of wonderful friends who have kept me going with their love and emotional nurturance over the years and I would now like to acknowledge and thank them for all they have done for me: Delys Bird, Diane Burrows, Melanie Cariss, Trish Crawford, Tanya Dalziell, Harriet Einsiedel, Hilary Fraser, Gail Jones, Prue Kerr, Judy Johnston, Tin Yi Loh, Sue Midalia, Heather Mutch, Sue Ramsay, Joan Shellien and Judy Skene. I would not have made it without you all.

Finally, I thank my family, especially my mother and my three children, but also my brothers and their families, my aunt and my cousin, Emily, all of whom I love very much. Each of them, in different ways, gave me the strength to continue.

Introduction: Unravelling the Knot

I Laying out the strands

> teach me to survive my
> momma
> teach me how to hold a new life
> momma
> help me
> turn the face of history
> *to your face.*
>
> June Jordan[1]

I open by asking my readers to imagine a densely threaded knot, one loosely entangled so that three-dimensional spaces are visible between the looped strands. This visual image has a double purpose. On one hand, the knot suggests both the dense complexity and relational circuitry of the mother–daughter relationship which comprises separate subjectivities that are loosely tied together, bodily and psychically. These subjectivities are interwoven and intertangled with one another, joined but separate, the same and *other*, ambivalently fused by a sense of difference and commonality. On the other hand, the metaphor implies that there are untapped imaginative and theoretical spaces that can be brought into being when constitutive threads are unwound and re-configured. Thus the visual power of the metaphor evokes the passionate, ambivalent strength and changing dimensions of the mother–daughter bond, as well as being suggestive of the relational politics, both theoretical and personal, that are made possible by applying a metaphorical perspective. I employ feminist readings of three texts, Jean Rhys's *Wide Sargasso Sea*, Jamaica Kincaid's *Lucy* and Toni

Morrison's *Sula*. These novels provide the literary grounding for my argument, which proposes to interweave trauma and whiteness theories through the already existing strands of race, gender and, to a lesser extent, issues of class. The historical contexts that together both bind and separate the mother–daughter relationships in these novels are also crucial to my discussion.

I shall argue that the application of the metaphorical logic of the knot contributes substantially to the disruption of a range of prescriptive binaries, particularly those connected to gendered and raced power differentials. As is becoming increasingly clear, dismantling a binary is much more complicated than moving hierarchies up or down, which is why the interwoven complexity of the knot structure with its overlapping, entwining strands is particularly useful. A knot can be disentangled and re-knotted in different figurations while the central thread holds firm. Clifford Ashley describes the possibilities evocatively:

> The simple act of tying a knot is an adventure in unlimited space. A bit of string affords a dimensional latitude that is unique among the entities. For an uncomplicated strand is a palpable object, that for all practical purposes, possesses one dimension only. If we move a single strand in a plane, interlacing it at will, actual objects of beauty and utility can result in what is practically two dimensions; and if we choose to direct our strand out of this one plane, another dimension is added which provides opportunity for an excursion that is limited only by the scope of our imagery and the length of the ropemaker's coil.[2]

As knots can be untied and re-tied, they are not only processual and dynamic but their structuring is also relational and ambivalent. They can be knots of strength that hold things together, or snarls and obstructions that impede or hinder, or even both at once. Knots bind one to one's own history – individual and collective – but the unravelling process provides a means of analysing historical, socio-cultural and maternal genealogies that shape female subjectivity, a positionality always multiply mediated through the axes of race and class as well as gender.

However, in order to theorise the mother–daughter relationship, feminist scholars have to remain very aware of two potentially disabling problems. Firstly, we risk the danger of valorising mutual bonding, nurturing, reciprocity and intersubjective empathy, while omitting the fact that this relationship is often infused not just with love, joy and sharing of identities, but also aggression, ambivalence and even hate. As Sara Ruddick states in her essay, 'Maternal Thinking': 'What we are pleased to call "mother-love" is intermixed with hate, sorrow, impatience, resentment and despair; thought-provoking ambivalence is a hall-mark of mothering.'[3] Indeed, it can be argued that the mother–daughter dynamic is the most ambivalent of all woman-to-woman relationships. I am therefore going to interconnect the idea of the trope of ambivalence as a reading strategy to that of the mother–daughter relation as an essentially ambivalent alliance.

The second, and more worrying, dilemma concerning theorising the mother–daughter relationship is that while Western feminists have enriched ways of thinking about sexual difference and subjectivity in the context of the mother–daughter dynamic – to the extent that Rosi Braidotti sees 'the mother–daughter image ... [as] a new paradigm in feminist thought' – exclusionary mechanisms exist when such theories are universalised by taking white women's experiences and ideas as normative.[4] The mother–daughter relationship is always already embedded in a socio-cultural and racialised context, and yet in general, white feminists have failed sufficiently to recognise race and class as differentials in mothering experiences. For instance, Nancy Chodorow's pathbreaking book, *The Reproduction of Mothering*, remains one of the most influential and most-quoted texts that has framed, and continues to frame, the predominant theories in feminist discourse on mothering.[5] Yet, Patricia Hill Collins stresses that Chodorow's text also 'exemplifies how decontextualisation of race and/or class can weaken what is otherwise strong feminist theorising'.[6] In her important essay, 'Shifting the Center: Race, Class, and Feminist Theorizing About Motherhood', Hill Collins argues that non-white mothers frequently experience different forms of relationship with their daughters as a result of factors that range from poverty and racism to the structural injustices of workplace practices, and therefore apply different theoretical insights and new angles of vision to their mother–daughter experiences and practices.[7] However, these are excluded from feminist theorising that relies solely on white middle-class women's experiences and analyses of gender differences that are falsely separated from issues of race. As long as white feminist theorising of motherhood continues to emphasise the themes of gender and sexual difference, it can only reaffirm white domination of theory, and obscure the racial domination that often accompanies white-skin privilege in material life.

My title is in a sense borrowed from a combination of Jane Lazarre's early feminist text about her relationship to her son, entitled *The Mother*

Knot[8] and Marianne Hirsch's *The Mother/Daughter Plot*.[9] However, while my theoretical background began with white feminist texts on the mother–daughter relationship, I aim to start where Hirsch ended by stressing the need to concentrate on the contradictions and ambivalences of the mother–daughter relationship to which she gestures in the conclusion of her work.[10] Even more importantly, I shall address the problematics of racial exclusion in feminist theory by applying a whiteness reading both to the theory I utilise and the three novels under examination. Indeed, I hope that by introducing a critical focus and strong critique of whiteness – the position from which I write – that I will earn the right to participate in an inter-racial dialogue, the aim of which is to disassemble historical, social and racial injustices with the hope that laying issues bare can help bring about transformation and change.

The knot metaphor has been used previously by other feminists. For instance, Gayatri Spivak employs the image to suggest the multiplicity of contradictions that occur when the subject-in-process is bound within the complex entanglement of race, class and gender in her description of the subaltern subject effect.[11] Diana Fuss uses a knot in her edited anthology of lesbian and gay scholarship – both as a figurative representation on the cover and as a theoretical metaphor[12] – and Susan Rubin Suleiman evokes it to signal the entanglements that surround the multiple forms and representations of love.[13] Both Fuss and Suleiman acknowledge their debt to Lacan, as does Elizabeth Grosz, who refashions his associated symbolisation of the Möbius strip.[14] However, while similar in methodological implications, the knot is significantly different from the Möbius strip because, as already stated, it is open-ended and therefore available both to re-knotting and the amalgamation of different re-threadings. The knot metaphor avoids the fixity of closure for the ends are not necessarily tied inextricably to anything else.

Grosz evokes the image of the Möbius strip – an inverted three-dimensional figure eight – in order to theorise an embodied feminist subjectivity that is constituted by 'the inflection of mind into body and body into mind, and the ways in which, through a kind of twisting or inversion, one side becomes another'.[15] Interestingly, Grosz's subject is corporeal feminism, and yet in her theory of differentiated bodies, despite her statement that '[e]very body is marked by the history and specificity of its existence',[16] the body as marker of race becomes merely a rhetorical disclaimer. This is the only moment in Grosz's book which refers to the racialisation of corporeal experience, and represents one example of the sort of white feminist exclusion that I aim to disavow. In a chapter entitled, 'The Body as Inscriptive Surface' Grosz states:

> The more or less permanent etching of even the civilized body by discursive systems is perhaps easier to read if the civilized body is decontextualised, stripped of clothing and adornment, behaviorally displayed in its nakedness. The naked European/American/African/Asian/Australian body (and clearly even within these categories there is enormous cultural variation) is still marked by its disciplinary history, by its habitual patterns of movement, by the corporeal commitments it has undertaken in its day-to-day life. It is in no sense a natural body, for it is culturally, racially, sexually, possibly even as class distinctive, as it would be if it were clothed.[17]

Sara Ahmed, commenting on this paragraph, contends that Grosz introduces race as a signifier of difference merely as an illustrative point to authenticate her argument that there is no natural body as such, that it is always 'clothed' by cultural prescriptions.[18] As Ahmed continues, '[t]his metaphoric reliance on race to signify the differentiated body has quite clear theoretical and political implications'.[19] Naked or not, it is the colour of a person's skin which to a large extent positions every body in the social system of constitutive meaning.[20] Aside from the problematics of referring to the 'civilized' body without explication in a passage that includes the image of the naked African body – when the inhumanity of slavery grew out of the binarised logic of free white bodies held in radical contra-distinction to the enslaved African black body – the exchange of clothing for skin colour as cultural signifier continues to eradicate the ever-pervasive power structure and domination of unacknowledged whiteness. As Ahmed states: 'Race becomes a means by which Grosz illustrates a philosophical shift in thinking about bodies. It appears (and also disappears) as a *figure* for the differentiated body'.[21] What is missing – what disappears under the figurative displacement – is the whole history that underwrites the dichotomising of racial bodies in the socio-political order of what became known as the New World.[22]

I carefully chose the novels *Wide Sargasso Sea*, *Lucy* and *Sula* because each, in completely different ways, illustrates mother–daughter relationships that are imbricated in either the historical specificity of the New World and its politics of slavery, or its traumatising legacies. All three texts incorporate the powerful dynamics of figurative language and the logic of metaphor that on one hand politicises gender, yet on the other veers between distanciation from the social injustices of racial meaning (*Wide Sargasso Sea*), to an ambivalent complicity yet gradual resistance to imperialist ideologies (*Lucy*), and finally, to a rewriting of black history through what Toni Morrison calls the 'gift for metaphor' (*Sula*). The painful mother–daughter dyad in Kincaid's novel is knotted around the ambivalent effects of colonial education, as represented by the enchanted space of Western literature, while the mother–daughter relationships in Rhys's novel, and to a much greater extent in Morrison's *Sula*, circulate around the metaphor of veiling and unveiling in relation to the iconography of clothing as a means of exposing what Ahmed describes as the 'encounter' with the racial body.[23] Indeed, metaphors of clothing and needlework are very much one of Morrison's lyrical trademarks, as evidenced by her Nobel Prize acceptance speech in which she pronounced: 'Don't tell us what to believe, what to fear. Show us belief's wide skirt and the stitch that unravels fear's caul'.[24] However, while there is a trope in Western philosophy of the 'unconcealing of being' (termed *aletheia*), that suggests the exposure inherent in an unveiling or unmasking which lays bare a hidden inner core,[25] my reading of the trope of unveiling is indebted to the work of feminist theoreticians and literary critics such as Ann duCille, Sara Ahmed, Karla Holloway and Toni Morrison and the whole tropological symbolisation of masking and unmasking, veiling and unveiling in Black English that grew out of and in resistance to the dehumanisation of racialised slavery in the plantations of the New World.

In her monograph, *Strange Encounters*, Sara Ahmed explores the interlinked notions of strangers, embodiment and the concept of community in the contemporary Western world from a feminist and postcolonial perspective. Central to her argument is the term 'encounter', which 'suggests a meeting, but a meeting which involves surprise or conflict'.[26] Ahmed's chapter entitled 'Embodying strangers', from which I took her discussion of Elizabeth Grosz's passage on corporeal feminism, begins with an example of a distressing racial encounter that happened to Audre Lorde as a child on the New York subway.[27] As a result of this incident, in which her small black body was pinned down by the traumatic impact of the white gaze reading her body as repulsive, Lorde began to query both the construction and the meaning of racial hatred. Karla Holloway, also tells of similar encounters experienced by herself and her friends, and in her *Codes of Conduct: Race, Ethics, and the Color of Our Character* she argues that black women have to be aware of the stereotypes that code their bodies because the trauma imposed by racism and sexism often materialises as a 'disfiguring assault' in the form of a gaze of prejudice.[28] She continues:

> As varied as our stories are, it seems that at some point African American women are forced into a confrontation with the confounding physical reality our bodies represent. *This moment of facing* is so critical to our psyches, and so frequently rehearsed in our everyday lives, that unless we have a response (like 'turning it out') ritualized into the patterns of our daily lives, we are likely to find ourselves [crucially] underprepared.[29]

As I understand it, 'turning it out' means speaking out or answering back in defiance of an authority figure who has demeaned a black woman in racist and/or sexist terms. Holloway quotes Lorene Cary's depiction of turning it out as 'not a matter of style; cold indignation worked as well as hot fury. Turning it out had to do with will.'[30] In the examples I have read, turning it out is a communal experience, in the sense that the women who describe it have always been in the company of another woman, often a mother and her daughter.[31] However, resistance is not always possible, as Morrison demonstrates in a very painful scene in *Sula*, when a black woman accompanied by her ten-year-old daughter is faced with a moment of racial exposure that forces her into a position of abject humiliation. Because she has so distanced herself from her maternal heritage, Helene Wright can no longer turn it out. However, many years later, the daughter, now in her fifties, begins the process of what is both an individual and communal reclaiming of her lost history.

I mention the trauma of the embodied racial encounter in association with the concept of voicing resistance because my aim is to bring these two notions together in my last chapter on Morrison's novel *Sula*. But I have also focused on reading the black (female) body at length for two reasons: to set up my future argument and to place my credentials on the table, as it were, for writing as I do from the position of a white feminist, I feel hesitant that I may be appropriating black feminist work as a means, however unconsciously invoked, of gaining access to some kind of higher moral position to which I have no right, and to which I am in no way seeking access. Valerie Smith draws attention to the fact that white feminists' continual association of black women with embodiment and ' "the material" seems conceptually problematic' because of its earlier connections to white women's complicity in constructions of black womanhood,[32] and there is ample evidence of white feminists 'using' the black female body as example and then moving on, or back, to universalistic theories of woman.[33] In the section on whiteness later on in the introduction I shall delve more deeply into the power politics of positioning, but for the moment I want to say that I am both mindful of the problem of appropriation while simultaneously believing that retreating into either white disavowal or intellectual paralysis is not helpful to the problems that surround the politics of difference in feminist theory.

Part of my unravelling process is to examine the role of metaphor as an aesthetic mode of figuration that can both oppress and liberate, and in particular its scope in what Holloway describes as '[t]he colonizing habit of linguistic dominance' which affects, she contends, both the psyche and the spirit.[34] In a witty analogy, Patricia Williams exposes the impact of conscious and unconscious ideological whitewashing that contributes to the erasure of black subjectivity in the conclusion to one of her 1997 Reith Lectures, 'The War Between the Worlds':

> I sit at my desk, I am writing this lecture. I reach for a little bottle of a correctional fluid called White-out, I start brushing it over the last few sentences. My fingers start to dissolve. In seconds, my index finger and the little finger of my right hand are almost completely melted away, to the knuckle, and the others are down to the first joint. There is no pain; I just watch them disappear quietly, quickly, as though they were no longer part of me. It is the subtlest of sensations.[35]

Williams gave five lectures on the topic of racism, concentrating on the 'small aggressions of unconscious racism, rather than the big-booted oppressions of bigotry'.[36] She asks: 'How precisely does the issue of colour remain so powerfully determinative of everything from life circumstance to manner of death, in a world that is, by and large, officially "colour-blind"?'[37] Further, '[w]hat metaphors mask the hierarchies that make racial domination frequently seem so "natural", so invisible, indeed so attractive?'[38] These are some of the questions I seek to answer.

II The mother–daughter dyad, ambivalence and whiteness

> [T]he racially fractured mother–child relationship is the site at which we glimpse the *wounds of history*[39]

Each of the three novels delineates a mother–daughter relationship or relationships damaged by both racial and gender positioning at a particular moment in history. The mother–daughter knot, always entangled by its relationship to patriarchal oppression, racial and class domination and the exploitation inherent in white capitalist society, can never be separated from its own historicity. Rhys's text, with which I begin, has a strangely doubled history. It is an imaginative reconstruction of the unknown life of Bertha Mason – the madwoman in the attic of Charlotte Brontë's *Jane Eyre* – and as such would seem to exemplify a revisionary postcolonial de-scribing of empire. Like Judith Raiskin, I want to underscore Rhys's theoretical and imaginative contribution to contemporary postcolonial theory and culture in her novel *Wide Sargasso Sea*, as she depicts the social and psychological fracturing that accompanied the mid-nineteenth-century dismantling of the British Empire on the Caribbean island of Jamaica.[40] However, while Rhys's focus on the tortured relationship between a white creole mother and daughter provides a poignant analysis of the ambivalent complexities of white-on-white racism, her mobilisation of a trauma narrative to explain the construction of Bertha's madness conceals the far greater traumatic historical conditions of enslaved African-Caribbeans. Indeed, Rhys's novel subtly ensures that the wounds of black history are covered over by her appropriation of the historical concept of *marronage*, or marooning, which signifies the revolutionary activity central to the Caribbean in which runaway slaves fled their enslavement to the inhospitable mountains, from whence they fought back against the white plantocracy, often with great success.[41] In *Wide Sargasso Sea* marronage becomes a metaphor ideologically appropriated to represent both the intersubjective politics of a fraught mother–daughter relationship and the abandonment of white creole colonials by the 'mother-country'.

My second section, on Jamaica Kincaid's *Lucy*, radiates out from the first, interweaving, echoing and extending what has gone before. I have based my argument around the metaphor of 'creative marronage', a term that grows out of historical marronage, as I shall explain. In Édouard Glissant's *Poetics of Relation*, his translator, Betsy Wing, argues that Glissant 'sees imagination as the force that can change mentalities; relation as the process of this change; and poetics as a transformative mode of history'.[42] In his poetic theoretical paradigm, the physical rebellion of the maroon fugitives (*historical marronage*) 'intensified over time to exert a *creative marronage* whose numerous forms of expression began to form the basis for a [resisting imaginative] continuity'.[43] The Caribbean, as far as Glissant is concerned, 'may be held up as one of the places in the world where Relation presents itself most visibly, one of the explosive regions where it seems to be gathering strength'.[44] It is through regaining the empowerment of a heritage of both historical and creative or imaginative marronage that Kincaid's protagonist, Lucy, is finally able to turn the face of imperial history around and reconnect with her maternal history, reflected, as it were, in her mother's face.

In the context of postcolonial theory, fictionalised mother–daughter relationships also provide an important space for a critical re-reading of the familiar colonial trope of the family and its tensions allegorised as the nation, and imperial powers as mothers of their colonised children.[45] This is the case in both *Wide Sargasso Sea* and *Lucy*, but with the tropes reversed. By analogy, the white creole mother–daughter relationship in Rhys's novel is represented as colonial daughter/island deserted by the 'mother' England. In Kincaid's novel, the young black protagonist leaves her Caribbean island when she is 17 partly to escape her mother's Anglophilic tendencies. Interestingly, the daughter in both these novels has a surrogate, or other-mother, from another race, to whom each of them becomes inordinately but ambivalently attached. Both texts take place largely in a white world. The third novel, Morrison's *Sula*, almost entirely excludes any white presence, and delineates the results of mother–daughter relationships irreversibly damaged by the racism and poverty crucial to the implementation of slavery in the United States. Audre Lorde speaks openly and with pain of the impact of America's racist white society on her relationship with her mother in a passage that has great resonance for the mother–daughter relationships in *Sula*:

> My mother taught me to survive from a very early age by her own example. Her silences also taught me isolation, fury, mistrust, self-rejection, and sadness. My survival lay in learning how to use the weapons she gave me, also, to fight against those things within myself, unnamed.
>
> And *survival is the greatest gift of love*. Sometimes, for Black mothers, it is the only gift possible, and tenderness gets lost. My mother bore me into life as if etching an angry message into marble. Yet I survived the hatred around me because my mother made me know, by oblique reference, that no matter what went on at home, outside shouldn't oughta be the way it was.[46]

I have brought these three texts together, one by a white author and two by women-of-color, all of which register traumatised mother–daughter relationships, in order to explicate the way history can wound and incapacitate, and will continue to do so if we do not critique 'the way it was'. This history must include not just a critique of the socio-historical context of the fiction about which literary critics write, but also of the continuing domination of whiteness in feminist theory and the ways in which marginalised feminist 'others' continue to be excluded despite the much lauded tactics of inclusivity that were thought to accompany the politics of difference. As Michele Wallace argues, '[b]lack women writers and critics are routinely kept from having an impact on how the fields of literature and literary criticism are defined and applied'.[47] This results in the edging out of women-of-color from the production and shaping of feminist knowledges.

While needing to be wary of the dangers of a politics of coalition as an excuse to slide back into the exclusionary practices that accompanied the familial metaphor of universal sisterhood, I want to explore a new approach to the possibilities of reforming a feminist solidarity not predicated on an implicit reliance on the binaries of differences. I believe that a *deliberate* (and therefore open) use of a trope or figure of thought which involves turns or conversions in thinking can help disrupt the logic of dichotomies which has played its part in the divisive practices inherent in the notion of universal sisterhood and the collectivity of woman. I offer the possibility that *ambivalence* is a great unrecognised dynamic in feminist theory. While it may not be immediately apparent why anything as tendentious as ambivalence could have any form of heuristic power, it is necessary to look at its source. The negative implications of ambivalence in fact stem from its use in positivist psychology and psychiatry where it is conceptualised as a situation in which a person overwhelmingly experiences a simultaneity of both negative and positive emotions towards a person, persons, object or action, and is unable to *choose* between these opposed attitudes, feelings or sets of values, thereby creating a source of undesirable stress, anxiety, irresolution or inertia. In its extreme form unresolved ambivalence is regarded as one of the four cardinal symptoms of schizophrenia.[48] However, just because ambivalence has been pathologised it does not necessarily entail that a choice *has to be* made. The term merely signifies that a person can experience intense oppositional emotions that co-exist and can remain in fluctuating opposition to each other. Perhaps ambivalence itself is not the problem. Maybe the difficulty lies more in the position of positivist science in the binary framework of Western thought, which disavows the existence of intrinsically contradictory ideas, emotions or wishes because they transgress and disrupt apparently mutually exclusive polar opposites that idealise fixity and closure. This inheritance has been transposed into common linguistic use, and it is this legacy that deems ambivalence a negative emotion. However, needless to say, such a position also encourages a subversive feminist (re)reading of ambivalence as a creative model of circuitry that breaks down prescriptive polarities.

One way of re-signifying a term that is made up of both negative *and* positive elements is to deconstruct and reconfigure its creative potential. Its synonyms include equivocalness, ambiguity and contrariety which, together with ambivalence, all suggest doubleness and an ability to think and negotiate between two voices, and thus an openness to interpretation and constant re-evaluation; and the potential of tolerating contradictions and uncertainties in diacritical opposition. Thus, ambivalence is not a static state, but a dynamic *process* that holds within it an ability to entertain dual perspectives. Indeed, to be capable of ambivalence is to be able to sustain the paradox without falling permanently to one pole or the other.[49] Ambivalence, then, is radically anti-polar and disruptive of binary oppositions because it transgresses and blurs the very boundaries these oppositions create by suspending the choices they imply or dictate. Read in this way as a positive force, the trope of ambivalence provides a way of seeing contradictions, tensions and differences as creative strengths. Above all, it is a relational state, that if analysed and thought through, can energise a linguistic and mental shift towards intersubjective and overlapping thinking. In other words, the use of ambivalence as a strategic trope within feminist theory could perhaps provide one small intermediary rhetorical space in which to meet across difference.

Thus the mother–daughter knot of my subtitle is bound up with both literary representations of the emotional depth and ambivalent intensity of the mother–daughter dyad *and* an attempt to re-theorise what have come to be seen as impossible contradictions in feminist epistemologies of race. In response to an article by Deborah McDowell that addresses, among other issues, the liberating possibilities of ambivalence in Morrison's novel *Sula*, Hortense Spillers speaks of the need 'to articulate the *spaces* of contradiction' in order to move beyond being '*arrested in a stage of ambivalence*'.[50] I would therefore like to acknowledge that it was from reading this short article by Spillers that I was able to extend my attempts to rethink the positive dynamics inherent in the concept of ambivalence. In any case it seems that ambivalence has always been a part of African-American life and its politics of resistance: it is in evidence in W.E.B. Du Bois's theory of double-consciousness as a form of socialised ambivalence to which I shall refer later, as it is in Geneva Smitherman's more contemporary reading of this experience as the 'push–pull syndrome . . . that is *pushing* toward White American culture while simultaneously *pulling* away from it'.[51] Ambivalence is also one of the most important tropes in postcolonial theory, adapted from psychoanalytic theory by Homi Bhabha to suggest the simultaneous complicity and resistance that exists in the fluctuating relation between the coloniser and the colonised subject.[52] Anne McClintock admonishes Bhabha for his reinscription of both ambivalence and mimicry as male strategies, and importantly, also problematises what she sees as his insistence on the 'transhistorical ubiquity of ambivalence'.[53] I shall therefore expand and diversify the concept in a range of ways, attending to historical and cultural specificity. Firstly, by reading the trope through mother–daughter narratives, the issue of gender will be of paramount importance; secondly, by historicising and contextualising the concept and using a materialist feminist approach, I hope to lessen the gap between discursive ambivalence and its lived experiences; thirdly, by underwriting my methodology by constantly interrogating issues concerning the unwritten ambivalence of whiteness, I hope to offer a new way of beginning to map the diversity and energy of feminism as we move through the first decade of the twenty-first century.

Ambivalence does not mean lack of direction or apolitical abstraction. I believe that there is something very politically enabling about the revelation of contradiction and ambivalence. Both can be politicised, located, gendered and given a history. As a heuristic reading strategy that belongs to the heritage of deconstruction, ambivalence is particularly easily transferred to the wider frame of a race-cognisant feminist politics. Indeed, Wahneema Lubiano talks about reading (as a first year graduate student at Howard University) C.L.R. James, Frantz Fanon and Aimé Césaire and the theories of language in which Black Aesthetic critics engaged, and then discovering poststructuralist theories, principally in the work of Jacques Derrida and Roland Barthes: 'Deconstruction . . . seemed to me to be an extension (within the dominant discourse) of the project of those already engaged in Afro-American or Black Studies – the project of theorizing about difference, absences, presences, and oppositionality. My response to the cultural studies discourse has been much the same.'[54] Acknowledging the reality of the possibilities of holding contradictory views without constantly striving for their eradication offers the potential for a shift in terms and a relational politics that holds within it explicit – rather than implicit – tensions that can then become productive. This is important in a context in which Cheryl Wall argues that for black women to make their 'positionality explicit is not to claim a "privileged" status for our positions ... Making our positionality explicit is, rather, a response to the false universalism that long defined critical practice and rendered black women and their writing mute.'[55] It is in relation to this white-enforced 'muteness' that I hesitantly offer my interpretation.

Avtar Brah maintains that 'categories such as "black feminism" and "white feminism" are best seen as non-essentialist, historically contingent, relational discursive practices, rather than fixed sets of positionalities'.[56] To move into a new discursive realm that remains aware of the long-standing existence of paralysing ethnocentrism in feminist theories and politics also necessitates a study of the enactment of power and ideologies that are also relational but often concealed under a cloak of whiteness.[57] As Toni Morrison attests in *Playing in the Dark*: 'The world does not become raceless or will not become unracialized by assertion. The act of enforcing racelessness in literary discourse is itself a racial act.'[58] Morrison's literary heritage emanates, as she frequently stresses, from the Black English oral tradition, in which, as Yvonne Atkinson makes clear, 'the surface meaning of words is rarely the complete meaning. Definitions of words and word usage are derived from the Black English oral tradition of linguistic reversal, using negative terms with positive meanings as well as contextual meaning, a practice of exchanging or masking one linguistic process with another language.'[59] Indeed, it is Morrison's writing – both fictional and critical – that drew my attention to the political and theoretical implications of the use of metaphor, as well as its ambivalence and the importance of both its concealed *and* overt imaginative gestures:

> Race has become metaphorical – a way of referring to and disguising forces, events, classes, and expressions of social decay and economic division far more threatening to the body politic than biological 'race' ever was ... racism is as healthy today as it was during the Enlightenment. It ... has assumed a metaphorical life so completely embedded in daily discourse that it is perhaps more necessary and more on display than ever before ... I remain convinced that the metaphorical and metaphysical uses of race occupy definite places in American literature ... and ought to be a major concern of the literary scholarship that tries to know it.[60]

Morrison is also a central figure in the instigation of whiteness studies and I use both her critical writing and her fiction as central to my critique.[61] In many senses, she is the moral centre of this book.

Ruth Frankenberg was one of the first white feminists to insist on the intrinsic importance of dismantling the ubiquitous, unmarked power contained within the '"racialness" of white experience'.[62] Since then it has become a subject that is often mentioned, but it is still rare to find the theory substantially put into practice in any kind of complex reading of fiction. However, there is an ambivalence at the heart of whiteness studies itself that must be addressed at the outset. Maulana Karenga has this to say on the subject:

> The new focus on the study of Whiteness by Whites and other schol-ars engenders *ambivalence* on several levels. It immediately raises questions about its intent, methodology and effect. As a Black studies scholar, my tendency is to be ambivalent about new calls for the study of White people when the majority of the curriculum is about them and usually in the most Eurocentric and vulgarly self-congratulatory forms.[63]

The point of whiteness studies should be to fight racial prejudice and racism across the board – in the world, in the academy, in ideological representations in all its forms, and so on. It is not just a theoretical fad, but an important epistemological enterprise, the aims of which are to expose racial injustices that emanate from the invisible normativity of white privilege that structures all forms of institutionalised power in Western societies, and this certainly includes academic enterprises, fem-inist or otherwise. However, while it is true that dismantling whiteness keeps the focus where it always has been, as Karenga states, it perhaps even more problematically offers white people who feel disparaged by affirmative action, reverse discrimination policies or what is incorrectly thought of as reverse racism, an opportunity falsely to claim the posi-tion of the victim. For these reasons, my selection of novels is both fun-damentally political and aims to demonstrate that there can never be a simplified reading of whiteness. Whiteness is a concept deeply riven and interwoven with racial prejudice, gender and class privileges, and as such needs to be exposed to critical unveiling. This applies also to many theoretical paradigms, of which trauma theory is just one, as I shall go on to discuss.

I am not going to spend much time outlining the complexities of whiteness theory here in the introduction, as part of my methodology is to expose its invisibility as I provide close readings of the novels. What I do want to stress is that no part of the ideology of whiteness is benign. It always concerns domination to a greater or lesser degree. Whiteness cannot be separated from hegemony, and this is why whiteness-as-privilege *has to be* addressed.[64] Barbara Flagg maintains that, '[a]ny serious effort to dismantle white supremacy must include measures to dilute the effect of whites' dominant status, which carries with it the power to define as well as to decide'.[65] The 'power to define' carries a devastating political saliency that has resulted in acts of unspeakable suffering, such as the regime of racial slavery and continuing acts of racism and sexism. Moreover, as whiteness is a socio-historical construct with immeasurable powers it constantly shifts its power bases, both ideological and material, as it adapts to changing historical circumstances such as the abolition of slavery and the rise of independent post-colonial nations. This is why critical, historically specific readings of traumas inflicted by the many variants of the ideology of whiteness are vital to refashioning the 'burden[s] of a negated history'.[66]

III Trauma and the power of the literary text

Analogous to the rise of whiteness studies is an almost unprecedented rise in trauma theory, not only in the humanities and especially in literary criticism, but as a genre that is widespread throughout the Western societies. As a recently published academic journal outlines in its opening paragraph: 'The desire to testify now pervades contemporary culture. The imperative to speak out and tell one's story operates across the traditional boundaries of public and private spaces, and is mobilised by disenfranchised subjects and celebrities alike.'[67] However, it is my contention that trauma theory continues the disciplining of knowledge within the constrictive paradigm of normative whiteness. The twentieth century is frequently invoked as the century of trauma: it also became, as Du Bois mournfully predicted in 1903, a period in which the 'problem of the color-line' would hold devastating sway in the divisive social policies of Western nations because of the white hegemony's refusal to come to terms and work through the entangled legacies of imperialism and industrial capitalism.[68] Thus, when Ruth Leys prefaced her recently published Foucauldian-based exposition, *Trauma: A Genealogy* with two examples of contemporary trauma that were positioned within the racial paradigm, it seemed (at least initially) as if the much-needed critical amalgamation of issues of trauma and race had finally begun to have an impact on this academic discipline.[69] Leys's first example refers to an article in the *New Yorker* which describes in extraordinarily harrowing and brutal detail a tendentious example of black on black violence in Uganda.[70] Her second example concerns the sexual harassment case Paula Jones brought against President Clinton, in which her lawyers claim that as a result of Clinton's actions, 'Jones now suffers from post-traumatic stress with long term symptoms of anxiety, intrusive thoughts and memories, and sexual aversion'[71]. Leys uses these examples, both of which were reported in the American media in 1998, to illustrate the extreme diversification of issues raised by the concept of psychic trauma. At one extreme lies the indispensability of trauma theory and its practices to deal with genocidal horrors of the twentieth century, the other suggests how such theory and its praxis can become a superficial and 'debased currency'.[72]

Leys's monograph is, as the title suggests, a genealogical reading of trauma theory that begins with Freud and ends with Cathy Caruth, of whose work she is rather dismissive. My project does not involve a critique of this work, except to emphasise the limited focus of Leys's new book, a text that is premised entirely upon a Eurocentric reading solely indentured to a middle-class whiteness built on concepts of Western individualism. The notion of a genealogy sets up a claim for a breadth of vision and a comprehensive analysis of trauma history in which it would be expected that there should be a substantial exploration of racism, one of the major traumas of the twentieth century. However, the interrelation of race and trauma – the subject of the opening paragraph – is never again referred to except in a gestural nod to Freud's own naming of his 'race'.[73] Surely – and especially now we have entered the twenty-first century which is shaping up to be one of almost unimaginable racial tension and acts of repeated trauma – we need a comprehensive remapping of trauma theory that is not white-centric and gender blind.

In any event, almost every black text, fiction or theory, testifies to the 'trauma of racism' to which Toni Morrison refers, as the continuing and ever present factor in the lives of people of colour.[74] In an article delineating a feminist perspective on psychic trauma, Laura Brown observes how narrow definitions of trauma have been constructed from the experiences of dominant groups in Western culture, which means 'white, young, able-bodied, educated, middle-class, Christian, men'[75]. Brown admits to being protected by her white skin, her upper-middle class status, her education and her access to language and resources, but as a Jew and a lesbian she also deals with the small violences of the spirit that can so often accompany these subject positions in her everyday life.[76] In this essay she builds on Maria Root's concept of 'insidious trauma' that refers to the 'traumatogenic effects of oppression that are not necessarily overtly violent or threatening to bodily well-being at any given moment, but which do violence to the soul and the spirit'.[77] Such a reading applies to the experiences of any non-dominant group of society, such as racial others (anyone non-white in America), lesbians or gays, people with disability, and so on. Their psychic traumata, often outside the definitions of what is deemed traumatic to mainstream (white) society, are therefore ignored. Brown also discusses intergenerational trauma that can 'spread laterally throughout an oppressed social group as well when membership in that group means a constant lifetime risk of exposure to certain traumata',[78] a concept which is very applicable to my reading of *Sula*.

If one side of the problem within trauma studies is the erasure of race, the other is what Dominick LaCapra terms 'vicarious victimhood', whereby the oppressors take over the position of the oppressed by shifting the focus of empathetic identification back onto themselves.[79] Empathy in the arena of trauma theory means being responsive to the traumatic experiences of others and, crucially, it involves affectivity as a central aspect of attempting to understand the others' pain. However, empathetic understanding must not become conflated, as LaCapra emphatically stresses, 'with unchecked identification, vicarious experience, and surrogate victimage'.[80] Such an action not only constitutes an appropriation of the distress of others who are often in the victim position, but also obscures vital historical distinctions between aggressors and victims which more often than not are related to the power differentials that structure racial hierarchies. This is certainly the case in *Wide Sargasso Sea*. Interestingly, however, LaCapra problematises the blurring of the crucial aggressor/victim distinction by raising the issue of what he sees as the necessary differentiation between structural and historical trauma. Structural trauma concerns transhistorical absence and appears in different ways in all societies and in all lives. On the other hand, historical trauma is specific in that it relates to an event or events that are locatable in historical time.[81] This may include a 'founding trauma – the trauma that paradoxically becomes the basis for collective and/or personal identity'.[82] One such trauma LaCapra names as the historical experience of slavery. My understanding of LaCapra's concept of structural trauma is that its problematic transhistoricism on one hand arises out of readings that apply no sense of importance to the historical specificity of the traumatic experiences that are being interpreted. This is certainly often the case. However, he frequently refers to this 'transhistorical notion of trauma which is structural or in some sense originary'.[83] In what sense can trauma ever be originary? Does this mean that historical and structural trauma can be divided – like the characterisation of clinical depression which is so often associated with post-traumatic experiences – into 'reactive' trauma which occurs in response to a specific environmental and therefore historically specific loss, or, 'endogenous' trauma which occurs in the absence of such environmental/historical stress and is reputed to be the result of purely internal causes?[84]

Two problems lead on from such a reading. In the first place it is impossible to differentiate between structural and historical trauma – they are inevitably knotted together to a greater or lesser degree. Again, this is something that becomes very clear in my reading of *Wide Sargasso Sea*. The second problem is that there is no factoring in of race in LaCapra's trauma theory beyond his reference to slavery as a foundational trauma. If structural trauma contains aspects of the originary, would this not result in a reading that could not escape from a discriminatory (race-biased) essentialism? For instance, if Morrison's theory of the trauma of racism is to be taken into account, then structural trauma as it stands in LaCapra's schema would rely on a reading of essentialised black – or any non-white bodies – as the originating, innate, and therefore immutable, factor of their (necessarily embodied) trauma. Moreover, if structural trauma is to be separated out from historical trauma, all causal factors that are the result of institutionalised racism would be excised. I do not mean here to discredit LaCapra's important and extensive work on the relations between trauma and history which is fundamental in reminding us that trauma theory has a tendency to blur the categories of who are the aggressors and victims of history. Yet, until the daily occurence of racial trauma becomes an important part of trauma theory, it will be addressing neither the structural nor the historical traumas of the twentieth century, nor will it provide a viable theoretical paradigm for the twenty-first. It seems to me that his abstract working through of existential dilemmas relating to historicist readings of trauma become difficult to translate into a particularised socio-historical context.

Nevertheless, LaCapra's evocation of the Freudian theories of acting out and working through are particularly useful, provided, as he himself insists, that psychoanalytic concepts such as these are linked to economic, social and political analyses and do not become a substitute for them.[85] *Acting out* is a form of melancholia, characterised by stasis and an affective state of arrested process, in which the traumatised person or collection of people are 'caught up in the compulsive repetition of traumatic scenes – scenes in which the past returns and the future is blocked or fatalistically caught up in a melancholic feedback loop'.[86] In *Wide Sargasso Sea*, the protagonist, Antoinette Cosway, is entrapped in a melancholic state of impossible mourning. While the text suggested that the mother–daughter relationship in this novel is predicated upon structural trauma, such a reading silences the historical causes and reactive traumas that are bound up with the axiomatics of imperialism. In Kincaid's novel, *Lucy*, the protagonist is suspended in the lingering and difficult space between colonialism and postcolonialism, between acting out and working through and between melancholia and mourning. Both these novels read trauma as individualistic. In Morrison's *Sula* there are three central characters. Only one, Nel Wright, moves into a state of mourning on the final page of the novel, and importantly her catharsis evolves out of a sense of community, and here I would like to relate Morrison's evocation of a coming to terms with historical trauma with LaCapra's understanding of mourning as 'not simply . . . isolated grieving or endless bereavement but as a social process'.[87]

With the idea of *process* in mind, I turn now to the work of Cathy Caruth who is one of the most influential and exciting of contemporary trauma theorists, and as a literary critic her work is, in any case, most relevant to readings of fiction. Caruth suggests that in this age of violence and natural and technological catastrophe, trauma itself may 'provide the very link between cultures: not as a simple understanding of the pasts of others but rather, within the traumas of contemporary history, as *our ability to listen* through the departures we have all taken from ourselves'.[88] Most trauma theory is based on the psychoanalytic/psychological model, and while I use these theories as a base, my methodology concerns a materialistic cultural reading of the *effects* of trauma on those who live within a specific socio-historical and racial context. Thus my project comprises reading history and trauma as threaded one through the other, which is why LaCapra's adaptations of psychoanalytic concepts such as melancholia and mourning are particularly useful. I want to suggest that if merged with LaCapra's work Caruth's *theory of belatedness* helps to unravel some of the more complicated paradoxes of trauma theory. From Caruth's perspective: '[T]he attempt to understand trauma brings one repeatedly to this peculiar paradox: that in trauma the greatest confrontation with reality may also occur as an absolute numbing to it, that immediacy, paradoxically enough, may take the form of belatedness.'[89] Again, this is something that I shall progressively unravel in my literary explications, but here would like to draw attention to the main issues that arise from Caruth's belatedness theory. While the concept primarily invokes a psychic rupture in the form of a withholding of traumatic memory from consciousness, it has consequences for the structuring of form and style in literary texts that leads both to innovative writing and new possibilities for *working through* trauma – as will become apparent in my readings. Caruth maintains that we begin 'to hear each other anew in the study of trauma . . . because they [here she refers to the main disciplinary fields that utilise trauma theory] are *listening* through the radical disruption and gaps of traumatic experience'.[90] While this is certainly the case, I would like to extend the idea of the 'radical disruption' of belatedness into a different way of addressing the notion of postcolonialism.

Together with the psychic implications and repercussions, belatedness also entails the idea of disjuncture in historical time which raises important questions about both the periodisation of colonialism and *post*colonialism and the long-term psychic effects of this imagined closure suggested by the prefix 'post'. In terms of the colonial/postcolonial binary, the question of who gets to be fortunate enough to effect closure on historical traumas is bound up with the imagined dismantling of colonialism. There are ongoing traumas for many millions of peoples whose lives are still disproportionately circumscribed by the often intense suffering created by the changing face of power structures that have transmogrified into neo-colonialism, cultural imperialism and now the injustices (racial, gendered and classed) inherent in the universalistic notion of global capitalism. Only those who can ignore 'the belated scar[s]' – both metaphorical and literal – inscribed on the lives of millions who *live the consequences* of colonialism can retreat, in the words of Robert Young, into the 'safety of its politics of the past'.[91] Belatedness then, also concerns the politics of relation, as Ruth Frankenberg and Lata Mani suggest in a provocative article from which I now quote:

> 'Post' means 'after in time'. But what happened during that time – presumably in this instance a time between 'colonialism', or 'coloniality', and now? In what senses are we now situated 'after' 'coloniality' in the sense of 'coloniality' being 'over and done with'? What, about 'the colonial', is over and for whom?[92]

The politics of location involve both the territorial (the physical location of the body mapped by ownership of land or nation) *and* the abstract (the psychic mapping of interpellation(s)). Moreover, the whole idea of *who will listen* is not only intrinsic to trauma theory and the outcomes of the possibilities of resolution through testimony, but also to the politics of the postcolonial arena. In postcolonial theory the question was raised by Gayatri Spivak, most notably in the words of the title to her now famous essay, 'Can the Subaltern Speak?'[93] Two years and much controversy later, she answered her own rhetorical question: 'For me, the question "Who should speak?" is less crucial than "Who will listen?"'[94] Amalgamating trauma theory and postcolonialism is not, therefore, just about traumatic experiences not being assimilated at the time of the occurrence: it is complicated by the cultural imbalances bound by issues of psychic and material domination inherent in the invisible whiteness of power structures – the differences between rulers and ruled (both psychic and material) – and the length of the time frame that is itself involved in historical disjuncture. Although on the positive side, the radical disruption of time unsettles the notion of historical progress, it must be remembered that for there to be any form of listening, there has to be a voicing of unresolved historical loss and pain. Hence the importance of fiction as a means of bearing witness and of the figurative language of metaphor as a way to confront the unspeakable. Through its ambivalent structuring, metaphor provides both the safety of a distancing mechanism and simultaneously, a linguistic strategy to speak about something unspeakable, as if by analogy.

Caruth strongly advocates 'the language of literature' as the exemplary genre that encourages a shift into forms of narrative that enables movement beyond the belatedness effect of trauma. This is because literary fiction gestures beyond itself, the figurative language offering an imaginative leap that moves beyond the denotative meaning.[95] However, the possibilities of *how* to envisage the actual psychic movement between traumatic memory that has previously been withheld from narrative coherence and its processing as a belatedly assimilated narrative, evaporates into vague gestures towards healing once a narrative is attainable. My argument will be that it is primarily through metaphor – both in its structure and its content – that trauma can be worked through, provided the metaphors that are utilised are both historically grounded and contextually orientated. Importantly though, it is the heritage of the double-voice of black oral traditions – Black English and in particular African-American literature – that most clearly supports such an interpretation. I would suggest, then, that it is in black literature that the emotional and psychic effects of racism and sexism on embodied subjectivity are most passionately and clearly articulated. The multiple levels of fictional narrative differs from the writing of theory or history because while all three combine images of social groups and relations and their interactions with each other and the outer world within which they live, fiction adds in much greater complexity the inner depth of emotional and psychic responses that cannot easily be encompassed within the other two genres. It is in the pages of fiction or poetry that we are imaginatively empowered and sometimes healed by understanding how it *feels* to be somebody else. It is in literature that the effects of racism on subjectivity can be most clearly discerned and renegotiated. As Sherley Anne Williams attests that although '[b]lack women as readers and writers have been kept out of [the] literary endeavor . . . literature . . . is about community and dialogue; theories or ways of reading ought to actively promote the enlargement of both'.[96]

It is my belief that the most effective way for white feminists such as myself to assist in the work of disassembling racism is to deconstruct inwards – to keep exposing whiteness in its many protean forms in order to dismantle it. Valerie Smith maintains that 'critical work, no less than the artistic, bears the imprint of the conditions under which it was produced and articulates the writer's relation to culture'.[97] Taking criticism seriously, and especially when engaged in interpretations that hinge on the emotive issue of race, means moving beyond confessing that I am a white middle-class feminist which acts, as Leslie Roman suggests, as 'little more than disclaimers of privilege'.[98] It concerns ethical and political responsibility. I hope that through lack of knowledge or some form of cultural or personal insensitivity that I have not caused offence or harm in any form but, if I have, I take full responsibility for my work. I close this introduction with reference to Anne duCille's wonderful essay, 'The Occult of True Black Womanhood', which has been instrumental in my thinking about writing about feminism and race, and in which she begins by describing how it feels to be 'a kind of sacred text. Not me personally, of course, but me black woman object, Other. Within and around the modern academy, racial and gender alterity has become a hot commodity that has claimed black women as its principal signifier.'[99] duCille goes on to describe the 'critical stampede' that has been attached to black women writers, and the frequent blindness of white feminists over matters of race.[100] She ends, however, on a note of hope about the possibilities of what one of her colleagues terms, 'complementary theorizing', a collaborative feminist scholarship in which 'women of color [are] talked *with* rather than about'.[101] It is on this note of the possibilities of such relational theorising that I begin my chapters.

1

'The White Hush between Two Sentences': The Traumatic Ambivalence of Whiteness in *Wide Sargasso Sea*

> In their faint photographs
> mottled with chemicals . . .
> they have drifted to the edge
> of verandahs . . .
> bone-collared gentlemen
> with spiked moustaches
> and their wives embayed in the wickerwork
> armchairs, all looking coloured
> from the distance of a century . . .
>
> And the sigh of that child
> is white as an orchid on a crusted log
> in the bush of Dominica
> a V of Chinese white
> meant for the beat of a seagull
> over a sepia souvenir of Cornwall,
> as *the white hush between two sentences* . . .
>
> Derek Walcott, 'Jean Rhys'[1]

'Jean Rhys' by West Indian poet, Derek Walcott, invokes the lost world of the white creole plantocracy through a reading of some old colonial photographs. It is a vivid and imagistic description of the decaying grandeur of early nineteenth-century white creole society in which the people pictured have 'drifted to the edge', as if marginalised and dispossessed in both time and space. The white creoles appear transfixed – 'embayed' is Walcott's word – in their wickerwork furniture, suspended between the world of their lost prestige and power and the beckoning anxiety of never again belonging. For they are neither imperially white

25

nor Dominican black, and they are entering a time of radical historical change. The poem is suffused with a mild irony. Both the men and the women (or it could be the mottled photographs at which the poet gazes, or even the aging furniture, for the wording is purposefully ambiguous) are 'all looking coloured/from the distance of a century', and the drifting of these creoles from the seat of the power of their located whiteness is merely a slow movement to the edge of verandahs. It is a depiction of cultural stasis, stagnation, and slow physical and mental disintegration. The only life affirming gesture, 'the white hush between two sentences', is a sigh emitted by the child, Jean Rhys.[2] This timeless sigh floats, bird-like, between the cultural divide of the vividly present(ed) landscape of Dominica and the far distant English county of Cornwall, which is represented by a sepia image of a souvenir photograph as somewhere always absent, perhaps longed for, but only ever visited in the imagination. The poem, with its fleeting but intense glimpses of the young Jean Rhys, forsees the literary impact she will have with 'her right hand married to *Jane Eyre*', thereby interweaving the focus between individual and historical narrative. The child who stares at 'the windless candle flame' in the poem will become the adult who rewrites this white creole historical trauma in her brilliant novel, *Wide Sargasso Sea*. In the process Rhys will relate 'the traumatic ambivalences of a personal, psychic history to the wider disjunctions of political existence'.[3] The white hush then, moves beyond a simple sigh.

Walcott's poem adumbrates many of the themes I shall address in the three chapters on *Wide Sargasso Sea*, though most notably a sense of cultural entrapment. It locates the unbelongingness of the white creole position caught between two racially divergent cultures. In Rhys's novel this position becomes a position of anxiety which makes manifest not a direct confrontation, but the ephemeral qualities of a melancholic sigh that strives to make connection across the rhetorical hush that divides the two sentences, or two rapidly dividing cultures. I shall argue that what the poem hints at is the thematic focus of Rhys's novel. The psychohistorical dislocation that accompanied the dismantling in the mid-1800s of the British Empire in the Caribbean resulted in a form of collective stasis among the white creole population who believed they had been deserted by the imperial motherland. The sense of entrapment induced a form of damaging melancholia that is represented, if somewhat ironically, in Walcott's verses. The poem also affirms the haunting qualities of metaphor and figurative language which will come to play such an important role in the poetics *and* politics of Rhys's novel. For this is a text in which what lies beneath in the subterranean economy of the unconscious or the figurative images, inference, allusions and unseen logic of the metaphorical unsaid is as significant, or perhaps even more significant, than what is explicitly enunciated.[4] A hush is an ambivalent concept, and indeed, there is always an ambivalence in metaphor and a politics to its usages. For instance, while the word 'hush' evocatively represents the suppression of sound, it can be a momentary stilling that is chosen *or* enforced. It is also a temporary space of silence in which some kind of vocal movement has been and will continue to be. The hush in Walcott's poem begins with a sense of movement, suggesting as it does that the child's sigh can carry across the seas between England and Dominica, but by the end of the verse the 'white hush is *caught* between two sentences'. The adjectival marker of colour is very strong in this stanza – it is repeated three times – the *white* sigh, the *white* painted V (the standard painterly symbol for a flying bird) and the *white* hush. It is a prelude to the underlying focus of whiteness of *Wide Sargasso Sea* which is, I shall argue, a trauma narrative of white-on-white victimhood that occludes and renders invisible the othered history of black Caribbeans on which it is predicated.

Historical trauma and its echoes: the whitewashing of history

> [H]istory, like trauma, is never simply one's own . . . history is precisely the way we are implicated in each other's traumas
> Cathy Caruth[5]

Wide Sargasso Sea is a mother–daughter trauma narrative encrypted within the outer framework of the white creole historical trauma to which Walcott alludes in his poem. It is a mother–daughter story of personal and historical fragmentation and dispossession, a narrative infused with loss, abandonment, racial hatred and a lingering melancholia. The textual ambivalence of whiteness begins with Rhys's own positioning as a fourth generation white creole, brought up on the West Indian island of Dominica in a period when classic colonialism was being dismantled. Rhys is, as Helen Carr states, 'a colonial in terms of her history, even though she could be considered a postcolonialist in her attitude to the Empire and in her employment of many postcolonialist strategies'.[6] She is in the ambiguous position of being part of colonialism *and* of the resistance to it. Indeed, her representation of the problematic and fluctuating positionalities of *Wide Sargasso Sea*'s protagonist, Antoinette Cosway Mason Rochester, as ambivalently caught between the ideologies of coloniser and colonised, oppressor and oppressed, and the menacing anxiety of being neither white nor black, bears some similarities to elements of Rhys's own upbringing. While many critics point out the ambivalences of the historical and personal positioning of both Rhys and her character Antoinette, they do not go on to provide an in-depth critique of what this positioning implies in the construction of the text. This will be the aim of these chapters.

My understanding is that ambivalence plays a crucial and multifac-eted role in Rhys's novel, much of it arising from the confusions and paradoxes of situatedness. However, I also wish to argue that *Wide Sargasso Sea* is a trauma narrative of lost whiteness. In an early inter-pretation of the novel, Kenneth Ramchand, adapting a phrase from Frantz Fanon's *The Wretched of the Earth*, indicates that 'we might use the phrase "terrified consciousness" to suggest the White minority's sensations of shock and disorientation as a massive and smouldering Black population is released into an awareness of its power'.[7] Using Ramchand's statement as a point of departure, I will explore the notion that Rhys's novel primarily revolves around the profound *cultural ambivalence* of being fixed in a historically inflected moribund white-ness that is itself, as Sanford Sternlicht states, 'trapped between two disdainful cultures'[8] at a crucial moment of imperial dismantling. It is this historical background that exacerbates, or perhaps even creates, the deep *intersubjective ambivalence* of the particularised mother–daughter relationship of Annette Cosway Mason and her daughter, Antoinette.

The setting of Rhys's *Wide Sargasso Sea* is Jamaica, the time-frame approximately 1834 to 1845.[9] This was a period of great political and social instability, and in particular a time in which the local meaning of *white* was in great flux as power relations shifted in England's colo-nial domains as a result of the passing of the British Emancipation Act of 1833 and its ratification in 1834. With the abolition of slavery, West Indian plantations fell into a temporary state of ruin. It was a point in imperial history when colonial whites discovered to their dismay that there were different levels within the power structure of whiteness, and that their place within this system was largely dependent on their position within the capitalist/imperialist enterprise. One of the text's central ironies is that it is only in her enclosed space of 'madness' at the end of the novel that Antoinette suddenly realises that for imperialists such as her husband, 'Gold is the idol they worship'.[10] Without it, as she has now learnt to her cost, the credibility of white creole position-ing is lost.

The looming ruin of the plantocracy meant erosion of their white-based power. Racial tension and bitterness were especially pervasive in the four years (1834–38) of the so-called apprenticeship system, established as a transitory measure between the abolition of slavery and the implementation of a waged-labour structure.[11] Disowned by England, the white creoles were now openly hated by the newly freed slaves. For the white creole slaveowners, slaves were property that with the passing of the Act became worthless, and without a workforce the slide into bankruptcy was inevitable. Adding to their financial woes, English promises of financial restitution did not materialise for a number of years. The suicide of Annette's only friend and white neighbour in *Wide Sargasso Sea* is symbolic of the results of white creole post-Emancipation desertion by the English. Those that remain of the once powerful and rich plantation owners, such as the widowed Annette Cosway and her children, around whom the narrative revolves, are overcome by poverty, and now black hatred mingles with utter contempt: 'Old time white people nothing but white nigger now, and black nigger better than white nigger' (10). The whites are derided, openly jeered at and despised. However, it is the act of abandonment by their own race that adds the extra edge of bitterness and despair.

Rhys constructs this white-on-white desertion as a historical trauma enacted upon a group of whites who are literally left stranded when they no longer fulfil the function allocated to them by the imperial centre. The ambivalent ideological underpinning of their abandonment is infused with resentment of the English and their wealth that the white creole Jamaicans no longer share, as well as the English attitudes of superiority towards them, yet these feelings of acrimony exist alongside a simultaneous longing *to be* English. It is to imperial whiteness that white creole ideological loyalty lies: but they are *white but not quite*.[12] They are disappointed, bitter, and in part repulsed by the English. Even as a child, watching the interrelation between her white creole mother and Mason, her new English stepfather, Antoinette knows her heritage is negatively defined as lacking and thus different from the English: 'Mr Mason, so sure of himself, so without a doubt English. And my mother, so without a doubt not English, but no white nigger either. Not my mother. Never had been. Never could be' (18). Yet as an adult, English is what Antoinette desperately desires to be, believing that the shift from periphery to metropolis will radically alter both her and the ideological burdens of white outsidership: 'I will be a different person when I live in England and different things will happen to me' (70), she tells her black nurse, Christophine. This, then, is the single-strand reading of a complexly knotted history from the victimised white creole perspective. This is the narrative that unfolds in the first two or three densely packed pages of the novel.

However, as Cathy Caruth contends, 'history is precisely the way we are implicated in each other's traumas', both personally and collectively. Because of the novel's concentration on the lost history of post-Emancipation white creoles, what is perhaps implicit – but still largely elided in the novel – is that white creoles, white imperialists *and* black Caribbeans all have complexly *interwoven* histories. And despite, or because of, the power differentials, these histories cannot be read separately. It seems to me that in her attempt to construct Antoinette Cosway as driven mad by trauma – as opposed to *inheriting* the presupposed white female creole traits of sexual depravity and manic drunkenness of the Brontë narrative – Rhys gets caught up in the thematics that such a reading implies. Her narrative of historical trauma reconfigured as individualised trauma actually participates in side-stepping the history of the more traumatised other, or examining the ways in which white and black histories of the West Indies overlap and interconnect.

Such reciprocal influences in modes of representation and historical and cultural practices come together in differing theories of transculturation and colonial/postcolonial contact zones, concepts which may be used to address the particularised world out of which Jean Rhys wrote. With specific reference to the Caribbean, Jamaican poet and historian, Edward Brathwaite outlines two distinct cultural processes of colonisation: '*ac/culturation*, which is the yoking (by force and example, deriving from power/prestige) of one culture to another (in this case the slave/African to the European); and *inter/culturation*, which is an unplanned, unstructured but osmotic relationship proceeding from this yoke.'[13] Inter/culturation is a more reciprocal process of 'intermixture and enrichment, each to each'.[14] I intentionally quote Brathwaite here because of his close relationship with Caribbean politics, both theoretical and literary, and because his wide-ranging exposition of cultural diversity focuses, as his title *Contradictory Omens* suggests, on heuristic possibilities of *creative ambivalence* in the Caribbean context.[15] Brathwaite accords *Wide Sargasso Sea* quite a substantial textual space in this essay, in part to outline the intriguing polarisation of opinion that has a particular (and well-known) history in relation to the reception of Rhys's Caribbean novel.[16] However, he ends his section on the novel by stating quite emphatically: 'White creoles in the English and French West Indies have separated themselves by too wide a gulf and have contributed too little culturally, as a group, to give credence to the notion that they can . . . meaningfully identify or be identified, with the spiritual world on this side of the Sargasso Sea'.[17]

For these reasons, I think Edward Said's notion of *contrapuntal* reading, which takes account of both the processes of imperialism and of resistances to it, is paramount in a reading of a text such as *Wide Sargasso Sea*.[18] To read colonial history contrapuntally means exposing the intertwined and overlapping histories in their plurality, and from a constantly interwoven and relational point of view. Among other things, a contrapuntal reading, Said reminds us, includes being aware that Western writers until the middle of the twentieth century wrote with 'an exclusively Western audience in mind', and that, for instance, references to India in *Jane Eyre* 'are made because they *can be*, because British power (and not just the novelist's fancy) made passing references to these massive appropriations possible'.[19] Indeed, a contrapuntal reading exposes a structural irony that is very much part of the literary history of the intertextual (mother–daughter) relationship between *Jane Eyre* and *Wide Sargasso Sea*. Over a century after Brontë's depiction of Bertha Mason as a mute, grovelling, creature, 'the clothed hyena . . . [with] a pigmy intellect',[20] Rhys gives 'Bertha' a speaking voice and a history in *Wide Sargasso Sea*, thus effectively describing a text of empire.[21] However, as I shall go on to explain, out of one appropriation came another (albeit of a different kind) which is one of the reasons why Gayatri Spivak reads '*Wide Sargasso Sea* as *Jane Eyre*'s reinscription'.[22]

From my reading of *Wide Sargasso Sea* there are two extremely troubling forms of *cultural appropriation* which silently structure Rhys's novel. The first involves a direct appropriation of a form of slave resistance known as *marronage* and the African-Caribbean notion of the *zombi* or *zombification*; the second is the installation of a central black voice in the novel to espouse the white creole point of view with a strong sense of empathy. By arrogating African-Caribbean tropes of resistance and reassigning them meaning from a white Jamaican perspective centring around individual trauma, and by positioning the ex-slave Christophine as the white creole spokeswoman, Rhys creates an aura of sympathy for the much-maligned creoles in her textual world, who effectively become the victims of history, rather than the slaves and ex-slaves on whom their fortunes had ridden.[23] However, before exploring the ambivalent characterisation of Christophine, I shall begin disentangling the metaphorical appropriations by demonstrating how two seemingly insignificant metaphors, if removed from their socio-historical context and used in a generalised and ahistorical vacuum, can effectively erase the existence of another history. The first, and most significant inappropriate borrowing is the notion of *marooning*, for it is the metaphor that sustains the pathos around which the novel turns. It is a concept-metaphor that has a situated Caribbean etymology which Rhys chose to disregard. It is this textual cover-up – or metaphorical *hushing* – of black Caribbean historical agency around which my argument revolves. Rhys's second metaphorical appropriation concerns the obeah practice of *zombification*. Although inextricably interwoven with the historical ethos of marooning, zombification is not quite as important to a postcolonial reading of this novel because the metaphor is made explicit in the text – it is not concealed in the same way as marooning.[24]

The earliest definition of the word *maroon*, in use by the early seventeenth century, refers to fugitive or runaway slaves and their descendants in the West Indies, and all other islands of the New World in which slavery was practised.[25] A hundred years later, the term had come to refer to the act of putting a person ashore, leaving him or her on an island or coast as punishment for an infraction on a voyage, abandoned without resources or hope to almost certain death. It is this second usage that Rhys employs as a metaphor for the white creole historical trauma of post-Emancipation. The word, however, is neither politically neutral nor static, and in the West Indies has a valency that has become depoliticised in today's language use. Indeed, the etymology of this word represents the normative processes inherent in the power of the white hegemony's assumption of the universalising normativity of whiteness in language that in turn renders invisible other grammars and other histories.[26] This is particularly regressive in the Caribbean context, where, according to Antonio Benítez-Rojo:

> We must conclude that the historiography of the Caribbean, in general, reads like a long and inconsonant story favouring the legitimation of the white planter ... I think [however] that the Caribbean's 'other' history ha[s] begun to be written starting from the *palenque* [the settlements of runaways] and the *maroon*, and that little by little these pages will build an enormous branching narration that will serve as an alternative to the 'planters' histories' that we know.[27]

Of course Jean Rhys writes not history but fiction, but the power of metaphor resonates through both disciplines, and in any case each is imbricated in the other. Rhys implies the outward event of historical trauma has in internal impact, a psychic wounding. But the outside events of *Wide Sargasso Sea* are not the trauma of slavery, or even the trauma of white on black racism, but the forced abandonment of white creole luxury with the collapse of the plantation system, a system of oppression which had inaugurated maroon flight in the first place. I shall argue then, that in Rhys's novel the flight of the runaway maroons is reformulated as the inward flight of trauma of her white characters.

Rhys's elision of maroon history is especially significant because she grew up in the West Indies. Her grandfather and great-grandfather owned large numbers of slaves, so she was aware of both the history of slavery and its accompanying cruelties and the wealth and prestige that accompanied white creole plantocracy status. This made for a kind of tormented ambivalence:

> I would feel sick with shame at some of the stories I heard of the slave days told casually even jocularly. The ferocious punishments the salt kept ready to rub into the wounds etc. etc. [*sic*]. I became an ardent socialist and champion of the down trodden, argued, insisted of giving my opinion, was generally insufferable. Yet all the time knowing that there was another side to it. Sometimes being proud of my great grandfather, the estate, the good old days etc. . . . Perhaps he wasn't entirely ignoble. Having absolute power over a people needn't make a man a brute. Might make him noble in a way. No – no use . . . the end of my thought was always revolt, a sick revolt and I longed to be identified once and for all with the others' side which of course was impossible. I couldn't change the colour of my skin.[28]

Yet, in *Wide Sargasso Sea*, the most obvious of all her novels in which she could have focused on the black down-trodden, Rhys instead aligns her story with white traumatisation. Moreover, slave resistance had strongly impacted on her own family, as their house on the family estate had been burned in 1844 by ex-slaves who feared a return to slavery. This scene 'returns' in the novel as the trauma that spiralled Antoinette's mother into madness. White individualised family trauma thereby replaces the collective subaltern history, and the many ways in which slaves fought back against the white ruling class.

In her historical monograph on the maroons of Jamaica, Mavis Campbell maintains that '[r]esistance was an integral part of Caribbean slave society'.[29] The most pervasive and disruptive oppositional practice in which the slaves participated in massive numbers was the act of running away to establish their own communities in the inhospitable country of the mountainous regions of the island, from where they conducted a highly successful campaign of guerilla warfare. In Jamaica and indeed throughout the New World, this act of escaping was known as *marronage*, and those that participated in it were called *maroons*. So great was this maroon defiance that it was considered 'the chronic plague' of New World plantation societies.[30] However, marronage was not just about a flight to freedom from lives of enslavement only to live a life of mere subsistence in the inhospitable mountain regions chosen for safety. Escaped maroons built elaborate settlements called *palenques* – which later became maroon towns.[31] These maroon societies then, as Richard Price describes them, were 'communities [that] stood out as an heroic challenge to white authority, and as the living proof of the existence of a slave consciousness that refused to be limited by the whites' conception or manipulation of it'.[32] Few slave societies had a more impressive record of revolt than Jamaica.[33] This was the 'dark' side of the history with which Rhys grew up while protected by her white creole status and its own version of events.

Colonial discourse 'takes over as it takes cover, revealing and concealing the appropriating impulse in the same rhetorical gesture', writes David Spurr.[34] As I see it, Rhys's *Wide Sargasso Sea* is implicated in the machinations of the colonial 'coverup', in the sense that the text's moral abstraction through the use of metaphor and metaphorical logic becomes an intricate part of the rhetorical act of the colonial appropriation to which Spurr alludes. Spurr argues that colonial discourse claims the other's territory as its own, covering this act of appropriation by converting the proprietary strategy into 'the response to a putative appeal on the part of the colonized land and people'.[35] This is what Rhys does with her appropriative use of the concept of *marooning*. In *Wide Sargasso Sea* it is the binding metaphor of the text that implies the historical dispossession and abandonment of white creoles: it is also a metaphor for the painful repression of the trauma that results from the actions of the racial other. The important difference is that Rhys reverses the power differentials, thus creating a vicarious victimisation not only of white creoles by their imperial superiors, but also by the island blacks. Indeed, the novel's first sentences draw us into a participatory reading of white creole persecution and an acceptance of Christophine's important role as protector of her white mistress: 'They say when trouble comes close ranks, and so the white people did. But we were not in their ranks. The Jamaican ladies had never approved of my mother, "because she pretty like pretty self" Christophine said' (5). Thus, by the end of the opening paragraph, the politics, thematics and tone are laid out, along with acceptance of the presence of Christophine's explanatory, empathetic voice.

This a text narrativised by associative connection: one memory immediately leads into another through parataxis not contiguity, and it is almost as if we are ourselves plunged into the tragedy which is presented with the vivid immediacy of traumatic vignettes. We proceed from the stated outsidership of white creoles in Jamaica, to Antoinette's father's death, to Mr Luttrell's despairing suicide and finally into the first incident of the white-washed version of marooning all within the first page. Antoinette, who is about eight at the time, unexpectedly comes across her mother's horse dead under a frangipani tree: 'I went up to him but he was not sick, he was dead and his eyes were black with flies. I ran away and did not speak of it for I thought if I told no one it might not be true' (6). She represses her horror in silent inward flight. Godfrey, the old groom who has stayed working for Annette because he is now too old to move on and make a new life post-slavery, also discovers the dead horse, and passes on the news to his mistress. The horse, which has been poisoned, was the last visible sign of her lost privilege, and Annette's response is one of hopelessness: 'Now *we are marooned* . . . what will become of *us*' (6, emphasis added). Godfrey replies: 'When the old time go, let it go. No use to grab at it. The Lord make no distinction between black and white, black and white the same for Him' (6). However, black and white are certainly *not* the same to Annette as her petulant use of 'us' amply demonstrates. Moreover, the appropriation of the African-Caribbean metaphor of marooning means that under the circumstances of Emancipation the white creoles take over the position of victim, implicitly merging black and white by implying that *both* are being victimised in the same way by the imperialists. The metaphor is pointedly repeated a few pages later, as I shall discuss later in greater detail, but at this stage I just want to draw attention to the emphasis on white marooning which pervades the exposition of the novel.

Much the same kind of argument applies to Rhys's metaphorisation of the *obeah* practice of *zombification*. Maroon societies and the practices of obeah were intimately interwoven, and both were strongly African-based. Maroon communities were based on African socio-political and military formations, and perhaps because slaves in the New World were captured from all over the coastal regions of West Africa,[36] Campbell maintains that:

[t]here appears to have existed a kind of 'Africanness' that transcended regionalism, ethnic or linguistic affinities, on which these

maroons based their existence . . . commonalities for the most part, are reflected in sex roles, attitude to warfare, familial arrangements, attitude to hierarchy, but above all in *religion, which was pivotal to all resistance in the area.* More than any other single factor, African religious beliefs gave the unifying force, the conspiratorial locus, the rallying point to mobilize, to motivate, to inspire, and to design strategies: it gave the ideology, the mystique, and the pertinacious courage and leadership to Maroon societies to confront the mercantilist society with its awesome power.[37]

Obeah fulfilled a practical and an ideological function of solidarity within both escaped and unfree slave communities. Legends built up around the great maroon leaders who were invested with almost magical powers.[38] One such was Tacky who led the 1760 Jamaican rebellion, one of the most notorious of Antillean uprisings.[39] This revolt created such widespread fear of obeah in the white plantocracy that a law was enacted which made its practice a capital offence.[40] However, this law neither prevented the custom nor the rebellions, both of which, bound in unison, helped to bring about the abolition of slavery. Jamaican maroon resistances are extremely important in the history of the unequal contact between Africa and the New World from the fifteenth century on, because the maroon rebels were the heroic freedom fighters who literally and symbolically earned the title of the 'Slaves Who Abolished Slavery'.[41]

The vital cultural role played by obeah and the politicisation of African religious beliefs as resistance practices has as its centrepiece the phenomenon of possession known as zombification. As with Rhys's use of the metaphor of marooning, in *Wide Sargasso Sea*, references to zombification are circumscribed and controlled by a Eurocentric interpretation. In its own cultural context, the figure of the zombi represents the African view of death.[42] However, once the symbol of the zombi was transferred into the enslaved condition of the African in the Caribbean, it became the *symbol of the slave*, 'the alienated man [sic] robbed of his will, reduced to slavery, forced to work for a master'.[43] Zombis can be recognised, Maximilien Laroche informs us, by their 'vague look, their dull almost glazed eyes, and above all by the nasality of their voice'.[44] In *Wide Sargasso Sea* the zombified Antoinette carries all these characteristics. As a result of Rochester's 'possession' of her she becomes a puppet incapable of independent action, a doll with a smile 'nailed to her face' (111). As with Antoinette's fixated passivity, the docility of the

African-Caribbean zombi is absolute. Zombis have no memory of their previous life and so are completely unaware of their condition as slaves to their masters. In the Caribbean, the symbolic meaning of the figure of the zombi, or living-dead, is in a sense reversed in that it was completely reformulated by African-Caribbeans to represent their economic, social and political *lived* embodiment of slavery.[45]

I have digressed at length to describe and contextualise what must be understood as strongly Africanist tropes of marooning and zombification, which in Rhys's novel become metaphors of white alienation and psychic numbing. These metaphors evoke the results of the enforced trauma that bring about Antoinette's fall into a state of derangement. Rhys's motivation in creating the character of Antoinette was, as I have stated, to provide Bertha Mason with a history before her incarceration in the attic at Thornfield Hall. Thus, from an intertextual point of view, Bertha's madness now has a causal narrative, but this is based on the misappropriation of black tropes of resistance. In Rhys's text, these tropes of subversive rebellion which have a history of their own become anglicised, whitened and reformulated and African-Caribbean resistance politics are effectively disarticulated, even erased. Black suffering and the trauma of slavery is rewritten as white suffering, and that is where the textual empathy lies. Moreover, and very importantly, while there is substantial material available on maroon resistance history and its religious underpinnings, or at least enough to make some connecting suppositions, on the whole this material continues to be glossed over in literary-critical expositions of *Wide Sargasso Sea*.

Considering the nearly 40-year gap since the novel was published and the rise of postcolonial feminist theory this is particularly worrying, and perhaps has more to do with the history of white middle-class feminist politics which has a tendency to culturally displace what cannot be worked through, as Rhys does in her novel. In a wide-ranging and fine essay on the marginalisation of the work of black women intellectuals in the white Eurocentric academy, Ann duCille raises the issue of how white feminists have often explored their own pain through an explicit identification with a range of oppressions depicted in black women's texts, especially those of Toni Morrison, Alice Walker and Gayl Jones.[46] Citing a specific example which stated: 'We, as white feminists, are drawn to black women's visions because they concretize and make vivid a system of oppression',[47] duCille concludes that one of the effects of such a practice is that white feminists connect to their own pain at the expense of black women's own suffering, which then becomes peripheral. One method, conscious or otherwise, of marginalising black women's texts, whether theoretical or literary, duCille suggests, is through the use of 'white metaphor'. She puts it this way:

> [B]lack culture is more easily intellectualized (and canonized) when transferred from the danger of lived black experience to the *safety of white metaphor*, when you can have that 'signifying black difference' without the difference of significant blackness.[48]

The 'safety of white metaphor' plays a prominent, and doubled, role in Rhys's text, for while *safety* of self, literally and figuratively is the goal of the trauma cure,[49] it is also a very important, if not obsessive, displacement trope in Rhys's trauma narrative. In the first instance, Antoinette's actions, vocabulary and traumatic memories are all bound up with a yearning for lost safety and this longing is, for the most part, always connected to her mother whose continual acts of rejection create a profound sense of vulnerability and aching to be loved in the child, a heritage that she carries into adulthood. However, at the same time, this trauma narrative is immensely complicated because Antoinette has another mother-figure who is both the only signifier of black difference in the novel and simultaneously the preserver of white safety, a textual positioning that results in occlusion of the traumatic lived experiences of slavery, and thus a de-signifying of the politics of significant blackness.[50] This then, is Rhys's second crucial textual appropriation in *Wide Sargasso Sea*.

Christophine, the powerful black *obeah* character, the only woman in the text with 'spunks' (63), is chosen as the enunciator, even the defender, of the white trauma. It is left to Christophine to critique imperialist white masculinity, but *not* from the point of view of her own people. Her critique, a defence of Antoinette, her much-loved surrogate daughter, is from a white creole perspective. Moreover, while Christophine's presence and voice resound with an indignant strength, her speech is always filtered through the consciousness of the white characters. Newly freed, Christophine has spent most of her life as a commodified gift, given from white to white, the 'gift' of an enslaved woman's life of servitude.[51] The narrative focus of her loyalty to her white mistresses gives little credence to the fact that Christophine was taken from her own family as a child, or that this forced dislocation may well mean that now, newly freed from slavery, she has literally nowhere else to go.

However, the intriguing point about Rhys's ambivalent narrative is that instances of appropriative borrowing occasionally become self-reflexive and interrogating of her own thematics. At times her narrative participates in imperial ideology and a belief that its history can be separable and therefore ethically distanced from black history: at other times, the black and white histories are acknowledged to be inseparable. For instance, in answer to Antoinette's anxious questioning about Christophine's history before she came to work with the family – the child is worrying Christophine may leave after the passing of the Emancipation Act – her mother replies: ' "Does it matter? Why do you pester and bother me about all the things that happened long ago?" ' (8). The child thus learns from an early age that this history of racial dispossession is unimportant, and indeed it is a lesson of ideological avoidance that Antoinette carries into her adult life. When her new husband inquires into the strange naming of a village called Massacre: ' "And who was massacred here? Slaves?" ' Antoinette replies: ' "Oh no . . . Not slaves. Something must have happened a long time ago. Nobody remembers that now" ' (39). The massacre that Antoinette 'forgets' refers to the murder in 1674 of 60–70 Carib men, women and children, including Thomas 'Indian' Warner, the half-Carib son of Sir Thomas Warner, the Governor of St Kitts.[52] However, a little further on, in trying to tell her mother's story, Antoinette seems aware of the racial entanglement of post-Emancipation Jamaica and the universality of death that crosses between races with little discrimination: 'It was Christophine,' she tells Rochester, 'who brought our food from the village and persuaded some girls to help her sweep and wash clothes. We would have died, my mother always said, if she had not stayed with us. Many died in those days, both white and black, especially the older people, but no one speaks of those days now' (83–4). Yet a sense of the absolute rightness of Christophine's role as slave/servant still lingers in this telling.

However, understanding that Rhys was a product of a certain historical and racial positioning is only part of the story. The role of an ethically responsible (postcolonial) critic is to expose and then read beyond the historically inflected authorial complicity, but at the same time ensuring that the racial othering imbricated in past ideologies is not replicated in contemporary interpretations. In this vein, Elaine Savory recently claimed in her monograph on Rhys: 'it is imperative that critics, especially white critics, recognise and identify those failings, not glossing over Antoinette's ambivalent position nor the power structure which enables her to lack "spunks" which Christophine, as a poor black woman and slave, has had to find in herself to survive.'[53] Yet Savory does not follow her own advice, often writing from a Eurocentric perspective that disregards the interwoven ambivalence of the history out of which Rhys wrote. For instance, in a reference to Rhys's use of marooning, Savory assumes the universal definition (as do the majority of critics), but goes further by suggesting that while this metaphor merely means that Antoinette and her mother are now cut off from society, Antoinette in her adult 'defiance against a husband and a culture that oppresses her . . . becomes a maroon in the Caribbean sense'.[54] This example is just one of many I could have picked from the race-blind genealogy of much white middle-class feminism.[55] How far then have literary critical readings progressed around issues of otherness? Captive in the imperial attic, Bertha Mason's otherness became standardised by early white feminist readings of her as 'Jane's truest and darkest double'.[56] However, if feminist theoretical thinking continues to concentrate solely on sexual difference in the reading of literary texts, then Bertha Mason's 'race' will always be disremembered.[57] She will remain the *'closet monster of ethnocentrism'* in white feminism,[58] and the figure around whom the oscillations between ideological positions of race and its historicity are left unwound. In the words of Patricia Williams: 'it is imperative to think about [the] phenomenon of closeting race',[59] because otherwise the result is uncritical acceptance of textual and cultural appropriations and, by extension, the continued silencing of othered experiences, narratives and histories.

To move into a critically circumspect racial analysis then, it is vital to keep in mind that while trauma narratives are cultural constructs of personal and historical memory, hegemonic cultural tropes and social normatives serve to conceal or highlight these memories and construct which versions of the past become legitimated knowledge.[60] As Iain Chambers states in an essay on the possibilities of postcolonial histories: 'History is not merely partial, it is also partisan'.[61] The unmitigated *whiteness* of trauma studies today still binds the ideological framework of what is considered traumatic in the historical past or in contemporary acts of traumatic violence. My aim then is to demonstrate that the invisible whiteness of trauma studies provides the possibility of political avoidance by allowing a space for the white victim position.

2
Keeping History Safe

A 'special type of forgetting': trauma's inward flight[1]

Thus far I have strategically separated the outward events of historical trauma from their internal impact on the characters of Annette and Antoinette Cosway Mason in *Wide Sargasso Sea*. This was in order to demonstrate how Rhys's use of the metaphor of marooning discursively appropriates and simultaneously conceals the central dynamic of black resistance and its long history in the Caribbean. My title for this chapter also has a doubled meaning. At one level, the inward flight of trauma signifies a defence mechanism such as repression or dissociation which the mind activates – most often unconsciously – in the face of intolerable external physical or mental suffering. It becomes a flight into the self which is also, paradoxically, a withdrawal from the self. However, on the second level, in the narrative form of Rhys's novel, this self-protective escape into the mind itself becomes a flight from, and de-politicisation of, historical context. In an article that challenges the notion that psychological effects of trauma are somehow ahistoric and universal, Laurence Kirmayer explores the role of the cultural construction of traumatic memory narratives and their reception. He argues that the context of retelling is crucial to the nature of collective memory and that its public reception is always dependent to some degree on 'an audience primed by history'.[2] There is a crucial distinction, Kirmayer maintains, between 'the social space in which the trauma occurred and the contemporary space in which it is (or is not) recalled'.[3] The ideological contours of the social space into which a trauma narrative is inserted is intrinsic then to its reception.

Given the crucial importance of the role of the listener in trauma studies, I return to Spivak's famous query. She points out that her

41

rhetorical question, 'Can the subaltern speak?' presupposed her answer, 'Who will listen?'[4] A postcolonial reading of trauma theory exposes the racialised division of access: firstly, who gets to be the speaker and who the listener; secondly, if there is no space allocated within whitened theories to othered speakers, trauma surrounding issues of racism and racial terror will remain silenced; and finally, the problematic conjunction of historical trauma with victimhood will remain unaddressed.[5] But there are different ways of listening. Sometimes the stories are not overt, which means having to read against the grain of history for the unsaid, for the metaphorically organised, but nonetheless real shape of the acts of remembering.[6]

Rhys's novel is highly tropological, its textual economy constituted by interconnecting tropes that are themselves deeply laden with connotative meaning. Indeed many of the symbols are *overdetermined* to an extraordinary degree. In the first place there is the restaging of both concepts and situations of *Jane Eyre* to the extent that it is the revenant text that ideologically haunts Rhys's novel. Secondly, there is an underlying dialogue with the iconography of white Christianity. Biblical imagery and allusions pervade the text, from the Edenic imagery of the garden at Coulibri with its prominent tree of life which returns so vividly in the third section, to the traditional symbology of betrayal through the crowing of the cockerel and direct allusion to the infamous deed of Judas Iscariot. The third, and most diffuse level, is the ambivalent relationship between colonial and postcolonial ideologies and representations. However, in a paradoxical fashion, the novel also displays the fragmented nature of a dissociative narrative, the coherence of which is ruptured by narrative gaps and lesions. What Antoinette remembers are fragmentary episodes of dissociation, isolated and unconnected visual images and feelings that are shrouded in a sense of unreality. These intrusions are haunting and often frightening because they make no narrative sense, they have no sequential meaning because the connecting links are removed. Dissociation works by compartmentalising overwhelming emotion thus creating a gap in the continuity of experience. There is a break in consciousness; with repeated dissociative experiences, consciousness is punctuated by numerous gaps. Memories may be clouded or occluded completely, and isolated fragments, visual images, and body sensations may intermittently haunt consciousness and intrude on everyday awareness.[7] Intrusions and amnestic gaps often co-exist in the same individual.[8] Dissociation is a defence against unbearable anxiety, pain or traumatic experience and one that may produce an overwhelming need to escape what is, in reality, unescapable. It is thus a 'special type of forgetting – unexpected and precipitous'.[9] This is what I call trauma's inward flight, and in many ways it is an ambivalent choice and one that will prove fatal for Antoinette. For while dissociation can radically increase control over the seemingly uncontrollable and thus provide a sense of safety, at the same time this same shutting-out of pain can induce dislocation, isolation from others and in the extreme, complex forms of identity fragmentation.[10]

Kirmayer interestingly connects the defence mechanism of dissociation with narrative conventions:

> Dissociation is a rupture in narrative, but it is also maintained by narrative because the shape of the narrative around the dissociation protects (reveals and conceals) the gap. Dimensions of narrative relevant to processes of dissociation include *coherence, voice, and time*: that is, the extent to which the narrative of self is integrated or fragmented, univocal or polyvocal, and whether the flow of narrative time is progressive, regressive, or static.[11]

Wide Sargasso Sea's three-part structure reflects both radical distortion of time and polyvocal points of view. Part I, written from Antoinette's point of view, is seemingly chronological in the manner of the *Bildungsroman,* and takes the narrative from when Antoinette is eight or nine until she is almost 17. It covers only 30 pages, and is bound together by extremely vivid vignettes which are imagistic recollections of the repetitive traumas that define Antoinette's young life. However, in marked contrast to the tradition of the *Bildungsroman,* in which the protagonist's preparation for life is represented as a heroic narrative of progress, Antoinette's life is reduced and constricted by her experiences. Each vignette, always grounded in Antoinette's reaching for safety in love of person or place, is an encapsulated whole small episode which then leaps directly into the next one. It is the dissociation of traumatic images that enables Antoinette to survive, to keep moving forward. In contrast, Part II – Rochester's neurotic control narrative of the foreshortened honeymoon which lasts only a few weeks at most – is over 70 pages long. Written from his point of view, the section begins: 'So it was all over, the advance and retreat, the doubts and hesitations. Everything finished for better or for worse' (39). With its military metaphors connected with a quotation from the Anglican marriage service, this opening – so different from the hesitant anxiety and outsider status that begins the novel itself – exudes a sense of mastery, conquering masculine imperialism and an assertive statement of rights over the female body, which in Rochester's metaphor-making gradually becomes inseparable from the virgin territory of the honeymoon island.[12] Finally, and again in contrast, in Part III Antoinette's narrative space from the attic takes up a mere ten pages and is packed with what initially appear to be cascading and inchoate images that have no temporal sequentiality or narrative cohesion. What do have meaning, as I shall discuss, are a dream and a dress, and both images are connected to the mother–daughter trauma.

Deborah Kelly Kloepfer makes the point that 'Antoinette seems able to articulate only those portions of her life which deal with her mother; she can narrate her childhood (which centres on her mother's madness) and the period of time she spends imprisoned (like her mother) preparing to reenact and retell her tale.'[13] Building on Kloepfer's argument, with which I agree, I would add that despite the prominence in length that is accorded to Rochester's point of view, the second part of the novel in fact is Antoinette's failed belated attempt to deal with the trauma of rejection and loss that grew out of her relationship with her mother. It, too, is an intrinsic part of the mother–daughter narrative, although this is not immediately apparent. As Antoinette moves from the safety of the convent to an unchosen married life, she gradually allows herself, against all her instinctual hesitations, to love another person. However, Rochester's paranoid and callous treatment of this tentative love reactivates her traumatic past. Christophine, the only person to understand the nature of traumatic experience in the novel, tries to help Antoinette by encouraging her to unburden herself of this legacy by speaking its pain. As part of her bargain of providing the obeah potion for Antoinette, Christophine asks her to tell Rochester what really happened to her mother. Thus, while her psychic harming at the hands of Rochester is the catalyst for belatedly reactivating a traumatic past, it is Antoinette's attempt to retell her mother's traumatic history – always inseparable from her own – that is the subject of this long second section of the novel. Despite Rochester's focalisation, I would emphasise the point that the mother–daughter relationship is still the traumatic kernel of this middle section of the novel.

Indeed it is my argument that two seemingly insignificant and overlooked feminine symbols carry the weight of Antoinette's trauma. The representations of these two tropes of trauma, which return again and again throughout the course of the novel, always in relation to maternal loss are those of *hair*, and a *dress*. The first time each trope appears in the text it is in relation to a traumatic scene between mother and daughter, but progressively they also become aligned with loss that accompanies both racial and sexual discord. In Rochester's section of the narrative they become more involved in the thematics of sexual and racial disruptions, but nevertheless these tropes always intrusively return Antoinette to the abandonment by her mother in early childhood. Generally, critics assume the burning of Coulibri to be the central trauma of the novel. However, I read *Wide Sargasso Sea* as the narrative of a daughter's cumulative trauma, much of it carried over from her mother's own traumatic life, and as such never far removed from racial politics. Antoinette, who is literally scarred by the rock thrown by Tia at the scene of the burning, is already deeply psychically wounded by her previous history of trauma and loss.[14]

While the feeling of lost safety is central to Antoinette's relationship with her mother, its early history lies in the death of her father. On the first page of the novel, one sentence including the full stop is curiously encircled by the safety of brackets: '(My father, visitors, horses, feeling safe in bed – all belonged to the past.)' (5). From the very outset, personal loss and trauma is always implicated in the outer framework of dispossession and historical trauma. Without the authority of patriarchal and neo-imperial endorsement, racial jeering and threats from the newly freed blacks begin in earnest. Her widowed mother, Annette, is a figure of profound isolation as she paces on the verandah of Coulibri, stared and laughed at by those passing. Her body reflects the pain of her estrangement, as she stands, long after the jeering echoes have passed, with her eyes shut and her fists clenched. Antoinette, anxiously watching her mother's withdrawal, seeks to comfort and be comforted, but is met by cold indifference:

> A frown came between her black eyebrows, deep – it might have been cut with a knife. I hated this frown and *once* I touched her forehead trying to smooth it. But she pushed me away, not roughly but calmly, coldly without a word, as if she had decided once and for all that I was useless to her. She wanted to sit with Pierre or walk where she pleased without being pestered. (7, emphasis added)

This passage carries within in it all the seeds of personal trauma and the interrelatedness of the traumatic relationship between mother and daughter, and indeed, the relational structuring of trauma itself. Antoinette reaches to smooth over the outward marking of her mother's psychic wounding, only to be met by double rejection. First, the physical rebuff, the pushing away, but then, in a gesture that will create more significant long-term damage, her mother's psychic dismissal which is calmly, chillingly conclusive. In juxtaposition with the child's repudiation is her mother's obvious preference for her disabled son, Pierre, which means that Antoinette is doubly shut out from the safety of her mother's love. This scene does not stand alone: it constantly repeats in different but similar forms. A page later Antoinette describes her only conversation with her mother in the novel. This has an undertone of desperation as the child strives to keep the dialogue going by asking questions that annoy Annette. When she sees beads of perspiration appear on her mother's forehead, Antoinette:

> started to fan her, but she turned her head away. She might rest if I left her alone, she said.
> *Once* I would have gone back quietly to watch her asleep on the blue sofa – *once* I made excuses to be near her when she brushed *her hair, a soft black cloak to cover me, hide me, keep me safe.*
> But not any longer. Not any more. (8–9, emphasis added)

Her mother's repetitive turning-away in its various forms wounds the child. Antoinette's yearning to be close to her mother becomes tied in with the image of her mother's hair as a shelter to which she no longer has access. In her pain she learns to define her relationship with her mother in negatives ('But not any longer. Not any more'), and the unconscious placing of the ideal of safety into the past with the repetition of the adverb 'once' in both passages are both defence mechanisms that help create a protective shield against this hurt.

The distress of Antoinette's private life is magnified by her social isolation and meetings with other children who continually taunt her: 'Go away white cockroach, go away, go away . . . Nobody want you. Go away' (9). Christophine, as always, intervenes on Antoinette's behalf, finding her a friend, the little black girl, Tia, who is the daughter of her own friend, Maillotte. A short interlude of happiness ensues for Antoinette as she and Tia spend their days by the bathing pool, swimming, cooking over an open fire and sleeping side by side. Rhys's depiction here is Edenic, both in her descriptions of the landscape and in the suggestion of this utopian space as one in which two small girls of different races can co-exist in harmony. Yet one sentence provides a condensed representation of an underlying contradictory reading of difference: 'Tia would light a fire (fires always lit for her, sharp stones did not hurt her bare feet, I never saw her cry)' (9). It is always Tia who lights the fire – in the manner of a black servant – and yet the brackets contain the exoticisation of the wild and brave savage other who can transcend pain because of a 'natural' fortitude gained by living an 'uncivilised' life. At the end of their day together they always part 'at the turn of the road' (9). There can be no overlapping of their shared time together in the wider framework of the society in which they live, and indeed their friendship is suddenly and devastatingly ruptured by their unthinking repetition of the racial hatred and divisions that surround them. They have a childish squabble over a dare and their small fight quickly degenerates as they fall into predetermined patterns of racial denigration. Antoinette calls Tia a 'cheating nigger' and Tia retaliates with the accusation that white creoles most fear: 'Old time white people nothing but white nigger now, and black nigger better than white nigger' (10). One of the interesting things about this important scene, is that while their interracial friendship is very short-lived, Antoinette's memories of these idyllic days will remain invested with a preponderant significance for the rest of her life, as will become clear at the end of the novel.

After their argument, Antoinette turns her back on Tia and so does not see that Tia departs wearing her 'starched, ironed, clean' dress, and leaving her ragged one in its place. Arriving back at the big house in Tia's dress, she is met by visitors, two women in beautiful clothes and a 'gentleman', each of whom laughs at her bedraggled and somewhat dirty appearance (10). The gentleman is Mr Mason, soon to become her stepfather, and he laughs loudest and longest. After the visitors leave her mother stares at her for quite some time (a highly unusual occurrence, for part of Antoinette's deep-seated feelings of rejection result from never being gazed upon). Annette demands to know why Antoinette looks like she does, but when told it is Tia's dress that her daughter is wearing, reacts with the stereotypical manifestations of colonial racism. 'Which one of *them* is Tia?' (11, emphasis added) implying the endless similarity of the feared unknown other. This is combined with an instantaneous revulsion: 'Throw away that thing. Burn it' (11), as if wearing the dress of the other is a contaminating act. This scene has fascinating correlations with Ahmed's concept of the racial encounter which I outlined in my introduction, and in particular her reading of Grosz's naked (undifferentiated) body that is always 'clothed' by cultural prescriptions. In this encounter, Antoinette's body takes on the denigratory racial inscriptions of blackness by her skin having come into contact with Tia's dress that is described as *dirty* as against Antoinette's own stolen one which is starched, ironed and *clean*. Moreover, her arrival back at the plantation house that precipitates her

mother's reaction throws the encounter into one of 'surprise and conflict' (thus connecting with Ahmed's configuration of the term) for two
reasons. They never have visitors, and now when they do Antoinette
stands out as aberrant because she has had to attire herself in the (dirty)
clothing of the other which places her in radical contradistinction to
the visitors: 'They were very beautiful I thought and they wore such
beautiful clothes that I looked away down at the flagstones' (10). The
lack of punctuation in this sentence means that the distinction between
beautiful people and beautiful clothes is lost so that their clothing
becomes a signifier both of all that is attractive about the strangers, and
also what plunges the child into a scenario of shame.

This extended scene – the first that involves a dress – signals the beginning of Antoinette's doubly traumatic childhood. It begins with a racial
encounter (Antoinette and Tia at the bathing pool), moves through a
short engagement with white-on-white politics (the shaming episode
on the steps of the plantation house) but then entangles these traumatising moments with maternal rejection. Significantly, this defining
moment also encompasses both the inappropriate use of the metaphor
of marooning and the child silently witnessing her two 'mothers' fight-
ing over her moral degeneration, which inexplicably (at least to a child)
seems as if it can only be re-dressed, as it were, by what covers her body:

> 'She must have another dress,' said my mother. 'Somewhere.' But
> Christophine told her loudly that it was shameful. She run wild, she
> grow up worthless. And nobody care.
> My mother walked over to the window. ('Marooned,' said her straight
> narrow back, her carefully coiled hair. 'Marooned.').
> 'She has an old muslin dress. Find that' [Annette commands
> Christophine]. (11)

By selling off one of her few remaining possessions, Annette is able to
procure enough muslin to make beautiful new dresses for herself and
her daughter, and out of this reclothing comes the marriage to Mason
and a dramatic change in their lives. Ironically, however, this marriage
brings disaster, for Mason's inability to read the cultural codings on the
island directly result in the fire that burns Coulibri, kills Pierre and
spirals Annette into grief and madness. However, the point I want to
stress here is that in Rhys's novel the iconography of clothing is used
both to denote the status of superiority and inferiority, but also, and
more importantly, while implicitly imbricated in issues of gendered dif-

ference, clothing (and also hair), are the devices by which issues of *racial* difference are displaced or evaded.

However, what remains central is the symbolism of clothing which binds together personal and historical trauma. In *Wide Sargasso Sea*, this is prefigured by the scenario that unfolds around Tia's dress. Antoinette has become friends with Tia because her mother ignores her: now Tia, her only friend, has betrayed her. Maternal and racial rejection now commingle: 'All that evening my mother didn't speak to me or look at me and I thought, "She is ashamed of me, what Tia said is true"' (11). Immediately afterwards the text moves into the first of Antoinette's three repeating dreams, which is most often read as a premonition of her life ahead. Instead, I see it as a traumatic flashback of the events of the day. In recounting this memory from an adult perspective, the immediacy and haunting visuality of both the drama of the dress and the dream are connected by the mother's presence, in mind and body, not by conjunctional grammar. The imagistic scenes are simply laid side by side:

> . . . what Tia said was true.'
> I went to bed early and slept at once. I dreamed that I was walking in the forest. Not alone. Someone who hated me was with me, out of sight. I could hear heavy footsteps coming closer and though I struggled and screamed I could not move. I woke crying (11).

Antoinette walks in the forest, perhaps somewhere close to the bathing pool. The 'someone' who hates her but remains out of sight is an entangled condensation of the ongoing trauma of her mother's indifference – now magnified by the dress scene and her mother's accompanying shame – and Tia's recent derision and rejection. It is not a premonition but a reliving of the trauma of the day, for in sleep the self is only too often overwhelmed by traumatic remembering. In accordance with Freud's later theory of the traumatic dream, this would appear to be some kind of re-enactment.[15] However, the meaning of the dream symbolism is not available to Antoinette. What haunts her is a waking image of the presence next to her bed of her mother whom she believes is there to assuage her fears.[16] Annette appears by her bed in response to her screams, but merely sighs in exasperation saying she has woken Pierre, and leaves to comfort him instead. Antoinette, in her abandonment, clings to the material surety of place. Lying in bed she recites to herself: '*I am safe* . . . There is the tree of life in the garden and the wall green with moss. The barrier of the cliffs and the high mountains. And the barrier of the sea. *I am safe. I am safe*' (12, emphasis added).

So great does the repressed impact of the traumatic confrontation with her mother over the dress scene become, that years later, in trying to speak her trauma to Rochester when urged by Christophine, Antoinette has introjected the shame. Shifting from an earlier understanding that it was after the doctor's diagnosis of Pierre's illness that left mother changed, becoming thin and silent and refusing to leave the house (6), now as Antoinette retells the story it is as if she is re-experiencing the dreadful day of double rejection all over again. As in the earlier scene, racial shame is conflated with her mother, but now she strongly blames herself, emphasised by the compulsive repetition of the words of blame:

> Then there was that day when she saw I was growing up like a *white nigger* and she was ashamed of me, it was after that day that everything changed. Yes, *it was my fault, it was my fault* that she started to plan and work in a frenzy, in a fever to change our lives. (84, emphasis added)

Any attempt to release trauma from its encapsulated security – and thus its assimilation into consciousness – is best worked through by narratavising this event to an empathetic listener or witness in the safe rhetorical and physical space this provides.[17] Rochester is far from this ideal listener. Antoinette starts trying to unburden herself of some of her fragmentary stories, only to be met by Rochester's indifference, the indifference of a white male imperialist to the traumas of white creole women. She admonishes him to little effect: 'You have no right . . . You have no right to ask questions about my mother and then refuse to listen to my answer' (82). Because Antoinette can never find such a self-protected space in relation to an empathetic other, the newly assimilated knowledge can only (re)turn inward to again psychically wound. It also accounts for her attachment to the ideal of safety.

Racial ambivalence comes to interact more strongly on personal trauma when Antoinette's beloved safe space, the house and garden at Coulibri, is burnt to the ground. This scene is the turning point of trauma. Fearing Mason's intention to import coolie labour, the ex-slaves are driven to vent their rage with the only option left open to them: 'A horrible noise swelled up, like animals howling, but worse . . . They all looked the same, it was the same face repeated over and over, eyes gleaming, mouth half open to shout' (20, 22). While it can be argued that this description depicts fear of the terrifying solidarity of the antagonistic mob from a child's point of view, it also verges on racist discourse. To dehumanise and animalise is a strategy that legitimates persecution. The outcome of the rebellion is terrible: Pierre dies and Annette descends into tortured self-blame and madness. There is, however, one moment of stillness in these two or three pages of agitation and racial bitterness during which the violence spirals out of control. Annette suddenly disappears and Aunt Cora puts her arms around her niece, saying: '"Don't be afraid, you are quite *safe*. We are all quite *safe*"' (20, emphasis added). Antoinette rests her head on her aunt's shoulder, inhaling her comforting vanilla scent. Suddenly another smell intrudes into this sense of safety. It was the smell of 'burned hair' and it accompanies her mother's return into the room carrying a prostrate Pierre: 'It was her loose hair that had burned and was smelling like that' (20), Antoinette remembers. It is the image of her mother's hair so loose and disordered in total contrast to its normal state of being 'carefully coiled' (11), together with the overwhelming smell of its burning, that for years will carry the weight of the terrifying chaos and trauma of that night.

The climax of the scene is one of the most well-known moments of the novel when Antoinette runs towards Tia who is part of the rioting crowd: 'I ran to her, for she was all that was left of my life as it had been . . . As I ran, I thought, I will live with Tia and I will be like her' (20). Tia throws a stone which cuts Antoinette's forehead, and the scene abruptly ends.[18] There is an elliptical textual space instead of a connective link and then another imagistic fragment, again intermixed with maternal imagery of hair and loss. Antoinette, scarred within and without, has been seriously ill for six weeks. Because of her illness her hair has been cut off. As she slips in and out of consciousness she repeatedly dreams of a coiled snake near her bed, but now discovers it is her discarded plait. In her almost death-like state she hears her mother's screaming, 'screams so loud and terrible' that she had to cover her ears (25). It is as if her cropped hair (which she fears will grow back darker) severs her connection to the destroyed Coulibri and now her physically displaced mother.

Antoinette's dissociation from her mother is exacerbated by a harrowing visit she pays her. Annette has been placed under house arrest by Mason and is minded by a 'coloured' couple who abuse her. The fact of their coloured status, rather than being named black, foreshadows later depictions of racial abhorrence aimed at mixed-race hybrid characters that surface at various points later in the text.[19] In her mind

Annette is part of Coulibri and now that is gone Antoinette does not really expect to see her mother again. Partly for this reason she does not immediately recognise the 'white woman sitting with her head bent so low that I couldn't see her face' (26). Antoinette knows her only by the two outward markings that connect her to her internalised symbols of trauma: 'I recognised her hair . . . And her dress' (26). Annette initially effusively welcomes her daughter, hugging her so hard she can hardly breathe. But she keeps looking over Antoinette's shoulder to where Pierre might have been:

> I could not say, 'He is dead,' so I shook my head. 'But I am here, I am here,' I said, and she said, 'No,' quietly. Then 'No no no' very loudly and flung me from her. I fell against the partition and hurt myself. (26)

This time the rejection comes with words: the repeated and loudly enunciated negative and the physically inflicted hurt. However, of many visits Antoinette pays her mother in her imprisonment, one particular episode haunts the rest of her days. It is an intensely traumatic moment in the novel: what she overhears and sees has a devastating impact. However, it is not until she is trying belatedly to experience this event in her enforced telling of it to Rochester, that the readers – like Antoinette – encounter it for the first time. Her belated psychic re-engagement with the event begins with Rochester accusing her of forgetting her mother, to which she answers:

> I am not a forgetting person . . . But she – she didn't want me. She pushed me away and cried when I went to see her. They told me I made her worse . . . One day I made up my mind to go to her, by myself. Before I reached her house I heard her crying. I thought I will kill anyone who is hurting my mother. *I remember the dress she was wearing – an evening dress cut very low, and she was barefooted.* There was a fat black man with a glass of rum in his hand. He said, 'Drink it and you will forget.' She drank it without stopping . . . I saw the man lift her up out of the chair and kiss her. I saw his mouth fasten on hers and she went all soft and limp in his arms and he laughed. (85–6, emphasis added)

In hiding from view and witnessing her mother's sexual and racial degradation it is as if Antoinette watches this unimaginable act from outside herself, a characteristic of extreme dissociation.[20] This event also has an immediacy that represents the absolute presence of the past intruding into the present as if it had only just happened as she relates the fragmentary episode. It is, I believe, the most traumatic moment in the novel with regard to the mother–daughter relationship, and one that simultaneously raises the spectre of unconscious racial ambivalence.

The final re-imaging of Antoinette's witnessing of her mother's sexual and racial abjection reappears in a condensed, almost hysterical form in her state of rapid mental disintegration in the last section of the novel. It is now not connected to (and therefore evades) the uneasy racial undercurrent that pervaded the original scene. Antoinette, at this stage, is obsessed by something she must do. She believes she has been brought to England for a reason and is troubled that she has yet to discover what that might be (116). She is suddenly struck by a vivid flashback. In accordance with her maternal inheritance, the condensed imagery of the returning memory encodes a *recognition* of her mother by the particular dress she had been wearing that day long ago. But for Antoinette this dress unconsciously represents both her mother's *mis-recognition* of her *and* the frozen image of the repeating moment of dismissal (117). Only in death will Antoinette escape this traumatic returning of her mother's endless abandonment.

However, this same episode has another haunting return, but this time it projects a more explicit racial ambivalence. It returns us to the scene in which Antoinette speaks the 'original' traumatic vignette to Rochester as part of her bargain with Christophine before the night of the aphrodisiac and its disastrous results.[21] Afterwards, in a cruel act of revenge and mastery, Rochester openly seduces the coloured servant, Amélie. Rochester's betrayal pushes Antoinette into unconsciously seeking a sense of safety in her white creoleness, the subject position from which she now speaks:

'You like the light brown girls better, don't you? You abused the planters and made up stories about them, but you do the same thing. You send the girl away quicker, and with no money or less money, and that's all the difference.'
'Slavery was not a matter of liking or disliking . . . It was a question of justice' [Rochester replies].
'Justice . . . I've heard that word. It's a cold word. I tried it out . . . I wrote it down. I wrote it down several times and always it looked like a damn cold lie to me. There is no justice . . . My mother whom you all talk about, what justice did she have? My mother sitting in

a rocking-chair . . . a black devil kissing her sad mouth. Like you kissed mine'. (94)

This is an extraordinarily pivotal passage. It begins with Antoinette differentiating between the ideologies of white imperialists and white creoles, which then merge in the act of white buying of black women's sexual favours. White sexual mastery and domination then becomes not an ethical question, only a mere differentiation in the amount of money paid by the men positioned by different hierarchies of whiteness. Then the passage suddenly reverts to the ideological disjunctures between metropolitan whites and those of the colonial island.

Rochester's catachrestical equation of slavery with justice is another example of metaphoric appropriation in the text. The 'abuse' of language inherent in the concept of *catachresis* demonstrates the 'positional power inherent in language', says Paul de Man.[22] 'Something monstrous lurks in the most innocent of catachreses', he continues,[23] and this is certainly the case in Rhys's conceptualisation. This appropriation has a double logic which represents the divisions of whiteness. As an imperialist, Rochester's catachrestic claiming of slavery as a judicial act in order to override his sexual appropriation based on financial exchange also has its ideological framework invested in colonial capitalism. It is 'just' as long as there is financial gain regardless of the dehumanisation of the other that is a 'necessary' component of slavery. However, in contrast, but effectively espousing the same point of view, Antoinette connects the idea of injustice, not to slavery – for white creoles the injustice was slavery's demise that accompanied the Emancipation Act – but to her mother. There still exists an implicit assumption that slavery is just. It is ironic, then, that while the discursive construction of her mother's madness is here alluded to, it is Christophine, an ex-slave, who will later fiercely articulate the injustice of Annette's position to Rochester.[24] Antoinette's unconscious disquiet is much to do with the *racial* degradation into which her mother is forced. In much the same way as her mother interpreted her wearing of Tia's dress as a contaminating act (the touching of the other's skin), now Rochester's sexual liaison with Amélie has retrospectively contaminated her. In a strange racial slippage, Rochester simultaneously *becomes* the sexually exploitative 'black devil' who had kissed her mother, who then kisses her in the same contaminating way. However much these two repeating passages are bound up with her mother's loss, they also represent a textual maze of racial contradictions and ambivalences.

Perhaps this explains why the only place after Coulibri in which

Antoinette feels safe is in the convent, a space of apparent asexuality and racial harmony. Initially, Antoinette luxuriates in the excessive binaries of the Catholic religion: 'Everything was brightness or dark . . . That was how it was, light and dark, sun and shadow, Heaven and Hell' (32). LaCapra maintains that as difference operates ideologically through the structuring of binaries, shoring up identity by opposition to othered outsiders, 'binaries may [also] be seen as excessively rigid defences against the incidence or recurrence of trauma'.[25] The radical dichotomies of Catholicism – based around shades of colour and white and black ideological associations with purity and evil – gradually enclose Antoinette in a sense of safe community. However, this is destroyed when Mason announces she will be leaving soon to marry. The other girls are curious, the nuns ever cheerful, for they do not realise, Antoinette believes, the importance of the fact that, '[t]hey are safe. How can they know what it can be like *outside?*' (34, emphasis in original). It is in this state of anxiety that Antoinette re-enters the outside world.

From this moment on, the rhetoric of safety is overtaken by Rochester. He allays Antoinette's fears when she tries to back out of the arranged marriage by seducing her with promises of 'peace, happiness, safety' (48). Throughout the honeymoon Rochester plays a dangerous discursive game of promised safety with Antoinette while indulging in brutalising forms of sex, verging on sadism. Death, sex, and both his discursive manipulation of the rhetoric of safety and its dubious enactment, come together in their physical union:

> 'You're safe,' I'd say. She'd liked that – to be told *'you are safe'* . . .
> [I] wonder if she ever guessed how near she came to dying . . . *It was not a safe game to play* . . . Desire, Hatred, Life, Death came very close in the darkness. Better not to know how close . . . *'You are safe,' I'd say to her.* (58–9, emphasis added)

Robert Young unravels the ambivalences of cross-race desire in his monograph on colonial desire and hybridity in which be repeats a number of times the axiom 'disgust always bears the imprint of desire'.[26] Soon after Rochester and Antoinette arrive on the Windward Island, Rochester observes that despite her beauty Antoinette has, '[l]ong, sad, dark alien eyes. Creole of pure English descent she may be, but they are not English nor European either' (40). She is beautiful, but she is other. The contradictory force of repulsion/attraction at the heart of colonial desire is also at the heart of colonial racism. However, Young states, there is a disjunction, paradoxically also the link, 'between discursive desire and the violence of colonial desire in its execution'.[27] White males in positions of colonial dominance and power enact their ambivalent desire toward exotic black sexuality by indulging in relationships of sadistic imperative that require a masochistic submission on behalf of subordinated black or mixed-race females.[28] It is this ideological dialectic of dominance and servitude that Rochester seems to participate in, especially as he unconsciously assumes from the beginning that his new wife's white creole status is very far from being within the bounds of racially-superior Englishness. His sexual aggression also seems to include doubts about his masculinity. One morning early in the honeymoon, Rochester returns to the bedroom to find Christophine hovering over Antoinette. 'Taste my bull's blood, master' (52) Christophine says to him, the implication being that the two women may have talked about his sexual prowess, or his lack of it. That the words come from the mouth of a black woman only add to his sexual and racial paranoia. After the intervention of Daniel Cosway – an embodied symbol of hybrid monstrosity in the novel – Rochester's ambivalent tendencies accelerate into cold, calculated brutality that accompanies his assumed outright ownership of Antoinette's mind and body. Jealousy ensures that even though he does not want her she will belong to no one else: 'my lunatic. She's mad but *mine, mine*' (107).

As a result, by the end of Part II, Antoinette retreats into the supposed psychic safety of the state of *zombification*.[29] Zombification as a stand-in for trauma becomes a simplified anglicised knowledge that Rhys relays to her readers through the representation of Rochester's reading of sections of *The Glittering Coronet of Isles* from which a section is quoted (67). Through Rochester's recounting it is suggested that zombification is a problem that is conquerable rather than a concept to be feared. Represented as an uncivilised act of black magic that has to be controlled or curtailed, its power is defused by white law which attempts to disassemble its spiritual power. Rochester takes over the role of the *bokor* and possesses Antoinette's mind and body, or 'soul-case' (69), Christophine's term for the facticity of the body. Rochester locks her away in the safety of the attic, where she becomes the living embodiment of 'a memory to be avoided' (112).

Escape into the safety of white metaphor signified as trauma has a different and highly ambivalent role yet to be discussed. It concerns the symbolic logic contained in the image of *hair*. It is possible that any latent white guilt or anxiety that could not be made explicit in a text that relies on a reading of the traumatisation of white creoles will be apparently resolved through the denial and disavowal mechanism of projection. This psychic strategy, when employed as a defence, can serve to protect the subject from knowledge of its own ambivalence.[30] The traumatic image of hair, as represented so far, has related to Antoinette's sense of maternal loss, often in association with ideas of safety. However, at one particular moment in *Wide Sargasso Sea* this image becomes implicated in an almost palpable racial abhorrence. On her way to the convent for the very first time, Antoinette encounters a young boy and girl who follow and taunt her about her mother at a particular moment in her life when she is devastated by the loss of her mother. Initially it appears as if racial revulsion is reserved for the hybrid body of the half-caste:

> There were two of them, a boy and a girl. The boy was about fourteen and tall and big for his age, he had white skin, a dull ugly white covered with freckles, his mouth was a negro's mouth and he had . . . the eyes of a dead fish. *Worst, most horrible of all, his hair was crinkled, a negro's hair, but bright red* . . . The girl was very black and wore no head handkerchief. *Her hair had been plaited and I could smell the sickening oil she had daubed on it,* from where I stood on the steps of Aunt Cora's dark, clean, friendly house. (26–7, emphasis added)

It is the boy's *white* body with negroid features that is represented as physically repulsive because he suggests the polluted outcome of miscegenation.[31] The 'horrible' imperfection of the albino body carries with it the threat of contagion around which so much imperial ideology revolves. But the striking visual images of this passage that are most indicative of an almost nauseous loathing *and* a simultaneous denial of their racist underpinnings revolve around their hair. What appears to be the most affronting of the boy's features ('worst, most horrible of all') is the fact that he has negro hair and it is *red*, a hair colour usually associated with ultra-white skin colouring. In visible contrast to the albino, the girl is very black. She is reduced to a mouth that taunts and an image of hair that exudes a *sickening smell* from the oil she had daubed on it. The verb 'to daub' signifies an in-built denigration in meanings, which range from unclean defilement with mud or oil, a smearing, coating over, to cover (the person or dress) with finery or ornament in a *coarse*, tasteless manner, a crude painting over, even a manner of bribery.[32] The girl's taunting hits at Antoinette's most vulnerable inner spaces, that she is crazy like her mother, her aunt is so frightened of her she wants her shut away, and worst of all, a reference to her mother's unbridled

sexuality, that she walks around '*sans culottes*' (27, emphasis in original).[33] Antoinette runs away in racial terror, her 'terrified consciousness'
inscribed on body and text by the stigmata of a 'mark on the palm of
my hand and a stain on the cover of my book' (27). However, it is not
the sneering *words* that follow her up the street. What haunts her is the
lingering smell of the girl's hair, and a glimpse of 'my enemy's red hair'
(28) as he runs from her cousin, Sandi, who steps in to help her.

In Rochester's section of the text, *hair* becomes implicitly associated
with both racial degeneracy and disordered sexuality. This begins with
discursive connections between the racial legibility of the body and
ideological assumptions. The servant girl, Hilda, wears a dress that is
spotlessly white, 'but her uncovered hair . . . gave her a savage appearance' (44); Antoinette requests Christophine to stop putting so much
perfume on her hair as, 'He doesn't like it', a silent association perhaps
with the notion of the other's oiled and daubed hair (48); Amélie, 'a
little half-caste servant' (39) who comes to play such a pivotal role in
the failed honeymoon, has 'white girl's hair' (75) for which Antoinette
immediately makes a grab when they physically fight over Amélie's
accusation that as a *white cockroach* Antoinette has had to buy Rochester
as a husband (63).[34] When references to hair are connected with
Antoinette in this section, Rochester's escalating paranoia as to her
racial heritage still reveals a sexual and racial ambivalence, but also participates more strongly in the ongoing intertextual dialogue. The
morning after the night of the obeah potion, 'I woke in the dark after
dreaming that I was buried alive, and when I was awake the feeling of
suffocation persisted' (87). This is an oblique reference to *his* zombification, a situation he will later revengefully re-master by using white
law to defeat *obeah* rebellion. What in fact is suffocating him is
Antoinette's hair 'lying across my mouth; hair with a sweet heavy smell'
(87–8). It had been a night of brutal love-making, as Christophine later
discovers when she sees the markings of Rochester's 'savagery' all over
Antoinette's body. The symbol of suffocating, out-of-control sexuality
lies not with Rochester, however, but with Antoinette and the image of
her hair. Gradually they exchange places of zombification as Rochester
regains control, and Antoinette's maternal legacy is seen to be taking
hold, in a crystallised, forceful image: 'Her hair hung uncombed and
dull into her eyes which were inflamed and staring, her face was very
flushed and looked swollen. Her feet were bare' (93). It is an ambivalent condensation of the image of a zombi caught between the living
and the dead, a re-presentation of her mother's trauma, accompanied
by her abusive jailer, broken glass and her bare feet, and a gesture toward

an ephemeral consanguinity to Bertha Mason, whom Jane Eyre describes thus: 'a woman . . . with thick and dark hair hanging low down her back . . . I never saw such a face . . . It was a discoloured face – it was a savage face.'[35] In its final manifestation in this part of the novel, hair, madness, deviant female sexuality and allusions of race are fused into one: 'She'll loosen her black hair, and laugh and coax and flatter (a mad girl. She'll not care who she's loving). She'll moan and cry and give herself as no sane woman would . . .' (106).

What does it mean then to be possessed by an image? From Caruth's perspective: 'To be traumatized is precisely to be possessed by an image or an event.'[36] In *Wide Sargasso Sea*, Antoinette Cosway Mason Rochester is possessed by repeating traumatic images that are both personally and historically located. One cannot exist without the other, and these images range between the nineteenth century world of Brontë's *Jane Eyre* and post-Emancipation Jamaica, between Rhys's own ambivalent positioning between colonialism and postcolonialism, between white and black. They are in history and outside history, and in many ways this is where the problems of reading Rhys's novel from a postcolonial perspective arise. As LaCapra emphasises, '[i]t is dubious to identify with the victim to the point of making oneself a surrogate victim',[37] and this is what Rhys does with Antoinette. In an article on trauma and the neo-slave narrative which particularly focuses on Gayl Jones's *Corregidora* and Toni Morrison's *Beloved*, Naomi Morgenstern argues that what is at stake in Caruth's analysis of trauma and history is 'not so much the *possibility* of history as its *preservation*. If trauma endangers the subject, it would seem to keep "history" safe.'[38] It is my argument that Jean Rhys does indeed keep white plantocratic history 'safe'. Keeping history safe shuts down subaltern readings of white creole oppression, but it also denies a deconstructive reconfiguring of levels of whiteness that reveals differing levels of domination in the pecking order of power. As surrogate victims of English whiteness and its policies and ideologies, white creole history is preserved, while the profound historical trauma of African-Caribbean slavery remains unarticulated. There is, however, another side to the story to which Rhys gestures in a very contradictory fashion.

3

'Caught Between Ghosts of Whiteness': The Other Side of the Story[1]

> [E]mpire messes with identity
>
> Gayatri Chakravorty Spivak[2]

Although Christophine is the pivotal character in the novel around whom most of the textual contradictions fluctuate and shift, Rhys was always ambivalent about the other side to the story of white creole victimisation which the black woman represents. In a letter to her editor, just before publication, Rhys worries about the textual preponderance she accords Christophine: 'The most seriously wrong thing with Part II is that I've made the obeah woman, the nurse, too articulate. I thought of cutting her a bit, I will if you like, but after all no one will notice. Besides there's no reason why one particular negro woman shouldn't be articulate enough, especially as she's spent most of her life in a white household.'[3] Rhys's reluctance to move beyond the white creole standpoint is reflected in her colonialist reading of the reason that a black woman could possibly be articulate, and also in the fascinating contradictions and blindspots that actually constitute the character of Christophine DuBois.[4]

Christophine's forceful textual presence coexists in an uneasy simultaneity with her social place, which is, as Spivak states, 'the category of the good servant'.[5] Paradoxically, Christophine is always spoken through the consciousness of white characters – what she says is always screened through the point of view of Antoinette or Rochester – but she is also the only one who voices a critique (and an extremely potent one) of the appropriating power of imperial whiteness and its model of obdurate masculinity as symbolised by Rochester.[6] Indeed, Christophine – beginning with the opening paragraph – shapes how everyone else feels or acts throughout most of the novel and, ironically, is the site of affirmation for this white trauma novel. Christophine is the text's strong black matriarch, but she is endlessly loyal to her white mistresses and *never*, except for a couple of asides, does she outrightly resist her own positioning or that of her fellow ex-slaves. Instead, on a number of occasions she uses her obeah power to frighten servants such as Amélie into reluctantly obeying their mistress. She even takes the side of Antoinette's father – a slave-owner renowned for his sexual prolificacy – against Daniel Cosway's slave-mother: 'His mother was a no-good woman and she try to fool the old man but the old man isn't fooled. "One more or less" he says, and laughs. He was wrong. More he do for those people, more they hate him' (101). Thus although she will fight to the end over Antoinette's mistreatment at the hands of Rochester, her textual prominence is *always* reliant on the legacy of her role as a good black 'nigger' in service to her 'legitimate' owners. As a commodified woman she is not only expendable but all too easily dismissible for her 'savage' practices of obeah when her value is no longer employable to shore up white defences. Rochester only has to display a letter that symbolically represents the power of the white Law and Christophine abruptly disappears from the text.

This said, Christophine is the only person in the novel who engages Rochester in a face-to-face duel. There is a long sequence in Part II when Christophine confronts Rochester on behalf of Antoinette. 'Don't think I frightened of you either' (96), she announces as she engages him in a discursive show-down. Benita Parry argues that 'Christophine's defiance . . . constitutes a counter-discourse' and that she functions in the text as the 'free woman' she professes to be.[7] While there can be no doubt that Christophine's spirited interaction with Rochester is an outright discursive rebellion against the imperialist, I do not agree that this represents a counter-discourse. Christophine's daring verbal assault is always probing and protecting *on the behalf of her white mistress* and is always the reported speech, the 'she said,' of Rochester's re-statement. It is, furthermore, also a re-duplication of the white creole trauma narrative that belongs to Antoinette and her mother, not to Christophine and her people. Although her poignant description to Rochester of how Annette was driven mad occurs with a depth of understanding and love that goes far beyond the loyalty of a bought servant (101), it is also spoken from a white point of view. Despite her textual power, Christophine is caught between the discursive ghosts of imperial and white creole whiteness. The potency of her character is always undermined by the necessary double-consciousness that she has needed to internalise in order to survive.

The necessary mutability of Christophine's sense of self is complicated by her positioning as Antoinette's surrogate, or 'othermother'.[8] This term applies to women in African-American communities who assist 'bloodmothers' by sharing mothering responsibilities. This role, adapted from West African practices, and an extremely important survival strat- egy under slavery, is also a vital factor in today's African-American communities, giving, as Patricia Hill Collins states, 'credence to the importance that people of African descent place on mothering'.[9] It may seem presumptuous to use this term in relation to a former slave who mothers a surrogate white daughter, and indeed was a slave when this role first began. However, my aim is to stress the oscillating ambivalence of Rhys's representation of this cross-racial mothering relationship, and at the same time implicitly draw attention to the blindspots in white feminist theories on theories of the maternal. The 'mother–daughter' relationship of Christophine and Antoinette is bound not only by the trauma of Antoinette's loss of her biological mother's love and the trans- ference of this love to Christophine, but also by Antoinette's attitude of white superiority that reasserts itself in her dealings with Christophine whenever she feels insecure or threatened. It is from Christophine that Antoinette receives the attention and maternal love she craves, but it is always an ambivalent love for Antoinette, as contradictory as the learned racism she has ingested from birth.

How Antoinette treats her 'servant/mother' is reliant to a large degree on the white creole discourse that surrounds them.[10] Returning to the newly restored Coulibri after her mother's marriage to Mason, the place has lost some of its childhood lustre for Antoinette. It is not the newness bought by money, nor the strange faces (new servants have been employed): 'It was their talk about Christophine and obeah [that] changed it' (14). This menacing power of rumour driven by racial fear is introjected by the child. Soon after returning home she enters Christophine's room next to the kitchen, which for years has been her sanctuary:

> [W]hen I was waiting there I was suddenly very much afraid. The door was open to the sunlight, someone was whistling near the stables, but I was afraid. I was certain that hidden in the room . . . there was a dead man's dried hand, white chicken feathers, a cock with its throat cut, dying slowly, slowly. Drop by drop the blood was falling into a red basin and I imagined I could hear it. No one had ever spoken to me about obeah – but I knew what I would find if I dared to look. Then Christophine came in smiling and pleased to see

me. Nothing alarming ever happened and I forgot, or told myself that I had forgotten. (14–5)

I think this is a very important, and not often discussed, passage in the text. Antoinette's desperate love for Christophine is always tempered by what she overhears others say of her surrogate mother. In this time of racial tension and historical rupture – accompanied by the changeability of racial positionings – fear and alarmed talk become more excessive than ever. Much later in the novel, when fleeing to Christophine for help after Rochester's abrupt sexual and emotional abandonment, Antoinette again enters Christophine's space. It is an uncanny repetition of the earlier scene, except that the adult Antoinette now has the power to buy her way out of a difficult situation:

Her bedroom was large and dark . . . after I had noticed a heap of chicken feathers in one corner, I did not look round any more.
'So already you frightened eh?' [Christophine says]. And when I saw her expression I took my purse from my pocket and threw it on the bed. (74)

Herein lies the problem. Antoinette cannot face the reality of obeah practices – the real chicken feathers – yet she wants to use obeah 'magic' in a desperate attempt to hold safe her place within the upper rankings of whiteness to which she gained access by her marriage to Rochester. Christophine has already tried to offer another way out for Antoinette by suggesting that she leave Rochester and live with her in Martinique, but Antoinette makes her choice to remain within the privileges of whiteness. In reply to Christophine's wonderful critique of the internalisation of an idealised England and Englishness – a 'cold thief place' (70) with its unseen ideological power to steal your soul – Antoinette reverts to the stereotypical English thinking that Christophine decries: 'how can she know the best thing for me to do, this ignorant, obstinate old negro woman, who is not certain if there is such a place as England?' (70). Christophine is hesitant to use her obeah powers in this situation, telling Antoinette 'that is not for *béké* [white person]. Bad, bad trouble come when *béké* meddle with that' (71), but succumbs out of love for Antoinette, even though it is at great risk to herself, because of the outlawing of obeah on the island. Regardless of this, Antoinette is prepared to bribe Christophine, if necessary, with her 'ugly money' (75). Her action of throwing her purse on the bed displays her colonialist internalisation of the belief in the automatic ownership through money of any black knowledge. The implicit connection of money and the bed also foreshadows Rochester's buying of Amélie's body as an act of revenge against the use of the obeah potion against him. The double-standard in gender and racial coding is interesting here, as Rochester's sexual transaction is represented as in part excusable because Amélie 'offers' herself to him.

It seems therefore as if Rhys's openly expressed ambivalence about her characterisation of Christophine only results yet again in the recounting of one side of the story. Annette and Antoinette are traumatised by history, their personal identities fragmented by their collective and individual pain and loss: Christophine, the subaltern figure representing the other side of the story, stands strong and fierce, indeed she *is* the 'judge's voice' of the novel (98). Yet there is no interior reading of her interpellated subjectivity or of the constitution of self as imbricated in the traumatising legacies of slavery. But how much of Rhys's displacement and disavowal of the ambivalence of the white creole position is projected as a covert longing for blackness? Sometimes in Rhys's other fiction this yearning is explicit. In *Voyage in the Dark* the protagonist Anna Morgan admits: 'I wanted to be black. I always wanted to be black . . . Being black is warm and gay, being white is cold and sad.'[11] Rhys herself consciously acknowledges this long-standing desire as somehow associated with her own mother's indifference to her of which she wrote in one of her vignettes entitled 'My Mother' that appears in her posthumously published memoir, *Smile Please*. She writes: 'She [my mother] loved babies. Once I heard her say that black babies were prettier than white ones. Was this the reason why I prayed so ardently to be black, and would run to the looking-glass in the morning to see if the miracle had happened? And though it never had, I tried again. Dear God, let me be black.'[12] However, in *Wide Sargasso Sea*, her novel most associated with the constitution of colonial relations, Rhys's evocation becomes a hidden, ambivalent desire. As I see it, this has much to do with *appropriation*, its ambivalent origins and ambiguous results.

There is one space where Rhys's appropriation turns against itself, and this concerns the concept of *mimicry*, a term describing the ambivalent relationship between coloniser and colonised and an important concept in postcolonial theory because it offers a mode of resistance to the colonised. In Homi Bhabha's conceptualisation mimicry is:

> the sign of a double articulation; a complex strategy of reform, regulation, and discipline, which *'appropriates'* the Other as it vizualises

power. Mimicry is also the sign of the *inappropriate*, however, a difference or recalcitrance which coheres the dominant strategic function of colonial power, intensifies surveillance, and poses an immanent threat to both 'normalized' knowledges and disciplinary powers.[13]

Rochester's power is radically unsettled by Christophine to the extent that he starts involuntarily repeating what she says: 'every word she said was echoed, echoed loudly in my head' (98). When she speaks, his mimicking reaction is not spoken out loud: it is a fragmented interior monologue, bracketed off from direct engagement. Thus, temporarily at least, the menace of mimicry is spoken by a black female ex-slave who 'inappropriately' disarticulates his white English patriarchal power. But is Rhys's use of Christophine as the spokesperson of white creoleness a case of reverse mimicry? If the colonised respond to colonial domination by an ambivalent mimicry – which while aiming to efface differences, re-inscribes them, but at the same time unsettles the distinction between the dominators and the dominated – the act of mimicry as resistance becomes a kind of parody that forces the parodied to examine their position, status and use of power. However, the irony of this text is that Rhys's white creoles are the *white but not quite* who mimic black Caribbean culture, wanting in one sense to be like them because of their supposed freedom, but in the other unconsciously and consciously despising them for that very culture and colour and the fact that they are the racially dominated. In this way the ambivalence of mimicry has produced a double turn.

For instance, there is also an unsettling incident when Antoinette undermines Rochester by impersonating a black voice. Stung into defiance by Rochester's refusal to discuss his visit to Daniel Cosway or listen to her mother's story, Antoinette retorts: ' "You frightened?" . . . imitating a Negro's voice, singing and insolent' (82). Another time she exactly repeats Rochester's hectoring words, again using the taunting Negro voice: 'she mimicked me . . . in that mincing voice' (94). In the second example a white creole woman mimics the white masculine imperialist, but, in doing so, appropriates the black resistant voice which at any other time has most often been defending the white creole position. So really, who is mimicking whom in this text? Racial and class lines are crossed, binaries are unsettled, but only by re-appropriating – and thereby usurping – the whole idea of mimicry as a weapon of the colonised.

By the close of Part II, Christophine has been driven from the text and Antoinette has been removed to the attic in Thornfield Hall. The third and last part of the novel returns to the trauma narrative in which Antoinette is the quintessential victim. The racial tension and bitterness of the Caribbean context and the historical trauma that has contributed to both her and her mother's madness is left behind. Antoinette now lives entirely in an individualised state of traumatised imprisonment, both in her mind *and* within the cardboard covers of *Jane Eyre*. No such place as the idealised whiteness of the England she imagines exists, just as Christophine had warned her. The psychic numbness that had enshrouded her towards the end of Rochester's narrative is beginning to shift and stir. She knows there is something she 'must do', but she does not yet know what this is. However, her mind is still confused and clouded by ever-present images of her mother and the particular doubled trauma that had engulfed her young life – her mother's aban-donment and the dreadful repeating scene of Annette's abuse at the hands of her jailers:

> Looking at the tapestry one day I recognized my mother dressed in an evening gown but with bare feet. She looked away from me, over my head just as she used to do . . . and I saw Antoinette drifting out of the window with her scents, her pretty clothes and her looking glass. (117)

She sees herself drifting out of the only window that is so high up, Antoinette has just told us, that she cannot see out of it, symbolic of the traumatised gaze that cannot see herself or others with any sense of narrative understanding. Her disintegrating subjectivity and her help-less 'drifting' here represent the passivity and helplessness of the pro-foundly dislocated, traumatised by a history over which she has no control. She is entrapped in an endless melancholy and impossible mourning.

Much of this is the result of Antoinette's inability to mourn her mother's abandonment and death, a mourning impaired by having no one to listen and empathise with her story of profound grief and loss. Her mother's funeral, a ritual devised to enhance the chance of com-pleted mourning, was rushed and incomprehensible. Held early in the morning – suggestive of the shame of suicide – no one tells her how Annette died, and she does not ask. Christophine cries bitterly, but Antoinette has no tears. She tries to pray 'but the words fell to the ground meaning nothing' (35). The Sister Superior had no answer to her question about the terribleness of her mother's life and death,

Rochester refuses to listen to her belated attempt at catharsis through trying to tell her mother's story, so the trauma deepens and fixates in the repetitive image of her mother's helplessness. The impacted grief of her traumatised inheritance and the impossibility of escape from its psychic hold is enacted as a form of *abreaction*, ironically crystallised as the moment that they 'lost their way to England'.[14] It takes place on the *white* ship. Held captive in her cabin, Antoinette puts her arms round the neck of the young man who brings her food and begs him to help her. When he refuses, she smashes 'glasses and plates against the porthole' both in anger and in the forlorn hope that this 'would break open and the sea come in' (117).[15] A man and a woman clear up the broken glass, and a third person gives her a drink to make her forget. Sexual contact, broken glass, a suicide attempt, oblivion in a mind-numbing liquid, all are horribly reminiscent of the scene that haunts her regarding her mother's physical and mental entrapment.

A visit by Richard Mason radically changes Antoinette's previous responses to her prolonged trauma, although she is not immediately aware of his visit. After the description of the abreactive experience there is a gap in the narrative. She wakes aching and sore but has no recollection of the previous night when Richard had visited, until the scene is repeated to her by her keeper, Grace Poole, the listener who has now replaced Rochester. The minute Richard mentioned that he 'cannot interfere *legally* between yourself and your husband' (119–20, emphasis added), Grace tells Antoinette, she had attacked him with a knife. Initially it seems as if Antoinette's *re*-action is in answer to her powerless state as her husband's legal property, but from my reading the trigger is the sudden return of a previously dissociated trauma that relates back to her relationship with her mother. What causes Antoinette's traumatic regression is that Richard does not *recognise* her, which spirals her back into the endlessly repeating scene of her childhood. Importantly, however, this is the first time in the novel that Antoinette begins to question herself and her actions or lack of them. As she begins to narrativise and to make sense of her life, the symbol that has carried all the symbolic weight of Antoinette's cumulative trauma now returns and merges into a singular red dress, representative of her past life and her lost West Indian self.[16] 'If I'd been wearing that [dress Richard] would have known me' (120) she tells herself and Grace Poole.

Antoinette demands to see the red dress. As she stares at it she is transported back in time, suffused with embodied memories of the scent and colours of Jamaica. The temporal shift is marked by a textual space then an ellipsis, both suggestive of omission or suppression. She is back with

Sandi in the immediacy of the past that appears to be the present.[17] She is again the white creole woman who can only read things in binaries as taught by the imperial/colonial cultural system that has structured her life. On one hand, she can never see beyond her longing for real whiteness ('I shall be different in England'); on the other, there is her ambivalent love of blackness as symbolised by her feelings for Christophine. In between is Sandi, who *can* offer her safety and happiness (the two things Rochester so callously promised) and a place in the new hybrid world of post-Emancipation Jamaica. However, reared as a white creole, a group collectively interpellated as being on the periphery of Empire, for Antoinette this hybrid space is the place of insecurity and fear of what the in-between colour entails. Following her mother's legacy, Antoinette emphatically chooses the white path. She will not stay with Sandi but goes to England with Rochester, ensuring her fate as the madwoman in the attic:

> there was no time left so we kissed each other . . . We often kissed before but not like that. That was the life and death kiss and you only know a long time afterwards what it is, the life and death kiss. (121)

Now comes the belated interpretation of her past act, the switching of tenses from past into present and the repetition of the desperate embrace – the 'life and death kiss' – signalling the move into conscious assimilation of this memory. The bitter irony of belated understanding begins to seep through. 'The white ship' (121) that takes her away to England whistles the levels of her interpellation into imperial whiteness that meant she would not consider happiness with Sandi. It whistles 'once gaily' (the enticement of seduction); 'once calling' (the hailing of 'hey you'); 'once to say goodbye' (the loss of subjective agency and departure into the white system). However, the flash of recognition is lost as she returns to the present time – again conveyed by a gap in the text – and the circumscriptions of Brontë's text.

Antoinette takes the red dress out of the closet, holds it against herself and asks Grace: ' "Does it make me look intemperate and unchaste?" . . . That man told me so . . . "Infamous daughter of an infamous mother," he said to me' (121). Rhys's brilliant interweaving of quotations from both 'mother' and 'daughter' texts draws attention to the power of discourse to structure and control encompassing both gender and racial ambivalences.[18] However, the return to traumatic memory as a cathartic healing cannot be efficacious in a text in which the traumatised person is predetermined to die in madness. Antoinette's internal monologue now slides into that very madness against which she has fought all her life: 'I held the dress in my hand wondering if they had done the last and worst thing. If they had *changed* it when I wasn't looking. If they had changed it and it wasn't my dress at all . . .' (121). The repetitive 'they' not only suggests a rapidly fragmenting objectified self, but also a connection back to the opening paragraph of the novel in which the 'they' then demarcated the white ranks from which Annette and Antoinette were already excluded. Antoinette's last words before falling into her final dream are again of the dress and misrecognition: 'If I had been wearing my red dress Richard would have known me' (121).

From my perspective, Antoinette's leap in imagination to rejoin Tia by the pool at Coulibri is basically a return to an unchanged pre-Emancipation white creole world. Rhys transposes her Edenic imagery – and in particular the trope of the tree of life – from the first section of the novel into the attic of Thornfield Hall, suggesting the lure of nostalgic return to the pre-lapsarian plantocratic empire that had existed before the Fall of Emancipation. Yet, of course, the ending is totally ambivalent.[19] Pre-determined to end in death, Rhys's rewriting of Bertha's life parodies and in a way mimics the white imperial culture that historically othered white creoles, as represented in *Jane Eyre*. In the process *Wide Sargasso Sea* unsettles the imperial reading of history, so often replicated in the choice of what is or has been included in the literary canon. However, despite its resistance to the imperial metanarrative, what the text does not do is to provide a space for Christophine's own story, the story of enslavement and appropriation of people's lives for the greater profit of the white race.

In one sense then, Jean Rhys's appropriation of Afro-Caribbean resistance practices as metaphors of white trauma silences the history on which they are predicated: on the other, the unconscious ambivalences which structure her novel open up possibilities of re-readings, not just against *Jane Eyre*, but of the whole ambivalence of the postcolonial era, and its academic speculations and theories. The mutability of the category of whiteness in the time of decolonisation and the power differentials inherent in racial dissonances, come under Rhys's ambivalent scrutiny. She disrupts and disarticulates *all* identity formations of Empire. Christophine is the character chosen to enunciate the white creole position and not her own, returning the trauma to the white mother–daughter narrative in which she played so much part. Yet, in this very representation, Rhys also anticipates the difficulties inherent in the belatedness of postcolonial theory that can never be separable from colonial history. *Wide Sargasso Sea* is a particularly interesting text for a postcolonial reading, as the use of orthodox postcolonial theories produce perplexing results. Appropriation, catachresis, ambivalence, mimicry, hybridity and so on, the principles of a resistant postcoloniality, are confused and sometimes almost reversed in Rhys's novel. Yet, the text's refusal of ideological closure, its focus on a mother–daughter relationship and its ambivalent unresolvability, open up the sometimes narrow confines of postcolonial theory and its gender imbalances.

To return to the poem that opens my reading of Rhys's novel, Antoinette Cosway Mason Rochester is literally caught in an untenable position *between two sentences*: between *Jane Eyre* and *Wide Sargasso Sea*, between black and white, between coloniser and colonised, between the tenets of Christianity and the power of obeah magic, between metaphors that appropriate and metaphors that proliferate. Jean Rhys's *white hush*, resonant with a temporary stillness, may be caught between two sentences, but a hush implies that the sigh will continue on. It is a transitory and creative stillness. *Wide Sargasso Sea* is a courageous novel that struggles with an historical trauma that haunted Jean Rhys all her life, in both a collective and individual sense. This resulted in a trauma narrative of extraordinary immediacy, both past and present, a 'wounded space'[20] that crosses the cultural divide(s), and in the suspension of ambivalent space begins a postcolonial renegotiation of the power structures of colonialism. As the sigh moves forward there is also a movement forward in time in the practice and theory of writing fiction. Rhys's novel lives on in its own mesmerising power, but very importantly, her work is taken up and reconfigured by black women Caribbean writers as diverse as Michelle Cliff and Elean Thomas, and poets, Olive Senior, Lorna Goodison and Jean Binta Breeze.[21]

Rhys's novel *Wide Sargasso Sea* is caught up in the axiomatics of imperialism, but her trauma narrative – riven as it is with ambivalence and contradictions – also opens up the difficult task of historical listening which Caruth describes thus:

> The attempt to gain access to a traumatic history, then, is also the project of listening beyond the pathology of individual suffering, to the reality of a history that in its crises can only be perceived in unassimilable forms.[22]

It is in literature that the 'unassimilable forms' of history can come alive, and it is the metaphorical image that in Elspeth Probyn's words, 'organizes the field of the unthinkable'.[23] However, it is of great political importance that metaphorical abstraction in theoretical criticism does not evade lived experience with all the racial, gender and class assumptions that this entails. Metaphors need to be historicised and contextualised so as to be aware of the possible powers of appropriation concealed in the normative axioms of whiteness. This, I believe, is made possible by approaching readings of literature through a contrapuntal relationship with what John Frow describes as 'a history that is rigorously committed to ambivalence'.[24] *Wide Sargasso Sea* is a novel that begins this process.

4
Lucy: Jamaica Kincaid's Postcolonial Echo

[T]here is nothing that ideology fails to touch

Deborah McDowell[1]

By her own admission, Jamaica Kincaid was an unruly student. At school in Antigua she was frequently punished for insubordination. One disciplinary infringement resulted in her having to copy out and memorise lengthy passages from Milton's *Paradise Lost*; another meant she had to write over and over again the lines, 'Ignorance is bliss; it's folly to be wise'.[2] In light of the rebellious postcolonial fiction Kincaid would come to write, these colonial punishments are profoundly ironic. *Paradise Lost*, Kincaid states, taught her the importance and the possibilities of articulating injustice in the face of overwhelming odds. Milton's anti-hero, the defiant and outcast Lucifer with whom she identified even as a child, inspired her and gave her a sense of worth. 'My version [of *Paradise Lost*] had a painting of Lucifer,' Kincaid confides in an interview. 'His hair was snakes, all striking. Oh it was fabulous! I was the wrong person to give it to.'[3] Lucifer – the Biblical symbol of evil, who, among other things, illustrates that there is a more complicated and ambiguous reading of right and wrong – is a figure that returns with a strange and echoing impact at the end of Kincaid's second novel, *Lucy*.

The contradictory interpellations of the British colonial curricula that indoctrinated children throughout the Empire with a sense of inferiority and alienation – while simultaneously inculcating a love/hate relationship with Englishness and English literature – is a frequent trope in the fiction of postcolonial Caribbean writers from Césaire, Naipaul, Lamming and Walcott to Rhys, Cliff and Kincaid herself. The psychic displacement that existed between the embodied experiences of the colonised and the imposed phantasmic economy of the plays, poems and fiction of such luminaries of the Western literary canon as Shakespeare, Milton, Keats and Wordsworth has been termed the 'daffodil gap' in contemporary postcolonial theory.[4] In her second novel, *Lucy*, Jamaica Kincaid has much to say about both daffodils and the split subjectivity – what she calls 'two-facedness' – that results from this educational imperialism.[5] Many critics have commented at length on Kincaid's focus on the daffodil, both its literal representation in Wordsworth's poem that the young colonial child, Lucy, recites on the school dais, and its psychic repercussions. Indeed, so central is the concept of the daffodil in readings of Kincaid's *Lucy* that there is hardly an article or book-length discussion of this novel that does not allude to the daffodil iconography in some shape or form.[6] I will align this emphasis on the daffodil gap with an exploration of the ambivalent ideological effects of a colonial education and the possibilities of a subversive postcolonial return that is intricately threaded through Kincaid's text.

The politics of Kincaid's adult postcolonial fiction makes the enforced repetition of lines of canonical poetry – the second of Kincaid's childhood penalties – a doubly ironic choice. For the sentence that she was forced to write, juxtaposing ignorance and bliss, folly and wisdom, is a quotation from the last two lines of Thomas Gray's 'Ode on a Distant Prospect of Eton College'.[7] Eton College, one of the oldest and most prestigious schools in Britain, was and still is, a bastion of white upper and middle-class masculine traditions, privileges and power, and an ideal space for the dissemination of imperial and neo-colonial ideologies and their disciplinary practices. The poem, in which Gray's school days at Eton College, and indeed Eton itself, acquire a 'prelapsarian innocence' shaped by echoes of Milton's description of Eden from *Paradise Lost*, is a lamentation on the loss of times past.[8] What the poem does not say, but the commentaries disclose, is that Gray was an outsider at this school, much despised for his delicate health and his aversion to the compulsory sport deemed so necessary to the creation of white manhood. His psychic survival depended on the banding together of himself and three like-minded boys who became known as the 'Quadruple Alliance'.[9] However, Gray's idealisation of his schooldays was written at a particular moment of anguished nostalgia. Of the four boys, the only one with whom he had remained close had recently died, while the other two refused connection with him. Gray's melancholic ode is thus perhaps an attempt to disavow the distress of his estrangement from the 'imagined community' that had sustained his sense of self, and simultaneously a requiem for his lost youth and the very particularised sense of naturally assumed white privilege that accompanied his positioning as an old Etonian.[10] In this way, ignorance can become bliss because it offers a comforting amnesia. However, there is a pivotal word missing from Gray's quotation with which the schoolgirl Kincaid was forcibly engaged, for the lines in fact read, '*where* ignorance is bliss, /Tis folly to be wise'.[11] By omitting this one small word – a positioning adverb of placement – the meaning of the sentence is radically altered. Yet, as it will turn out, little matters more than a subject's positioning, which, as Kincaid's protagonist in *Lucy* so aptly demonstrates, is always entangled with the power differentials that structure race, gender and class placements.

Yet it is also next to impossible to avoid the ambivalent binding power of the ideology that surrounds the colonial education system, a structure intimately related to interwoven and internalised aspects of both pleasure and power. Ketu Katrak maintains that aggressive physical acts of conquest and literal appropriation of land and peoples constitute only one aspect of colonial aspirations: 'mental colonizations perpetuated in a colonizer's language, education, and cultural values are often more devastating and resilient.'[12] As Elleke Boehmer avers, 'empire was governed as much by symbolism as by real distinctions in the world, which is to say, because colonial authority expressed its dominance in part through the medium of representation, a colonialist work of imagination functioned as an instrument of power'.[13] Indeed, the pleasure of the text was ultimately what held the recipients of a colonial education in thrall, and Western canonical literature occupied what Gayatri Spivak calls a 'kind of enchanted space'.[14]

Gauri Viswanathan sees both John Milton's treatises on colonial education and his great work of poetry, *Paradise Lost*, as responsible for the development of a significant part of imperialist ideology.[15] Ironically, while Milton's verses were central to the formulation of colonial loyalty – and in this respect it seems that for Kincaid Milton holds a particular eminence – *Paradise Lost* is also a key component of Kincaid's strategy of literary *backchat* and postcolonial reversal, as I hope to demonstrate.[16] In interviews, Kincaid freely admits to a deep-seated allegiance to Milton's epic poem, yet while her knowledge was the result of a British colonial education that she much resented, she is also adamant that she is 'not going to make myself forget John Milton because it involves a painful thing. I find John Milton very beautiful . . . I am sorry that the circumstances of how I got to know it were horrid . . . but since I know it, I know it and I claim every right to use it'.[17] In another interview, Kincaid goes as far as admitting that she had modelled her 'entire literary life so far on *Paradise Lost*... almost all of my work centres on the beginning of a paradise from which one falls and to which one can never return'.[18] Interestingly, Sharon Achinstein argues that 'Milton's poetry has proven capable of supporting *either* an anti-imperial *or* pro-imperial stance', and Kincaid's reworking of the power of Lucifer clearly engages with what Achinstein terms 'the dialectical nature of ideological writing'.[19] Where Kincaid totally diverges from any other post-colonial rewriting of *Paradise Lost* that I have encountered is that the paradise from which the young female protagonist always falls is inevitably the very gendered symbolic space of 'the paradise of mother'.[20] This is true of the majority of stories in her anthology, *At the Bottom of the River*, her first two novels, *Annie John* and *Lucy*, and also the oxymoronically titled *Autobiography of My Mother*.

Lucy, the focus of this chapter, is the story of a Afro-Caribbean young woman, aged 17, who leaves her home island of Antigua to work as an *au pair* in America for a rich middle-class white family that consists of the mother, Mariah, her husband, Lewis, and four young daughters. We assume the protagonist is called Lucy, but she is in fact not specifically named until the last pages of the novel with carefully orchestrated dramatic intent. The American family has no patronymic, indicative of its symbolic status as representative of white American liberal humanism. The young woman has been reared on a colonial education, and arrives on American soil with her head full of the books she has read – the canonical classics of Western 'civilisation' – sure that her life now is really to begin. She has left behind a fractured relationship with her mother fissured by an almost pathological ambivalence that manifested itself as an intense 'feeling of hatred'. In many respects this novel follows on and echoes the themes of Kincaid's first novel, *Annie John*. There is a continuation of the themes of both the tempting yet enraging indoctrinations of each protagonist's colonial education and also a profound maternal ambivalence. However, *Lucy* is unique in Kincaid's oeuvre in that this is the novel which represents what Edward Said describes as, 'Jamaica Kincaid in the white world'.[21] Apart from her recent book on gardening, *My Garden (Book)*, which follows her latest interest in forms of conquest, both literal and imaginative, that accompany acts of ecological imperialism, Kincaid's other fictional and non-fictional work meditates upon the black world of her cultural home, the Caribbean island of Antigua. It is only in *Lucy* that she directly interrogates the intoxicating power of contemporary whiteness, and it is a novel that is less overtly rebellious than the rest of her work, and in many ways more painful.

In *Annie John* the young protagonist literally throws off the shackles of history when she defaces a picture of Christopher Columbus that appears in her history book, a text of Empire entitled *A History of the West Indies*.[22] In *Lucy*, Kincaid is engaged with the subtle entanglements of ideology and its internalisation bound up as it is in the living out of this very history and its traumatic inheritances. Christopher Columbus again features at the moment of belatedness in this text, but now Kincaid satirises with a forceful but subtly biting irony the long-lasting echoic legacies of Columbus's 'foul deed' (135) that resulted in the transportation of African slaves to the Caribbean. While the end of the novel circles back to a confrontation with Lucy's ancestral history, which until then has been psychically subsumed under confusions of positionality, the context of the novel is contemporary North America. In particular, it concerns her relationship with her employer, Mariah, whom Lucy grows to love as a substitute mother with a love seemingly devoid of ambivalence, an emotion reserved for her own mother whom she has gladly left behind in Antigua. Kincaid focuses intensively in all her work on the mother–daughter relationship, but this is complicated beyond readings of maternal ambivalence by her symbolic correlation between the damaging effects engendered by the 'mother-country' on the 'daughter' colony. The personal, and often antagonistic, relationship between mother and daughter is problematised by the mother having internalised the cultural mores of the colonialists. Resembling in some form the ideological machinations of the colonial education system, Kincaid's mothers in both *Annie John* and *Lucy* act as agents of colonial assimilation who try to mould their daughters into properly disciplined colonial subjects.[23] In *Lucy*, although the protagonist is now physically separated from her mother by the vast expanse of the Atlantic ocean, her ambivalent psychic bond remains profoundly connected. Relocated and rehoused physically and mentally within the cocoon of white liberal humanism as espoused by Mariah, Lucy works for a year, has two love affairs with white men, forms a friendship with a young Irish immigrant named Peggy, and gradually begins to break free from the ideology of whiteness that has so enthralled her.

Considering the centrality of the mother–daughter relationships in this text – that is, both real and surrogate – one of the ironies that will slowly unfold in a close reading of the novel is that the literary texts in which Lucy is most immersed (specifically named in the novel as *Paradise Lost* and the Bible, especially the Book of Genesis) are explicitly gendered 'stories of the fallen' (152). Both Milton's opus and the biblical story of the Fall from grace on which it relies are tales of shame, grief and the punishment of women. Eve's temptation into 'original sin' in the Book of Genesis – or into the desire for knowledge, depending on the perspective of the reader – precipitates not only the fall from Paradise, but also brings about the creation of shame. In *Lucy*, the first chapter is suffused with oblique references to the Bible, and in the last of the five chapters there are a number of allusions to shame as the protagonist moves into a newly developing mode of self-consciousness.

It is interesting, then, that in Milton's rereading of the Fall from grace, with which Kincaid is avowedly familiar, the primal scene of shame – when Eve and Adam realise that they are naked in the eyes of God and reach for fig leaves to cover their nakedness – is textually connected with the discovery of the New World:

> Hide me . . . hide . . .
> The Parts of each from other, that seem most
> To shame obnoxious, and unseemliest seen,
> Some Tree whose broad smooth Leaves together sew'd,
> . . . Those leaves
> They gather'd, broad as Amazonian Targe,
> And with what skill they had, together sew'd,
> To gird their waist, vain Covering if to hide
> Their guilt and dreaded shame; O how unlike
> To that first naked Glory. Such of late
> Columbus found th'American so girt
> With feather'd Cincture, naked else and wild
> Among the Trees on Isles and woody Shores.[24]

The fall into shame is often blamed on Eve for succumbing to temptation and eating the forbidden fruit, then seducing Adam to follow her lead. Yet, ironically, while they then suffer the punishment of banishment from Paradise, they also gain access to knowledge. They can now tell the difference between good and evil, right and wrong, inside and outside, naked and clothed, shame and innocence, and so on.[25] Perhaps, if the question is posed from a postcolonial perspective, it becomes more complicated. Interestingly, in Milton's rendition (or at least in these few lines) gender drops out of equation – 'with what skill *they* had, together [they] sew'd'. As Colombus reformulated the notion of discovery in the New World by the genocide of the Arawak and Carib Indians that led over time to the importation of slave labour from elsewhere, the question then becomes: who is falling from Paradise, and who should engender and suffer from notions of shame?

However, among the extraordinary wealth of intertextual references and allusive echoes for which *Paradise Lost* is famous, there is also a small scene that interlaces Eve's story with another of the founding myths of subject formation, the classical tale of Narcissus and Echo.[26] Still innocent, as she has yet to eat the forbidden fruit from the Tree of Knowledge, Eve is represented by Milton as possessing the narcissistic vanity for which the hero of the myth is famed, suggesting perhaps the inevitability of the Fall at the hands of a woman.[27] This is particularly ironic because, as Gayatri Spivak caustically remarks in her essay on Echo, 'Narcissus was a boy'.[28] This classical myth is almost always read as Narcissus's story alone, as if Echo had no part to play in the unfolding drama.[29] In much the same manner, it is also 'naturally' assumed, as with the case of the biblical story of creation, that the protagonists are white.

As I see it, the classical myth of Echo and Narcissus has a particular resonance in *Lucy*, and indeed I will argue that Kincaid utilises the story as a strong sub-textual undercurrent. Yet, while a close reading of this novel reveals the power of the white text to reduce the othered woman to an echo of herself, it also delineates Lucy's resistance. Her subversive postcolonial echo uproots the haunting impact of white canonical texts and creates a new self-conscious form of contemporary race and gender conscious re-troping of both the notion of the echo and its foundations in the classical Western myth. It is both an acknowledgement of the past that has been overlaid by echoes emanating from the intoxication of Western literature, and a refiguring of its ideological pull as a form of subversive return that ironically utilises the very form and lure of its 'enchanting' containment. The question that Kincaid's novel implicitly raises then asks is: is it ever possible psychically to disengage from the binding pleasure of the texts of one's youth, or do they always remain diffusely positioned as constantly recurring nostalgic echoes that blind the recipient to their ideological calling?

Echoic ambivalence

A textual echo (or any echo for that matter) has a precursor. As *Wide Sargasso Sea* echoes and rewrites *Jane Eyre*, Kincaid herself is haunted by Brontë's text, which she read over and over again as a child. Books, she says, provided the greatest happiness in her difficult adolescent years that were overshadowed by her growing alienation from her mother, and *Jane Eyre* was one of her favourites. Reading the novel for the first time when she was ten, Kincaid notices and then becomes captivated by Brontë's representation of that languorous extended moment of European dusk when she uses the word 'gloaming'. There is, of course, no period of twilight in the Caribbean where light shifts very quickly from sunset into darkness thus, as Kincaid muses from an adult perspective:

> She's describing something, English, something I would never see until I was thirty-odd years old. I got stuck on that word, and eventually found a way to use in *At the Bottom of the River*. Then I was free of it. It was important to me to have written those stories, because it freed me of an obsession with a certain kind of language. I memorized Wordsworth when I was a child, Keats, all sorts of things. It was an attempt to make me into a certain kind of person, the kind of person they had no use for anyway. An educated black person. I got stuck with a lot of things, so I ended up using them.[30]

Inserting and refashioning the very English word into one of her own stories diffracts and to some extent lessens the interpellative power of the white literary echo. However, its distortions, as Kincaid intimates, had lingered on in her mind for 20 or so years, suggesting that metaphorical systems bind those educated through the colonial curriculum in incalculable ways. This internalisation of the Western echo can play a substantial role in suppressing or even denying alternative readings and the possibilities of developing a self-conscious black subjectivity uncontaminated by such symbolic processes.

Words can wound and heal, enthral and subjugate, and they are intrinsic to constructions of both the interiority and exteriority of the self. This is in part the subject of Spillers' famous essay, 'Mama's Baby, Papa's Maybe', which addresses the destructive power of the American grammar, and in particular the impact that white stereotyping has had on generations of African-Americans.[31] The ongoing pathologising that first justified the capturing of African bodies through the Atlantic Slave Trade has metamorphosed into a linguistic strategy that uses the black body as a 'resource for metaphor' Spillers argues, thereby turning the literal possession of the 'captive body' into an abstract ownership through the power of language. One of her examples is the infamous Moynihan Report, which 'freezes in meaning' an extremely negative understanding of the composition of the Negro family of the late 1960s, thus continuing the literal marking and branding that had originally been inscribed directly on the bodies of slaves.[32] This prescriptive othering and its internalised echoing then transfers down through generations, impacting on African-Americans in ways that are seen and unseen. The effects Spillers critiques by re-troping one of the founding proverbs of the American grammar: 'We might concede, at the very least that sticks and bricks *might* break our bones, but words will most certainly *kill* us.'[33]

Powerfully negative aspects of symbol-making, which play so great a role in what Spillers elsewhere calls the 'Manichean frieze',[34] have their counterpart in the story of Narcissus and Echo. In allegorical form, it outlines the power of language in the construction of identity. Indeed, John Hollander, in his evocative book, *The Figure of Echo: A Mode of Allusion in Milton and After*, to which I owe much of my interpretation, draws attention to the fact that the Echo and Narcissus myth is centrally a story about language.[35] Echo, punished by the goddess Juno for distracting her by keeping her talking while the rest of the nymphs cavort with her husband, Jupiter, is deprived of the power of normal speech: she is forever condemned merely to echo the last words of others. Moreover, unable to originate discourse, neither can she forbear from reply. As Ovid puts it, Echo 'repeats the last words spoken, and gives back the sounds she has heard'.[36] Echo then falls hopelessly in love with the beautiful youth Narcissus. Because of her punishment she cannot approach him with declarations of love, having to wait instead for him to speak with words that she might re-use to echo her longing. One day, discovering him alone and calling out to his lost companions, Echo grasps the opportunity cleverly to participate in the dialogue. Invited by her own echo of his words, Echo comes out of hiding and embraces him, but Narcissus violently rejects her with the words: 'Away with those embraces! I would die before I would have you touch me!' Her poignant echoing reply, 'I would have you touch me', omits the words 'I would die', a phrase that will have important echoing repercussions in Kincaid's novel, as I shall discuss.[37] Thus scorned, Echo conceals herself from all others, hiding her shamed faced in the woods. With the pain of rejection, her body slowly wastes away and finally turns to stone, leaving only her voice. From that time on, Echo's plaintive voice can be heard compulsively answering the calls of others that she hears echoing around the mountains. In the meantime, punished by Nemesis for his self-obsession and disregard for others, Narcissus is condemned to fall in love with his own watery reflection. He lies beside a beautiful pool staring at his face in the water until he too gradually pines to death, mourned forever by the watching Echo. This is the Western myth that pathologises women into a state of petrification with its allegory of silencing, abjection and passivity. One small resistance is left to her for while Narcissus pines away and metamorphoses into a flower: Echo 'survives as a consciousness and a voice'.[38] Like Narcissus, she too loses her body, but her voice lives on in both mourning and mockery. In the place of his body, and as a visible representation of his absence, grows the beautiful flower that bears his name. Coincidentally, the narcissus belongs to the same genus as the daffodil, synecdochic of Empire, as I have argued, in much postcolonial fiction.

There is then, a tangential but resonant connection that enables a reading of Narcissus as a symbolic white male coloniser in love with his own image and seductive power, whose self-fixation ensures an almost complete disregard for others, and Echo as his gendered subaltern subject. Moreover, Kincaid's reconstituted Echo is particularly subversive as it reconfigures a founding Eurocentric myth of identity formation, a myth that has become a part of Western popular discourse through its understanding of the concept of narcissism. However, Kincaid's remodelling of the negative aspects of the mythic Echo comes from a completely different ideological and race-positioned perspective. The echoing voice of the subaltern subject, distorted by both the West's original texts' misrepresentations and the material traumas they have inflicted, introduces a form of mimicking *backchat* that in the postcolonial mode is a conscious act of belated acknowledgement and accusation concerning past distortions and injustices of the previously written. The subaltern echo may be able to repeat only a fragment of the utterance, yet that fragment is also a form of postcolonial mimicry: the echoing voice 'knows' the full utterance but only repeats the last few words. The female subaltern subject is not merely indulging in the mockery of mimicry (which is perhaps a lot less resistant than Bhabha's theory suggests, and certainly so for a woman) nor a form of passive echolalia, but the agency of call-and-response theory as proposed by a number of African-American theorists and writers, many of whom are women.[39] The protagonist in *Lucy*, as I shall go on to argue, is at first caught up in the passivity of the Western literary tradition to which Echo belongs, but gradually moves into participating in African-American traditions of resistance that signify agency, though often in a necessarily veiled form.

Importantly then, the echoic subaltern voice is a female voice. Even more importantly, it connects in with the long tradition of African oral culture that was carried over in and through the unimaginable trauma of the Middle Passage, the event that Barbara Christian defines as 'the dividing line between being African and being African American'.[40] Despite the trauma of disjunction of the Middle Passage, the slaves carried with them their African cultural traditions which, in the words of Cornel West, included a 'kinetic orality, passionate physicality, improvisational intellectuality, and combatative spirituality [that] would undergo creative transformation when brought into contact with European languages and rituals in the context of the New World'.[41] Once in the New World newly captive slaves lived in a culture of pain in which they were deprived of all basic dignities and fundamental human rights, but one that they fought against with a fierce resistant power. In the American Plantation system they created a veiled African-based culture that was a forced synthesis of African cultural history, traditions and memory with an appropriation of the only language now available to them – the English language, and with it the rhetoric and symbolism of the Christian Bible. Using the newly acquired white discourse and in order to survive attempts to dehumanise them, slaves sang work songs and spirituals while they worked in the fields. These helped to alleviate suffering and loss but also masked codes of resistance and escape that were unintelligible to white ears. Placed in the most disempowering position ever imaginable, they turned the words of their oppressors' own songs against them with what W.E.B. Du Bois calls 'veiled and half-articulate' messages.[42] In the final chapter of his highly significant work, *The Souls of Black Folk*, Du Bois eloquently describes the beauty and pain of the 'sorrow songs' of the slaves, arguing that, 'the Negro folk-song – the rhythmic cry of the slave' was the oral voice of exile through which 'the slave spoke to the world'.[43] In *Liberating Voices*, Gayl Jones demonstrates how African-American writers gradually came to shape and modify their oral resistances into a canonical literature that used models and literary techniques not only from European and European American traditions, but also from their own distinctive oral and aural forms.[44] It is a literature that has always retained its roots in African oral/aural traditions – the mainstay of their cultural heritage – a tradition which the slaves transformed in the New World into spirituals, work songs, proverbs, blues and jazz, which then in turn transformed white American culture in often unacknowledged ways.[45]

In my reading of Kincaid's novel, I want to try and participate in Cheryl Wall's suggestion that the impulse to define a distinctive sound which was central to the formulations of a Black Aesthetic remains a primary trope for Afro-American literary criticism today.[46] My aim is to follow the politics and poetics of Kincaid's text that as I see it offers a fascinating interweaving of the Western story of Narcissus and Echo, and the antiphonal resistance of the African-American technique of call-and-response, which Jones describes thus:

Call-and-response is an antiphonal back-and-forth pattern which exists in many African American oral traditional forms, from sermon to interjective folktale to blues, jazz and spirituals, and so on . . . In oral storytelling the listeners may interject their commentary in a modified call-and-response pattern derived from African musical tradition. *In the literary text both dialogue and plot structure may demonstrate this call-and-response pattern: one scene becomes a commentary on a previous scene while a later scene becomes a commentary or response to that one.*[47]

One of the most moving literary representations of what I understand as call-and-response is Baby Suggs's calling out to her black audience in the Clearing in *Beloved*, demanding of them that they learn to love themselves, love their bodies and their flesh in all their fractured parts.[48] Gradually men, women and children start laughing, crying, singing and dancing – they verbally and physically respond, building up to a triumphant *collective* voice – and in so doing, a significant shift in their sense of themselves takes place. This scene highlights the importance of the call-and-response pattern, which began with collective work songs and spirituals, becoming a highly sophisticated affirmation of collective voice as antiphonal phrases repeat and respond to each other, the participants assenting to membership in a group and affirming that their experience is shared.

In Kincaid's novel *Lucy* the pattern of call-and-response is mostly implicit, encoded more in the structuring of the text. This is because the young protagonist is engulfed in the white world, separated totally from her Caribbean roots and her family and friends she has left behind in Antigua. Her passage across the Atlantic is a very different one from the one I have just described. It appears at first as if this is a journey that Lucy herself has chosen, but her struggle to find her own voice involves a sense of personal loss and incomplete mourning that is in part the result of 500 years of cumulative cultural loss and grief, which has to be healed on both a personal and cultural level. For Lucy's life in Antigua has been consumed by two almost overwhelming love/hate relationships, one with her mother, the other with Western canonical literature, which in their complex entanglement have together compromised her sense of agency. Lucy's story then, is not just a simple story of resistance, for it involves a doubled-sided discourse in which ambivalence is necessarily enfolded, a doubled heritage and pain of double-consciousness, what Lucy calls her 'two-facedness: that is, outside I seemed one way, inside I was another; outside false, inside true'

(18). Leaving aside for a moment the fact of Du Bois's gender bias typical of his era,[49] his original definition of double-consciousness speaks in many ways to Kincaid's character, Lucy: 'It is a peculiar sensation, this double-consciousness, this sense of always looking at one's self through the eyes of others . . . One ever feels his [*sic*] two-ness, – an American, a Negro; two souls, two thoughts, two unreconciled strivings; two warring ideals in one dark body.'[50] Since Du Bois, the term has become one of the most important concepts of African-American criticism, and indeed for literary criticism in general. For instance, in *The Signifying Monkey*, Henry Louis Gates Jr explores the connection between double-consciousness and the inherently double-voiced and parodic nature of the African-American text, but Gates remains wedded to the masculinity of Du Bois's original formulations.[51] If, however, the notion of double-consciousness is used to provide a paradigm for understanding issues of identity within the framework of the power structures that dominate cultural and racial conflicts and the differences they espouse, then I think it can be very useful, provided that the intersections of gender, and to a lesser extent perhaps class, are always present.

Theorised as a form of imposed *socialised ambivalence*, and utilising the positive as well as the negative aspects of the resulting tensions, the concept of double-consciousness provides a methodological paradigm through which to explore ways of articulating the many forms of often painful resistance by and through which African-Americans and others have voiced a coming to self-definition, self-determination and self-consciousness. Furthermore, as Jones remarks, not only is double-consciousness a recurring theme in twentieth-century African-American literature, particularly in character depiction, motivation, and revelation, '[i]t is also a mechanism for elucidating the relationship between personal experience, history, and society'.[52] Importantly too, Du Bois himself conjoins double-consciousness with the structural pattern of call-and-response. He ends *The Souls of Black Folks*, a text suffused with an Enlightenment world-view and ethos, with a call for a participatory response: 'HEAR MY CRY, O God the Reader; vouchsafe that this my book fall not stillborn into the world-wilderness.'[53]

With this in mind I chose a metaphor that connects in with Jones's notion of the 'liberating voice' and its heritage within the oral traditions that evolved through the enforced synthesis of cultures that began in the Caribbean and American plantations of the Deep South – that of *creative marronage*. This is a term of Édouard Glissant's that signifies the cultural opposition that began with the physical resistance of the maroon fighters of the eighteenth and nineteenth centuries of which I wrote in the first chapter – what Glissant terms *historical marronage*.[54] As colonialism moved into the postcolonial, historical marronage evolved into differing forms of discursive resistance known as creative or imaginative marronage, such as music, literature and so on, as a means of continuing to counteract and subvert renewed forms of re-appropriation by dominant white cultural values. Kincaid's *creative marronage* represents one of the newest forms of innovative writing that has its roots in the Caribbean.

5

The Search for a Voice

Lucy's antiphonal backchat

The structure of Jamaica Kincaid's novel, *Lucy*, is an important component of the attempt to recover the voice and self-conscious interiority of the black female subject. It consists of five titled chapters that appear in the following order: 'Poor Visitor', 'Mariah', 'The Tongue', 'Cold Heart', and finally, 'Lucy'. The first chapter covers Lucy's arrival from Antigua and her unexpected homesickness as she settles in with Mariah and her family. The protagonist's attempt to move beyond her fragmented identity takes place in the numbing environment of self-congratulatory wholeness of being that accompanies the privilege of whiteness:

> The household in which I lived was made up of a husband, a wife, and four girl children. The husband and wife looked alike and their four children looked just like them. In photographs of themselves, which they placed all over the house, their six yellow-haired heads ... smiled out at the world, giving the impression that they found everything in it unbearably wonderful. (12)

Mariah, a strong exponent of liberal humanism, tells Lucy to make herself at home and become part of the family, rhetorically disregarding the seemingly obvious differences in positions of class and race. Yet her actions quite often belie her 'good' intentions. This recalls bell hooks's argument that the ideology of liberalism – by merely asserting a universal subjectivity (we are all just people) without making any changes in the structuring of society will automatically bring about the disappearance of racism – in fact masks a 'deep emotional investment in the myth of "sameness", even as their actions reflect the primacy of whiteness'.[1] Lewis, Mariah's husband, is not even this accommodating, but he veils his responses in derogatory remarks. He ridicules Lucy for staring at them while they eat, asking her if she has never seen anyone eat 'French-cut green beans' before (which of course is not very likely), all the while keeping a look of concern on his face (14); and he repeatedly recounts to her a monkey story, ostensibly blind to its racist implications. Lucy has little to do with him as he is a peripheral character in the story, but as a symbolic WASP male he exerts the ultimate authority on his family from behind the scenes. However, most of the young *au pair*'s time is spent with Mariah and the children. Mariah is the focus and foil of Lucy's developing sense of self, and with the opening of the second chapter – significantly titled 'Mariah' – Lucy's quest for identity begins.

In this chapter Lucy will ask a question five times, the core of which is: 'How does a person get to be that way?' but it alternates between this and the more personal, 'How do *you* get to be that way?' (emphasis added). The searching inquiry is always asked in relation to Mariah. My suggestion is that this is an adapted form of the call-and-response pattern that I outlined in the last chapter. However this is complicated by Lucy's deep immersion in the 'books [she] had read' (6), and which, at the outset at least, provide the template for her reading of American society. With her sense of self buried by both the effects of double-consciousness that have resulted from her past colonial education and her present position as servant, Lucy's first attempts at calling Mariah to respond to the very real differences between them are both internal and individualistic. Contrary to the thematics and politics of call-and-response, which has at its heart a calling in of additional voices that will respond to the caller and a gradual building up to an empowering communal response that is intrinsic to becoming part of a collective voice, Lucy can only begin by reaching out towards this heritage. Her questing voice cannot initially be spoken aloud. However, both the repetition of the question, its variations, and the response that occurs when Lucy finally speaks, intensifies the meaning of the repeating call.

The chapter begins with the ambivalent subject of daffodils. It is March, and Mariah talks excitedly of the coming Spring, a season that Lucy has yet to encounter, and a season that is symbolised for Mariah by the flowering of daffodils. Her description of them is ridiculously rhapsodic: 'when they are in bloom and all massed together, a breeze comes along and makes them do a curtsy to the lawn stretching out in front of them. Have you ever seen that? When I see that, I feel so glad to be alive' (17). It is almost a parody of Wordsworth's famous poem that comes to play such a pivotal role in the novel. Lucy is reduced to a wondering amazement: 'So Mariah is made to feel alive by some flowers in the breeze. How does a person get to be that way?' (17). At this stage the question is merely a generalised query, for Lucy has yet to interconnect Mariah's effusive enthusiasm and idealisation of nature with her ability to depoliticise and decontextualise racialised social injustices. Directly after this moment, Lucy tells Mariah with subdued anger the story of how she had to recite Wordsworth's poem on the school podium, which at the time had engendered in her a disconcerting feeling of being split in two. Mariah listens to Lucy's story of psychic alienation, but it has no impact on her way of seeing the world. The first day of spring finally arrives, and any hope of daffodil watching is buried under a huge fall of late snow, an event that Mariah takes as an almost personal insult. Inwardly laughing, Lucy wonders to herself for the second time: 'How do *you* get to be a person who is made miserable because the weather changed its mind, because the weather doesn't live up to your expectations? How do *you* get to be that way?' (20, emphasis added). Again the questions are represented as internal dialogue, but this time it is varied by the use of the second person interrogative aimed at someone who is not herself. The inquiry is becoming more personal.

By the time Lucy comes to ask the question for the third time, things have become much more complicated. She is beginning, albeit unconsciously, to confront the elitism of Mariah's aura of easy perfection, and she is also having to deal with memory echoes from her past, memories, as we shall see, that always connect back to her mother. Kincaid then inserts a scene that is bracketed off by ellipses and covers exactly two pages – beginning top left and ending on the bottom right, so they are also divided off from the rest of the text by the mechanism of page-turning. It is an ambivalent scene because it lays the imagined purity of whiteness under a piercing spotlight, but it also bathes Mariah, the subject of the questioning and also the symbol of white middle-class femininity, in a setting that exudes love, benevolence and empathy. Lucy is alone in the kitchen when Mariah enters lightheartedly dancing and singing, swirling wildly but with a grace that ensures she avoids banging into the 'many things on her path' (26). She stops, announcing with a flourish how she has always wanted four girl children and that she loves them wholeheartedly. Lucy thinks to herself:

Mariah was beyond doubt or confidence. I thought, Things must have always gone her way, and not just for her but for every body she has ever known from eternity; she has never had to doubt, and so she has never had to grow confident; the right thing always happens to her; the thing she wants to happen happens. Again I thought, *How does a person get to be that way?* (26, emphasis added)

Now, 'how does a *person* get to be this way' has come to mean how does a *'white* person come to be this way?' Lucy's unspoken interrogation is really about the normativity and unacknowledged presumption of white-skin privilege and its matrix of naturalised power. However, it is a question which Lucy cannot yet voice aloud, especially as this privileged whiteness is symbolised throughout the text by Mariah, the beautiful 'golden mother' who loves her children and Lucy, and whom Lucy herself 'grows to love' (46). Moreover, not only is Mariah a surrogate mother, but she seemingly offers an uncontradictory acceptance of Lucy's difference in both race and class status. Furthermore, while Mariah not only outwardly expresses her love for Lucy, an understandably seductive offering for a young woman alone in a foreign world, she is also her employer. But Mariah is not just a perfect mother bathed in a light of blinding whiteness, she becomes the white mother of Christianity, represented at this moment in the text as the Marian symbol of goodness, femininity, loving maternity and selflessness:[2]

She looked so beautiful standing there in the middle of the kitchen. The yellow light from the sun came in through a window and fell ... on Mariah with her pale-yellow skin and yellow hair, [She] stood still in this almost celestial light, and she looked blessed, no blemish or mark of any kind on her cheek or anywhere else. (27)

The idealised image, however ambivalently treated, and especially one bound up in the dynamics of love, gratitude or grace, is hard to confront. This is also one of the reasons that the liberal humanist approach is so difficult to gainsay, especially if the one seeking to ask the questions is, like Lucy, shrouded under the mantle of a servant. Tactics of evasion under the guise of civility are, in the words of Toni Morrison, 'further complicated by the fact that the habit of ignoring race is understood to be a graceful, even generous, liberal gesture. To notice is to recognize an already discredited difference'.[3] This is the ideological approach that Mariah pursues, that is, until Lucy displeases her and the mask of liberalism is replaced by an angry employer who demands the hierarchical black and white relationship of master/slave and the humility and subservience that it entails.

What is also extremely significant is that directly before this isolated vignette is a strange story from Lucy's childhood about a friend of her mother's called Sylvie who has a scarred cheek, the result of a bite, 'an embrace of hatred', from another woman whom she had enraged. This is an allegorical story of a fall from grace, connected to Eve by the biblical imagery: 'It was as if her cheek was a half-ripe fruit and someone had bitten into it, meaning to eat, but then realized it wasn't ripe enough' (24). As a child Lucy was always sure that the 'mark on [Sylvie's] face was a rose . . . and it was as if the mark . . . bound her to something much deeper than its reality, something that could not be put into words' (25). Lucy was sure that when she grew up she too 'would end up with a mark somewhere' (25), a statement echoingly reminiscent of the opening of Spillers' essay, 'Mama's Baby: Papa's Maybe' that I have already mentioned and which begins: 'Let's face it. I am a marked woman, but not everyone knows my name'.[4] So the story-line moves from the story of the marked black woman and the assumed inheritance of this scarring, through the distinctly separated Madonna scene, to one of the climactic moments in the text when Lucy is faced for the first time in her 19 years with the reality of 'A host, of golden daffodils . . . fluttering and dancing in the breeze', and a confrontation with the scars that she cannot yet voice.[5]

In a caricature of a colonial act of capturing, Mariah insists on blindfolding Lucy and leading her into the midst of 'her beloved daffodils' (30). Despite now knowing of Lucy's aversion to this paradoxical flower – insignia of Empire and a symbol of mourning for her lost self – Mariah assumes that in the end she will be able to charm Lucy into finally seeing things from her perspective. 'There was such joy in her voice,' Lucy recounts, 'how could I explain to her the feeling I had about daffodils – that it wasn't exactly daffodils . . . Where would I start? . . . I tried to talk I stammered and by accident bit my own tongue' (29). Mariah, thinking she is overcome with joy, reaches out to hug Lucy. Lucy moves back in anger, and this physical act reactivates her speaking self: 'Mariah do you realize that at ten years of age I had to learn by heart a long poem about some flowers I would not see in real life until I was nineteen?' (30). They walk home in silence.

The first three 'calls' come towards the beginning of the 'Mariah' chapter. Then after the catalyst scene, there is a gap in the pattern. Lucy, Mariah and the children travel to the family holiday house on the Great Lakes, where Mariah had grown up and to which she has great nostalgic attachment. They spend a number of weeks there, playing on the beach, walking, planting a garden and generally living a country life.

On the whole Lucy is distracted from her quest for self for she has embarked on a pleasurable love affair, but while she experiences flashes of intense resentment, these are still internalised responses. At one moment she wants to say to Gus, a Scandinavian who has worked for Mariah's family all his life, 'Do you not hate the way she says your name, as if she owns you?' (34); another time Mariah, returning proudly with some fish she has just caught says to Lucy, 'Let's go feed the minions' (37), and Lucy thinks bitterly to herself:

> It's possible that what she really said was 'millions' not 'minions'. Certainly she said it in jest. But as we were cooking the fish, I was thinking about it. 'Minions.' A word like that would haunt someone like me; the place where I came from was a dominion of someplace else. (37)

Lucy caustically reframes the meanings of both dominion and its derivative minion by placing them firmly in a postcolonial perspective. She aligns the words with the phrase 'racial *domination*', and with her homeland, a place long haunted by its colonial ownership. But she says nothing to Mariah, and instead tells her a story from her childhood. What finally liberates Lucy's interrogatory voice is an extraordinarily insensitive race-blind statement by Mariah.

One evening, as the two women are about to go to bed, Mariah says to Lucy: 'I was looking forward to telling you that I have Indian blood, that the reason I'm so good at catching fish and hunting birds and roasting corn and doing all sorts of things is that I have Indian blood. But now, I don't know why, I feel I shouldn't tell you that. I feel you would take it the wrong way' (39–40). Underneath Mariah's statement, the masked assumption of white privilege that permits the owning of anyone's identity (though ironically the one drop of blood policy in America would have meant that if this was the case Mariah could be considered coloured), to Lucy who is struggling to find hers, is almost incomprehensible in its arrogance. Not least because Lucy herself has a Carib Indian grandmother. Her anger now visibly rising, Lucy says to herself:

> If someone could get away with it, I am sure they would put my grandmother in a museum as an example of something extinct in nature, one of a handful still alive. In fact, one of the museums to which Mariah had taken me devoted a whole section to people, all dead, who were more or less related to my grandmother.

Mariah says, 'I have Indian blood in me,' and underneath everything
I could swear she says it as if she were announcing her possession of
a trophy. How do you get to be the sort of victor who can claim to
be the vanquished also? (40)

The latter part of the quotation pinpoints a worrying trend of those
privileged by the unacknowledged power attached to whiteness theory,
claiming of the victim position as a way of avoiding ethical repsonsi-
bility in relation to issues of racial injustice. The irony is that Mariah
can enact a performance of liberal guilt which appears truly to have
consumed her, while at the same time she is writing a book of 'vanish-
ing things', which to her means only the local flora. Native Americans,
whose lands the Puritans originally bartered for a pittance and who have
either been slaughtered or forced to vanish into reserves, play no part
in Mariah's historicising of things lost from the past.

So far Lucy has said nothing aloud. Perhaps sensing Lucy's inner
turmoil, Mariah lets out a 'long breath, full of sadness, resignation, even
dread' (41), but Lucy is angered enough finally to confront her surrogate mother and employer with the direct question, twice repeated:

'All along I have been wondering how you got to be the way you are.
Just how it was that you got to be the way you are.' (41)

Mariah tries a new disarming tack. She moves to hug Lucy. But Lucy
steps out of her path, and repeats: '"How do you get to be that way?"'
(41). The anguish on Mariah's face 'almost broke my heart,' Lucy admits,
'but I would not bend. It was hollow, my triumph. I could feel that, but
I held on to it just the same' (41).

This ends the second chapter. Lucy has finally called the question she
has been building up to voice throughout this chapter. But it provides
her with no sense of triumph. Call-and-response is a collective enterprise, a joining in solidarity and communal resistance, and Lucy is alone
in the white world, cut off from her cultural roots. Reclaiming a self
signifies a self-conscious developed sense of interiority. It is about connection, conjoining affect to event, and about reconnecting to a self
that is allowed to *feel*. While Lucy's political consciousness and voice
are beginning to surface, she has to shut out, even as an echo, her profoundly ambivalent feelings towards her own mother. What she has to
do now is to learn to feel again, which is the subject of the remainder
of the novel.

The third chapter is named 'The Tongue', the organ of speech, of taste, of sensuality and of feeling. It is also the fleshly agent of the voice. 'Taste is not the thing to seek out in a tongue,' the adolescent Lucy decides after experiments in kissing, 'how it makes you feel – that is the thing' (44). Importantly though, the tongue, voice and an ability to feel are all intrinsic to the notion of double-consciousness and the sense of interiority so long erased by white readings of black culture. The masking performance of double-consciousness teaches a person to divorce herself from her true feeling that Kincaid refers to earlier as 'two-facedness'. From Toni Morrison's point of view, if she has made the reader *feel* the event she is describing, it means she has succeeded in her work. When asked in an interview whether she had read many slave narratives in order to write *Beloved*, Morrison answered that she had read a number of them, but because they could not alienate their audience which was usually white, these 'narratives had to be very understated. So while I looked at the documents and felt *familiar* with slavery and overwhelmed by it, I wanted it to be truly *felt* . . . I wanted to show the reader what slavery *felt* like'.[6] So a resistance narrative is not just about having a tongue but about being able to give voice to inner trauma and pain, the self-conscious ability to *feel* one's interiority and to be able to voice this. As Kincaid implies through her character, Lucy: 'to feel is the thing'.[7]

How to feel, then, could be said to be the existential quandary of this novel, but beyond that, how to speak what the protagonist feels, to be able to name and speak of the 'bad feeling' for which she had no name, but 'only knew it felt a little like sadness but heavier than that' (3–4). However, first Lucy has to circumnavigate the cold heart of a self negated and othered by her own mother who has adopted the cultural mores of the British imperial nation that has colonised their home island of Antigua. Thus Lucy's self-abnegation is complicated not just by her sense of cultural doubleness, the lines of which are blurred by the internalisations from her schoolday teachings and then furthered by the seductions of English literature and American white liberalism, but also because this double-consciousness is so profoundly bound up within the complications of her deeply ambivalent relationship with her mother who sides ideologically with all that Lucy is trying to combat.

The maternal echo

While most adolescent girls fight strongly against becoming like their mothers as a means of forming a separate identity, Kincaid's obsession with her mother dominates all her work and sometimes criss-crosses unnervingly between biography and her strongly autobiographical fiction. Indeed, there is a particularly intriguing point of contiguity between Kincaid's autobiographical fiction, her own enunciatory voice represented in a number of interviews conducted with her, and her memoir, *My Brother*. However, it is through a reading of the latter that we encounter the story of Kincaid's and her mother's symbiotic relationship. We also, in a particularly vivid traumatic vignette, learn of their alienation from each other which is clearly bound up around the subject of books and literature. It is Kincaid's mother who teaches her to read at three and a half and is then very proud of her ability and her love of reading, and who gives her an Oxford Dictionary for her seventh birthday.[8] But then, as Kincaid becomes immersed too deeply into Western literature, her mother revokes her endorsement and loving encouragement. This happens after the birth, in quick succession, of Kincaid's three male siblings, when her mother begins to demand her help in the home, another recurring theme in her fiction. In *My Brother* Kincaid recalls a devastating scene of her childhood in which she becomes so absorbed in her reading that she fails to look properly after her small brother whom she is minding for the day. On discovery, her mother piles all her daughter's treasured books in a great pyre, douses them with kerosene, and sets them on fire.[9] Indeed, so painful is this memory that Kincaid tells and retells it over a number of pages. In *Lucy,* this is re-presented as the traumatic moment when her Edenic world is shattered, and the 'paradise of mother' is dramatically ruptured.[10]

Betrayal by the beloved mother, then, is a theme that echoes throughout Kincaid's work, and this treachery is matched by another, that of the British colonial power which dominates their lives.[11] To complicate this, the protagonist's mother symbolically represents the despised yet alluring mother-country against whom the colonial daughter must inevitably rebel, thus conflating mother–daughter antagonisms with the power imbalances inherent in the relationship between the imperial nation and its colony. Thus, in Kincaid's work double-conscious alienation from self is always relational, based on an anguished intersubjective relationship between mother and daughter, which in some sense is always the story of Kincaid's troubled relationship with her own mother endlessly replayed. 'I've never really written anything about anyone except myself and my mother' Kincaid has said.[12] The contradictions of her feelings for her mother are reflected in the many comments Kincaid makes in interviews. On one hand, she can state that 'the fertile soil of my creative life is my mother': yet elsewhere in the same article she disparages her mother for her Anglophilia and the 'middle-class English upbringing' she forced upon her daughter.[13] Kincaid's fictional attempts to come to terms with psychic alienation of the colonised is complicated by the agonising disparity, loss, even hatred, that drive mother and daughter apart: indeed they are often inseparable in the text. Yet neither can they can ever break free of their psychic circuitry because each is also simultaneously caught in an entanglement of deep longing for reconnection that at times resembles a physical pain. The character of Lucy's mother – only ever focalised from the daughterly perspective – appears to be a deeply compromised colonised subject who has been seduced into complete acceptance of colonial cultural mores and English ways of being that she then tries to impose upon her daughter. Conspicuously unnamed in the novel, she is both an agent of empire, and symbolically rendered as the loving and rejecting mother-country.[14]

Thus the theme of the echo which threads through the novel is not only one of literary enchantment alternating with deep resentment. A love/hate relationship with English literature, a numbed and fragmented sense of self that is entangled with the effects of colonisation, and the repression of feeling that in moments of resurfacing always echo back to the mother, combine into the maternal echo, which collectively concerns loss, incomplete mourning and a reaching out to an incomprehensible sadness. This is the context in which Mariah, Lucy's white employer, becomes a substitute mother. The two mothers echo each other. Sometimes the echoes meld together; more often they reverberate one against the other, causing Lucy pain and inner conflict. Her surrogate mother carries far less cultural baggage for Lucy: it is with her biological mother whom she has left behind that her psyche is more constantly engaged. Yet the conflict between the two always lies in juxtaposition in the text. At one moment Lucy tells us:

> Mariah wanted all of us, the children and me, to see things the way she did . . . The children were happy to see things her way . . . But I already had a mother who loved me, and I had come to see her love as a burden . . . I had come to feel that my mother's love for me was designed solely to make me into an echo of her; and I didn't know why, but I felt that I would rather be dead than become just an echo of someone. That was not a figure of speech. (35–6)

She is not just refusing to become an echo of her mother: she is refuting her mother's passive mimicry of the imperial mother country. It is only in the final pages of the novel that Lucy begins to move towards understanding that it is not her mother's love that burdens and suppresses her but the burden of colonial history that has damaged their relationship.

However, for most of the novel Lucy expends a great deal of energy in repressing all feeling toward her mother. The fourth chapter, entitled 'Cold Heart', opens with the metaphor of 'iron bars twisted decoratively into curves and curls' (85) that cling and bind around the organ of affect. Lucy had believed that 'a change of venue would banish forever from my life the things I most despised' (90), that once she had physically crossed the 'vast ocean', she could leave her past behind. But whatever she's doing, and however hard she tries to immerse herself in her new position in the white world, echoes of her mother always intervene. She may be feeding Miriam, the youngest of the children in her charge and the one she loves the most, when she is suddenly reminded of her mother feeding her when she was exactly the same age (44–5); or she may be walking in the woods with the children when a memory from the past suddenly intrudes into the present, this time a recollection of how when she was a child she would sit in her mother's lap and fondle the scar on her mother's temple, a wounding from which she had nearly died, and would have, if her own mother had not been able to save her with her *obeah* healing powers (54–5). Time and time again associative thinking somehow connects her back to her mother, until one day it dawns on her:

> My past was my mother . . . Oh, it was a laugh, for I had spent so much time saying I did not want to be like my mother that I missed the whole story: I was not like my mother – I was my mother (90).

To try and counteract her enormous psychic presence in her life, Lucy refuses to open the 19 letters she has received from her mother, 'I knew that if I read only one, I would die from longing for her' (91). 'I would rather die' – Echo's missing words to Narcissus – now echo through Kincaid's text in a series of repetitions. Having made love to Mariah's best friend's son, Hugh, for the first time, and immediately realising that she has forgotten to use contraception, her thoughts ricochet to a time years before when her mother had taught her about abortifacient herbs. She now wonders if she will contact her if she has to, as she 'had always thought I would rather die than let her see me in such a vulnerable position' (70). The psychic force of their connection is so strong that Lucy begins to suffer from violent headaches exactly like the ones that used to afflict her mother (93), and it is when she is describing her mother's first paralysing migraine headache that the origins of this echoing repetition become apparent. Once, in a bitter argument with her mother, she had turned to her and said,

> 'I wish you were dead.' I said it with such force that had I said it to anyone else but her, I am sure my wish would have come true. But of course I would not have said such a thing to anyone else, for no one else meant so much to me. (93–4)

The outcome of this had been days of childish terror. For her mother was overcome by such a powerful headache that she retired to bed for days, and during the night Lucy would hear strange sounds which she imagined to be the undertaker come to remove her mother's body. Each morning when 'I saw her face again,' Lucy recounts as an adult,

> I trembled inside with joy. And so now when I suffered from these same headaches which no medicine would send away, I would see her face again before me, a face that was godlike, for it seemed to know its own origins, to know all the things of which it was made. (94)

While this is an adult recollection of a childhood memory, it still seems, at this stage, a trifle melodramatic. Elsewhere, Lucy tells Mariah with an even greater intensity that 'for ten of my twenty years, half my life, I had been mourning the end of a love affair, perhaps the only true love in my whole life I would ever know' (132). It is only with the arrival of Maude Quick – her mother's much-loved god-daughter, a bully who has always been held up as a shining light of perfection in direct contrast to Lucy's 'evil' ways – that we begin to understand both the psychic intensity of her obsessive love for her mother and the link with the statement, 'I would rather die'. This is a citation that turns out to represent her repressed and incomplete mourning for her lost relationship with her mother that had resulted from a traumatic and constitutive instance of mother–daughter betrayal.

Maude arrives unannounced at Mariah's house bearing a letter from Lucy's mother that she is to hand-deliver on her way back from the Caribbean. The letter contains news of Lucy's father's death a month before. Lucy is devastated. She cannot cry or speak, until, that is Maude says:

'You remind me of Miss Annie, you really remind me of your mother.'
I was dying, and she saved my life. I shall always be grateful to her
for that. (123)

Lucy launches into a litany of complaints against her mother, which is
only really stopped by Maude's departure. Maude leaves behind a smell
of clove, lime and rose oil, a scent that makes Lucy 'almost . . . die of
homesickness' (124), for the scent draws her into the immediacy of her
past with the image of her mother bathing her in water in which she
had boiled the leaves and flowers of those plants in order to ward off
evil spirits. The deep contradictions of Lucy's behaviour now manifest
themselves in her writing a 'cold letter' to her mother that 'matched
my heart' (127), yet in which she also encloses all the money she has
been saving to move out into a flat of her own.

Ironically, it is Mariah who brings about the possibility of catharsis.
She asks Lucy a piercing question: '"Why don't you forgive your mother
for whatever you feel she has done? Why don't you just go home and
tell her you forgive her?"' (129). This reactivates a haunting memory,
and 'with the memory came a flood of tears that tasted if they were
juice squeezed from an aloe plant' (130). The release of the traumatic
memory concerns the birth of her three brothers that began when Lucy
was nine. Until that time she has received her mother's undivided love
and attention. In her mind there is an abrupt cessation of love with the
birth of the first boy. Each male child is adored and their futures as a
doctor or lawyer trained in England is a subject of much discussion and
immense pride between her parents:

I did not mind my father saying these things about his sons, his own
kind . . . But my mother knew me well, as well as she knew herself:
I, at the time, even thought of us as identical; and whenever I saw her
eyes fill up with tears at the thought of how proud she would be at
some deed her sons had accomplished, I felt a sword go through my
heart, for there was no accompanying scenario in which she saw me,
her identical offspring, in a remotely similar situation. (130, emphasis added)

It is a very gendered betrayal. Her mother now expects her to neglect
her own schooling to help at home, and her future possibilities are
limited to some form of domestic service, or at best being a nurse when
she had wanted to be a doctor. Lucy can to some degree feel again, and
she tastes the bitterness of belatedly encountering this memory of her

mother's treachery on her tongue as her tears run into her mouth. She now reads all her mother's unopened letters, acknowledging that, 'if I had seen those letters sooner, one way or another I would have died. I would have died if I did nothing; I would have died if I did something' (139). She then burns them, writes a final letter, lying to her mother pretending she will come home soon, tells her she is moving out of Mariah's house and finally, in an act of symbolic severence, gives her a false address to ensure that she will never receive a reply. Lucy has erased, she thinks, the maternal echoes in her head. Now she has to divest herself of the shroud of whiteness.

The deadening impact of whiteness

The maternal echo and the internalised impact of whiteness come together in Kincaid's ambivalent metaphor of snow. Her use of this trope is hardly unusual, but Kincaid moves beyond its orthodox allusions to the purity of whiteness by accentuating instead snow's seductive power, leaving hidden (initially at least) the co-existing dangers of paralysis from the cold, blindness from its devastating bright glare, even the possibility of death:

> When the snow fell, it hung on the trees like decorations ordered for a special occasion . . . even I could see that there was something to it – it had a certain kind of beauty . . . [it made] the world seem soft and lovely and – unexpectedly, to me – nourishing. (22–3)

In Lucy's first winter in America there had been innumerable snowstorms, but she only notices the snow's impact when she has to make her way 'through the mounds of it that lay on the sidewalk' (22). Without any break in sequence, and reflecting the use of associative thinking, the next sentence proceeds straight into a memory of a story her mother had told her that connects both the deadening effects the ideology of whiteness can have on colonised subjects and a sense of the immense pleasure it offers:

> My parents used to go every Christmas to a film that had Bing Crosby standing waist-deep in snow and singing a song at the top of his voice. My mother once told me that seeing this film was among the first things they did when they were getting to know each other. (22)

As insidious as the daffodil that produces a reading of nature totally alienated from their Caribbean island, Bing Crosby's singing of 'White Christmas' becomes an annual nostalgic ritual that provides Lucy's parents with a momentary psychic escape from the impoverishment of their own material reality and the sun-drenched drought-ridden land-scape that has been denuded of its tropical rainforests in the name of white capitalist expansion and profit.[15] Waist deep in nostalgia and celebrating the Christian story of rebirth, her parents are pictured as immersed in an unseen ideology that is so normative that it is an intrin-sic part of the ritual of their lives. Crosby can sing at the top of his voice with no impediments to either sound or content because he is part of the (celebratory) culture of whiteness. Finding a voice to counter this is not so easy.

While the engulfment of whiteness that faces Lucy in America – or at least the part that is the hardest for her to resist – is symbolically rep-resented in the maternal persona of Mariah, Kincaid's other characters cleverly illustrate different characteristics of whiteness that impact on Lucy in subtly different ways. In *Playing in the Dark*, Toni Morrison's study of whiteness in American literature, she outlines the ways in which black characters are used as a foil in the construction of white identity, while simultaneously being deprived of their own interiority and constitution of selfhood.[16] All the adult white characters in *Lucy* – Mariah, Dinah, Hugh, Paul, Lewis and Peggy *need* Lucy to oppose and help construct their own sense of identity. Hers means nothing, or very little, except to Mariah, who genuinely seems to love her.

Mariah's husband, Lewis is an apt symbol for the narcissistic or self-obsessed nature of white masculine power. Interestingly, he is repre-sented as lacking a voice: 'He was the sort of person – a cultivated man, usually – who cannot speak his mind. It wasn't that speaking frankly had been bred out of him; it was just that a man in his position always knew exactly what he wanted, and so everything was done for him' (119). He is the man with the deceitful tongue who can simulate sexual desire when touching Mariah's neck with his tongue, and then, in an almost replica scene caress the neck of his wife's best friend, Dinah, with the tongue that will 'attack in an underhand way' when it suits him (119). For instance, he manoeuvres Mariah into asking him to leave, thus making him blameless over his affair. He is a user, a man of power, a manipulator, who is then 'kind' to Mariah in her misery, for as Lucy caustically remarks in an aside, 'it is so easy to be kind when you are in his position, the winning-hand position' (112). This statement also con-tains a masked contestation of colonial paternalism. Moreover, Lewis has no sense of beneficence: it is he, not Lucy, who represents the cold-heart and callous behaviour, and an oblique connection can be made here between Lewis and Narcissus, both of whom have stared too long and lovingly at their own images.

Dinah, Mariah's best friend, and Lewis's lover, appears proprietary in all areas of her life. She wants what Mariah has although she already has so much of her own, her predatory arrogance symbolising a contrasting position to Mariah's liberal well-meaningness within the ideology of whiteness in American culture. Dinah makes it quite clear to Lucy that to a person such as herself, 'someone in my position is [always] "the girl" – as in "the girl who takes care of the children"' (58). From Dinah's perspective, Lucy is merely the newest manifestation of the Mammy figure of preceding eras and, as such, easily dismissed: she is just another black girl performing a different form of 'involuntary servitude', to use a phrase of George Lipsitz.[17] Indeed, among the many iniquities of white capitalism is the labour structure that continues to allocate black female immigrants such as Lucy to the position of domestic labour in white American middle-class homes. It is quite beyond Dinah's comprehension to imagine that, in the words of bell hooks, 'Many of the [whites] are shocked that black people think critically about whiteness because racist thinking perpetuates the fantasy that the Other who is subjugated . . . lacks the ability to comprehend, to understand, to see the workings of the powerful'.[18] This arrogant blindness is humorously disrupted by Lucy's unspoken aside: 'It would never have occurred to her that I sized her up immediately, that I viewed her as a cliché, as something not to be, a something to rise above' (58).

Lucy also meets Dinah's brother, Hugh, at a party in the holiday home organised by Mariah in part to entertain her employee. This party is the epitome of a white masquerade. It consists of impeccably dressed and behaved people, 'their clothes, their features, the manner in which they carried themselves were the example all the world should copy. They had names like Peters, Smith, Jones, and Richards – names that were easy on the tongue, names that made the world spin' (64). During this event, Hugh becomes Lucy's first lover in America. For Lucy this relationship represents the enjoyment of sex with someone who has enough courtesy to ask *which* island she comes from in the Caribbean, and importantly, the fact that he was about five inches shorter than she especially pleased her. However, despite his attraction, he unconsciously speaks the language of privilege: '"Isn't it the most blissful thing in the world,"' he says to Lucy, '"to be away from everything you have ever known – to be so far away that you don't even know yourself anymore and you're not sure you ever want to come back to all the things you're part of?"' (66). His privileged position in society means that he does not have to examine the great difference between the position of a wealthy young white man who can travel the world for as long as he is enjoying it, and that of a young West Indian woman who travels into this white world, her shoulders cloaked under the 'mantle of a servant' (95).

If a cold heart and narcissistic behaviour is epitomised by Lewis, it is Lucy's second lover Paul, who is connected in the text with direct references to the classical Narcissus myth. He is an artist, textually aligned to Paul Gaugin (unnamed in the novel but obviously referenced), and indeed he seems to have inherited the earlier Paul's fetish of visual ownership through representations of exoticised, but docile, black women.[19] The younger Paul's paintings are not 'straightforward . . . the people [in them] looked like their reflections in a pool whose surface has been disturbed' (97). With instant attraction redolent of the myth, on meeting him all Lucy can think about is that she wants 'to be naked in a bed with him. And I wanted to see,' she says, with the second reference to Narcissus, 'what he really looked like, not his reflection in a pool' (97). Consummated lust prevails in their relationship (unlike Echo's celibate and passive longing), and Lucy dismisses Paul as soon as he becomes overly possessive of her. While Gaugin exoticised and sexualised Tahitian women through his paintings, Paul fetishes Lucy's hair and colouring (100) and reproduces photographic images, such as one of her, naked from the waist up, standing over a boiling pot of food (155). Both are examples of othered women's positionality within the global system of white male ownership, whether by gaze and its representations, or in the figurations of literal bondage, as the photograph of Lucy implies. It comes as no surprise that Paul has a penchant for violent sex (113), the feats of the great explorers (129) and also has a fetish for 'things that came from far away and had a mysterious history' (156). If this is not alienating enough for Lucy, his idea of an outing is to take her to visit the ruined Plantation house of a rich slave-owner.

However, none of the males is represented as having good qualities in this novel: only the women really matter. Peggy, Lucy's closest friend, and the second most developed white character in the text, plays an important role in that her *white trash* heritage places her in between Mariah's WASP liberalism and Lucy's black immigrant/servant status. Mariah's attitude toward Peggy is particularly interesting. She gives Lucy 'lectures about what a bad influence a person like Peggy could be. She said that Peggy was never to come to the house and should never be around the children' (63) as if her presence would pollute and contaminate. Her strong disapproval of Peggy accentuates the class bias of the WASP hegemonic consciousness that is an important part of the denigration of white trash who act as the border between working-class whites and blacks.[20]

Peggy is disconcertingly different to other white Americans with whom Lucy forms a relationship, for she does not participate in defining identity through the legibility of the racial body: indeed, she does not even notice the difference between the colours of their skins. To her, it is about *voice*: 'You're not from Ireland, are you? You talk funny' (62), Peggy says on meeting Lucy. Ironically, Lucy and Peggy end up sharing a flat for the very reason that they have nothing at all in common except that they recognise in each other, as Lucy states: 'the same restlessness, the same dissatisfaction with our surroundings, *the same skin-doesn't-fit-ness*' (145, emphasis added). While it is the distance that grows between her relationships with both Peggy and Paul that provokes Lucy to move into a different psychic space at the end of the novel, there is perhaps a suggestion of the possibilities of an alliance of solidarity between lower classes of both black and white who are conventionally separated by the powerful ideologies of the white hegemony.

While both Peggy and Lucy are disempowered by their position at the lower echelons of the American class structure, Peggy's stress on the voice over skin colour could suggest that whatever happens, however much she is distanced from the hegemonic power base by virtue of her class status, Peggy still has access to the normative privilege that she has accrued merely from being *white*. Displaced Caribbean-British writer, Caryl Phillips, also suffers from a profound sense of alienation that has resulted from his British schooling, one that he acknowledges at the beginning of his moving memoir, *The European Tribe*, with these words: 'If the teaching of English literature can feed a sense of identity, then I like many of my black contemporaries in Britain, was starving.'[21] Phillips also repeatedly articulates how being or not being at home in one's skin produces a complex relation to the power to speak and to be heard.[22] It is the connection between access to a liberating, resistant voice and racial positioning that is important here, I think. Lucy experiences a psychic shift when she is able to tell the story of her traumatic loss of her mother's love when she was nine to Mariah, but disillusionment sets in when Mariah's final answer is to produce a classic tome of white feminism, Simone de Beauvoir's *The Second Sex*, as the answer to all Lucy's problems with her mother. Lucy reads the first sentence:

'Woman? Very simple, say the fanciers of simple formulas: She is a womb, an ovary; she is female – this word is sufficient to define her.' I had to stop. My life could not really be explained by this thick book that made my hands hurt as I tried to keep it open. My life was at once something more simple and more complicated than that. (132)

This great feminist text has no way of speaking to Lucy or approaching the complexities of her racial existence, for de Beauvoir's 'Woman' is always unspokenly white.[23] This moment of estrangement between Mariah and Lucy ends the fourth chapter, 'Cold Heart', and it is the defining moment for Lucy to make 'a new beginning again' (133). Indeed, it is only when her frustrated expectations with whiteness – and by extension with her surrogate mother – set in, that Lucy can finally begin the painful return towards her own mother and her ancestral history.

6

'The Sea is History'

... in the salt chuckle of rocks
with their sea pools, there was the sound
like a rumour *without any echo*

of History, really beginning.

Derek Walcott[1]

It was the oceans of the globe that enabled the discovery of the New
World and the implementation of slavery through the Middle Passage.
As described by Édouard Glissant in his *Poetics of Relation* (in which he
uses the title of Walcott's poem as an epigraph) cries of unbearable suffering emanating from thousands of slave-ships were only audible to
their captors. The plaintive echoes of torment and mourning dispersed
unheard over the vast Atlantic ocean, mingling only with the cries of
wheeling seabirds. Thus the reclaiming of that lost history is tied up
with the acknowledgement that sea and history overlay one another in
an ambivalent symbiotic relationship. Indeed, the symbolism of loss of
voice and the ocean as destroyer could be seen to merge in what Cornel
West describes as the 'metaphorical association of black hearts, black
people, and black culture with water (the sea or a river) [which] runs
deep in black artistic expression'.[2] It is interesting then that in Kincaid's
novel, from the very beginning, there is a strong presence of water
imagery that is connected to the divisions between the young protagonist's past and future:

I was no longer in the tropical zone, and this realization now entered
my life like a flow of water dividing formerly dry and solid ground,
creating two banks, one of which was my past – so familiar and

predictable that even my unhappiness then made me happy just now
to think of it – the other my future, a gray blank, an overcast seascape
on which rain was falling and no boats were in sight. (5–6)

Imagery that could be connected to the Middle Passage continues to be
entangled with Lucy's unhappiness on her arrival in America where she
is to sleep in a room 'like a box – a box in which cargo traveling a long
way should be shipped. But I was not cargo' (7). However, the body of
water that divides Lucy's past from her future is both physical and
mental. There is as yet no present, for this, as she will discover, is caught
up in the belatedness of both historical and personal trauma: 'I was
unhappy. I looked at a map. An ocean stood between me and the place
I came from, but would it have made a difference if it had been a teacup
of water? I could not go back' (9–10).

However, the rupturing of the past from the future needs to be healed
if the promise of a future can be implied. At the beginning Lucy
attempts to repress the past, believing that a 'change of venue' will
ensure that the things she wants to banish from her life will remain on
the other side of 'the vast ocean' she has just crossed (90). What she
has not taken into account is the binding form and force of the echoes
of her past, echoes that always relate, consciously or unconsciously, to
her mother, and by extension to her lost maternal ancestry: 'As each
day unfolded before me, I could see the sameness in everything; I could
see the present take a shape – the shape of my past. My past was my
mother' (90). Yet she also realises that '[e]verything remains the same
and yet nothing is the same', a gradual understanding that she had first
discovered a long time ago but has forgotten: 'When this revelation was
new to me, years ago, I told it to my mother, and when I saw how deeply
familiar she was with it I was speechless' (78). Yet away from the politics of the Caribbean and the backchat between herself and her mother,
much of Lucy's resistance takes place unconsciously, and in silence, in
a series of haunting dreams. The last of these is a repetitive dream that
connects her obliquely to the theme of maternal loss, but in the form
of a patterning she cannot yet break. The sense of profound bereavement is condensed into the image of a beautiful present that her mother
leaves for her at the bottom of a murky pool, but it is a gift she cannot
grasp because it keeps suddenly disappearing in the deep, sullied water
(87).

The last chapter, 'Lucy', is a circular return centring on change, both
personal and historical:

The person I had become I did not know very well. Oh, on the outside everything was familiar. My hair was the same . . . My eyes were the same. My ears were the same. The other important things about me were the same.

But the things I could not see about myself, the things I could not put my hands on – those things had changed, and I did not yet know them well. *I understood I was inventing myself,* and that I was doing this more in the way of a painter. (133–4, emphasis added)

This is the depiction of an awakening consciousness. Lucy is becoming aware that she has been previously reading herself through the inter-pretations of others. This shedding of double-consciousness means seeing that her body parts have been fractured in surface readings that have occluded any interiority or subjective depth. Possibilities of future agency are now linked to a self-conscious, albeit painful, process of intentionality which means breaking through the deadened feelings that have been veiled under unacknowledged experiences of shame. When Lucy breaks open the traumatic silence of the melancholy long held within her – when she finally admits to Mariah something she has never spoken of before, that 'I was not an only child but it was almost as if I was ashamed of this, because I'd never told anyone' (130) – she begins to release her story, and as a result 'all sorts of little details of my life on the island where I grew up came back to me' (131). This em-bodied traumatic memory and its belated return is full of the colour and imagistic presence for which such memories are renowned. But, sud-denly, just as she remembers how one of her brothers had nearly choked to death swallowing a plum he had found, Lucy is forced by an inner compulsion to speak no more: '[M]y mouth was empty, my tongue had collapsed into my throat. I thought I would turn to stone just then,' she says (131). In a reversal of the Western Echo myth, in which her body turns to stone, but her voice lingers on, Lucy's painful recollection is interrupted by Mariah's presence. It is at this moment that Mariah then produces de Beauvoir's white feminist text, and Lucy's cathartic moment of telling of her shame is swallowed up again by the white echo.

The second shaming incident happens when Lucy meets an Ameri-can who has just returned from holidaying in Antigua. This tourist is blind to the poverty and the material legacies of slavery that are only too visible on Lucy's home-island with its economy built on distress and deprivation and the ownership of people. To the holiday-maker, it is just 'a beautiful place' (134): she cannot see what British Guyanian poet,

Grace Nichols, describes in one of her poems on the Caribbean as 'islands/fertile/with brutality'.[3] But what disconcerts Lucy even more is that the woman 'named a village by the sea and then went on to describe a view that was unknown to me. At that time I was so ashamed I could hardly make a reply, for I had come to believe that people in my position in the world should know everything about the place they were from' (134–5). Yet, the fact that Lucy knew little of her island is embedded in the political history of Antigua: white colonialists owned all the banks, offices, and resorts such as the exclusive Mill Reef Club, and all the island's most beautiful beaches were reserved for whites only.[4] Shame again almost interrupts her answer, but a new sense of belonging to her island's subaltern history makes Lucy realise:

> I know this: it was discovered by Christopher Columbus in 1493; Columbus never set foot there but only named it in passing, after a church in Spain. He could not have known that he would have so many things to name, and I imagined how hard he had to rack his brain after he ran out of names honoring his benefactors, the saints he cherished, events important to him. A task like that would have killed a thoughtful person, but he went on to live a very long life.
>
> I had realized that the origin of my presence on the island – *my ancestral history – was the result of a foul deed* . . . (135, emphasis added)

Columbus's 'discovery' of the West Indies in 1492 began a period of genocide of Amerindian peoples which was followed by the mass importation of African slaves. The humorous stress on the importance of names honouring Columbus's white heritage emphasises how imperial ownership by naming is in itself a 'foul deed'. Tzvetan Todorov describes it this way: 'The first gesture Columbus makes upon contact with the newly discovered lands . . . is an act of extended nomination . . . the declaration according to which these lands are henceforth part of the Kingdom of Spain.'[5] It is a written deed of ownership. Columbus landed, as Todorov ironically states, 'armed with his inkwell'.[6] Todorov's metaphor also applies to the writing of imperial histories, which when joined with imposed phantasmatic economy of Western literature, plays such a powerful role in creating the 'two-facedness' of double-consciousness. But Lucy has begun to feel again:

> One day I was living *silently* in a personal hell, without anyone to tell what I felt, without even knowing that the feelings I had were

possible to have; and then one day I was not living like that at all. I had begun to see the past like this: there is a line; you can draw it yourself, or sometimes it gets drawn for you. (136–7, emphasis added)

Shamed by her lack of localised knowledge into contemplating the realities of her history, Lucy no longer constantly relives the traumatic past. She has gradually learned this in her year away, by 'trying to explain it to myself, [through] speaking to Mariah, how I got to feel the way I even now feel' (137). She has recently disengaged from a relationship with her mother by sending her the lying letter with the false address. Now she leaves Mariah's employ and moves into an apartment with Peggy. She has not, however, divested herself entirely from her traumatic attachment to her mother, as is clear by the obsessive stress on the books she will take with her (143).

It is not surprising, then, that the climactic tension builds around an image of water in the shape of one of Lucy's photographs taken of the Great Lakes, which she has pinned on her bedroom wall in her new room:

> it was a body of water . . . no boats, no people, no signs of life – except the water, its surface of uniformly shaped ripplets, its depths dark, treacherous and uninviting. It was the very opposite of the water I was surrounded by on the island where I grew up. The water was three shades of blue, calm, inviting, warm; I had taken it for granted, so much so that it became one of the things I cursed. (148)

As Lucy disengages from Mariah, she reunites imaginatively with her island and its beautiful surrounding sea. It is a psychic return built on adjectival differences. She opens a drawer and takes out a collection of documents that define her life in the white world: her passport, immigration card, permission-to-work card, birth certificate and a copy of the lease of the apartment. These documents, she thinks, show 'everything about me . . . where I was born . . . my birthday . . . They showed my skin and my eyes were the same color brown' (149). Indeed, the identificatory photographs show everything and nothing, for they are all surface readings bound by skin colour, official documentation reminiscent of the classificatory role photography played in imperial dominance.

What they do not illustrate is the internal impact of the power of naming and labelling. Startled by seeing her name repeated again and again on the documents, Kincaid's protagonist is finally provided with the name we as readers have so far only assumed: 'These documents all said that my name was Lucy – Lucy Josephine Potter' (149), and so begins a four-page meditation on the origins of her three names, two of which have been chosen by her mother, and all of which she hates. Her hatred of her patronymic is understandable: it is an inherited slave ownership name. Josephine was chosen in relation to her mother's uncle, Mr Joseph who was reputed to be rich and might, her mother thought, leave Lucy some money in his will. The ironic moral of this tale is that he had lost all his fortune and was forced to live in an old tomb in the Anglican churchyard, the spiritual home of the imperialists. It is, however, the first name that matters. As a child Lucy had hated her name, thinking it 'slight, without substance' (149). She had not received an answer when she asked her mother the origins of her name years before, and it is important that when she gets a response her mother is pregnant with the last of her three sons, a time of extreme alienation between mother and daughter: '"I named you after Satan himself. Lucy short for Lucifer. What a botheration from the moment you were conceived"' (152), her mother finally replies.

This is not only a very ambiguous statement, it is the peripeteiac sentence of the novel in many ways. Lucy is illegitimate, her brothers legitimate. Lucy has to ask twice, the second time her mother answers 'under her breath', so it is quite possible that this reply is a projection of Lucy's bound up with her profound sense of her mother's betrayal that had occurred after her first brother was born. Yet, despite its negative connotations, Lucy declares: 'I was transformed from failure to triumph. It was the moment I knew who I was' (152). Lucy immediately goes on to tell how she was taught to read through the Bible, *Paradise Lost*, and that part of her education involved having to memorise parts of *Paradise Lost*. As I see it, this is the moment in the novel when the two cultures merge together. Her joy is in part a response to her deep affinity with this great poem, thus representing the white literary echo that has resounded through her life; however, it is extremely important that Satan was also the favourite anti-hero of slave folklore, work songs, spirituals and slave narratives.[7] Lucy now renames Milton's Lucifer as her own: 'The stories of the fallen were well known to me, but I had not known that my own situation could even be distantly related to them' (152–3). Having always despised the name Lucy, she now affirms the appellation her mother gave her, which she can now connect to a reading of the Caribbean and maybe a rereading of the passage in which Milton ambivalently connects Columbus's discovery of the New World as an afterword to the biblical scene of shame. Milton's canonical echo has now merged with the resistance Satan has provided for African oral traditions in the New World.

All this time Lucy has been lying in her bed. She gets up and looks out of the window onto the white world below where she notices a broken clock: 'it made me even more conscious of a feeling I had constantly now: my sense of time had changed . . . For a very long moment I wondered what my mother was doing and I saw her face; it was the face she used to have when she loved me without reservation' (154–5). The very long moment is a distillation of trauma and its passing into consciousness. Lucy moves out of the latency of belated time. Instead of the stilling of time around the moment of trauma of her mother's rejection in which the past had continually forced itself into an endless repeating possession of her present, the past can now be aligned with a future that can stretch ahead.

In her final act in the novel, Lucy is alone one night in the apartment. She picks up a leather notebook with blank white pages that Mariah had given her as a parting present:

> It was on the night table next to my bed. Beside it lay my fountain pen full of beautiful blue ink. I picked up both, and opened the book. At the top of the page I wrote my full name: Lucy Josephine Potter. At the sight of it, many thoughts rushed through me, but I could write only this: 'I wish I could love someone so much that I could die from it.' And then as I looked at this sentence a great wave of shame came over me and I wept and wept so much that the tears fell on the page and caused all the words to become one great blur. (163–4)

The only other occasion in the book where Lucy cries was the profound moment of belated understanding *why* her relationship with her mother was scored with such a profound sense of ambivalent hatred and desperate longing for reunion. It was the moment when she finally admits *out loud* that she was not an only child as her previous silence suggested, but one with a traumatic past, a past haunted by her mother's sudden expiration of maternal love. But one of the echoing memories of that terrible time was that her mother's eyes also constantly filled with tears. However, they were not tears of mourning for her lost love for her daughter, but tears of pride at the thought of what great deeds her sons might very well perform when they grew up. Lucy's tears that flow as she tells the story to Mariah tasted as if they were squeezed from an aloe plant. In the Western pharmaceutical industry, aloe is used as a bitter purgative. But the label *aloe* means that the plant belongs to the genus of the African lily. The entangled trope of taste and feeling has threaded through this novel, and Lucy's will-to-feel must always be as ambivalent as the tears that taste of aloe. Now, Lucy's tears flow again. She begins to mourn the lost relationship with her mother, but her future life and the self she is crafting will always hold that sense of loss at her centre. She can never be totally free of either the literary or the maternal echoes that haunt her life.

Separated from her African cultural roots by her mother's assimilation into the cultural mores of the colonists, Lucy's method of call-and-response has been partly subsumed by the deadening whiteness of the responding echo that returns from Mariah, the only person she has an empathetic face-to-face relationship with in the novel. I began this section by describing two colonial punishments that Kincaid endured as a child. I have already discussed the reconstitution of the echoes of Milton's *Paradise Lost*. However, the lines of Gray's poetry, 'Ignorance is bliss: It's folly to be wise', which Kincaid was forced repeatedly to copy follow a different trajectory which contains a wonderfully ironic justice. In an essay entitled, 'The Muse of History', Derek Walcott describes how in the Plantations of the New World 'the slave [gradually] wrested God from his captor'[8] and with extraordinary dexterity reformed the only language and imagery available to them into differing forms of oral backchat. One such act of resistance was the Afro-Caribbean proverb which turned the ideology behind the biblical proverb into one of mimicry or mocking subversion. In the plantation fields of Jamaica the slaves retaliated by reconfiguring the master's language in a manner that was all their own. The biblical proverb which reads: 'Answer not a fool according to his folly, lest thou also be like unto him. Answer a fool according to his folly, lest he be wise with his own conceit'[9] became, according to Orlando Patterson, one of the slaves' favourite proverbs, but now reading, 'Play fool, to catch wise.'[10] Stereotyped as lying, cowardly, lazy, subhuman and utterly unintelligent, the slaves re-troped the ideological prescription imposed upon them by turning it into a double-coded subversion that echoed, but rewrote, the original. As African traditions of orality provided a way of projecting a resisting voice through and across the dualistic world that silenced them, so too has it enabled the creation of a distinctive literary form. The socio-historical context of Jamaica Kincaid's *Lucy* is contemporary America, but the force of its call is grounded in Glissant's theory of 'creative marronage' which explodes outwards from the Caribbean to become part of that subversive tradition.

Importantly, however, Kincaid's racial reconfiguring is specifically gendered; her protagonist's subjectivity is a relational identity fashioned, painfully and tentatively, out of her maternal heritage and ancestry. Barbara Christian, in her significant essay, 'Race for Theory', argues that 'people of color have always theorized – but in forms quite different from the Western form of abstract logic. And I am inclined to say that our theorizing . . . is often in narrative forms, in the stories we create, in riddles and proverbs, in the play with language, since dynamic rather than fixed ideas seem more to our liking. How else have we managed to survive with such spiritedness the assault on our bodies, social institutions, countries, our very humanity?'[11] Kincaid's narrative form itself can be seen to be a writing back against the abstract prescriptions of a colonial education and its double-conscious heritage through instigating a subversive response to the pull of the 'white world' and the interpellative pleasures of its literary echoes.

7

'Knots of Death': Toni Morrison's *Sula*

'Gotta make a way out of no way' – Traditional black folk saying[1]

The short untitled prologue of Toni Morrison's second novel, *Sula*, powerfully delineates the devastating potency of white American society to create, structure, name, then destroy, a black community merely on a whim. Her carefully crafted opening sentence expresses both the violence and loss that will permeate the novel: 'In that place, where they tore the nightshade and blackberry patches from their roots to make room for the Medallion City Golf Course, there was once a neighborhood.'[2] 'The violence lurks', Morrison states elsewhere, 'in having something torn out by its roots – it will not, cannot grow again.'[3] The capricious destruction of the rural community by the ubiquitous 'they' also suggests a sense of the black community's alienation and exclusion from any participation in the history that had, and continues to have, so much impact on the lives of African-Americans. However, the connection between racial violence and white history becomes more apparent when immediately after describing its death, Morrison explains the story of the community's beginnings, for she illustrates quite clearly that the inhumanity and capitalist impulse of slavery were not halted by Emancipation:

> A good white farmer promised freedom and a piece of [fertile] bottom land to his slave if he would perform some very difficult chores. When the slave completed his work, he asked the farmer to keep his end of the bargain. Freedom was easy – the farmer had no objection to that. But he didn't want to give up his land. (5)

114

The 'good' white farmer therefore tricks the slave into believing that the infertile land up in the hills really is 'the bottom of heaven – the best land there is' (5). Thus the black community becomes called the Bottom 'in spite of the fact that it was up in the hills...where planting was backbreaking, where the soil slid down and washed away the seeds, and where the wind lingered all through the winter' (4, 5). This cruel reversal of fortunes the narrator describes as a 'nigger joke', a survival technique that inverts and masks the profound existential pain hidden beneath the laughter, '[t]he kind [of joke] colored folks tell on themselves when...they're looking for a little comfort somehow' (4–5).[4] However, as is already clear before the reader is more than two pages into the novel, there is very little spiritual or material comfort to be found cushioning the lives of the black characters in this novel, who are often reduced to an existence of mere survival. As the narrator describes it, 'the laughter was part of the pain' (4).[5] Indeed, the repression of pain masked by laughter acting as solace is a recurrent trope in the novel, as is an interweaving of laughter and death.

While Morrison, as Barbara Christian suggests, 'weaves a fable about the relationship between conformity and experiment, survival and creativity', death has an overwhelming presence in this novel, beginning with the death of the black community itself.[6] As Maureen Reddy argues, 'Each of the ten major chapters includes a death, sometimes metaphoric but more usually actual'.[7] The literal deaths are often almost incomprehensible in their violence, and always involve a family member or someone known to those involved; the spiritual deaths are long and drawn out and equally as painful. While the novel's surface construction appears to be contained within the conventions of a chronological timeframe, the text is divided exactly in half, with the two almost identically sized parts separated by a 10-year interval. It begins with an untitled prologue, then the chapters are titled by the dates 1919, 1920, 1921, 1923, 1927 – the 10-year temporal rupture registered as pure absence – then 1937, 1939, 1940, 1941, and finally 1965, which serves as an epilogue. However, the deep structure of the novel does not progress along the assumed teleological ethos of traditional historical time but moves in the rhythms of the psychic time-frame of trauma. Morrison's methodology involves placing each death at a moment in history suggested by the chapter title: at first it is merely described by the omniscient narrator – often in horrific detail, but also, paradoxically, in evocative and hauntingly lyrical language. Then an explanation from the character that has been most involved in each death appears later in the text, usually in another chapter altogether.

These knots of traumatic grief Morrison unties and reconfigures at a later moment in the text, with the dénouement breaking through the sequence of repeating death with an epiphanic moment of belated experience. More than *Wide Sargasso Sea* and *Lucy*, *Sula* exhibits the formal devices of *belatedness* – the protective numbing that initially accompanies a traumatic experience, the repeating intrusions that are unavailable to conscious assimilation, and the moment of belated recognition that can unexpectedly occur, thus moving the traumatised person out of a perpetual melancholia and into the possible healing of mourning. Even more importantly, in Morrison's text belatedness is intrinsic to the novel's formal properties; its figuration is subtle, original and the knots' unravellings are profoundly affected by the logic and ethics of metaphor.

However, if death and time are inextricably interwoven with the concept of belatedness in the novel, neither can they be separated out from the presence of nature, for Morrison's characters' philosophy of life is also bound up with the cyclical patterns of nature. Not only does their survival depend on it in certain ways, but reading the signs of nature is an intrinsic part of life in the Bottom.[8] Hot and freezing winds, uncanny frosts, sudden rises of temperature in the dead of winter, plagues of birds and so on, charge the text: even promises are repeatedly 'leaf-dead' (161, 162). These unfulfilled promises emanate from white society, and the effects of their withdrawal result in yet more deaths. However, the adjective 'leaf-dead' also holds within it both a configuration of the complexity of the ever-changing, ever-damaging relationship between black and white Americans, but also the suggestion that with spring's renewal there is a hope of redemptive possibility. Nevertheless, such a possibility must be kept at arm's length as a tactic of survival, and more often the black community's attitude suggests an interweave of ideas of nature with a notion of determinism:

> They did not believe Nature was ever askew – only inconvenient. Plague and drought were as 'natural' as springtime. If milk could curdle, God knows robins could fall. The purpose of evil was to survive it and they determined (without ever knowing that they had made up their minds to do it) to survive floods, white people, tuberculosis, famine and ignorance. (90)

The problem with the enforced victim status of the community in the face of omnipotent white manipulation is that it results in a resigned obstinacy, which means that the inhabitants no longer have the strength to determine the difference between the ills inflicted by nature and the social ills inflicted by the white system. Tolerating evil is a passive means of survival, as the community cannot fight back against the enormity of the oppression that surrounds them. As I shall go on to argue, the Bottom has all the hallmarks of a *traumatised community*. It is the notion of a communal response to trauma – or trauma that cannot be separated out from the embodiment of a raced and gendered existence that is knotted into community life – that differentiates this novel from the other two I have discussed.

The story of the Bottom's birth, then, is the outcome of what Barbara Christian describes as the 'result of a White man's inversion of the truth, and it is destroyed years later when Whites again alter the truth, [and] the worth of the land, to suit their own desires. Thus, a tradition evolves during the life-span of the Bottom that is inextricably connected to its beginning, a tradition that is rooted in the nature of the land as the bottom on the top.'[9] The Bottom becomes a community of devastating economic poverty: the inhospitable land cannot support the black families, there are few jobs available for the men, and only low-paid domestic work in the white houses of the valley for the women, with the result that husbands frequently desert their families.[10] In turn, this political economy of distress and deprivation gives rise to emotional, psychic and physical trauma that engenders repeated familial patterns of violence, oppression and hate.

The space between the Bottom's birth and death and its struggle for survival is central to *Sula*; it is also the 'black' history of the Bottom that Morrison unravels and re-ravels in the course of the novel. As a consequence of the pressure exacted by the invisible force of whiteness, the black community's principal survival strategy is to shore up seemingly impermeable boundaries governed by strict unspoken rules to which both individuals and the community must conform. This necessarily creates an insular black society, but one that is, as Wendy Harding and Jacky Martin suggest, brimming with a 'richness and intensity of life'.[11] Indeed, the community of the Bottom is a paradigmatic ambivalent space, and as with all Morrison's fictitious communities, is in her words simultaneously 'a support system and a hammer'.[12] Interestingly, and in accordance with this status of ambivalence, 'the Bottom' is both a generic term for a black suburb *and* a particularised example of enforced segregation that gave birth to blues, jazz and new forms of dance. Geneva Smitherman explains that the label 'bottom' or 'bottoms' describes an area of any city or town where African-Americans live, and which over time has come to refer to a run-down or slum area in the black community.[13] However, Zora Neale Hurston, in a wonderful article entitled 'Characteristics of Negro Expression', also refers to a specific black community which had existed in 1920s in the 'Jook section of Nashville, Tennessee . . . a tough neighbourhood known as Black Bottom – hence the name', which was a particularly famous spot where black music and dance grew and flourished.[14] Here then, we have both the positive and the negative: the segregated black communities of endless Bottoms but within which black-created jooks sparked an artistic creativity that spread back outward into American white society in ways that forever changed and rejuvenated 'American' culture.[15]

It is this kind of masked resistance built out of African-American cultural traditions that underwrites Morrison's novel. This is signalled by a small incident on the second page which will only alert a reader who can read the cultural reference.[16] It occurs when the narrator seamlessly switches the description of the violent uprooting of the community to a nostalgic remembrance of the neighbourhood as it had once been:

> [O]n quiet days people in valley houses could hear singing sometimes, banjos sometimes, and if a valley man happened to have business up in those hills – collecting rent or insurance payments – he might see a dark woman in a flowered dress doing a bit of *cakewalk*, a bit of black bottom, a bit of 'messing around' to the lively notes of a mouth organ . . . The black people watching her would laugh and rub their knees, and it would be easy for the valley man to hear the laughter and not notice the adult pain that rested somewhere under the eyelids . . . somewhere in the sinew's curve. (4, emphasis added)

The intrusion of the generic white man on capitalist business into the apparently carefree atmosphere of the black community offers the first sign of a masked critique. However, the more obvious allusion to the white man's objectifying, sexualised gaze, the superiority of his financial position and his inability to see the pain that lurks below the skin – a distress which must be *mis*recognised in order to justify its continued existence – is accentuated by the fact that the white valley man also fails to register the mimicking power of the dance known as the cakewalk, a Sunday dance that originated in the plantation system. This was a parodic performance undertaken for pleasure, a masked but public satire in which, according to black musician and former slave, Shephard Edmonds, slaves 'would dress up in hand-me-down finery to do a high-kicking, prancing walk-around. They did a takeoff on the high manners of the folks in the "big house", but their masters, who gathered around to watch the fun, missed the point'.[17] Eric Sundquist maintains that Edmonds was mistaken in asserting that the white masters always missed the satire at their expense, but whether the mimicry was silently acknowledged and then ignored by the white owners, is not really the point.[18] As I see it, this makes the impact doubly subversive, but it does not necessarily, or only momentarily, lessen the existential pain of the slaves. However, this example of subversive upstaging has a wonderfully resonant energy because it also illustrates the 'indomitable power of slaves to assert their human agency in closely restricted circumstances', as Paul Gilroy says in relation to another form of resistance, Morrison's use of the Margaret Garner story for *Beloved*.[19]

Morrison's vignette of the white valley man subtly evokes the oppressive structure of the objectifying look and the reliance on exterior body signs that feeds the otherness of racial prejudice. It also foreshadows one of the most metaphysically difficult scenes in the novel when Helene Wright, one of the women from the Bottom, is publicly humiliated and punished for being black and female by both a demeaning racial censure and the lingering sexualised look of a repulsive white conductor, when she mistakenly gets into the whites-only carriage of a Jim Crow train. This episode, as I mentioned in the introduction, is emblematic of Sara Ahmed's reading of the racial encounter and, importantly, is the politicised reversal of the encounter in *Wide Sargasso Sea* in which the white creole child, Antoinette, is shamed by donning the 'dirty' dress of Tia's blackness. In *Sula*, Helene's humiliation is witnessed by her 10-year-old daughter, Nel, an experience that will haunt the impressionable girl for the rest of her life. It is a scene as piercing and echoic as Frantz Fanon's important work on the constitutive white gaze and repeated trauma of being derisively singled out by the pointing finger, and the accompanying words, '"Look a Negro!"', which results in the sprawling, distorted black body riven with psychic pain that is returned to him 'clad in mourning'.[20] Yet, Fanon's brilliant exposition of the suffering black body distorted by ideological prejudice and 'legends, stories, history, and above all *historicity* . . . [metaphorically] battered down by tom-toms, cannibalism, intellectual deficiency, fetishism [*sic*], racial defects, slave-ships'[21] and so on, was of course also famously masculinist. In contrast, Morrison states in *Playing in the Dark*, '[m]y work requires me to think about how free I can be as an African-American *woman* writer in my genderized, sexualized, wholly racialized world'.[22] Thus, while Morrison, like Fanon, is interested in confronting her readers with the damaging embodied effects of white dominance of American society – strongly implying that white control of history has created unbearable suffering – she adds a radically gendered critique. In particular, she unravels, often in intricate detail, how the dominant social order of whiteness in its various mutations is internalised by her black female characters.

Racial suffering is pin-pointed in *Sula* as beginning with the traumatic historical experience of slavery, an experience that crippled African-American bodies and minds. The story then shifts to World War I when black bodies were again considered an economic necessity, but this time as cannon fodder in the wider historical framework of a white man's war, and then continues in what appears, initially at least, to be a linear progression towards 1965. However, after the prologue and first chapter, Morrison concentrates on the female members of the black community. My argument is that the psychic suffering of this continuing legacy can never *literally* be seen unless rhetorically (re)presented and imaginatively visualised.[23] In this novel, psychic traumas are literally written onto the bodies of the main characters, and as a result many have bodies that are physically marked in some way, whether by birthmark, self-mutilation, or through the process of violent death. 'Freedom was easy' (5), the text tells us, but relinquishing ideological control of black lives was not something that was going to be so easily given up. After Emancipation, the continuation of white supremacy shifted from material to ideological ownership – from the corporeal to the abstract.

The freedom to tell stories, whether fiction or the writing of history, is based on the structures of power, and in the case of the disempowered, both the ability to tell stories and the thematic content is very often, as Obioma Nnaemeka tells us, about 'survival (to live beyond/after the event) . . . one must outlive/survive the event in order to engage in its telling'.[24] From the perspective of Chinua Achebe, whom Nnaemeka quotes to illustrate her point: 'It is the storyteller, in fact, who makes us what we are, who creates history. The storyteller creates the memory that the survivors must have – otherwise their surviving would have no meaning.'[25] And, as Nnaemeka goes on to state, Toni Morrison is 'one of the greatest storytellers of all times'.[26] But African-American storytelling, whether fiction or history, has been immeasurably complicated by what black historians and other anti-racist intellectuals term the 'African Holocaust', the *repressed* history of the Middle Passage, black slavery in the New World, and its long-term effects that have continued on in differing forms to the present day, in what Morrison herself terms, the 'trauma of racism'.[27] From Morrison's perspective, '[t]he trauma of racism is, for the racist and the victim, the severe fragmentation of the self, and has always seemed to me a cause (not a symptom) of psychosis'.[28] Yet this form of trauma, Morrison continues, holds little interest for the institutions of white-controlled psychiatry, or indeed, most generally for the still white-dominated discipline of literary criticism.[29]

The foundations of trauma theory, formulated by Sigmund Freud in 'Beyond the Pleasure Principle', were written under the shadows of World War I. The context of this work and the focus on the psychic effects of war, have a particular relevance for a reading of *Sula*, especially as the first chapter concerns a black soldier's traumatised experiences in this same war.[30] As Freud struggled to understand the phenomena of war neuroses, he came to believe that the trauma of witnessing horrific violence and the mutilations of death in war instigated repeated traumatic reactions that were relived in the mind. But he argued that it was not so much the horrific visions of death itself, but death's utter unexpectedness that the mind could not fathom and incorporate into consciousness. Because the mind withholds assimilation of the horror of the traumatic event, from Caruth's contemporary perspective, 'the outside has gone inside without any mediation'.[31] This means that sufferers have continually to wake in, and into, fright, to a repeating state of consciousness of their survival. It is the repeating experience of the realisation of survival itself that causes the ongoing structure of psychic trauma. This is the peculiar and perplexing experience of *survival* which is intrinsic to the lived experience of the inhabitants of the Bottom.

Of all trauma theorists, Caruth provides the most intriguing and illuminating understanding of the direct effects external violence can have on both the individual and the collective psyche. Moving beyond Freud's notion that response to a traumatic event most often occurs in delayed and uncontrollable ways, repetitive dreams, flashbacks, hallucinations and other intrusive phenomena, Caruth maintains that the 'problem of trauma is not simply a problem of destruction but also, fundamentally, an *enigma of survival*'.[32] The intricate relationship between trauma and survival is 'through the very paradoxical structure of *indirectness* in psychical trauma ... trauma is suffered in the psyche precisely, it would seem, because it is *not* directly available to experience'.[33] While the body can protect itself by means of a spatial boundary between inside and outside, the mind reacts to trauma by creating a 'break in the mind's experience of time',[34] what is called in the metaphoric logic of this text, 'the closed place in the middle' (118).

[A]lthough history should not become a straitjacket, which overwhelms and binds, neither should it be forgotten. (Toni Morrison)[35]

In this section then, I shall address the notion of indirectness in psychic trauma (the mind's protective act of creating a suspension in consciousness and time) and the idea of a history of trauma both as an individual and collective attempt to claim one's own survival as the necessary experience of waking into consciousness. Such a reawakening must be identified with some means of reliving that trauma in a way that requires events of the past to be acknowledged and assimilated into the conscious life of an individual. Once reclaimed – as opposed to being the unclaimed experience of the traumatic past – this previously silenced history, whether individual or collective, needs to be articulated, so that survival is not just mere survival, but becomes a possibly transformative measure that will alter not just how the past can be read, but can radically change perceptions of the future. The extraordinarily powerful metaphoric logic inherent in Morrison's literary fiction offers, I believe, a particularly imaginative conduit between repressed traumatic experience(s) and an awakening into consciousness of the previously excised experience of black historical trauma which is, in its many personalised configurations, continually damaging to the psyche. In the first section on *Wide Sargasso Sea*, I discuss how metaphor can be used as a 'safety' valve, a means of shutting oneself off from the realities of historical injustices. In the second section on *Lucy* I maintain that the metaphor of echoing evoked the notion of an interpellative complicity with what has been, and also prefigures the possibility of moving beyond once the pull of the echo is mediated. With a close reading of *Sula*, I move into the final stage of my argument by suggesting that Morrison's exquisite use of the indirectness of metaphorical structuring provides a creative method of *breaking through* to unacknowledged traumatic material. Borrowing from psychoanalytic use of metaphor, I contend that 'inasmuch as repression represents an inability to understand unconscious meaning in abstract literal terms, a metaphorical statement may represent this unconscious meaning in concrete figurative language'.[36] In particular, I want to address Morrison's evocative creation of a conceptual metaphor of unique force which both structures and drives the text – her brilliant rendition of *'gone things'* (174, emphasis added) which are never gone but linger and echo in the minds of all the main characters. Indeed, *Sula* is overwhelmingly a story of loss, of 'gone things' historically and collectively imposed on

African-Americans, and individually on the lives of those who suffer the trauma of racism. In fact, the whole narrative structuring is based on the notion of belated assimilation and retelling as the way to salvage a lost past of 'gone things' and, in conjunction with the notion of belatedness, this echoing metaphor is only explicitly named on the last page.

However, in my reading of *Sula* I shall stress, as I did with *Lucy*, that the awakening into consciousness associated with white-dominated trauma theory can never be separated from double-consciousness, internalisation of racist ideologies and the need continually to mask the impact of psychic pain. But I shall now argue that the masking, inversion, double-coding and the structuring of metaphorical language and logic that is threaded through the double-consciousness heritage of the African-American tradition can be played out in a literary text *in unexpectedly cathartic ways* by utilising the very same linguistic strategies that perhaps had initially been more centred around strategies of survival. This is particularly relevant because, as Geneva Smitherman argues in her important book, *Talkin and Testifyin: The Language of Black America*, American Black English is not only highly innovative and often deeply subversive, but is also a verb-driven, profoundly metaphoric and imagistic evocation of the English language.[37] This is the narrative impulse that Hurston had described 50 years earlier as the 'will to adorn', which from her perspective is the 'second most notable characteristic in Negro expression'.[38] The constitutive force of black semantics comprises metaphor and simile, the use of the double descriptive, and finally, creative verbal nouns (such as to 'funeralize'), which together form 'the Negro's greatest contribution to the language'.[39] What I hope to demonstrate is that the will to adorn is also a highly visualised form of will-to-narrative, both spoken and written, that provides a bridge between traumatised affect and event.

Trauma, imagery of knotting and the death-like binding of white history, psychic loss and its inversion, psychic comfort and the power of metaphor, all converge in *Sula* in the enigmatic figure of Shadrack, a young black soldier traumatised by the events he witnessed in World War I. The first chapter, entitled '1919', tells his story. Shadrack is in fact psychically damaged in 1917, but it is as if time stills; he is held within a numbing stasis, which lasted, 'for more than a year, only eight days of which he fully recollected' (11). As if mirroring this encapsulation of time, this chapter appears initially to be moving seamlessly on from the description of the violent destruction of the black community and into Shadrack's individual, but equally violent destruction of self. However, the shift from prologue to first chapter also represents a radical temporal disjuncture, for, as we later realise, the death of the Bottom has been told from the perspective of the time of the epilogue, as if it were the present tense. Returning now to an experience that took place 50 years earlier, we are abruptly plunged into a different form of trauma. This time it concerns the white masculinist violence of World War I which leaves Shadrack '[t]wenty-two years old, weak, hot, frightened, not daring to acknowledge the fact that he didn't even know who or what he was . . .' (12). Persistent and delayed responses to combat stress occur because the traumatic events of the war damage the foundations of his identity: 'he didn't even know who or what he was . . . with no past, no language, no tribe, no source, no address book, no comb, no pencil, no clock, no pocket handkerchief, no rug, no bed, no can opener, no faded postcard, no soap, no key, no tobacco pouch, no soiled under-wear and nothing nothing nothing to do' (12). The double-coding inherent in this description of a shattered identity (rendered in repeated negatives) applies to the experiences of a traumatised ex-soldier, and may also recall a sense of obliteration that could be related to the long-term effects of the Middle Passage, slavery and its ongoing racist aftermath.

Unlike his biblical forebear, a Hebrew dissident who emerges a hero, whole in body and spirit from Nebuchadnezzar's fiery furnace because of his unshakeable faith in his God,[40] Morrison's shell-shocked and dis-orientated Shadrack emerges psychically wounded from the furnace of war. He is literally 'bound in a straitjacket' (9), tied up in the knots of white male history that he cannot undo, when he becomes violent with fear in the mental ward of a hospital where he has been incarcerated suffering from shell-shock. His psychic trauma is the result of his first experience on the battlefield, when he 'saw the face of a soldier near him fly off . . . [while] the body of the headless soldier ran on, with energy and grace, ignoring altogether the drip and slide of brain tissue down his back' (8). He develops an irrational fear that his hands are growing 'higgledy-piggledy fashion like Jack's beanstalk' (9), and the 'unchecked monstrosity of his hands' (12) make them not only terrify-ing, but useless. The poignancy of straitjacket metaphor is wonderfully rendered. On one hand, the narrator acknowledges that '[w]hen they bound Shadrack into a straitjacket, he was both relieved and grateful, for his hands were at last hidden' (9), but at the same time, because of the problem with his hands, Shadrack cannot, however much he desires, disentangle himself from the straitjacket in which he has been bound, even though he is unconsciously aware that 'his very life depended on the release of the knots' (12). The straitjacket is a space of safety, a comfort and a trap. Shadrack is then callously, and to him inexplicably, ejected from hospital with his trauma unhealed, and with nothing but a fleeting memory of home and a longing 'to see his own face . . . [so that he can] tie the loose cords of his mind' (10). This yearning to reclaim his lost identity, to see his face, directly results from his sense of invisibility as mere cannon fodder in the wider historical framework of a white man's war. Shadrack, a black man with no patronymic, is a generic symbol of trauma.[41] However, and very importantly, while his experiences were a common feature of trauma theory symptoms registered by the inordinate number of shell-shocked soldiers in World War I, Shadrack's adaptation to and resistances against his trauma, and the story that grows out of it, are both class and race-driven.[42]

Thrown in prison as a vagrant, Shadrack finally recognises his lost self. Overwhelmed by a recurring desire to see his face, and as there is no other mirroring surface to look into, he is forced to search for a sight of himself in the water of his toilet bowl. Significantly, as if offering a premonitory warning to his black community to which he is about to return, Shadrack has first to shut out the contaminating white light that surrounds him in his cell, by placing his prison blanket over his head. In an ironic reversal of the Narcissus myth, he then catches a glimpse of his face, which reveals not only that he is 'real', that he 'exists', but 'the indisputable presence' of his own blackness (13).[43] Instead of falling in love with his own reflection and pining away and dying by a forest pool, Shadrack rediscovers life through acknowledging the 'joy' of his blackness in a filthy cell of a country jail, and starts his personal fight back against the straitjacket of white history, a trauma in which he has been enmeshed by a force greater than himself. Finally back in his community of the Bottom, he inaugurates an annual National Suicide Day which 'had to do with making a place for fear as a way of controlling it. He knew the smell of death and was terrified of it, for he could not anticipate it . . . [so] he hit on the notion that if one day a year were devoted to it, everybody could get it out of the way and the rest of the year would be safe and free' (14). Paradoxically, Shadrack, the only male figure in *Sula* to gain an inner strength and sense of self, is thought to be mad by the rest of the community, and yet his madness is imbued with a strong sense of power that is almost Christ-like: as the Reverend Deal, the minister who presides over the black church in the Bottom says quite explicitly, '[m]ay's well go on with Shad and save the Lamb the trouble of redemption' (16). Moreover, '[t]he terrible Shad who walked about with his penis out, who peed in front of ladies and girl-children [was] the only black who could curse white people and get away with it' (61–2). Thus, Shadrack is both black victim *and* resister. He is almost incoherently mad, yet he can still curse and thus intimidate white people, and the self-exposure of his black body, and in particular his penis, confronts a long-standing white fear and fetishistic preoccupation with black masculinity.

At first the inhabitants of the Bottom are frightened of the very different Shadrack who has returned from the war, but 'once the people understood the boundaries and nature of his madness, they could fit him so to speak, into the scheme of things' (15). Gradually his annual holiday becomes 'absorbed . . . into their thoughts, into their language, into their lives' (15). To a lesser extent, it is as if Shadrack is also woven into the natural fabric of the environment. In America the signifier 'shad' is applied, usually with a defining word, to many forms of fish, the creatures he relies on for material survival and a species he loves along with the river. His profound spiritual connection to the protagonist Sula Peace involves his reading of her birthmark: 'She had a tadpole over her eye (that was how he knew she was a friend – she had the mark of the fish he loved)' (156).[44] But much more importantly, Shadrack and Sula are also conjoined through his only conscious, heartfelt action in the novel: when the tear-stained face of the 12-year-old Sula appears in his immaculately tidy hut (one of the many ways in which he tries to ward off the disorder in his mind) he looks at her face, sees the skull beneath and knows instinctively that she is as deeply afraid and traumatised by death as he had once been:

> he tried to think of something to say to her to *comfort* her, something to stop the hurt spilling out of her eyes. So he had said 'always,' so she would not be afraid of the change – the falling away of skin, the drip and slide of blood, and the exposure of bone underneath. He had said 'always' to convince her, assure, her of permanency. (157, emphasis added)

The violence underpinning Shadrack's singular word is hidden from the child, for his interior vision of war-torn horror is not reflected on his body. Ironically, his hands are now stilled, and the limbs which had once been a source of such terror to him, reassure Sula: 'no one with hands like that, no one with fingers that curved around the wood so tenderly could kill her' (62) she believes. She has no concept of his inner trauma, just fears him for his reputation. From Shadrack's point of view, this child wants something from him which he, and only he, can provide and his intuitive word of 'always' to the crying Sula is offered as a loving gift of comfort. It is the only word he speaks in the text, and it is of intrinsic importance. However, his comfort word is interpreted by the young Sula not as a 'promise that licked her feet' (63), but as a lifetime threat of trauma and overhanging guilt.

I have taken a long time to introduce both the death of the community and Shadrack, who importantly frames the text. After his tale is told at the beginning, he becomes only a shadowy figure in the narrative, but one around whom the plot threads. Although the novel is named after the protagonist, Sula Mae Peace, and tells the story of Sula's entwined friendship with her closest companion, Nel Wright, Sula does not appear until 30 pages into the text and then dies about three-quarters of the way through. This positioning and the amount of early narrative space given to Shadrack and the community signals the tripartite entanglement of Shadrack, Nel *and* Sula as crucial, together with the absolute centrality of the black community as socio-political, historical, cultural and psychic context for both agency and victimisation for every black character in the text. Thus, although Sula's life quest is to seek a self that necessarily lies outside the rules of her black community, this searching is always in relation to the wider framework of race and gender oppression in American society, in which the Bottom is necessarily immersed. Each main character has a double that inverts and contradicts the other: the white town of Medallion is juxtaposed to the black community of the Bottom; the stunted deweys, the 'trinity with a plural name' (38), offset Shadrack, Nel and Sula; and the intergenerational matrilineal members of the Wright and Peace families are constituted in a complex interwoven opposition to each other. First there are the grandmothers, Helene Wright and Eva Peace, then the daughters, Rochelle and Hannah, and finally, the most important pairing of the granddaughters, Nel and Sula. This is not a narrative that proceeds on binary dichotomies, but one that consists of relational cross-overs and entanglements.

As the second chapter begins, Morrison suddenly and abruptly transposes the traumatic violence of the white male public sphere onto the interior lives and material worlds of the black female private sphere, focusing her (re)vision on the matriarchal Wright and Peace families. By translating the historical into the personal, the public into the private, and actual male violence and grand historical traumas into repeated patterns of oppression, self-mutilation, and violence between women, she draws all her readers into the untying of the patterning of hierarchical and prescriptive binaries, thereby implicating us in her rereading of history and its structures of representation and meaning.

For it is no longer possible to distance ourselves from the impact of racism and sexism, if, as Morrison says: 'the historical becomes people with names'.[45] Her radical shift in perspective from public to private, from outer to inner, has been ironically signalled by Shadrack himself. Waking in fright from his year-long catatonic state of paralysed trauma in the hospital after the war, he does not recognise himself under the de-individualising, white-institutional army label of 'Private', a label often repeated to him by the exasperated white nurses who have no interest in understanding his trauma:

> He wanted desperately to see his own face and connect it with the word 'private' – the word the nurse (and the others *who helped bind him*) had called him. 'Private' he thought was something secret, and he wondered why they looked at him and called him a secret. (10, emphasis added)

The secret, or unknown quality that is Shadrack, as he discovers in the epiphanic moment in the cell, is a self that is tied to race and bound to community. This is the binding grace, the small thread of strength gained against all the odds that Morrison transfers from the masculine dominated prologue and first chapter to the remainder of the novel that centres on the black women of the Bottom community.

8
Ambivalent Maternal Inheritances

When reading a novel like *Sula*, we need to keep in mind, as Mary Helen Washington reminds us, that 'motherhood, complicated and threatened by racism, is a special kind of motherhood'.[1] This comment is especially relevant to a text in which the greatest acts of maternal love are represented through the black matriarch, Eva Peace, who fights past her inner pain and ignores the beckoning lure of the 'comfort' of death in order to stay alive for the sake of her three young children, and then offers a sacrificial leg as the only possible indemnity for their collective survival. These are not the usual actions of motherhood, but ones that result from the brutalities of poverty and pervasive social distress. This does not mean that love between mothers and daughters does not exist, just that it is transmitted in other forms. At one moment in the text Eva is tentatively asked by her adult daughter Hannah: ' "Mamma, did you ever love us? . . . I mean, did you? You know. When we was little?" ' (67). Eva abruptly answers: ' "what you talkin' 'bout did I ever love you girl I stayed alive for you can't you get that through your thick head or what is that between your ears, heifer?" ' (69). Unable verbally to express the protective tenderness she feels, Eva hides her fierce maternal love under her disparaging language and angry, ambivalent tone. The lack of punctuation suggests an onrush of confusion and hurt at the question, mingled with an instinctive self-protective defiance. The fight for physical and mental survival for herself and her children, in itself a supreme *act* of maternal love, leaves her with no time or energy to articulate or to encompass maternal nurturance in conventional terms.[2] In her book on trauma and recovery, Judith Herman argues that the 'damage to relational life is not a secondary effect of trauma, as originally thought. Traumatic events have primary effects not only on the psychological structures of the self but also on the systems of attachment and meaning'.[3] Both Nel and Sula grow up in maternal households distorted and traumatised by the external pressures of racial, class and sexual oppression, and this drives a wedge between the successive generations of women. As Spillers suggests, these echoing circles of sorrow are 'transmitted from mother to daughter, female to female by mimetic, unspoken gesture'.[4]

Morrison's choice of narrative strategy exposes the unspeakability of psychic crippling associated with physical survival in an inimical world by creating the contrastive parallelism of the matrilineal inheritances of the Wright and Peace families. This doubling is then emphasised by paired antithetical character development.[5] On one hand, the Wrights are a family rigid with repression, righteousness and a yearning for assimilation with white middle-class ideals. On the other, the Peaces represent a three-woman household of happy-go-lucky chaos in which female sexuality can be pleasurably indulged without confining commitment, a freedom entwined with a sense of resistance to white capitalism through community responsibility – in this case caring for others who have been cast adrift by the system, such as Tar Baby and the deweys.[6] Yet, the first is not right, and the latter far from rewardingly peaceful from either inner or outer turmoil. What then is the purpose of this complicated, interwoven narrative strategy? Why are we asked to contemplate the profound physical and internalised distress of loss by involvement in the lives of a domineering matriarch who murders her own son, or her granddaughter who passively watches her own mother burn to death? Why compare the seeming indifference and brutality of one family on the one hand, with the good behaviour and acquiescence of the other family, who live a death-in-life of conventionality and such strict adherence to the mores of the community that they are stifled into silence? It is, I think, an elaborate and brilliant narrative manoeuvre that entices readers into confronting the trauma of racism and sexual oppression.

In *Sula*, it is the *community* that moderates individual pain, provides a context of shared resistance against the omnipresence of whiteness and serves as a repository for binding traditions, with the Reverend Deal's black church as its heart and sanctuary. However, the Bottom is also a community that suffers from *collective trauma*.[7] It is a damaged social organism, what Cathy Caruth would term, 'a symptom of history'.[8] The inhabitants are collectively *possessed* by the long-term insidious effect of racism: they are psychically 'owned' to a greater or lesser degree by events beyond their control. Kai Erikson strongly believes that '[t]raumatized people often come to feel that they have lost an important measure of control over the circumstances of their own lives and are thus very vulnerable . . . they also come to feel that they have lost a natural immunity to misfortune and that something awful is almost *bound* to happen'.[9] It is interesting then, that there are three telling references to vulnerability in this novel, each of which is central to comprehending the different ways that the women characters survive by displaying various forms of adaptive behaviour.[10] The word is used in reference to the matriarchs of both Wright and Peace families as they try to strengthen or protect themselves against 'routine vulnerabilites' (36); and inversely to Sula who is said to be evil in part because she possesses *no* visible sign of such weakness. '[W]here were the scars? Except for a funny-shaped finger and that evil birthmark, she was free of any normal signs of vulnerability', the narrator comments (115).

I will examine in detail the two references that connect vulnerabilities to the contrastive personalities of Helene Wright and Eva Peace, but first I want to draw attention to the fact that for them the noun is always in the plural, while for Sula, the only woman in the text referred to as being free of vulnerability – and this, the narrator suggests, is one of the reasons she is both hated and feared – the noun is used in the singular. The adjectives attached to the noun are 'old', 'routine' and 'normal', the choice implying that the plurality of vulnerabilities is what all the women of the Bottom face, yet it is Sula alone who fights against the numbing presence of racial and sexual vicissitudes, which results in her being singled out to be the community's 'pariah' (122). The derivation of the word vulnerable is from the Latin verb *vulnerare*, to wound, and suggests ideas of covering over in order to protect the self, a self open or susceptible to being wounded or hurt. Trauma's etymological source is the Greek word for *wound*. So the thrice repeated word *vulnerability* in *Sula* serves an important synecdochic function in that it connects the outward manifestations of racial and sexual trauma to individualised psychic wounds of a specific character.

Helene Wright has succumbed to the internalisation of whiteness. In a desperate attempt to distance herself from her own maternal heritage – she is the 'daughter of a Creole whore' (17) – Helene Sabat *becomes* Helen(e) Wright and thrives on her new life of repression and empty pretentiousness that merely masks the psychic distortion that has arisen because she has distanced herself from any sense of racial pride. Helene's self-protection manifests as an obsession with social order that mimics white values and customs. Like Shadrack, but reversed – Shadrack is bound to his blackness, while Helene is trying to disavow hers – she devotes herself to creating a façade of ritualistic order. This is reflected in her neat and oppressive home, but more alarmingly in the way she moulds her only daughter's imagination, character, and even her body. 'Any enthusiasms that little Nel showed were calmed by the mother until she drove her daughter's imagination underground' (18) the narrator tells us and, indeed, 'calm' becomes the emotional state around which the adult Nel binds her righteous life. Thankful that Nel has not inherited her 'dusky' beauty,[11] Helene nevertheless tries to erase her daughter's negroid features, her father's flat nose and wide lips. Her daughter must not 'look' like her own mother Rochelle, but neither must she appear as negroid as her father. Nel is blissfully unaware of all this until the train journey south to visit her dying grandmother. On this journey to death she has to confront the lived effects of Jim Crow laws, and her mother's profoundly abject behaviour that is so incredibly different from the mother she knows who rules the most conservative black church in the Bottom.

Nel is only ten when Helene receives the letter summoning her back down South to say goodbye to her dying grandmother – 'the woman who had rescued her' from her mother and their life in the brothel (19) – but it is an experience that will scar and haunt Nel for the rest of her life. In keeping with the physical and emotional veil with which Helene has shrouded herself as a protection,[12] she overcomes her heavy misgivings about returning to the racially segregated South – and the possibility of re-meeting her mother, Rochelle – by believing that 'her manner and her bearing' and also a beautiful new 'elegant dress' (19) would best protect her. They are late arriving at the station and, in their haste to board the segregated train, by mistake Helene and Nel enter a whites-only coach.[13] Quickly moving to the 'right' section of this train, as Helene opens the door marked 'COLORED ONLY' (20) they are confronted by a repulsive, sweaty white conductor, who publicly humiliates Helene. The ensuing scene is watched helplessly by a group of black soldiers, who mask their own humiliation at not being able to intervene 'with closed faces [and] locked eyes' (21). The conductor demands:

"What you think you doin', *gal*?"
Helene looked up at him.
So soon. So soon. She hadn't even begun the trip back. Back to her grandmother's house in the city where the red shutters glowed, and already she had been called '*gal*'. *All the old vulnerabilities*, all the old

fears of being somehow flawed gathered in her stomach and made her hands tremble. *She had heard only that one word* . . . (20, emphasis added)

The ineffectiveness of Helene's psychic cloak of self-righteous distancing is immediately apparent. Her fear and anguish in the face of inevitable humiliation now becomes inscribed both internally and externally in and on her body: a sense of overwhelming helplessness floods her stomach, her hands tremble. Her mimicking of white middle-class respectability and repression cannot help her now. Later in the novel, Morrison connects this painful scene of symbolic death with the grief surrounding the very real death of a little boy when the narrator describes the depth of feeling of the collectivity of black women in the congregation at Chicken Little's funeral: 'They did not hear all what he said; *they heard only one word*, or phrase, or inflection that was for them the connection between the event and themselves' (65, emphasis added). The women here are in the safe space of the black church where they can be themselves and enact their pain.[14] Helene Wright, cut off from connecting with her racialised self, cannot begin to merge affect with event. The racially inflected 'gal' – a word, according to Smitherman, to which black women take particular exception because of its suggestive white denial of black womanhood and connotation of white notions of ownership[15] – directly and unexpectedly throws Helene back into the realities of her despised heritage and buried self, a self not tied to race or to the black community from which she has distanced herself with all her affected ways.

So far, the staged spectacle only alludes to the fact that the racial humiliation is also gendered. However, Helene's response to white male bullying is one of obsequious sexual abasement, a scene to which Nel bears witness:

[F]or no earthly reason, at least no reason anybody could understand, certainly no reason that Nel understood then or later, she [Helene] smiled. Like a street pup that wags its tail at the very doorjamb of the butcher shop he has been kicked away from only moments before, Helene smiled. Smiled dazzlingly and coquettishly at the salmon-colored face of the conductor. (21)

Ironically, while Helene has attempted to dissociate herself from her mother's contaminating public sexuality and heritage of prostitution, in her performance with the white conductor she unconsciously turns to 'acting out' her despised maternal inheritance. Indeed, Morrison draws attention to the inescapability of each woman's matrilineal heritage and heightens the connection between bodily rejection, sexual betrayal and loss of self-identity by repeating the same imagery when many years later Jude (Nel's husband) betrays her by having sex with Sula. Nel finds them 'on all fours (uh huh, go on, say it) like dogs' (105) and when Jude looks at her in silent guilt, all Nel can see is that 'your eyes looked like the soldiers' that time on the train when my mother turned to custard' (106). Morrison's use of simile to liken Helene's servility to a starving street dog and the idea of a black couple having sex in an animalistic manner is of great interest to the argument towards which I am working – the possibilities of recuperation inherent in the figurative structure of metaphor. However, whereas metaphor merges two things being compared into a new non-literal conceptual compound which allows for a space of imaginative connection and reconnection, simile keeps the comparison direct and explicit, and in many ways binds the two figurative elements within something like a rhetorical straitjacket. The connection is harder to evade and more binding. In this way, the grovelling woman *becomes* the grovelling puppy. Animal imagery is used by both white male characters in the novel who are discussed with more than just a passing reference: the conductor and, later, a white bargeman refer to black people as animals (63).

The lacing and binding imagery introduced in the Shadrack chapter now reappears.[16] Yet while the young black man is bound and knotted inside, something he cannot undo, Helene's body is seemingly exposed by the white male gaze. Nel believes that if she raises her eyes above the fall of the skirt of the 'elegant dress', she too will see the nakedness that this gaze imposes. The feminine detail of 'hooks and eyes' – the tiny and most often invisible fastenings that hold together the opening or slit at the top of a dress (the placket) – is juxtaposed with the child's overwhelming fear that all the world will see her mother's body. The image, with its connection between binding imagery and vision, is a very feminised and beautifully apt metaphor for intense shame in which the eyes look down, and the self is exposed in ritual humiliation.[17] Nel projects her own feeling of shame onto her mother's body. The metaphor also imaginatively employs the domestic vocabulary of needlework, the meaning of which would probably exclude many men, providing a clear example of Morrison's reconfiguring of the masculinity of the Black Aesthetic to which I referred in the introduction. Nel, looked deeply at the folds of her mother's dress. There in the fall of the heavy brown wool she held her eyes. She could not risk letting them travel upward for fear of seeing that the *hooks and eyes* in the placket of the dress *had come undone* and exposed the custard-colored skin underneath. She stared at the hem, wanting to believe in its weight but knowing that custard was all that it hid. If this tall, proud woman . . . were really custard, then there was a chance that Nel was too. (22, emphasis added)

Helene's elegant disguise is effectively destroyed by 'the stretch of her . . . foolish smile' (22). Yet the metaphorical undoing of the hooks and eyes is also connected at a deeper level to the oppressive power of white stereotyping in which Helene *becomes* Jezebel, the oversexed and always available black woman, the fantasy of white male prejudice and assumed sexual superiority. Moreover, the thrice repeated reference to 'custard' carries the connotative negatives of moral cowardice, sexual consumption and miscegenation.

Nel is only 10 but she has learned a very adult lesson. Yet her own life of repression is built upon this foundational trauma – the unveiling of her mother's vulnerabilities. As a result of this journey (an inversion of the usual allusion to spiritual growth), Nel 'resolved to be on guard – always. She wanted to make certain that no man ever looked at her that way' (22). Paradoxically, however, the immediate impact was an affirmation of self and 'her newfound me-ness [that] gave her the strength to cultivate a friend in spite of her mother' and her previous dismissal of Sula's 'sooty' heritage (29). From that moment on until she marries at 17, Nel Wright and Sula Peace are inseparable, for 'they found in each other's eyes the intimacy they were looking for' (52). The previously meek and docile Nel lets down her guard in her adolescent years with Sula: 'Her parents had succeeded in rubbing down to a dull glow any sparkle or splutter she had. Only with Sula did that quality have free reign' (83), and they roam the neighbourhood 'in the safe harbor of each other's company' (55). They are always together: that is, until Jude Greene comes along and 'selects' Nel away from Sula. Before they had shared everything, including the boys, but now, at 17, Nel wants to be seen 'singly', despite the fact that from Jude's point of view she would only ever 'be the hem – the tuck and fold that hid his raveling edges' (83). Again the recurrent trope of the sewing metaphor stresses a radical gender imbalance, and in this case foreshadows the predictable outcome of Nel's retreat into the conventional subservient female role of 'someone sweet and industrious and loyal' whose wifely duty will be to 'shore up' her new partner who marries her in a vain attempt to have his 'adulthood recognized' (83, 82).[18] Nel's wedding marks the final pages of the first half of the novel. Ominously, her wedding veil is too heavy for her to feel the core of Jude's kiss pressed on her head (85). It is not only that the veil represents a mantle of social convention and identity erasure that will negatively overlay the rest of her life, but in marriage she has relinquished the one person who saved her imagination from being permanently driven underground. During the wedding, Sula leaves the Bottom, and it will be 10 years before she and Nel see each other again. When she returns, she will be accompanied by a plague of robins, and will be dressed in the 'manner that was as close to a movie star as anyone would ever see. A black crepe dress splashed with pink and yellow zinnias, foxtails, a black felt hat with *a veil of net lowered over one eye*' (90, emphasis added).

The repeated reference to veiling is particularly intriguing in a novel that places a great deal of credence on the visual economy. There is even a command to look, 'Voir! Voir!' (27),[19] and textual emphasis is placed on the different ethics between the active verbs *see*, *watch* and *look*.[20] This I read as a strategy to make the reader look deeper, in order to consider the ethical questions Morrison raises by the comparison between these verbs. Subtly directed to what is veiled or masked, we begin to 'see' the double message that has always been not just a matter of survival for African-Americans in the white world, but a means of resistance and subversion of the dominant culture and its constitutive ideologies.[21] Importantly, the veil metaphor has both an ideological and literary history in the African-American tradition. In her essay entitled 'The Site of Memory', Morrison discusses her own literary heritage and its relationship with the 'print origins of black literature (as distinguished from the oral origins) [which] were slave narratives'.[22] Written to enlist the support of white audiences to help in the fight to abolish slavery, these narratives necessarily avoided explicit renditions of the most violent and demeaning details of this experience. 'Over and over,' Morrison relates, 'the writers pull the narrative up short with a phrase such as, "But let us drop a veil over these proceedings too terrible to relate".'[23] Given the shift in time, Morrison sees her participation in this literary heritage this way:

> For me – a writer in the last quarter of the twentieth century, not much more than a hundred years after Emancipation, a writer who is black and a woman – the exercise is very different. My job becomes how to rip that veil drawn over 'proceedings too terrible to relate.'[24]

In *Sula* then, Morrison takes us behind the veil of the distortions of white ideology and shows us the black world as it is, a world of survival against all the odds, but one with profoundly painful individual and collective consequences. Ripping the veil also means exposing vulnera-bilites. This is not to suggest that the women of the Bottom are weak and their behaviour ineffective, but to emphasise their enormous courage and perseverance in the face of their powerlessness amid the exigencies of the dominant white world. Helene's lighter skin speaks of her whitened heritage, but instead of banding together with the rest of the community against white oppression, Helene protects her vulnera-bilities by becoming the ultimate assimilationist who tries to 'git ovah' by leaving her blackness behind.[25]

Eva Peace follows a completely different path as she tries to overcome her particular vulnerabilities. As undisputed head of the three-woman household at 7 Carpenter's Road, built with insurance money she earned from self-mutilation, Eva becomes its powerful 'creator and sovereign' (30). However, her empire is built not on love, but upon a base of 'liquid hatred'. When her deserting husband unexpectedly returns, and stands before her, a 'picture of prosperity and goodwill. His shoes were a shiny orange, and he had on a citified straw hat, a light-blue suit, and a cat's-head stickpin in his tie' (35), instead of anger, disgust, or a rush of love, Eva feels no emotion at all. All feeling has been excised in the will-to-survive. The visit is amicable, that is, until BoyBoy goes outside, bends down and whispers something in the ear of the woman in the pea-green dress who has accompanied him, and she laughs aloud:

> A high-pitched big-city laugh that reminded Eva of Chicago. It hit her like a sledge hammer, and it was then that she knew what to feel. A liquid trail of hate flooded her chest . . . Hating BoyBoy, she could get on with it, and have the safety, the thrill, the consistency of that hatred as long as she wanted or needed it to define and strengthen her or protect her from *routine vulnerabilities*. (36, emphasis added)

It is not just BoyBoy's sartorial finery that sparks Eva's hatred – for she sees that it merely masks the 'defeat in the stalk of his neck' (36) – or even jealousy at his attention to the other woman. It is, I think, the 'big-city laugh' that plunges Eva into a traumatic memory that has to do with the loss of her leg. There are two adjectives that refer to the city, and although it is not defined in the text, it seems likely that in the mysterious 18 months of her absence she would have had to be in a city, both to survive the event of self-mutilation in a hospital, and to be on hand to claim the insurance money. This city could easily have been Chicago. Moreover the laughter here is not the community's answer to masking pain, but a singular, perhaps derisive laugh of (an)other, that manifests separation not solidarity. Thus for Eva the impact of BoyBoy's return does not provide comfort through a belated relinquishing, and perhaps acceptance, of the past. Instead, 'hit like a sledge hammer' she is slammed into a bodily centred traumatic memory, and this 'gone thing' transforms into bitterness and the driving force of hate.[26] The result is a kind of psychic stunting, the obliterated feelings of tenderness or love corporeally represented in the text by her 'lost' leg and vulnerable body.

While Eva thrives on hate, her daughter Hannah, whose 'laughing' husband dies when Sula is three, subsumes her grief under a mask of indifference, and spends her days in domestic tasks in her mother's house interspersed with 'some touching every day' (44). Despite constantly wearing the 'same old print wraparound', Hannah 'rippled with sex' (42) the narrator tells us, and her casual and frequent encounters with men 'taught Sula that sex was pleasant and frequent but otherwise unremarkable' (44). Both the form of dress and sexual abandon will become intrinsic to the maternal heritage within which Sula becomes unconsciously bound. Although Hannah does not remain in the text for very long, she is a character created with a great deal of warmth and allure (and in this she resembles Rochelle).[27] 'Nobody but nobody, could say 'hey sugar' like Hannah' (42–3) the narrator continues, but her promiscuousness is damaging and, not suprisingly, she has few friendships with women. Most important of all, her relationship with Sula seems one of indifference, registered in the text by an almost total absence of closeness, or even communication, between them. Not surprisingly then, Sula clings to Nel 'as the closest thing to both an other and a self' (119) that she can ever have, and indeed Nel provides the stability and closeness that she cannot find in her home.

The reason for Sula's self-protective displacement and her seeming 'lack' of vulnerability has a history. With Nel as her friend, Sula negotiates her childhood quite happily until one fateful day when she is 12 two events happen that shake the very foundations of her growing self. En route to swim in the river with Nel, Sula drops into 7 Carpenter's Road, and as she passes the kitchen she overhears Hannah telling two women: '"I love Sula. I just don't like her. That's the difference"' (57). Although she is accustomed to her mother's indifference, this betrayal is particularly destructive as it is *spoken aloud,* and thus shared publicly. '[T]he pronouncement sent her flying up the stairs. In bewilderment, she stood at the window fingering the curtain edge, aware of the sting in her eye' (57).[28] Nel calls to Sula, disrupting her 'dark thoughts' (57); they meet downstairs, and run towards the river. Then an incident occurs that embroils the two girls in a 'knot of death' from which neither will ever be able totally to unravel themselves. A small boy named Chicken Little approaches. Sula is playful and kind to the little boy, and helps him climb to the top of a nearby tree, then swings him round and round as he shrieks with joy. Suddenly, he slips from her hands, sails out over the nearby river, and he and his bubbly laugh disappear under the water:

> The water darkened and closed quickly over the place where Chicken Little sank. The pressure of his hard and tight little fingers was still in Sula's palms as she stood looking at *the closed place in the water* ... Both girls stared at the water ... There was nothing but the baking sun and *something newly missing*. (61, emphasis added)

The small detail of the indentation of his fingers in Sula's hand is as harrowing as any description of brutality, and the image of this deep but small imprint lingers long after reading the words, together with the sudden stillness as the childish laughter is swallowed by the concentric circles in the water. The vividness, immediacy and lyricism of the language almost replicates the structuring of the deep unconscious imprinting of traumatic unassimilated experiences that will return in flashbacks and haunting memories. Indeed, the two italicised phrases repeat continually throughout the remainder of the novel, especially 'the closed place in the water', which appears three times (61, 101, 141) and then in varying manifestations from 'the dark closed place in the water' (62), 'the closed place in the middle' (118), and finally 'the water closing quickly over the place' (170). 'Something newly missing' appears twice on the page that describes Chicken Little's drowning. The significance of this repeating phrasing is important. The 'closed place in the middle' comes to represent the moment of trauma that does not enter consciousness, because of its unexpectedness and incomprehensible horror. 'Something newly missing' symbolises the moment of revelatory belatedness when the trauma of Chicken Little's death enters Nel's consciousness and becomes mediated meaning in the final paragraphs of the novel.

After the initial shock, Nel tells Sula that someone has seen the drowning, and it can only be Shadrack whose riverside hut is close by.

Terrified, Sula goes up there, to be met by Shadrack in the scene I have already discussed, in which he pronounces the one word, 'Always' (62). Sula flees back to Nel, collapsing in tears (62). In contrast to Sula's hysterical crying, 'Nel has remained calm' throughout (170), enacting an emotional numbing that her mother has unconsciously passed on to her daughter as a means of self-protection against life's malevolence. From the beginning of the incident, the girls have behaved in completely different ways. Sula is friendly and welcoming and plays with Chicken Little; Nel is patronising and distant. Trained in possessiveness, Nel is possibly jealous that Sula's attention is diverted from her, and this may well be the cause of her hidden pleasure when he disappears under the water. But this is something that is not revealed until the last couple of pages of the novel, at the same moment as it enters Nel's own consciousness. However, Sula is unable to speak of the traumatic event ever again and, foreshadowing her internalised silencing, the narrator tells us that 'Sula covered her mouth as they walked down the hill' (63). This silence is bound up with both the symbolic death of what she perceives as the loss of her mother's love, and a physical death of which she was the cause. As if in further punishment, Chicken Little's death also ends any aspirations that Sula holds towards maternity – they drown 'in the closed place in the water' along with the little boy.

The death creates a temporary distance between the two young girls: they neither hold hands nor look at each other during Chicken Little's funeral. Sula cries ceaselessly but 'soundlessly' throughout the service, letting her tears run down her face, into her mouth and over her chin onto her dress (65). It is only after the little coffin is lowered into the earth, that 'the space that had sat between them in the pews ... dissolved' (66). They are reunited in an unspoken and probably unconscious acknowledgement that although he is dead, Chicken Little's 'bubbly laughter and the press of fingers in the palm would stay aboveground forever' (66). For Sula, the two events of the catastrophic day also revolve around the presence or absence of words. In the first scene, Sula *overhears* her mother's painful words, not intended for her ears. In the second, Chicken Little drowns in *echoing silence*, followed by Shadrack uttering his singular haunting word. Nel and Sula are bound together in the unspeakability of this trauma: each has her own separate 'dark closed place in the water'. They never tell what happens to the little boy, though Eva implies at the end that she always knew, and she may easily enough have connected Sula's silent but extreme distress with the disappearance of the boy.

However, Sula has yet to face the last monumental trauma of her childhood, the witnessing of her mother burning to death when she was 13. Although this occurs up to a year after Chicken Little's death, there is only one mention of Sula in the interim period. However, in Morrison's ambiguous style, her clipped reference to 'Sula's craziness' (75) just before her mother's death can be attributed to the hot dry wind that rattled roofs and loosened doors – one of the five natural omens warning of the impending death – or it could be that she is suffering badly from the traumatic aftershock of Chicken Little's death. On the terrible day, Hannah catches on fire in the backyard, runs frantically around, a 'flaming dancing figure' until a tub of water is thrown on her, the steam searing her flesh as she lay 'twitching lightly among the smashed tomatoes, her face a mask of agony so intense that for years the people who gathered 'round would shake their heads at the recollection of it' (76). The air smells of 'the odor of cooked flesh' (77). This is the scene that her grandmother accuses Sula of passively watching, 'because she was interested' (78). Whether this is the case, or whether Sula is paralysed by trauma, or a state between the two, the burning represents the second knot of death which threads through Sula's life.

Brooks Bouson argues that Morrison wants her readers to love and hate her characters, to feel intense sympathy and solidarity with them and then be repulsed by their actions.[29] Indeed, one of the complications of reading Morrison's fiction is that she grants the narratee the ambivalent reading position, thus in many senses disallowing a conclusive resolution, which is also of course one of the reasons why her writing is so compelling.[30] In particular, this applies to Sula,[31] who dies quite early in the novel, as if punished for her many dishonourable acts of resistance, the most notable of which are refusing to become a mother, and putting Eva 'away' in an old folks' home.[32] Yet, we are literally confronted by and urged to mourn her 'stunning absence', not Ajax's, to whom the phrase refers (134). Morrison's epigraph (to the future loss of her sons from her immediate family life) gives a clue to the importance of loss and absence as a core theme in the text. Sula is the most precious of the 'gone things' and the loss of her presence echoes the haunting despair with which the novel opens.

9

The 'Gift for Metaphor'

The epistemology of 'gone things'

In *Sula*, Morrison threads together the multiplicity of psychic and material impediments that circumscribe the lives of African-American women during the time-frame of the novel. She then attempts to untie the knots, ensuring that the relational complexity of the situation facing these women is placed within the strictures of the white system that invisibly dominates their lives, what Chimalum Nwankwo calls 'the potency of white absence in Morrison's work'.[1] Survival in the white world, to a large extent, depends on the strength of cultural mores manifested through familial and communal bonds. Thus, because she estranges herself from all close connections, Sula's courageous attempts to create a unique sense of self are predestined to fail. Spillers suggests that the 'possibility of art, of intellectual vocation for black female character, has been offered as a style of defense against the naked brutality of conditions. The efficacy of art cannot be isolated from its social and political means.'[2] However, while Spillers then maintains that Sula is specifically circumscribed by the 'lack of an explicit tradition of imagination or aesthetic work, and not by the evil force of "white" society', I would argue that Morrison's text seems to suggest that these two categories are hard to separate out in this way.[3] As Alice Walker delineated in her famous essay, 'In Search of Our Mothers' Gardens', even in the face of inhumanity, poverty and oppression, black women kept their creativity alive, through music, quotidian acts of beauty such as creating 'a screen of blooms', as Walker's mother did, or sewing beautiful quilts, but most of all by telling stories and passing them on.[4] '[S]o many of the stories that I write, that we all write, are my mother's stories' writes Walker, and with the telling of these stories, from childhood

142

onwards, she unwittingly absorbed her people's culture. As I read it, Sula's loss of creativity is the result of a rejection of her maternal heritage and her community. However, her rejection is also a complex entanglement of her individual loss of maternal love and a defiant stance against collective black cultural dictates that have themselves lost the art of creativity in the ceaseless struggle to survive white oppression and domination. The famous passage – on which practically every critic has commented – reads as follows:

> In a way, her strangeness, her naiveté, her craving for the other half of her equation was the consequence of an idle imagination. Had she paints, or clay, or knew the discipline of dance, or strings; had she anything to encourage her tremendous curiosity and *her gift for metaphor*, she might have exchanged the restlessness and preoccupation with whim for an activity that provided her with all she yearned for. And like any artist with no art form, she became dangerous. (121, emphasis added)

While there can be no doubt that as both Nel and Sula had discovered years before that as they 'were neither white nor male . . . all freedom and triumph was forbidden to them, they had [still] set about creating something else to be' (52). For me, what underwrites this text is the incredible strength of black women in the community of the Bottom who attempt some form of creative expression only too aware that it may well fail, such as Helene's careful crafting of her 'elegant dress with velvet collar and pockets' (19) to carry her safely down South. Writing on this passage, a number of years ago now, Renita Weems says that the artist without art form applies to every female character Morrison creates in her first three novels, and '[s]uch Black women are both mourned and praised'.[5] In the case of Sula, it is impossible not to want to praise her. Yet, ultimately, it is Nel, the survivor, who has not only to learn to grieve for the loss of Sula, but also to mourn for both their gone things.

Sula may be a frustrated artist, but her tendency to become restless and dangerous is more a result of her childhood traumas. Hers is not the monstrous ego so often attributed to artists. In fact she has no ego at all, the narrator tells us. With few avenues open to Sula, her artistry becomes the lived performance of her life:

> As willing to feel pain as to give pain, to feel pleasure as to give pleasure, hers was an experimental life – ever since her mother's remarks

sent her flying up those stairs, ever since her one major feeling of
responsibility had been exorcised on the bank of a river with a *closed
place in the middle*. The first experience taught her there was no other
that you could count on; the second that there was no self to count
on either. She had no center, no speck around which to grow . . . She
was completely free of ambition, with no affection for money, property or things, no greed, no desire to command attention or com-
pliments – no ego. (118–19, emphasis added)

Sula's closed place in the middle had its traumatic birth on that cata-
clysmic day and from this day on she becomes gradually disconnected
from all others as she struggles to maintain a sense of self. Judith
Herman believes that the 'damage to the survivor's faith and sense of
community is particularly severe when the traumatic events themselves
involve the betrayal of important relationships. The imagery of these
events often crystallises around a moment of betrayal, and it is this
breach of trust which gives the intrusive images their intense emotional
power'.[6] Despite Robert Grant's disclaimer that '[t]oo often Hannah's
comment is interpreted as a "determining" factor in Sula's personality
formation, as if this one remark betokened a socio-behavioral pattern
and "key"', I believe that what Sula perceives as a betrayal by her mother
is supported by the text.[7] It is her mother's remarks that taught her that
she has no significant other to count on. Chicken Little's death adds to
her loss of self. Together they crystallise into the imagery of traumatic
repression, the much-repeated 'closed place in the middle', a phrase that
carries immense resonant power. For the rest of her life her inner being
is overshadowed by this 'closed place'. She is still dreaming of it as she
dies.

Writing at much the same time as Weems, Deborah McDowell also
discusses what she calls the figure of the 'thwarted female artist',
quoting the passage from *Sula* as a classic example of one of a number
of thematic commonalities in the work of contemporary black female
novelists, citing Morrison and Alice Walker as prime examples.[8] However, it is McDowell's third example of thematic parallels – the use of
'clothing as iconography' – as central to the writings by black women to
which I now turn.[9] (Her second, which blends down from the first and
into the third is an obsessive 'ordering of things' for which McDowell
names Eva Peace's 'ordering the pleats in her dress'.)[10] In the days
following Sula's return to the Bottom after her 10-year absence, her conversation is marked by constant references to burning and a complete
change of dress. Surrounded by dying robins, Sula arrives back incon-

gruously dressed with city sophistication, which is possibly one reason why Eva reacts so strongly to her sudden and *unexpected* arrival. Both the unexpectedness of Sula's entrance and her citified glamour replicate the earlier scene of Eva's reunion with BoyBoy, and plunge Eva into a sudden recall of her time in the city when she is forced to sacrifice her leg:

> Eva looked at Sula pretty much the same way she had looked at BoyBoy that time when he returned after he'd left her without a dime or a prospect of one . . . 'Them little old furry tails ain't going to do you no more good than they did the fox that was wearing them.'
> 'Don't you say hello to nobody when you ain't seen them for ten years?'
> 'If folks let somebody know where they is and when they coming, then other folks can get ready for them. If they don't – if they just pop in all sudden like – then they got to take whatever mood they find'. (91–2)

This first moment of the meeting spirals grandmother and grand-daughter into an antagonistic relationship that probably neither would have wanted if their moods had been different. Sula tries to recapture what might have been by asking, 'How you been doing, Big Mamma?' (92), but Eva immediately slips back into a self-protective hatred, and they become involved in a mutually destructive repartee which revolves around accusing each other of murder. Sula accuses Eva of burning Plum to death; Eva in return retorts: 'Don't talk to me about no burning, You watched you own mamma . . . You the one should have been burnt' (93). Sula's answer is to threaten her grandmother with a fiery death of her own. There is then a complete shift in pace, tone and rhythm as the scene shifts from the bitter anger and confrontation between Eva and Sula to Sula's reunion with Nel, which is described with glowing warmth and images of benevolence and natural fecundity. The abrupt transition is also registered by the first of three signifiers of ellipsis, clearly marked out by ◉ ◉ ◉.

The next few pages describe Nel and Sula's reunification. For Nel the strangely magical quality of this May was 'all due to Sula's return to the Bottom. It was like getting the use of an eye back, having a cataract removed. Her old friend had come home' (95). Sula, divested herself of her flamboyant city apparel, visits Nel most afternoons 'wearing a plain yellow dress the same way her mother, Hannah, had worn those too-big house dresses – with a distance, an absence of a relationship to clothes which emphasized everything the fabric covered' (95). Patricia McKee reads this as an example of Sula's 'absence of relation' in all things: 'Clothing might represent or reform the body, making it look different . . . for Sula there is no relation between her body and her clothes, which therefore do not seem to contain or alter her body at all'.[11] I have been arguing that the point of clothes in this novel is that they matter as artefacts of veiling over of traumatic relations. For Sula, as McKee suggests, clothes mean nothing on one level, but I would add that they are extremely important as markers of trauma. It would seem that the detail of Sula's imitating of her dead mother's form of dress carries a sense of yearning for so many of the gone things of her life. However, there are three more examples of clothing, or pieces of clothing, as designators of psychic pain in the novel: the first concerns the traumatic triangle of Nel, Sula and Jude, the second the short but passionate relationship between Ajax and Sula and the third, the metaphysical connection between Shadrack and Sula.

The first example occurs near the end of the chapter that describes the joyful reconnection of Nel and Sula's friendship and concerns a thin length of fabric that will come to embody the symbolic weight of traumatic betrayal. The scene is contained within a two-page section that is specifically marked off in the text by the second ellipsis and an abrupt change of scene. It begins with the narrator's words: 'He left his tie' (104), and ends with Nel for the only time in the text taking the first person point of view, 'you walked past me saying, "I'll be back for my things." And you did but you left your tie' (106). The tie in question belongs to Jude, her husband, and the scene opens with the traumatic moment when Nel discovers Jude and Sula making love on the floor. In her trying to shut out the immediacy of her distress, Nel focuses on his 'fly' being undone which is repeated three times, stressing the *unveiling* of his penis, which is also connected further down the page to the unveiling of her mother's body all those years ago on the train, as I discussed earlier. Even though Sula does not bother to put her clothes back on she does not seem naked to Nel, only Jude does, because although he has re-dressed, he has forgotten to button the fly. But, finally, as the scene ends, Nel's agony refocuses on Jude's tie, and a scrap of material becomes a symbol of traumatic loss that hereafter will continue to echo through the text.

The second incident follows the third and final elliptical marker. After many alienating sexual encounters through which she desperately searches for herself, Sula falls deeply in love with the free-spirited Ajax, a man of 'sinister beauty' (50) and bearer of wondrous gifts. Now she discovers the meaning of 'possession' (131), an emotion about which she had always been so disdainful when it happened to others. Just before the ellipsis is a long and erotic celebration of Ajax's body, then the discovery of possession. Significantly, Sula marks this moment by 'tying a green ribbon in her hair [and] the green silk made a rippling whisper as she slides it into her hair – a whisper that could easily have been Hannah's chuckle, a soft slow nasal hiss she used to emit when something amused her' (131). The ribbon, the marker that adorns her body as a sexual enticement, is the first of the signs that Sula will proffer that day that alerts Ajax to the 'scent of the nest' (133), which he immediately deserts. Sula's death follows soon after. On the surface, the ribbon, coloured green, is suggestive of jealousy and its attendant feeling of possession. However, at a far deeper and ever-present level, there is always the whispering voice of her dead mother whose lifestyle Sula emulates, however unconsciously that may be. The first time she and Ajax make love, she pulls him into the pantry, a 'gesture [that] came to Hannah's daughter naturally' (125).

The final example, like the others, is of a piece of clothing that is cloaked in the iconography of gone things. When Sula visits Shadrack's hut immediately after the drowning of Chicken Little, unnoticed by her, the belt of her dress falls off. The missing item is not mentioned again until near the end of the novel, when it unexpectedly reappears as a marker of violent loss and death. On the day that Shadrack had offered the small crying child a word of benediction that to his mind would 'convince her, assure her, of permanency' (157), his reward had been finding her lost belt which he had pinned over his bed as a visible reminder that he had once had a visitor: 'It hung on a nail near his bed – unfrayed, unsullied after all those years, with only a permanent bend in the fabric made by its long life on a nail' (157). The small purple and white belt becomes his life-long symbol of connection: 'His visitor, his company, his guest, his social life, his woman, his daughter, his friend – they all hung there on a nail near his bed' (157). An uncanny ambivalence resides in this scene. On one hand there is the extreme poignancy and loneliness of the image of the belt, with all Shadrack's repressed longings and feelings transferred onto a scrap of cloth. On the other, the nail on which it hangs may well repeatedly return him to the facticity of experiential pain that overwhelmed him on the battlefield in 1917, when in the face of extreme trauma his mind concentrated on 'the bite of a nail in his boot' (8).

Each example connects clothing or a fragment of cloth to spiritual or physical death. The first example centres around Nel's spiritual death, for from the moment that Jude leaves his tie Nel is harassed by the haunting grey ball and the repression of a death-in-life existence. The green ribbon is the marker of Sula's final 'spirit damage'[12] that leads to her death. And the final example of the intense focus on Sula's belt only happens just after Shadrack has accidentally seen Sula's dead body in the mortuary, described as '[a]nother dying away of someone whose *face* he knew' (158, emphasis added). This sighting of death may well have triggered a series of flashbacks to his postwar experience in the mental hospital when he is overcome by an overwhelming and repeated longing to see his face because he now totally loses interest in the next National Suicide Day, which happens to be the following day: 'for the first time he did not want to go. He wanted to stay with the purple-and-white belt. Not go. Not go' (158). His instincts are right as this is the day when so many members of the Bottom community who have usually ignored his call to celebrate a day of death now follow him singing and dancing to what might be read as a multiple suicide.

The irony, of course, is that as a metaphor for the containment of traumatic experience the ritual behind National Suicide Day is to devote one day a year to death so that the 'rest of the year would be safe and free' (14). Members of the black community, the text informs us, 'knew anger well but not despair . . . and they didn't commit suicide [because] it was beneath them' (90). Yet, if so many well-known faces of the Bottom died by accidental suicide, as it were, is there also an argument for Sula's death as self-inflicted? When Ajax suddenly leaves, Sula seems to fall apart: 'His absence was everywhere, stinging everything . . . When he was there he pulled everything toward himself. Not only her eyes and all her senses but also inanimate things seemed to exist because of him' (134). Soon after, Sula becomes ill, and lies dying at 7 Carpenter's Road, alienated and alone. She receives a single visit from Nel, from whom she has been estranged ever since her brief fling with Jude, and the visit does little to change this. Yet, after she leaves, Sula thinks longingly of Nel and the loss of times past:

> [S]he will walk on down that road, her back so straight in that old green coat, the strap of her handbag pushed back all the way to the elbow, thinking how much I have cost her and never remember the days when we were two throats and one eye and we had no price. (147)

From the pain of this loss, Sula drifts into a jumble of remembrances, then abruptly, and following no particular sequence, an oblique reference to one of the founding traumas of her life flashes into her mind: 'I didn't mean anything. I never meant anything. I stood there watching her burn and was thrilled. I wanted her to keep on jerking like that, to keep on dancing' (147). However, the trauma of her mother's death has yet to be integrated into her consciousness. Sula immediately falls into a sleep and into her recurring nightmare of The Clabber Girl Baking Powder Lady, who smiles and beckons. However:

> When Sula came near she disintegrated into white dust, which Sula was hurriedly trying to stuff into the pockets of her blue-flannel housecoat. The disintegration was awful to see, but worse was the feel of the powder – its starchy slipperiness as she tried to collect it by handfuls. The more she scooped the more it billowed. At last it covered her, filled her eyes, her nose, her throat, and she woke gagging and overwhelmed with the smell of smoke. (147–8)

This is one of the most extraordinarily eloquent metaphorical representations of a forced reliving of a witnessed death and the intense grief and powerlessness both of the memory of that time and the unstoppable repetition of the traumatic re-enactment. The first sentence twice repeats Sula's name in full rather than using a pronoun, as if calling her into the swirling dust. A small child's act of trying to save her mother's disassembling body by stuffing the powder in her pockets mingles with the adult Sula's interpretation, for a 'housecoat' is not the garment of a child. The feel of the starchy slipperiness of cornflour is familiar to anyone who cooks, and it would be almost impossible to pick up a substantial amount as it would indeed slide out of your hands: it is a perfect depiction of enforced ineptitude. The dream, which in its final moments transposes the dust into Hannah's ashes, almost chokes and smothers Sula. She wakes in fright to her survival and the knowledge of her mother's death. A traumatised agony now takes hold of her body, and it is as if the community's last reading of her birthmark as 'Hannah's ashes marking her from the beginning' (114) is what she finally comes to believe in. For as her own death nears, her embodied pain becomes a 'kind of burning' (148), a corporeal inscription of psychic pain. This is not only from having watched her mother die, but also having internalised her grandmother's, and later the community's, interpretation of her as evil. Thrilled or not at the spectacle of her mother's death, it has still traumatised her all her life as this last scene so clearly demonstrates. As Jill Matus says: 'If anything, Sula's artistic sensibility – the interestedness, curiosity, aesthetic wonder – leaves her more vulnerable to pain than others who see more restrictedly and conventionally.'[13] However, as I see it, the existential problem that assails Sula right up to her death is that because this repeating trauma is unintegrated knowledge, she is unable to accept and mourn her mother's death and see that as a child it was not her fault that she had not tried to save her.

At the time of her death the narrator states that '[s]everal times she tried to cry out, but the fatigue barely let her open her lips, let alone take the deep breath necessary to scream' (148). It is not until the final pages of the book that we learn through Nel's reminiscence that Sula's mouth in death had looked like 'a giant yawn that she never got to finish' (172). This represents the gagged silence of her life. Sula *lived* her rebellion. Like her grandmother, it was her actions that counted far more than her words. Perhaps the saddest thing of all is that Nel never knew that Sula's final words *after* death were addressed to her. The poignancy of Sula's ' "Wait'll I tell Nel" ' (149) is compounded by the fact that in the last years of her life Sula never had the opportunity to speak her love aloud. Sula's inability to give words to her love had begun in her childhood as a defence against the loss and trauma she had suffered. If only she had been able to heal the breach with Nel things might well have been very different, because severed as she was from her maternal heritage, her closeness to Nel was what could have reconnected her to her lost subjectivity and, by extension, to her black community. Yet Sula's gift for metaphor, at least during her life, did have a positive impact on the Bottom. She becomes a catalyst for good and by her very existence lays down a methodology for healing.

Yet one of the problems of Sula's will-to-resist is her silence. Sula has, she believes, sung every song, but – and this is very important – she never voices her songs of rebellion to the community. She only lives them soundlessly by deed. There is no call and response. Her pride is that her mind and her loneliness are her own and not second-hand emotions, but by keeping what she feels to herself, by keeping her song internalised, she has ostracised herself from the community. Barbara Johnson argues that Morrison's most striking literary technique in *Sula* is the 'dissociation of affect and event', citing Nel's attempt to howl her pain as the 'most important example of affective discontinuity'.[14] While in total agreement with Johnson, I think that the silencing of Nel in the traumatic renunciation of her sexuality and her marriage is inseparable from Sula's traumatised silence, over and beyond, that is, the fact that Sula caused Nel's pain. What both Sula and Nel lose, for completely different reasons, is the capacity to acknowledge, assimilate, voice and mourn their traumatic grief within the community of women. Indeed, it is highly significant that Morrison prefaces Nel's howl that will not come with a long and evocative passage about how a collective of women can keen and outpour their grief:

> She [Nel] thought of the women at Chicken Little's funeral. The women who shrieked over the bier and at the lip of the open grave. What she had regarded as unbecoming behaviour seemed fitting to her now; they were screaming at the neck of God, his giant nape, the vast back-of-the-head that he turned on them in death . . . The body must move and throw itself about, the eyes must roll, the hands should have no peace, and *the throat should release all the yearning despair and outrage that accompany the stupidity of loss.* (107, emphasis added)

The implication is that the women can mourn because in the very physical act of their keening they can move from the state of melancholia and into mourning. Mourning is a forward moving and dynamic process while melancholia is static and self-destructive. Melancholia and depression are passive acts of aggression against the self. Mourning is a release of this repressed malignancy.[15] The repression ingrained in Nel's psyche by her mother's attempt to protect her daughter from the outside world and its attendant vulnerabilties means that she is unable to let herself go enough to keen aloud in her pain. Instead:

> Hunched down in the small bright room Nel waited. Waited for the oldest cry. A scream not for others, not in sympathy for a burnt child, or a dead father, but a deeply personal cry for one's own pain. A loud strident: 'Why me?' She waited. The mud shifted, the leaves stirred, the smell of overripe green things enveloped her and announced the beginning of her very own howl.
> But it did not come. (108)

Even though an attempt to keen her own internal agony, this contains a passing reference and longing for the solidarity of communal pain. 'Such a cry,' Alan Rice avers, 'would resemble a field holler, the cry by which slaves showed their deep private despair in the antebellum South.'[16] But it is a cry from which Nel has been disassociated, for her mother had severed any connection with her mother tongue and a matrilineal inheritance that was not contaminated by the effects of internalised whiteness. Nel's conscious legacy of maternal repression, which had been the basis of her emergent 10-year old 'me-ness', has merged with the unconscious repression of the 'closed place in the middle' that surrounds Chicken Little's drowning, but neither we nor Nel herself are aware of her traumatised withholding of that event until the last pages of the novel. Her howling cry cannot escape her and fill the small space in the bathroom with her grief because she has 'a flake of something dry and nasty in the throat' (108). The possibility of verbal relief is replaced by a striking visual symbol of silent containment:

> There was something just to the right of her, in the air, just out of view . . . A gray ball hovering just there. Just there. To the right. Quiet, gray, dirty. A ball of muddy strings, but without weight, fluffy but terrible in its malevolence. She knew she could not look. (108–9)

She refuses to look. The dirty ball's intrusive haunting *presence* is emphasised by the repetition of the phrase 'just there' and Morrison's use of verbs and nouns connected with vision.[17] It is a metaphor that could only apply to the highly-controlled and ever righteous, Nel. It is as if the hooks and eyes that earlier had simultaneously imprisoned and revealed her mother's body are converted here into a metaphor of psychic repression. The tight ball of muddy strings that is 'terrible in its malevolence' (109) is the maternal inheritance that Nel failed to escape; both metaphorically symbolise dissociation from the traumatised body. The maternal circuitry binding her psyche has become dangerously venomous because she no longer has Sula, the one person who could keep her restricted imagination alive, with whom to talk and laugh. Her repressed imagination shrivels in its containment of the grey ball, a colour that has connotations of whiteness in black American culture.[18] The lost history of gone things – the howl of history – both individual and cultural all have to be acknowledged if the move into mourning can take place. Yet as Cathy Caruth asks: 'How is it possible . . . to gain access to a traumatic history?'[19]

'Something newly missing' – the poetics of belatedness

Trauma, whether individual and collective, is not only experienced as repression or a defence mechanism, but also involves a temporal delay, a break in psychic time, that carries the individual(s) beyond the shock of the unexpected moment(s) of trauma. This is how the concept of 'belatedness' works. In Caruth's words: 'Trauma, that is, does not simply serve as a record of the past but precisely registers the force of an experience that is not yet fully owned.'[20] In order to move beyond psychic survival into a form of recovery, the traumatised memory must be moved from its recurring pattern of unconscious repetitions into the conscious mind where it can be integrated. Only then can withheld grief be mourned. If this is to be applied to the excised history of a trauma-tised people, that which is 'lost' or 'gone' has to be brought forward into consciousness and then publicly articulated in a form of collective witnessing that can assuage past wrongs. This offers hope of moving towards both an individual and collective form of psychic and literal reconciliation. I believe that the metaphoric logic of Morrison's fic-tional work offers a very special way of bridging some of the traumatic absences and gaps of black history and its repeated knots of death, for the dialogical structure of metaphor opens up a space for 'a testimony that can speak beyond what is already understood'.[21] I shall later discuss the transformative importance of the connection between traumatic narrative and metaphor, but first of all I want to examine in more detail the concept of belatedness which also involves trying to find a way past the psychic barrier that prevents the speaking of the unspeakable.

When previously dissociated unconscious trauma finally moves into consciousness through a triggering event, it is the moment when time returns back into the present but in a way that provides for a new separation from the traumatised past. A distinction can now be made between past and present, making possible the imagination of a future. It therefore becomes the moment when time is located and placed into a historical time-frame. However, as I outlined in the introduction, LaCapra believes that there is a risk of obfuscation and ethical evasive-ness in moving between the concepts of structural and historical trauma.[22] But if the movement of belatedness also involves a forming or reforming of identity out of a loss that now is specifically acknowl-edged, then I think a different form of ethical engagement is brought into play. In the African-American tradition of self as part of commu-nity, the articulation of even one identity (which in any case is rela-tional and concerned with doubleness or multiplicity) means that it will be part of a re-evaluation of the historical situatedness of the whole community. It is interesting that the epilogue, which is narrated from Nel's point of view, begins with Nel contemplating the community's loss in the static framework of melancholia. Following LaCapra's reading, her loss 'is converted into (or encrypted in an indiscriminately generalized rhetoric of) absence',[23] which would make mourning impos-sible. Yet in the last paragraphs of the epilogue and the novel, Nel passes through the moment of belatedness into an epiphanic revelation of self, and in this process moves beyond the stasis of melancholia and into the beginnings of mourning what has now reconverted back into the temporality of loss and 'gone things' which become specific, individualised and located. Now she realises it is not Jude, but Sula, whom she has missed all these years, and can begin to move into a state of accountable grief and mourning. Her feelings surrounding her estrangement from Sula, compounded by Sula's 25-year absence in death, are specified and named (spoken, or in this case howled) as her historically lost other. To mourn is to be able to place history (individual and collective) in the time-frame of gone things.

I believe that the location of metaphor as an act of transference (this is its etymological source) aids the shift into belatedness, though this is *not* the case in all metaphoric logic, as I demonstrated in the first chapters. Metaphor in *Wide Sargasso Sea*, and most centrally the concept of marooning, is divested of its historical specificity in order to justify an assumption of the victimised position of African-Caribbeans for the newly deterritorialised white creole family of the Cosway-Masons. Their situation became one of structural trauma, an inward flight that enabled evasion of the racialised socio-political ethics of that time. But as I have been emphasising, Black English is a highly metaphoric language, one created out of the ambivalent need to veil meaning while simultaneously providing a dissenting alternative.

The structure of a metaphor is inherently ambivalent. A metaphor provides a bridge between two opposing worlds, feelings, events, images and so on, but at the same time it can be – consciously and unconsciously – utilised only as a distancing measure or defence mechanism. Within the figurative language, of which metaphor is one of the most fundamental components, terms literally connected with one object are transferred to another and so achieve a new wider meaning, and one that may well remain ambiguously concealed. The use of metaphor provides a path to that which is too difficult and isolated but also untouchable, and thus offers a viable, indirect approach to traumatic histories:

> A metaphor is a descriptive statement with a double connotation. On the one hand it symbolically expresses the hidden emotion-laden content (a memory, a meaning, a dynamic conflict), and on the other, the metaphor fits an outer configuration of facts (or a fictitious or idiosyncratic, highly personalized interpretation of what is believed to be 'true' facts). In this way the metaphorical linguistic configuration bridges the gap between the inner and outer factors and carries a strong emotional content and impact. The metaphor

may be used therapeutically in circumnavigating resistance, at the same time symbolically uncovering hidden content.[24]

Until trauma is acknowledged and consciously assimilated, the person will remain frozen in the position of trauma. *Sula* is a text that is composed around the concept of belatedness, not only in the recurrent deaths (symbolic or real) that haunt those who have been involved, or in Morrison's manipulations of time. The actual structure of the text is an example of belatedness. The prologue covers a historical – and therefore collective – traumatic event in the far past that is represented as the immediate present in the manner of a flashback. The chapters that cover the 1920s (Nel and Sula's childhood), the late 1930s and early 1940s (the period of their adult estrangement), and then finally the 1965 epilogue (the end of the community), bring together both the principal characters, and by extension the wider community, in an act of remembrance and belated understanding. As Johnson states, 'the novel itself is written under the sign of "something newly missing" '.[25] The notion of belatedness involves both a distanciation between affect and event *and* a temporal disjunction, which is why trauma is sometimes referred to as a *'disease of time'*.[26] And Morrison, in line with her use of the iconography of clothing, has a particular idiographic metaphor that connects in with this idea of the psychic disease of historical time: the pleats of history and their invisible ironing.

Eva Peace's 'fastidious lining up of the pleats or pressing out of wrinkles on her skirts' (167) is Morrison's domestic metaphor for the profundity of personal loss and extreme psychic pain that can eventually turn into madness. Yet because it concerns a mother's killing of her own son – an act of maternal 'love' necessitated by Plum's psychic degradation that has resulted from his participation in the white man's war – personal trauma is implicated in the wider framework of American society. The first reference to realigning a pleat occurs at the beginning of the '1923' chapter when Hannah asks her mother if she had ever loved her children. Hannah has to repeat the question twice as Eva does not answer the first time. Then with the repetition of the query that cuts right to the repressed centre of her being, 'Eva's hand moved snail-like down her thigh toward her stump, but stopped short of it to realign a pleat' (67). Then she answers and we are figuratively catapulted into Eva's remembrance of Plum's murder, which had taken place two years earlier, and which Eva now describes to her daughter in great detail as if reliving the traumatic memory for the first time. 'Long after Hannah turned and walked out of the room, Eva continued to call his [Plum's] name while her fingers lined up the pleats in her dress' (72). By the end of this chapter Hannah too has burnt to death in a scene of appalling horror. Forty-four years later, Eva is trapped in her endless realigning of the pleats and 'dreaming of stairwells' (167). The metaphor of pleats has a double function: in the first place its patterning suggests the contraction of time into neat ordered segments that defy the intermingling of past, present and future in a continuous flow of narrative time. Eva orders and contains her past by a concertina-like repression, which means that while the past may constantly intrude into her present, it is contained within the folds of the knife-edged pleats of time. It is a means of overcoming chronological time and its effects. By the time Morrison reuses the metaphor near the end of the novel, the literal pleats have, in Eva's madness, become her tangible connecting psychic life-line with Plum. As she talks to him, and he to her, so she thinks, as she tells Nel: '"Plum. Sweet Plum. He tells me things"' (169). The metaphoric link between the fruit overlaid with suggestion of a delicacy ready for eating, adds to the already existing ambivalence of the whole mother–son relationship. Thus, figurative use of hems, hooks and eyes, pleats, fragments of clothing and dress itself are all part of Morrison's black female artistry that both hooks into and defies the straitjacket of white male history. It is an ambivalent figuring, however, because both Shadrack, who is associated with the straitjacket, and Eva, with the pleats, can only survive their pain in a state of devastating dissociation.

Indeed, the three main protagonists, Nel, Sula and Shadrack, all in their different ways are silenced by the displacement of trauma. Ironically, it is Nel Wright who moves beyond the impact of her own personal incomprehension of the 'stupidity of loss' and into the beginnings of belated understanding. 'Virtue, bleak and drawn, [has become] her only mooring' (139), and in her capacity as community carrier of extreme righteousness, towards the end of the novel she goes to visit Eva, who, now aged over 90, has outlived both her daughter and her granddaughter. It turns out to be a confronting visit for Nel. Eva suddenly accuses her of killing Chicken Little, and when Nel offloads the blame onto Sula, Eva replies: '"You. Sula. What's the difference?"' (168). Throughout the whole conversation between them, Eva continues pleating and her imaginary ironing. Nel extracts herself and thankfully escapes from the building, fastening her coat against the rising wind as she walks. 'The top button was missing so *she covered her throat with her hand*. A bright space opened in her head and memory seeped in' (169, emphasis added). The implication is that the 30-year-old flake in her throat is beginning to shift, and in her fear of what may unfold she covers the spot on her body where it is contained. Prompted by Eva's accusatory, ' "You was there. You watched, didn't you?" ' (168), Nel has a sudden and very vivid flashback of the scene of the drowning, and with its assimilation into her conscious thought finally admits to herself that she had experienced a 'good feeling . . . when Chicken's hands slipped' (170). With this 'new' knowledge she is forced to ask herself: ' "Why didn't I feel bad when it happened? How come it felt so good to see him fall?" ' (170). What she had always admired in herself is her calm, controlled behaviour that she first exhibited that day so long ago on the river and which had contrasted so strongly to Sula's hysterical sobbing: 'Now it seemed that what she had thought was maturity, seren- ity and compassion was only the tranquillity that follows a joyful stim- ulation' (170). Significantly, that reconnection occurs as she approaches the cemetery where Sula is buried, an area which McDowell sees as a metaphor for 'Nel's buried shadow'.[27]

As Nel walks along, her memory roams to the day that Sula was buried. After the white folks had left the cemetery, a group of black people from up in the Bottom enter with 'hooded hearts and filed eyes to sing "Shall We Gather at the River" over the curved earth that cut them off from the most magnificent hatred they had ever known' (173). This is a sorrow song that, in the words of Trudier Harris, 'is one that has traditionally brought comfort to black people and the expectation that life after this world would be much better than that lived here'.[28] Ironically, their singing is more a ritual-bound affirmation of their reli- gion and the spiritual comfort it provides than any heartfelt sadness at Sula's death, and as if in one last mocking gesture, the narrator suggests that perhaps Sula answers them from beyond the grave, 'for it began to rain, and the women ran in tiny leaps through the grass for fear their straightened hair would beat them home' (173). This is an ironic refer- ence to the fact that although it is now 1965, the era of Black Power and the slogan of 'Black is Beautiful', members of the Bottom are still worried about the effect of rain on their 'nappy' hair, suggesting that internalised whiteness is still paramount in the community.[29]

Nel continues walking and Shadrack passes her on the road. They move in opposite directions, 'each thinking separate thoughts about the past. The distance between them increased as they both remembered gone things' (174). Suddenly Nel stops. It is as if the trees are calling in Sula's voice: ' "Sula?" she whispered, gazing at the tops of the trees. "Sula?" *Leaves stirred; mud shifted; there was the smell of over-ripe green things*. A soft ball of fur broke and scattered like dandelion spores in the breeze' (174, emphasis added). The sentence I have italicised is a replica (although with the ordering shifted) of the painful moment 28 years before when Nel had slumped in her bathroom waiting for the howl that would not come (108). Now all the gone things press down on her and with a sudden surge of what is a mixture of mourning and joyful, but belated, understanding she realises that it was not Jude she has been missing all these years, but Sula, and a wild keening cry finally breaks out of her throat:

> 'O Lord, Sula,' she cried, 'girl, girl, girlgirlgirl.'
> It was a fine cry – loud and long – but it had no bottom and it had no top, just circles and circles of sorrow. (174)

This is the beginning of articulating the traumatic history that has impacted on her own life and all the inhabitants of the Bottom. It is important that the racially demeaning word 'gal' which had reduced her mother to custard all those years ago, now becomes 'girl' which is, Smitherman says, a term most often used by black women to denote close female friendship.[30] It is a moment of radical personal catharsis, moral transformation and coming to consciousness.[31] It may well become Nel's future role to take up where Sula left off and try to change the face of her community thinking. Her life has been one of refusing to look, of repressing pain, of ignoring her history. Through connecting back to Sula by admitting the vital nature of gone things, her life will never be the same again. She has lost Sula, but she now *has to* mourn that loss. The ending, then, is necessarily ambivalent.

One of the central questions the novel seeks to answer is how does a singular, personalised story become a communal one? How does Nel's story become a collective historical voice? Through the character of Nel the novel comes full circle. From a maternal heritage of repression, conventionality and assimilation to white middle-class values, it is as if Sula's voice whispering in the trees – as Hannah's voice had whispered in Sula's hair through the symbol of the green ribbon – could well be saying to Nel what Janie says to her best friend Phoeby in Zora Neale Hurston's *Their Eyes Are Watching God*: ' "You can tell 'em what Ah say if you wants to. Dat's just de same as me 'cause mah tongue is in mah friend's mouf." '[32] By unravelling the silenced knots of death, of existential pain and historical grief and by rebinding them as the 'hem of life',[33] Morrison voices black history that grows out of sharing both suffering and resistant knowledge.

In a continuation of Nel's maternal literary heritage, Morrison knots into the configurations of an African-American woman-centred text, in which Karla Holloway maintains '[i]n rejection of conventional histo-riography, feelings are proven more durable and trustworthy than history'.[34] By joining affect to events of the past in *Sula*, 'feelings' have *become* history, a black history both personal and collective. It is also a dynamic process of mourning, and therefore inverts and rewrites of the stasis of *Wide Sargasso Sea*, a text caught in the paralysis of melancho-lia. Sula has been dead for 30-odd years, and it is only belatedly that Nel can begin to mourn for the great loss of what was perhaps *the* most important relationship in her life. Yet it is hopeful, and reminds me of the ending of *Their Eyes Were Watching God*, when Janie sits up all night reciting and reliving the memories that make up her life to her oldest and closest friend Phoeby whom she has not seen for a number of years. Phoeby leaves and Janie is alone with her memories: 'Here was peace ... She called in her soul to come and see.'[35]

Conclusion: A Meditation on Silence

As my tongue unravels
in what pitch
will the scream hang unsung
or shiver like lace on the borders
of never   recording

Audre Lorde, 'Echoes'[1]

Audre Lorde believed in redemptive possibilities. All her life she actively and eloquently fought discrimination in all its permutations – racism, sexism, heterosexism and homophobia – in her essays, in her poetry, in the way she lived and spoke. And as a black feminist lesbian mother living in a society dominated by the social power of whiteness and patriarchal heteronormativity, her fight was more complicated than most. In 1977 she gave a paper entitled 'The Transformation of Silence into Language and Action' that was to come to exemplify her public stance against external and internalised pain that resulted from her positioning as a 'sister outsider'.[2] However, it was also immensely courageous on another level, for in this talk Lorde unveiled her private battle with breast cancer which was finally to take her life in 1992. But the breaking of silence always crossed between the public and private in Lorde's work and one gave strength to the other.[3] So when she says, 'My silence had not protected me. Your silence will not protect you',[4] she is also calling for a response from all of us, regardless of race, class, health or choice of sexuality:

The fact that we are here and that I speak these words is an attempt to break that silence and bridge some of those differences between

160

us, for *it is not difference which immobilizes us, but silence.* And there are so many silences to be broken.[5]

However, as Lorde constantly emphasised in her work and as my readings of Rhys's *Wide Sargasso Sea*, Kincaid's *Lucy* and Morrison's *Sula* suggest, the historical structuring of silence for women-of-color living in societies in which whiteness is the dominant discursive and material force has many layers, most of which are painfully hard to break. Despite revisionary readings of literature and history by a collection of eminent black feminist critics, the masked whiteness of theory – literary theory, theories of trauma, feminist theories, postmodernism, deconstruction, and so on – ensures that black voices continue to be marginalised. Indeed, in her poem that prefaces this conclusion, Lorde registers a deliberate gap between *never* and *recording*, thereby suggesting the continuing erasure of black identity under the continuing traumas of contemporary racial prejudice and exclusion. This spatial ellipsis also alerts us to the fact that as a result of trauma some memories are in fact irrecoverable. Nevertheless, Evelynn Hammonds, like Audre Lorde, maintains that '[t]he goal should be to develop a "politics of articulation" that would build on the interrogation of what makes it possible for black women to speak and act'.[6] In response, my focus has been on interrogating the unseen dynamics of power in figurative language *and* to emphasising the creative power of metaphor that can create a bridge between the unspeakable and the spoken. But because of the high incidence of racial disarticulation, I have concentrated on cultural readings of 'the closed place in the middle' – the silent space of repression of traumatic memories and traumatised histories, both personal and collective – across a range of historical contexts. This psychic silencing has so often meant that the 'scream [does] hang unsung'.[7]

Silence then, is an inherently ambivalent word. It can protect, dignify and honour, or it can erase, subjugate and oppress, and the spaces between the two are often blurred. As the conclusion to *Sula* suggests, for African-American women the breaking of years of repression and silence (Nel's ululating mournful cry) symbolically and literally takes place within and out of what Paul Gilroy calls the 'condition of being in pain'.[8] Yet the doubled-edged coding and metaphorical logic integral to African-American cultural traditions has played a large part in the politics of survival and resistance, which is why, as Valerie Smith maintains, close reading focusing on the 'figurative dimensions of the text within the context of its production', is an important mode of a politicised and historicised critical inquiry.[9] For instance, Lorde's strategic connection of the verb *hang* to the noun *scream* carries silently within it reverberations of historical trauma and the violence of death by lynching, and also recalls Billie Holiday's 1939 blues song, 'Strange Fruit', with its 'strange bitter crop' hanging silently in the trees, the outcome of excessive white violence and silencing.[10] However, read within the cultural paradigm of whiteness alone, despite her eloquence, the power of Lorde's race politics are significantly undermined.

While I have focused on whiteness, ambivalence and trauma in the chapters of this book – all of which compound acts of racialised silencing – I now want to offer a way to gesture beyond these difficulties. I thus end with a close reading of Toni Morrison's only published short story 'Recitatif', which is a complex meditation on silence and the difficulty of gaining a voice in a world structured by racial hierarchies.[11] As the musical metaphor of the title suggests, 'recitative' is a style of musical declamation, intermediate between singing and ordinary speech. The story is a riff on the traumatic ambivalence of silence that threads through the lives of two young girls named Twyla and Roberta, one black and one white, who meet for the first time when they are both eight in St Bonney's, a shelter for abandoned and orphaned children. They have both been removed from or abandoned by their mothers (it is purposefully ambiguous), Twyla because her mother 'danced all night' and Roberta because her mother was sick (243). Morrison's narrative concentrates on the working through of difficult (and previously silenced) knowledge, which so often accompanies experiences of cumulative trauma, and ends with a tentative speculation on how to engage in more open and equal, but still difficult, interracial dialogue.

'Recitatif' is, in many ways, an uncomfortable and demanding story to read, not least because all the anger, pain and hatred are projected onto the body of a mute woman named Maggie who has no recourse to spoken resistance: in the words of one of the young girls who taunt her, she 'wouldn't scream [because she] couldn't' (260). Moreover, in a story in which Morrison deliberately erases all linguistic colour coding in order to expose the hidden ideologies that are the mainstay of continuing racial prejudice in language, Maggie is the only 'raced' character in the narrative, and indeed the colour of her skin is a constant source of fascination.[12] It is an unsettling, ambivalent reading experience that meshes with my work for a number of reasons. The two female protagonists' self-definition, read over a 30-year span, is hinged on the knotted entanglement of their respective maternal inheritances and the material and psychic effects of racial divisions. It is a story of damage, but one engaged with the possibilities of belated healing. It is also, in many respects, a parable of the problematics of feminist politics that have, for some decades now, become paralysed around the emotive subject of difference.

Of the story's 24 pages, the first six describe the girls' incarceration in the institution, the remaining three-quarters narrate four subsequent chance encounters. The time-frame covers three decades, the 1950s, 1960s and 1970s, but it is as if time is condensed into one day in the manner of a traumatic vignette, because the four meetings occur at dawn, mid-morning, afternoon and finally, late at night.[13] The women's first reconnection – when they are 16 or 17 – takes place at dawn eight years after their stay at St Bonny's in one of the Howard Johnson chain of eateries that are replicated across the United States. At this stage Twyla (who narrates the story as an adult) is a Howard Johnson waitress and Roberta a customer on her way to a Jimi Hendrix concert. Despite their earlier friendship in the shelter, the encounter is a disaster: 'A black girl and a white girl meeting at Howard Johnson's on the road and having nothing to say' (253). Their next two accidental meetings happen approximately 12 years later, when they would be about 30 and are now themselves mothers. Twyla, with one son, is married to a fireman and their economic status is strained. Roberta has married a wealthy executive and has four step-children. They practically collide in the check-out queue of an upmarket gourmet store where Roberta is at home and Twyla the interloper, but their earlier estrangement at Howard Johnson's is temporarily overcome over a cup of coffee. Four months later they end up on opposite sides of picket lines as they demonstrate against the compulsory bussing of their children – the American government's attempt to enforce a reversal of their own implementation of the discriminatory Jim Crow laws – and the divisive politics become personalised. They part in a scene of semi-veiled hatred. Their last encounter – another eight years on when they would be about 38 – takes place on a snowy night just before Christmas, and it offers, as I shall infer, a tentative revisioning of the trauma that has shadowed and silenced their friendship.

This may seem a tedious retelling of the story without analysis, but the structuring has important political implications. Like *Sula*, the narrative's formal composition favours belatedness, both in its temporal and psychic aspects. The girls' life-long traumas unfold during their time in the shelter but the traumatic impact is not confined to the first quarter of the narrative space. Each subsequent meeting is in effect a replaying of these traumatic experiences through a reliving of traumatised memories that have remained encapsulated in a psychic time-lock. Thus, their childhood suffering is represented by repeating flashbacks that occupy most of the narrative space. But more than that, Morrison's narrative strategy draws us as readers into an imaginative engagement with these returning memories such that we both witness and participate in their re-enactments in truly disconcerting and unsettling ways.

As with all her work, Morrison deliberately structures this story to ensure an interactive and creative relationship between author and reader.[14] However, in this instance, she goes further by attempting to disarticulate the prescriptive racial codes invisibly present in language by removing them altogether and replacing them with contradictory readings of class-based mores. From the opening paragraph we are made aware that one girl is black and one white and that they are both traumatised by their mothers' desertion. Thrown together in an institution that can be read as symbolising a microcosmic representation of the outside world of institutionalised racism (or, and this is my tentative speculation, the imagined world of a feminist politics indentured to an empowering, but exclusionary, ideal of a universal sisterhood), the two young girls bond in a particularised form of silencing that necessarily erases the complexities of their racial positioning:

> 'Is your mother sick too?' [Roberta asks]
> 'No,' I said. 'She just likes to dance all night.'
> 'Oh,' she nodded her head and I liked the way she understood
> things so fast.
> So for the moment it didn't matter that we looked like salt and
> pepper standing there. (243–4)

However, what they appreciate in each other is a gestural but unspoken acceptance of the problems of the other, which means that they never get to understand the other's perspective or affective distress. Moreover, as Kalpana Seshadri-Crooks contends, '[t]he girls' willingness to maintain silence, to refuse curiosity, then also becomes the point of vulnerability that the two [will later] use against each other'.[15] Yet, despite their masked-over differences, Roberta and Twyla are encouraged into a deeper sense of solidarity by the external pressures that exist in their small society. In the institution they are resented by the majority of other children because even though they were 'dumped'[16] they do still have mothers, while the rest are orphans. They are also the youngest by a number of years and are frightened of the older girls, whom they nickname the 'gar girls – Roberta's misheard word for the evil stone faces described in civics class' (253). The ambivalence of the metaphor is start-lingly apt. On the one hand, gargoyles have open mouths as if emit-ting a silent scream (though ironically, the aim of their open mouths is to protect the buildings from which they jut by expelling excess water); on the other, the imagery suggests that these 'gar girls' are frozen in car-icatures of pain, a suffering which they in turn inflict on others less strong than themselves; among these, Twyla and Roberta, and especially Maggie. Indeed, Morrison does not shy away from depicting the spir-alling violence and abuse in the home or the reasons for the inmates' wounding. The gar girls, as Twyla remembers from the distance and understanding of her adult perspective, are themselves 'put-out girls, scared runaways most of them. Poor little girls who fought their uncles off' (244), but nevertheless they passed the violence on. At the time though '[w]e were scared of them, Roberta and me, but neither of us wanted the other one to know it' (244). When the gar girls chase them and twist their arms and pull their hair, they help each other but never speak between themselves of the shared intimidation. This then, is the other side of the protective silence with which they shroud themselves as an internal flight from the pain their mothers inadvertently inflict, yet both merely mask different manifestations of distress. They may bond together to protect each other or their inner selves, but because their distress is not consciously acknowledged, the only real resistance is running away, calling out 'dirty names' that echo back over their shoulders as they run (244).

We never know if the gar girls are white or black and that really is not the point. For if the 'hermeneutic impulse of the literary critic' – which is how Seshadri-Crooks describes Elizabeth Abel's 'playing the critic-as-detective [as a means of] trying to figure out who is white and who is black' in Morrison's story – concentrates solely on trying to work out which girl is of which race, the carefully constructed readings of the *causes* of racial prejudice and discrimination are lost. The story's diffi-cult knowledge is then elided. For instance, one of the more difficult aspects of the story with which it is necessary to come to terms, if reading from a race-cognisant feminist perspective, is that the daugh-ters' racism has been inculcated by their mothers:

The minute I walked in and the Big Bozo introduced us, I got sick to my stomach. It was one thing to be taken out of your own bed early in the morning – it was something else to be stuck in a strange place with a girl from a whole other race. And Mary, that's my mother, she was right. Every now and then she would stop dancing long enough to tell me something important and one of the things she said was that they never washed their hair and they smelled funny. Roberta sure did. Smell funny, I mean. (243)

As the story is focalised through Twyla's perspective, it is not known at first if Roberta also internalises racism through her mother's teaching. What the story stresses is that solidarity gained through the need to knot together against society's dictates can alter the tenets of learned racism, but that this path, though necessary, is far from easy. As the girls' friendship grows, they hear that their mothers are coming to visit, and they long for, discuss at length and plan a meeting between them. On the day, they curl each other's hair and dress in their best clothes, but when Roberta smilingly brings her mother over to where Twyla and her mother Mary are standing, Roberta's mother turns away in silent disdain as soon as she *sees* them, humiliating Twyla and embarrassing Roberta.

Interestingly, in her depiction of the mothers, Morrison appropriates one of the central stereotypes of white patriarchal discourse, the radically binarised madonna/whore dichotomy. Mary becomes the whore mother, unsuitably dressed in tight green slacks 'that made her behind stick out' (247) and a fur jacket with ripped pocket linings in which her hands get stuck.[17] The inexpediency of her attire is emphasised by the fact that one of the day's activities is to attend a chapel service, and in the church Mary lives up to her stereotyping, groaning, muttering in the silent spaces and then refusing to sing the hymns, instead checking her lipstick in her pocket mirror (248). In contrast, Roberta's mother is an imposing and excessive madonna figure: 'She was big. Bigger than any man and on her chest was the biggest cross I'd ever seen. I swear it was six inches long each way. And in the crook of her arm was the biggest Bible ever made' (247). The final touch of irony is that it is not only the whore mother who has tried to inculcate racial hatred in her daughter; it is the madonna mother who in the end refuses to shake hands with Mary who has been only too willing 'to yank her hand out of the pocket with the raggedy lining' and tangibly connect with Roberta's mother (247). The Christian edict of loving thy neighbour clearly means little when there are racial lines to be crossed, even when the other woman bears the traditional name of the madonna figure. This contemptuous and silent racial dismissal is a pivotal scene in the narrative and when repeated years later in one of their chance encounters as adults engenders the only italicised word in the text: 'Remember ... how we tried to *introduce* them?' (253) Roberta asks Twyla.

So the first level of silencing contains many layers. There is the individualised silence of repression or displacement through dissociation
which becomes so much a part of the lives of Rhys's Antoinette,
Kincaid's Lucy and Morrison's Nel, and now, Roberta and Twyla. In the
stories I have discussed, this traumatic silencing centres on profoundly
ambivalent relationships between mothers and daughters. However,
as I hope to have demonstrated, this repressive silencing can never be
separated out from racial positioning, and in particular from the psychic
and material effects of the oppression and domination inherent in
the ideology of whiteness. It is an ambivalent protection, of course,
because knowledge hidden from the self remains in a state of stasis or
impasse and stifles the psychic movement necessary to move into a
state of mourning, thus curtailing forms of resistance. Indeed, this
individualised silence, or inability to share deep self-knowledge with
similar others, radiates outwards into the public arena. But at the same
time, this form of silence is constructed very ambivalently in Morrison's
story:

> Two little girls who knew what nobody else in the world knew – how
> not to ask questions. How to believe what had to be believed. There
> was politeness in that reluctance and generosity as well. Is your
> mother sick too? No, she dances all night. Oh – and an understand-
> ing nod. (253)

However, 'politeness' and the liberal gesture can also mask white denial
(as is symbolised by Mariah in Kincaid's *Lucy*), which is really only a
more benign form of the contemptuous dismissal. In a race-driven
society silencing is a power tactic of the privileged: 'generosity' as a protective shield can become a form of displaced denial made possible by
the shield of power.

In Morrison's tale these forms of silence are shown to be socially constructed, as is racial prejudice, and the concepts are interwoven and
destructively tied together. The implication is that silent (or linguisti-
cally invisible) prejudices must be consciously confronted, disassembled
and laid bare in order that they may then be rethreaded in a different
configuration, one that makes the knots' figurations a binding of positive strength. The second level of silencing in 'Recitatif', and one much
more entrenched and hard to break, is an essentialist one, tied to the
body, with the accompanying implications (and complications) of the
biological and the innate – the feminist taboo, as it were. In the text,
this tabooed area is further complicated by the fact that the mute figure

in the text is Maggie who, as I stated earlier, is the only character explicitly connected to a racial positioning *and* the figure on whom all the girls in St Bonny's – regardless of race – vent their rage, violence and cruelty. Abel describes her as a 'figure of racial undecidability' (472) – she is variously drawn as 'sandy-colored' (245), 'black' (257) or even possibly 'pitch-black' (259) – she changes colour depending on the race of the beholder and the vagaries of traumatic memory. What never alters though is the fact that Maggie is punished for everybody else's pain. The gar girls push her down and tear off her clothes (254), Twyla and Roberta also taunt and ridicule her, as if obsessed by her muteness:

> '[W]hat if somebody tries to kill her?' I used to wonder about that.
> 'Or if she wants to cry? Can she cry?'
> 'Sure,' Roberta said. 'But just tears. No sounds come out.'
> 'She can't scream?'
> 'Nope. Nothing.'
> 'Can she hear?'
> 'I guess.'
> 'Let's call her,' I said. And we did.
> 'Dummy! Dummy!' She never turned her head. (245)

But one incident in particular becomes for both the girls a traumatic memory that will plague them for the duration of the story, overpowering happy reminiscences of their past friendship nearly every time they meet, as I shall demonstrate.

We first learn of Maggie's existence through Twyla's description of a repeating dream of the shelter's orchard in which '[n]othing really happened. Nothing all that important, I mean. Just the big girls dancing and playing the radio. Roberta and me watching. Maggie fell down there once' (244–5). The sudden and abrupt inclusion of Maggie into the narrative bespeaks trauma, but the depth of the repressed trauma and its connection with the maternal only gradually becomes clear. After a brief description of Maggie and a diversion into why she and Roberta 'got along' – it is a friendship almost entirely based on 'being nice about not asking questions' about each other (245) – there is a hint and foreshadowing of the interconnection in their minds of Maggie and their mothers who have silently shut them out of their lives: 'I think it was the day before Maggie fell down that we found out our mothers were coming to visit us' (246). The agonies of the maternal visit (symbolic of the many instances of distress that occur for both girls) become merged with the horror of the day that Maggie falls down and is kicked and abused. They become condensed into one memory. All the children's self-hatred, their woundings from their mothers' displacing behaviour and their fear of permanent abandonment are projected onto Maggie, whose mute coloured *body* becomes the repository for Twyla's and Roberta's wounded bitterness and for the hatred and confusion of the gar girls. Maggie becomes the abject, the object onto which all other subjects expel the unspeakable aspects of their psyches in order to survive.[18] However, as 'abjection is above all ambiguity', it also simultaneously represents the *failure* of an abject displacement, 'something rejected from which one does not part'.[19] Maggie has herself been raised in an institution: she is all they might themselves become and, as such, is loathed and persecuted. Yet ironically, it is the spectre of Maggie that they take with them into the outside world.

Despite their tentative attempts to rekindle their past relationship, three out of the four times Twyla and Roberta encounter each other over the following decades, they are overwhelmed by the haunting memory of the day Maggie fell down. At their first and disastrous meeting at Howard Johnson's, Roberta, falling back into her maternal patterns, contemptuously dismisses Twyla apparently on racial grounds. They part in anger and with a jibe about each other's mother – the shared part of them that is both a wound and a weapon. However, their next chance encounter starts off promisingly by their being able to laugh at what, at the time, had been a harrowing episode:

> 'Remember . . . how we tried to *introduce* them?'
> 'Your mother with that cross like two telephone poles.'
> 'And yours with those tight slacks.'
> We laughed so loudly heads turned and made the laughter harder to suppress. (253)

But their laughter turns to dissonance when the remembering shifts to the subject of Maggie and the day she fell down. Roberta argues that the gar girls knocked her over, and Twyla seems to have totally repressed the confrontation so that they cannot talk it through. They cover the differences over and depart with Twyla promising to contact Roberta, but knowing she never will.

Their third meeting centres around a scene of racial strife and flaring antagonisms. Twyla spots Roberta demonstrating against the introduction of bussing, and stops to talk to her. The political context quickly inflames their conversation, which ends with a threatening accusation from Roberta:

'Maybe I am different now, Twyla. But you're not. You're the same little state kid who kicked a poor old black lady when she was down on the ground. You kicked a black lady and you have the nerve to call me a bigot.' (257)

What is particularly interesting about this scene (and also what makes it hard to write about) is that what bothers Twyla about the incrimination is not that she is accused of bigotry, or that she has kicked an old black lady, but the fact that Roberta says that Maggie is black:

What was she saying? Black? Maggie wasn't black.
'She wasn't black,' I said.
'Like hell she wasn't, and you kicked her. We both did. You kicked a black lady who couldn't even scream.' (258)

Is this to be read as implying that a profound trauma will override questions of race? Or that the masking over and silencing of racial differences will end up in acts of violence both physical and psychic? In any event, it is a question that troubles Twyla for years and she provides the answer herself. She had not kicked Maggie but she had wanted to, because:

Maggie was my dancing mother. Deaf, I thought and dumb. Nobody inside. Nobody would hear you if you cried in the night. Nobody who could tell you anything important that you could use. (259)

With this epiphany, the story shifts into its final phase. On the way home from buying a Christmas tree late one night, Twyla stops into a diner, where she encounters Roberta, resplendent in a 'silvery evening gown and dark fur coat' (260). Roberta leaves her grand circle of friends and comes over and launches straight into an apology for her accusation all those years ago: 'I have to tell you something, Twyla. I made up my mind if I ever saw you again, I'd tell you' (261). Twyla is reluctant to re-enter this psychic space but Roberta insists:

'Listen to me. I really did think she was black. I didn't make that up. I really thought so. But now I can't be sure. I just remember her as old, so old. And because she couldn't talk – well, you know; I thought she was crazy. She'd been brought up in an institution like my mother was and like I thought I would be too. And you were right.

> We didn't kick her. It was the gar girls. Only them. But, well, I wanted
> to. I really wanted them to hurt her.' (261)

In an interesting article on trauma and race and the pedagogical imper-
atives of helping African-American students to work through the history
of slavery and the lingering and negative impact of its long term associations in contemporary America, Rinaldo Walcott argues that the
trauma of racism – historical and contemporary – is 'laden with the evidence of defeat and shame' which in turn articulates a kind of knowledge with which it is difficult to engage.[20] He therefore advocates
Deborah Britzman's notion of 'difficult knowledge', which suggests that
however confronting or difficult knowledge is to deal with, it must be
worked through at a psychic level in order to engage with the release
that accompanies the act of mourning.[21] Quoting Britzman, Walcott
states 'perhaps the greatest risk of learning is that lonely recognition
that knowledge of loss and our own insufficient response can be made
only in *belated time*'.[22] The breaking of psychic silence does not necessarily have to be spoken out loud, but it would seem that most
successful workings through of trauma take place within some form of
dialogue, whether this be through medical means, reconciliation tri-
bunals, private or public sharing of traumatic memories, or, as I have
been advocating, through the use of metaphoric understanding in literature, which returns me to Morrison's short story.

As Roberta has been talking she starts to cry and we move into the
story's conclusion. Importantly, it is Roberta's voice that for the first
time leads the narrative, which has until now been told from Twyla's
point of view:

> She wiped her cheeks with the heel of her hand and smiled. 'Well
> that's all I wanted to say.' . . .
> 'Thanks, Roberta.'
> 'Sure.'
> 'Did I ever tell you? My mother, she never did stop dancing.'
> 'Yes. You told me. And mine, she never got well.' Roberta lifted
> her hands from the tabletop and covered her face with her palms.
> When she took them away she really was crying. 'Oh shit, Twyla.
> Shit, shit, shit. What the hell happened to Maggie?' (261)

In the end the 'difficult knowledge' about their mothers is a final
healing gift to each other – an ambivalent acknowledgement of sharing

and voicing 'the condition of being in pain'. Nothing is resolved, least of all the problem of Maggie, but the interracial lines of dialogue are, for the first time in the narrative, opened and redolent with future possibilities.

I end by connecting the possibility of such a dialogue to Ann duCille's notion of complementary theorising that describes the ways in which black and white feminists '*think with*, rather than across, one another about the intersections of racial and gender differences'.[23] Working through difficult and previously silenced knowledge is, I believe, a means not only to participate in this vital dialogue but also to engage actively in the possibilities of cross-cultural healing.

Notes

Introduction

1. June Jordan, 'Gettin Down to Get Over', a poem dedicated to her mother, *Naming Our Destiny: New and Selected Poems* (New York: Thunder's Mouth Press, 1989) 75–6, emphasis in original.
2. Clifford W. Ashley, *The Ashley Book of Knots* (New York: Doubleday, 1946) 8.
3. Sara Ruddick, 'Maternal Thinking', *Feminist Studies* 6 (1980): 368.
4. Rosi Braidotti, 'The politics of ontological difference', *Between Feminism & Psychoanalysis*, ed. Teresa Brennan (London & New York: Routledge, 1990) 96.
5. Nancy Chodorow, *The Reproduction of Mothering: Psychoanalysis and the Sociology of Gender* (Berkeley, Los Angeles & London: University of California Press, 1978).
6. Patricia Hill Collins, 'Shifting the Center: Race, Class, and Feminist Theorizing about Motherhood', *Mothering: Ideology, Experience, and Agency*, eds Evelyn Nakana Glenn, Grace Chang and Linda Forcey (New York & London: Routledge, 1994) 63.
7. Hill Collins (1994), 45–65.
8. Jane Lazarre, *The Mother Knot* (New York: McGraw-Hill, 1976).
9. Marianne Hirsch, *The Mother/Daughter Plot: Narrative, Psychoanalysis, Feminism* (Bloomington & Indianapolis: Indiana University Press, 1989).
10. Future readings, Hirsch states, 'should relinquish their exclusive dependence on psychoanalytic models and will have to integrate psychoanalysis with other perspectives – historical, social and economic . . . They will have to include aggression, ambivalence, contradiction, even as they wish for connection, support, and affiliation. They have to include the body even as they avoid essentialism. See Hirsch (1989), 198–9.
11. As Spivak's use of the metaphor has many similarities to mine, I quote a central passage in full: 'A subject-effect can be briefly plotted as follows: that which seems to operate as a subject may be part of an immense discontinuous network ("text" in the general sense) of strands that may be termed politics, ideology, economics, history, sexuality, language, and so on. (Each of these strands, if they are isolated, can also be seen as woven out of many strands.) Different knottings and configurations of these strands, determined by heterogeneous determinations which are themselves dependent upon myriad circumstances, produce the effect of the operating subject.' Gayatri Chakravorty Spivak, 'Subaltern Studies: Deconstructing Historiography', *In Other Worlds: Essays in Cultural Politics* (New York & London: Routledge, 1988b) 204.
12. Diana Fuss ed. *Inside/Out: Lesbian Theories, Gay Theories* (New York & London, Routledge, 1991).
13. Susan Rubin Suleiman, 'Nadja, Dora, Lol V. Stein: women, madness and

narrative', *Discourse in Psychoanalysis and Literature*, ed. Shlomith Rimmon-Kennan (London & New York: Methuen, 1987) 124.

14. Elizabeth Grosz, *Volatile Bodies: Toward A Corporeal Feminism* (St Leonards, NSW: Allen & Unwin; Bloomington: Indiana University Press, 1994).

15. Grosz (1994), xii.

16. Grosz (1994), 142.

17. Grosz (1994), 142.

18. Sara Ahmed, *Strange Encounters: Embodied Others in Post-coloniality* (London & New York: Routledge, 2000) 42.

19. Ahmed (2000), 42.

20. Gayatri Spivak terms the discriminatory reduction of race to the question of skin colour 'chromatism'. See Gayatri Chakravorty Spivak, 'Imperialism and Sexual Difference', *Contemporary Literary Criticism: Literary and Critical Studies*, eds Robert Con Davis and Ronald Schleifer (New York & London: Longman, 1989) 526.

21. Ahmed (2000), 42 (emphasis in the original).

22. Hortense Spillers contends that for African-Americans, 'their New-World diasporic plight marked a *theft of the body* – a willful and violent (and unimaginable from this distance) severing of the captive body from its motive will, its active desire.' Hortense J. Spillers, 'Mama's Baby, Papa's Maybe: An American Grammar Book', *Diacritics* 17 (Summer 1987): 67 (emphasis in original). The troping of the captive body and the symbolic violence of its branding and marking as a cultural text through the discursive power of the American Grammar is the subject of Spillers's brilliant article, to which I shall frequently refer.

23. Ahmed (2000), 6–9.

24. Toni Morrison quoted in Cheryl Lester, 'Meditations on a Bird in the Hand: Ethics and Aesthetics by Toni Morrison', *The Aesthetics of Toni Morrison: Speaking the Unspeakable*, ed. Marc C. Conner (Jackson: University of Mississippi, 2000) 133. Morrison's metaphorical language (the veil, the caul and so on) is itself steeped in the metaphorical logic and idiom of W.E.B. Du Bois's *The Souls of Black Folk* [1903] (New York & London: Penguin, 1989).

25. See Jacques Derrida, *The Truth in Painting*, trans. Geoff Bennington and Ian McLeod (Chicago & London: University of Chicago Press, 1987) 324. See also 5, 367.

26. Ahmed (2000), 6. These surprise meetings do not necessarily involve a face-to-face encounter of two or more subjects. More generally, 'a meeting suggests a *coming together of at least two elements*. For example, we can think of reading as a meeting between reader and text' (7, emphasis in original).

27. Quoted in Ahmed (2000), 38. It is a description in which, as Ahmed intimates, 'Lorde uses the poetics of remembering to dramatise the operation of racism on her body, in the violence of its particularity' Ahmed (2000), 39. The scene describes the young Audre accompanying her mother home from a Christmas shopping trip. A white woman sitting opposite them in the subway car stares so hard at the child, her gazing moving all over Audre's body with such a look of disgust that she silently communicates 'her horror' to the child. Audre Lorde, 'Eye to Eye: Black Women, Hatred, and Anger', *Sister Outsider: Essays and Speeches* (Freedom CA: The Crossing Press, 1984) 147–8.

28. Karla F.C. Holloway, *Codes of Conduct: Race, Ethics, and the Color of Our Character* (New Brunswick, NJ: Rutgers University Press, 1995) 34.
29. Holloway (1995), 34, emphasis added.
30. Lorene Cary, *Black Ice* (New York: Vintage, 1991) 58–9. Quoted in Holloway (1995), 30. bell hooks has also written extensively of her notion of 'talking back', see *Talking Back: Thinking Feminist, Thinking Black* (London: Sheba, 1989), especially 5–9. Jamaica Kincaid has a version called 'backchat' which she uses in *Lucy* and which I shall discuss again in the chapters on her work.
31. See Holloway (1995), 30–6.
32. Valerie Smith, 'Black Feminist Theory and the Representation of the "Other"', *Changing Our Own Words: Essays on Criticism, Theory, and Writing by Black Women*, ed. Cheryl A. Wall (London: Routledge, 1990), 45.
33. Articles which draw attention to such forms of appropriation are Norma Alarcón, 'The Theoretical Subject(s) of *This Bridge Called My Back* and Anglo-American Feminism', *Criticism in the Borderlands: Studies in Chicano Literature, Culture and Ideology*, eds Héctor Calderon and José David Saldivar (Durham & London: Duke University Press, 1991) 28–39; Chela Sandoval, 'The Theory and Method of Oppositional Consciousness in the Postmodern World', *Genders* 10 (1991): 1–24; Paula M.L. Moya, 'Postmodernism, "Realism," and the Politics of Identity: Cherríe Moraga and Chicana Feminism', *Feminist Genealogies, Colonial Legacies, Democratic Futures*, eds M. Jacqui Alexander and Chandra Talpade Mohanty (New York & London: Routledge, 1997) 125–50; and Abby Wilkerson, 'Ending at the Skin: Sexuality and Race in Feminist Theorizing', *Hypatia* 12:3 (1997): 164–73.
34. Holloway (1995), 18.
35. Patricia J. Williams, *Seeing a Colour-Blind Future: The Paradox of Race, The 1997 Reith Lectures* (London: Virago, 1997) 57.
36. Williams (1997), 59.
37. Williams (1997), 13.
38. Williams (1997), 13.
39. Elizabeth Abel, Barbara Christian and Helene Moglen, 'Introduction: The Dream of a Common Language', *Female Subjects in Black and White: Race, Psychoanalysis, Feminism*, eds Elizabeth Abel, Barbara Christian and Helene Moglen (Berkeley, Los Angeles & London: University of California Press, 1997) 13, emphasis added.
40. Judith L. Raiskin, *Snow on the Canefields: Women's Writing and Creole Subjectivity* (Minneapolis & London: University of Minnesota Press, 1996) 98.
41. See Rosalyn Terborg-Penn, 'Black Women in Resistance: A Cross-Cultural Perspective', *In Resistance: Studies in African, Caribbean, and Afro-American History*, ed. Gary Y. Okihiro (Amherst: University of Massachusetts Press, 1986) 198–200.
42. Betsy Wing, 'Translator's Introduction', *Poetics of Relation*, Édouard Glissant, trans. Betsy Wing (Ann Arbor: University of Michigan Press, 1997) xii.
43. Glissant (1997), 71.
44. Glissant (1997), 33.
45. See, for instance, *Motherlands: Black Women's Writing from Africa, the Caribbean and South Asia*, ed. Susheila Nasta (London: The Women's Press, 1991); Vron Ware, *Beyond the Pale: White Women, Racism and History* (London & New York: Verso, 1992).

46. Lorde (1984), 149–50. The emphasis is mine. The interweaving themes of survival and maternal love is an important focus in *Sula*.

47. Michelle Wallace, 'Variations on Negation and the Heresy of Black Feminist Creativity', *Invisibility Blues: From Pop to Theory* (London & New York: Verso, 1990) 214.

48. See 'Ambivalence', *The New Fontana Dictionary of Modern Thought*, eds Alan Bullock and Stephen Trombley (London: Harper Collins, 2000) 26.

49. Muriel Dimen, 'In the Zone of Ambivalence: A Journal of Competition', *Feminist Nightmares, Women at Odds: Feminism and the Problem of Sisterhood*, eds Susan Ostrov Weisser and Jennifer Fleischner (New York & London: New York University Press, 1994) 379.

50. Deborah E. McDowell, 'Boundaries: Or Distant Relations and Close Kin', *Afro-American Literary Study in the 1990s*, eds Houston A. Baker Jr and Patricia Redmond (Chicago & London: University of Chicago Press, 1989) 51–70 and Hortense J. Spillers, 'Response', 71–3. Spillers' quotations appear on 72 and the emphasis is hers.

51. Geneva Smitherman, *Talkin and Testifyin: The Language of Black America* (Detroit: Wayne State University Press, 1977) 10–11 (emphasis in original). See Du Bois, (1989 [1903]) 5 for his concept of double-consciousness.

52. Homi K. Bhabha, 'Of Mimicry and Man: The ambivalence of colonial discourse' [1984], *The Location of Culture* (London & New York: Routledge, 1994(b)) 85–92.

53. Anne McClintock, *Imperial Leather: Race, Gender and Sexuality in the Colonial Conquest* (New York & London: Routledge, 1995) 65.

54. Wahneema Lubiano, 'Mapping the Interstices between Afro-American Cultural Discourse and Cultural Studies', *Callaloo* 19:1 (1996): 69.

55. Cheryl A. Wall, 'Introduction: Taking Positions and Changing Words', *Changing Our Own Words: Essays on Criticism, Theory, and Writing by Black Women*, ed. Cheryl A. Wall (London: Routledge, 1990) 2.

56. Avtar Brah, *Cartographies of Diaspora: Contesting Identities* (London & New York: Routledge, 1996) 14.

57. Leslie G. Roman, 'White is a Color! White Defensiveness, Postmodernism, and Anti-Racist Pedagogy', *Race, Identity and Representation in Education*, eds Cameron McCarthy and Warren Crichlow (New York: Routledge, 1993) 72.

58. Toni Morrison, *Playing in the Dark: Whiteness and the Literary Imagination. The William E. Massey Sr. Lectures in the History of American Civilization* (London: Picador, 1993(a)) 46.

59. Yvonne Atkinson, 'Language That Bears Witness: The Black English Oral Tradition in the Works of Toni Morrison', *The Aesthetics of Toni Morrison: Speaking the Unspeakable*, ed. Marc C. Conner (Jackson: University of Mississippi, 2000) 25.

60. Morrison (1993(a)), 63.

61. I refer throughout this book to Morrison's fiction, which aside from my close reading of *Sula* especially includes *The Bluest Eye* and *Beloved*, but also her essays such as 'Memory, Creation, and Writing', *Thought* 59:235 (1984): 385–90; 'Rootedness: The Ancestor as Foundation', *Black Women Writers: Arguments and Interviews*, ed. Mari Evans (London & Sydney: Pluto Press, 1985) 339–45; 'The Site of Memory', *Inventing the Truth: The Art and Craft of Memoir*, ed. William Zinsser (Boston: Houghton Mifflin, 1987) 103–24;

'Unspeakable Things Unspoken: The Afro-American Presence in American Literature', *Michigan Quarterly Review* 28 (1989):1–34; 'Toni Morrison: The Art of fiction CXXXIV', *Paris Review* 128 (1993(b)): 82–125; 'Home', *The House That Race Built: Black Americans, U.S. Terrain*, ed. Wahneema Lubiano (New York: Pantheon, 1997) 3–12; *Playing in the Dark*, as listed above, and a collection of her interviews, *Conversations with Toni Morrison*, ed. Danille Taylor-Guthrie (Jackson: University Press of Mississippi, 1994). My conclusion will be a meditation on her only published short story, 'Recitatif', *Confirmation: An Anthology of African American Women*, eds Amiri Baraka (LeRoi Jones) and Amina Baraka (New York: William Morrow, 1983) 243–61.

62. Ruth Frankenberg, *White Women, Race Matters: The Social Construction of Whiteness* (London & Minneapolis: Routledge and University of Minnesota Press, 1993) 1.

63. Robin Bennefield interviews Maulana Karenga, 'Whiteness Studies: Deceptive or Welcome Discourse?', *Black Issues in Higher Education* 16:6 (1999): 26, emphasis added.

64. Joe L. Kincheloe, 'The Struggle to Define and Reinvent Whiteness: A Pedagogical Analysis', *College Literature* 26:3 (1999): 162.

65. Barbara J. Flagg, '"Was Blind, But Now I See": White Race Consciousness and the Requirement of Discriminatory Intent', *Michigan Law Review* 91:5 (1993), 979.

66. This phrase is a quotation taken from Abel, Christian and Moglen, 'Introduction: The Dream of a Common Language', *Female Subjects in Black and White: Race, Psychoanalysis, Feminism* (Berkeley, Los Angeles & London: University of California Press, 1997) 10.

67. Sara Ahmed and Jackie Stacey, 'Testimonial Cultures: An Introduction', *Cultural Values* 5:1 (January 2001): 1. For an important work on testimony and its relationship with literature see Shoshana Felman and Dori Laub, *Testimony: Crisis of Witnessing in Literature, Pyschoanalysis, and History* (New York: Routledge, 1992). See also, *Tense Past: Cultural Essays in Trauma and Memory*, eds Paul Antze and Michael Lambek (New York & London: Routledge, 1996); and Kirby Farrell, *Post-traumatic Culture: Injury and Interpretation in the Nineties* (Baltimore & London: Johns Hopkins University Press, 1998).

68. Du Bois (1989 [1903]), 1.

69. Ruth Leys, *Trauma: A Genealogy* (Chicago & London: University of Chicago Press, 2000).

70. Leys (2000), 1.

71. Leys (2000), 2. The article to which Leys refers appeared in the *New York Times*, Saturday, 21 March 1998.

72. Leys (2000), 2.

73. Leys uses a quotation of Freud's about his race in which he in fact is referring to his Jewishness, Leys (2000), 289. Leys's only other reference to race is a brief reference to Walter Benn Michaels's article '"You who was never there": Slavery and the New Historicism, Deconstruction and the Holocaust', *Narrative* 4:1 (1996): 1–16, Leys (2000), 268, 285.

74. Morrison (1989), 16.

75. Laura S. Brown, 'Not Outside the Range: One Feminist Perspective on Psychic Trauma', *American Imago* 48:1 (1991): 121.

76. Brown (1991), 130.

77. Brown (1991), 128.
78. Brown (1991), 129.
79. Dominick LaCapra, 'Trauma, Absence, Loss', *Critical Inquiry* 25:4 (1999): 699.
80. Dominick LaCapra, *Writing History, Writing Trauma* (Baltimore & London: Johns Hopkins University Press, 2001) 40.
81. LaCapra emphasises it is very important to distinguish between the notion of absence and that of loss. In general terms he situates the historical past as the scene of losses which holds the possibilities of reconfiguration through narrative in ways that may transform the present and the future. He situates absence, on the other hand, in the realm of the transhistorical because in the way in which he is using the term it is not as a locatable event, so that it does not imply the temporal concepts of past, present and future. See LaCapra (1999), 699–700.
82. LaCapra (1999), 724. Other than slavery, LaCapra lists the Holocaust, apartheid, and the effects of the atom bombs in Hiroshima and Nagasaki as examples of founding trauma.
83. LaCapra (2001), xiii.
84. I have taken the distinguishing definitions of reactive and endogenous from Robert Jay Lifton's discussion of depression in his book *The Broken Connection: On Death and the Continuity of Life* (New York: Simon and Schuster, 1979) 182.
85. LaCapra (2001), ix.
86. LaCapra (2001), 21.
87. LaCapra (2001), 23.
88. Cathy Caruth, 'Introduction', *Trauma: Explorations in Memory*, ed. Cathy Caruth (Baltimore & London: Johns Hopkins University Press, 1995a) 11 (emphasis added).
89. Cathy Caruth, 'Introduction', *American Imago* 48:1 (1991): 5.
90. Caruth (1991), 2. The areas of study to which she refers include the fields of psychoanalysis, psychiatry, sociology and literature (emphasis added).
91. Robert Young, 'Neocolonial Times', *Oxford Literary Review* 13 (1991): 2. The first quotation in the sentence is also Young's from the same article (1991) 3.
92. Ruth Frankenberg and Lata Mani, 'Crosscurrents, Crosstalk: Race, "Postcoloniality" and The Politics of Location', *Cultural Studies* 7 (1993): 294–5.
93. Gayatri Chakravorty Spivak, 'Can the Subaltern Speak?', *Marxism and the Interpretation of Culture*, eds Cary Nelson and Laurence Grossberg (Urbana & Chicago: University of Illinois Press, 1988a) 271–313.
94. Gayatri Chakravorty Spivak, 'Questions of Multi-culturalism', *The Post-Colonial Critic: Interviews, Strategies, Dialogues*, ed. Sarah Harasym (New York & London: Routledge, 1990) 59.
95. Cathy Caruth, *Unclaimed Experience: Trauma, Narrative, and History* (Baltimore & London: Johns Hopkins University Press, 1996) 3.
96. Sherley Anne Williams, 'Some Implications of Womanist Theory', *Reading Black, Reading Feminist: A Critical Anthology*, ed. Henry Louis Gates, Jr (New York & London: Meridian, 1990) 74.
97. Valerie Smith, *Self-Discovery and Authority in Afro-American Narrative* (Cambridge, MA & London: Harvard University Press, 1987) 7.

98. Roman (1993), 78.
99. Ann duCille, 'The Occult of True Black Womanhood: Critical Demeanor and Black Feminist Studies', *Female Subjects in Black and White: Race, Psychoanalysis, Feminism*, eds Elizabeth Abel, Barbara Christian and Helene Moglen (Berkeley, Los Angeles & London: University of California Press, 1997) 21.
100. The quotation appears in duCille (1997), 23.
101. duCille (1997), 51 (emphasis added).

1 'The White Hush between Two Sentences': The Traumatic Ambivalence of Whiteness in *Wide Sargasso Sea*

1. Derek Walcott, 'Jean Rhys' in his *Collected Poems 1948–1984* (New York: Farrar, Straus & Giroux, 1986) 427–9 (emphasis added).
2. Walcott modifies the 'hush' with the racial marker white, for he is writing about the racialised culture of the white creole in a cultural context in which the meaning of the word *creole* changed along with the shifting forces of colonisation. The racial and linguistic fluidity of the term 'creole', its history and ambivalent status are outlined by Edward Brathwaite in his *Contradictory Omens: Cultural Diversity and Integration in the Caribbean* (Mona: Savacou Publications, 1974). I found while writing the chapters on *Wide Sargasso Sea* that having always to insert a racial modifier extremely problematic as this constantly reifies racial divisions.
3. This is a quotation from Homi Bhabha's 'Introduction' to his collection of essays published as *The Location of Culture* (London: Routledge, 1994a) 11.
4. Thomas Loe begins his essay, 'Patterns of the Zombie in Jean Rhys's *Wide Sargasso Sea*', *World Literature Written in English* 31:1 (1991): 34–42 with much the same line of argument about the suggestiveness of the unsaid in Rhys's Caribbean novel but with a different inference.
5. Caruth (1996), 24.
6. Helen Carr, *Jean Rhys* (Plymouth, UK: Northcote House, 1996) 18.
7. Kenneth Ramchand, *The West Indian Novel and its Background* (London: Faber & Faber, 1970) 225. Ramchand was referring to three novels by white West Indians: Jean Rhys's *Wide Sargasso Sea*, Phyllis Shand Allfrey's *The Orchid House*, and Geoffrey Drayton's *Christopher*.
8. Sanford Sternlicht, *Jean Rhys* (New York: Twayne; London, Prentice Hall, 1997) 118.
9. While Jean Rhys grew up in Dominica (hence Walcott's references), *Wide Sargasso Sea* is set in Jamaica.
10. Jean Rhys, *Wide Sargasso Sea* [1966] (London: Penguin, 1997) 122. This Penguin edition has a useful introduction, appendix and notes by Angela Smith. Gold was indeed the imperial idol, as is well documented by Eric Williams in his early classic text, *Capitalism and Slavery* (London: Andre Deutsch, 1964). The equation of wealth with the authoritative power of imperial whiteness is so omnipresent in this novel that even as a small child Tia says tauntingly to Antoinette: 'Plenty white people in Jamaica. Real white people, they got gold money . . . Old time white people nothing but white nigger now' (10).

11. From the point of view of former slaves, the apprenticeship system was just slavery in a new guise. They were effectively still owned by white masters, only now these were special magistrates paid by the government. See Sue Thomas, *The Worlding of Jean Rhys* (Westport, CN & London: Greenwood Press, 1999) 167–71. See also Angela Smith (*Wide Sargasso Sea* 1997) 133–4.

12. The phrase 'white but not quite' is an intervention into Homi Bhabha's theoretical exposition of his reading of the ambivalence of 'mimicry as ironic compromise'. See his essay 'Of Mimicry and Man: The ambivalence of colonial discourse', Bhabha (1994(b)), 85–92. See especially 86, 89 and 91 for variants of the phrase.

13. Brathwaite (1974), 6 (emphasis in original).

14. Brathwaite (1974), 11.

15. The notion of a creative ambivalence that radiates out from the Caribbean is a theme I explore in the chapters on Jamaica Kincaid's *Lucy*.

16. Brathwaite (1974), 34–5.

17. Brathwaite (1974), 38.

18. Edward Said, *Culture and Imperialism* (New York: Knopf, 1993). See especially 66–7, 295, 278–81, 316–17, 335–6. Importantly for my reading, Said's interpretative strategy stresses the importance of contradiction, ambivalence and the power of metaphor. Indeed, Said's metaphor of musicality echoes through this book which ends with a reading of a short story of Toni Morrison's entitled 'Recitatif'.

19. Said (1993), 66.

20. Charlotte Brontë, *Jane Eyre* [1847] (Oxford & New York: Oxford University Press, 1993) 307.

21. In an interview in the late 1970s, Rhys describes how when she read *Jane Eyre* she had wondered: 'Why should she [Brontë] think Creole women are lunatics . . . What a shame to make Rochester's first wife, Bertha, the awful madwoman . . . I thought I'd try and write her a life.' Quoted in Nancy R. Harrison, *Jean Rhys and the Novel as Women's Text* (Chapel Hill & London: University of North Carolina Press, 1988) 128.

22. Gayatri Chakravorty Spivak, 'Three Women's Texts and a Critique of Imperialism', *Critical Inquiry* 12 (1985): 244.

23. However, Dominick LaCapra, an important historian of trauma, also maintains that while *empathy* can be 'mistakenly conflated with identification or fusion with the other . . . it should rather be understood in terms of an affective relation, rapport, or bond with the other recognized and respected as such', *sympathy* implies 'difference from the discrete other who is the object of pity, charity, or condescension'. LaCapra (2001) 212–3. Here I have used the categories of empathy and sympathy interchangeably because in Rhys's novel they are affective weapons of power that *are* utilised in the same way for the same result.

24. This point is also made by Judith Raiskin but with a completely different focus from mine. Her reading of Rhys's cultural appropriation solely relates to the notion of *zombification* of which she writes interestingly and in great detail. Raiskin (1996), 129–43. Of *marooning* she says little, just a one sentence reference to the possibilities of the word's double reading (132). Mary Lou Emery is the only critic to my knowledge who discusses *marooning* in its fully developed Caribbean meaning. See her monograph *Jean Rhys at*

'World's End': Novels of Colonial and Sexual Exile (Austin: University of Texas Press, 1990) 39–45. However, Emery's reading of maroon history and its connections with Rhys's character Annette, focuses on the betrayals of maroon leaders and so has a completely different political focal point from mine.

25. *Oxford English Dictionary, Vol VI, L–M* (Oxford, Clarendon Press, 1961) 178.
26. See Spillers (1987): 65–81.
27. Antonio Benítez-Rojo, *The Repeating Island: The Caribbean and the Postmodern Perspective*, trans. James Maraniss (Durham & London: Duke University Press, 1992) 254 (emphasis added).
28. Cited in Teresa O'Connor, *Jean Rhys: The West Indian Novels* (New York & London: New York University Press, 1986) 36. The enigmatic insight of *Wide Sargasso Sea* is that racial positioning is *not* always reliant on skin colour that cannot be changed. Instead, the novel highlights the discursive construction of racial subjectivity in all its contradictions, especially the split subjectivity of the white, Caribbean, creole woman.
29. Mavis C. Campbell, *The Maroons of Jamaica 1655–1796: A History of Resistance, Collaboration & Betrayal* (Granby, MA: Bergin & Garvey, 1988) 1. See also Eugene D. Genovese, *From Rebellion to Revolution: Afro-American Slave Revolts in the Making of the Modern World* (New York: Vintage, 1981) especially Chapter 2, 'Black Maroons in War and Peace', 51–81.
30. The root of the word *maroon* is the Spanish *cimarron* which referred to domesticated cattle which escaped to the mountains. Carib Indians who avoided being massacred by the colonisers by also escaping to the mountains were then called *maroons*. However, it was when the African slaves started fleeing the plantations in sizeable numbers, forming communities and engaging with highly effective guerilla tactics against the plantation owners that the term *maroon* became synonymous with successful resistance. Maroon societies have survived on into the present day in Jamaica and Suriname. Continuation of the maroon tradition of resistance to oppression resonate in great freedom fighter icons of the twentieth century such as Marcus Garvey, whose father was a maroon. Campbell (1988), 12. The 'chronic plague' is a quotation taken from Lucien Peytraud, *L'esclavage aux Antilles françaises avant 1789* (Paris, Hachette, 1897) 373, and cited in Richard Price, 'Introduction: Maroons and Their Communities', *Maroon Societies: Rebel Slave Communities in the Americas*, ed. Richard Price (New York: Anchor, 1973) 2.
31. See Campbell (1988), 47.
32. Price (1973), 2.
33. Hardly a decade went by without some kind of large-scale revolt that threatened the white plantocracy. There were two Maroon Wars – the first beginning in 1725 and lasting 15 years, the second from 1784 until 1832 – both of which required the British to sign Treaties to end them. There was, of course, one outrightly successful slave rebellion in the Caribbean led by Touissaint L'Ouverture. See C.L.R. James, *The Black Jacobins: Touissant Louverture and the San Domingo Revolution* (London: Secker and Warburg, 1938).
34. David Spurr, *Rhetoric of Empire: Colonial Discourse in Journalism, Travel Writing, and Imperial Administration* (Durham & London, Duke University Press, 1993) 31.

35. Spurr (1993), 28.
36. Captured slaves came from all over the coastal belt of West Africa. In 1703 there were about 45 000 on Jamaica. By the time the Emancipation Act was ratified in 1834, the slave population on this island alone stood at an estimated 311 070. See Orlando Patterson, *The Sociology of Slavery: An Analysis of the Origins, Development and Structure of Negro Slave Society in Jamaica* (London: MacGibbon & Kee, 1967) 250. In contrast, a census of 1844 stated that only 4 per cent of the population in Jamaica were identified as white.
37. Campbell (1988), 3–4 (emphasis added).
38. These leaders were not always male. The most famous of the female fugitives who became a warrior of great ferocity and leadership was the celebrated Nanny, now a national hero of Jamaica. Campbell (1988), 5, 50–1. Nanny's resistant presence lives on in the fiction of writers such as Michelle Cliff and the poetry of Grace Nichols.
39. In the 1760s Tacky engaged an *obeah* man as a spiritual leader whose delegates spread out among plantations supplying the slaves with a magic powder that made them invincible against the whites' weapons. In the year of the rebellion's planning, the power of rebellious silence among the slaves (strengthened by all conspirators taking the Akan blood oath) meant that the whites were totally unprepared for the uprising. See Benítez-Rojo (1992), 160. However, the rebellion was crushed at great cost of life to the slaves, many of whom chose suicide rather than re-enslavement. As against 60 whites dead, 300–400 slaves were either killed or committed mass suicide. The planters exacted a savage revenge by executing or transporting 600 more slaves. Patterson (1967), 271.
40. Bryan Edwards, *The History, Civil and Commercial, of the British Colonies in the West Indies* (Dublin: Luke White, vol. 2, 1793) 87–8. Cited in Alan Richardson, 'Romantic Voodoo: *Obeah* and British Culture, 1797–1807', *Sacred Possessions: Vodou, Santería, Obeah, and the Caribbean*, eds Margarite Fernández Olmos and Lizabeth Paravisini-Gebert (New Brunswick, NJ: Rutgers University Press, 1997) 174–5.
41. See Richard Hart, *Slaves Who Abolished Slavery, Vol. I, Blacks in Bondage* (Kingston, Jamaica: Institute of Social and Economic Research, University of West Indies, 1980), *Vol. II, Blacks in Rebellion* (1985).
42. Maximilien Laroche describes a zombi thus: 'The zombi, or living-dead, dies only in appearance and is resurrected by those who have created the illusion of his death. Ordinarily, that is according to the most widely held beliefs, a spell is cast on someone who then "dies" and is buried. But in the night following his burial, the one who has cast the spell goes to the cemetery and there, with the aid of the appropriate incantations brings back to life, albeit a lethargic one, the dead man who is not dead but is simply lost in sleep. And from the point on, this dead man who has returned to life, but to a life without any real autonomy, to a larval existence is the property of the person who has killed him. He is thus chained to this master and forced to work for him.' Maximilien Laroche, 'The Myth of the Zombi', *Exile and Tradition: Studies in African and Caribbean Literature*, ed. Rowland Smith (London: Longman & Dalhousie University Press, 1976) 49.
43. Laroche (1976), 55.
44. Laroche (1976), 51.

45. Laroche believes that 'it was apparently the trauma of slavery, transportation from Africa . . . [and] the experience of colonial oppression, which led the Africans . . . to make adjustment in their conception of the living-dead' (58).
46. duCille (1997), 21–56.
47. This is a quotation from Patricia Sharpe, F.E. Mascia-Lee, C.B. Cohen, 'White Women and Black Men: Different Responses to Reading Black Women's Texts', *College English* 52 (February 1990): 146. It appears, and duCille's discussion of it, in duCille (1997), 49.
48. duCille (1997), 29, emphasis added.
49. Judith Herman, in her monograph on trauma written from a feminist perspective, argues that despite the fact that traumatic experiences are very varied, 'the recovery process always follows a common pathway. The fundamental states of recovery are establishing *safety*, reconstructing the trauma story, and restoring the connection between survivors and their community.' *Trauma and Recovery: From Domestic Abuse to Political Terror* (London: Pandora, 1992) 3 (emphasis added). Traumatic events destroy the victim's general belief in safety of self, a sense of safety that is initially established in earliest life in the relationship with the first caretaker, who is most often the mother. Herman (1992), 51.
50. In direct opposition to the idea of concealment in the white safety in metaphor is the key black trope of *testimony* which Henry Louis Gates Jr discusses at length in *The Signifying Monkey: A Theory of African-American Literary Criticism* (New York: Oxford University Press, 1988). See especially, 51–4.
51. Christophine was one of Annette's former husband's wedding presents to her.
52. This is a particularly bitter story of racial betrayal. The order for the massacre is thought to have been given by Philip Warner, Sir Thomas Warner's legitimate (white) son. See Thomas (1999), 173. See also *Wild Majesty: Encounters with Caribs from Colombus to the Present Day*, eds Peter Hulme and Neil L. Whitehead (Oxford: Clarendon Press; New York: Oxford University Press, 1992) 89–106. A related part of the forgotten history is that Massacre was one of the villages that was singled out by white authorities as a site central to the powers of obeah practices. Thomas describes how a 'moral panic' was engendered in the white population by outbreaks of obeah rituals in Massacre which pushed forward the promulgation of The Obeah Act 1904 amid much accompanying publicity. Rhys, Thomas tells us, was 14 at the time of the passing of the Act and would have been well aware of its implications and the fear it engendered among white creoles (158–9).
53. Elaine Savory, *Jean Rhys* (Cambridge: Cambridge University Press, 1998) 135.
54. Savory (1998), 136. Hereby a gender reading completely overrides the racial underpinnings of the metaphor and its power differentials and, in effect, reproduces the logic of Western imperialism in its unthinking appropriation of the difference of the other.
55. Another example that particularly struck me was a chapter on Rhys in a text of literary criticism that focuses on metaphor in women's fiction. The chapter is entitled ' ". . . marooned . . .": Jean Rhys's desolate women' and

yet it overlooks the importance of the metaphor's Afro-Caribbean cultural significance. See Avril Horner and Sue Zlosnik, *Landscapes of Desire: Metaphors in Modern Women's Fiction* (New York & London: Harvester Wheatsheaf, 1990) 133–80.

56. Sandra M. Gilbert and Susan Gubar, *The Madwoman in the Attic: The Woman Writer and the Nineteenth-Century Literary Imagination* (New Haven & London: Yale University Press, 1979) 360. It must also be remembered that the title, which has become iconic of 1970s feminist literary criticism, remains just that, an empty titular gesture. The references to Bertha Mason are always and only in relation to being Jane Eyre's angry and hidden self. Bertha herself was subsumed in her role as 'the dark double' (360) and was never discussed separately as a woman in her own right.

57. Deirdre David interestingly argues that although Bertha Mason is an 'insane, creole white woman from the West Indies [she is] figuratively described as having the obscene propensities of a *black woman*'. Deirdre David, *Rule Britannia: Women, Empire, and Victorian Writing* (Ithaca & London: Cornell University Press, 1995) 95. See also Susan Meyer, *Imperialism at Home: Race and Victorian Women's Fiction* (Ithaca & London: Cornell University Press, 1996) 67, for a similar reading of the narrative construction of Bertha as black.

58. I owe this phrase to Shaobo Xie and his article on postcolonialism in which he argues for an attempt to move beyond Eurocentric ideology, beyond colonialist binary structures of self/Other and, ultimately, beyond any forms of racism. He suggests that 'ethnocentrism [is] a closet monster in every ethnic community and individual'. Shaobo Xie, 'Rethinking the Problem of Postcolonialism', *New Literary History* 28:1 (1997): 17.

59. Williams (1997), 6.

60. See Michael Lambek and Paul Antze, 'Introduction: Forecasting Memory', *Tense Past: Cultural Essays in Trauma and Memory*, eds Paul Antze and Michael Lambek (New York & London: Routledge, 1996) xi–xxxviii. I found this a useful introduction to the social dimension of the psychology of trauma.

61. Iain Chambers, 'History after humanism: responding to postcolonialism', *Postcolonial Studies* 2:1 (1999): 38.

2 Keeping History Safe

1. The quoted phrase is used by Laurence Kirmayer to describe dissociation, a particular form of mental escape from overwhelming trauma. See Laurence J. Kirmayer, 'Landscapes of Memory: Trauma, Narrative, and Dissociation', *Tense Past: Cultural Essays in Trauma and Memory*, eds Paul Antze and Michael Lambek (New York & London: Routledge, 1996) 174.

2. Kirmayer (1996), 186.

3. Kirmayer (1996), 189.

4. Spivak, Sarah Harasym ed. *The Post-Colonial Critic: Interviews, Strategies, Dialogues* (New York & London: Routledge, 1990) 59.

5. Internalised victimhood as a result of the belittling and covering over of the very real traumas of slavery and its legacy of psychic wounding is the subject of my chapters on Toni Morrison's *Sula*.

6. Kirmayer (1996), 148.
7. Jon G. Allen, *Coping with Trauma: A Guide to Self-Understanding* (Washington & London: American Psychiatric Press, 1995) 86–7.
8. Kirmayer (1996), 188.
9. Kirmayer (1996), 174.
10. Elizabeth A. Waites, *Trauma and Survival: Post-Traumatic and Dissociative Disorders in Women* (New York & London: Norton, 1993) 117–18.
11. Kirmayer (1996), 181 (emphasis added).
12. The conflation of imperial ownership of virgin land and the othered female body is a classic example of the use of metaphor as imperial appropriation. See Spurr (1993), 29–31. See also McClintock (1995), 24–8.
13. Deborah Kelly Kloepfer, *The Unspeakable Mother: Forbidden Discourse in Jean Rhys and H.D.* (Ithaca & London: Cornell University Press, 1989) 147–8.
14. There are two types of trauma listed in the psychological literature. Single traumatic events that happen once only, often called 'single-blow trauma', and prolonged and repeated cumulative trauma that may lead the individual to resort to more elaborate strategies of dissociation and repression. Kirmayer (1996), 187. For the differences between repression, suppression and dissociation see Kirmayer (1996), 179.
15. Deirdre Barrett argues that '[d]reams constitute a unique window on trauma and its effects. The window is not clear, however, but prismatic, showing us a changed version of events that is frequently distorted but can also bring chaos into resolution.' Deirdre Barrett ed. 'Introduction', *Trauma and Dreams* (Cambridge MA & London: Harvard University Press, 1996) 1.
16. Caruth provides yet another evocative slant on theories of the traumatic dream that is useful in a reading of Antoinette's dream. In a close reading of Freud's description of the traumatic nightmare, she states: 'the trauma of the nightmare does not simply consist in the experience *within* the dream, but in *the experience of waking from it*. It is the experience of *waking into consciousness* that, peculiarly, is identified with the reliving of the trauma.' Caruth (1996), 64 (emphasis in original). I shall return to this supposition in my reading of *Sula*.
17. Dori Laub and Marjorie Allard maintain that '[t]he absence of an empathetic listener, or more radically, the absence of an *addressable other*, an other who can hear the anguish of one's memories and thus recognize their realness, annihilates the story and destroys the survivor again'. 'History, Memory, and Truth: Defining the Place of the Survivor', *The Holocaust and History: The Known, The Unknown, The Disputed, and The Reexamined*, eds Michael Berenbaum and Abraham J. Peck (Bloomington & Indianapolis: Indiana University Press, 1998), 804.
18. Tia and Antoinette are frequently referred to as two sides of one character, a form of racial *doppelgänger*. This is as reductive an interpretation as Bertha Mason as Jane Eyre's dark double and nothing more. Both readings smother difference into normative whiteness as if the black other could only exist as a shadowy double that enhances white luminosity, especially in a canonical text. It is this kind of literary construction that Toni Morrison deconstructs with her reading of 'American Africanism' in *Playing in the Dark: Whiteness and the Literary Imagination* (1993a). See especially her first essay, 'Black Matters', 1–28.
19. As is so often the case in Rhys's depictions of race, there is an interesting

textual contradiction around the issue of hybridity. Repulsion and abhorrence infuse the representations of Annette's jailers and the albino with negroid features who appears later in the text. However, Antoinette's cousin, Sandi, is also 'coloured', and yet he is affirmed as the only person who can save Antoinette, and the only character besides Christophine who exhibits a secure sense of self.

20. See Allen (1995), 75–6.
21. In the face of witnessing Antoinette's misery, and against her better judgement, Christophine agrees to supply Antoinette with a love potion provided she talks to Rochester and explains how she feels (71–3).
22. Paul de Man, 'The Epistemology of Metaphor', *On Metaphor*, ed. Sheldon Sacks (Chicago and London: University of Chicago Press, 1979) 19.
23. de Man (1979), 19.
24. The use of *catachresis* as a form of tropological resistance in postcolonial theory – as pioneered by Spivak – is informative here. 'Claiming catachreses from a space that one cannot want to inhabit and yet must criticise is, then, the deconstructive predicament of the postcolonial,' Spivak argues. A gestural politics of claiming 'the names that are the legacy of the European Enlightenment (sovereignty, constitutionality, self-determination, nationhood, citizenship, even culturalism) are catachrestical claims, their strategy a displacing and seizing of a previous coding of value.' Gayatri Chakravorty Spivak, *Outside in the Teaching Machine* (New York & London, Routledge, 1993) 64–5. Rhys's strategical use of catachresis, on the other hand, wrests a word from its normative meaning in a manner that, unconsciously or not, endorses the nineteenth-century white creole point of view of the 'rightness' of slavery.
25. LaCapra (1999), 699, n.5.
26. Robert J.C. Young, *Colonial Desire: Hybridity in Theory, Culture and Race* (London & New York: Routledge, 1995) 149.
27. Young (1995), 108.
28. Young (1995), 108.
29. Psychic numbing is an extreme form of psychic arrest. It is a complete cessation of feeling in the face of overwhelming traumatic impact. As a life-consuming feeling of inner deadness, it represents symbolic death, a state of radically impaired existence of an emotionless 'death in life'. Paradoxically, psychic numbing protects the person from a sense of degrading helplessness by keeping the inner self isolated and safe. As stated earlier, it resembles the enforced state of dehumanisation that was effected by slavery. See Robert Jay Lifton, *Death in Life: Survivors of Hiroshima* [1968] (Chapel Hill & London: University of North Carolina Press, 1991) 500–10.
30. See Claire Pajaczkowska and Lola Young, 'Racism, Representation, Psychoanalysis', *'Race', Culture and Difference*, eds James Donald and Ali Rattansi (London: Sage, 1992) especially 201 and 213.
31. Laura E. Ciolowski in her essay, 'Navigating the *Wide Sargasso Sea*: Colonial History, English Fiction, and British Empire', *Twentieth Century Literature* 43:3 (1997): 344–5 also focuses on this connection between racial degeneracy and the hybrid body of this albino boy.
32. *Oxford English Dictionary, Vol III, D-E* (Oxford: Clarendon Press, 1961) 44.
33. Rhys's use of the term *sans culottes* is another example of her colonialist-

constructed catachresis. The term was a class-based appellation used during the French Revolution to refer to extreme republicans. It referred to the fact that these revolutionaries wore long trousers instead of the fashionable knee-breeches worn by aristocrats. Smith (*Wide Sargasso Sea* 1997) 141, n. 49.

34. In her ethnographical exploration on the underground Africanist religious practices of voodoo and obeah in Haiti and Jamaica, Zora Neale Hurston comments on examples of black resistance through 'songs, their Anansi stories and proverbs and dances'. Zora Neale Hurston, *Tell My Horse: Voodoo and Life in Haiti and Jamaica* [1938] (New York: Perennial, 1990) 9. She continues: 'Jamaican proverbs are particularly rich in philosophy, irony and humour' and then provides 12 examples. One of these, which interrelates with Rhys's text, reads: 'Cock roach nebber in de right befo' fowl. (The oppressor always justifies his oppression of the weak)' (9).

35. Brontë (1993 [1847]), 297.

36. Caruth (1995a), 4–5.

37. LaCapra (1999), 722.

38. Naomi Morgenstern, 'Mother's Milk and Sister's Blood: Trauma and the Neo-slave Narrative', *Differences: A Journal of Feminist Cultural Studies* 8:2 (1996): 104–5 (emphasis in original).

3 'Caught between Ghosts of Whiteness': The Other Side of the Story

1. This phrase is Audre Lorde's. It is the second line of one of her poems entitled, 'A Song for Many Movements', which begins: 'Nobody wants to die on the way/caught between ghosts of whiteness'. Audre Lorde, *The Black Unicorn* [1978] (New York: Norton, 1995) 52.

2. Spivak (1993), 226.

3. *Jean Rhys Letters 1931–1966*, eds Francis Wyndham and Diana Melly (London: Penguin, 1985) 297.

4. Given the importance of naming in the novel, there is a certain sense of irony in Rhys's choice for Christophine's surname. Even if Rhys had not heard of W.E.B. Du Bois, many contemporary readers would be well aware of the significance of this name. Moreover, Christophine exhibits many of the hallmarks of Du Bois's exposition of *double-consciousness*, albeit transfigured into female (Caribbean) form. The notion of double-consciousness is a subject to which I shall return in greater detail in later chapters.

5. Spivak (1985), 252.

6. This point is also made by Caroline Rody, 'Burning Down the House: The Revisionary Paradigm of Jean Rhys's *Wide Sargasso Sea*', *Famous Last Words: Changes in Gender and Narrative Closure*, ed. Alison Booth (Charlottesville: University Press of Virginia, 1993) 307.

7. Benita Parry, 'Problems in Current Theories of Colonial Discourse', *Oxford Literary Review* 9 (1987): 38.

8. Patricia Hill Collins, *Black Feminist Thought: Knowledge, Consciousness, and the Politics of Empowerment* (New York & London: Routledge, 1990) see especially 119–23.

9. Hill Collins (1990), 121.

10. I borrow the phrase 'servant/mother' from Rody who states: 'Christophine holds the paradoxical authority of servant/mother to the white heroine'. Rody (1993), 307.

11. Jean Rhys, *Voyage in the Dark* [1934] (London: Penguin, 1969) 27.

12. Jean Rhys, *Smile Please: An Unfinished Autobiography* (London: Penguin, 1981) 42. Her mother's 'indifference' is taken from 43. The trope of the looking-glass textually associated with identity loss and issues of racial displacement is a recurrent theme in *Wide Sargasso Sea*.

13. Bhabha, (1994b) 86, (emphasis added). Mimicry is an especially important concept in the Caribbean partly as a result of the theory's referential relationship with V.S. Naipaul's novel *The Mimic Men*, London: André Deutsch, 1967. However, the concept of cultural mimicry of periphery to metropolis is also a much debated area. See Derek Walcott, 'The Caribbean: Culture or Mimicry?', *Journal of Interamerican Studies and World Affairs* 16:1 (1974a): 3–13.

14. *Abreaction* involves the vivid re-experiencing of a traumatic event or events and their associated effects. As a release of psychic tension that has built up around a trauma, verbalising or acting out the repressed trauma can be extremely painful, the re-enactment likely to be experienced as re-traumatising or re-victimising. See Waites (1993), 220–3.

15. The idea of the (Caribbean) sea as a force that might overcome the symbolic white ship has interesting echoing repercussions in my reading of Jamaica Kincaid's *Lucy*.

16. Sandra Drake, 'All that Foolishness/That All Foolishness: Race and Caribbean Culture as Thematics of Liberation in Jean Rhys's *Wide Sargasso Sea*', *Critica: A Journal of Critical Essays* 2:2 (1990): 97–112 also offers a complex reading of the symbol of the dress in Rhys's novel. However, Drake's focus is different from mine in that she connects the image of the dress with Antoinette's identity and her autonomy (102).

17. Sandi is her 'coloured' cousin with whom she was close until her new step-father forbade their friendship because he could not pass as white. Sandi has an invisible but haunting presence in the text. When Antoinette attributes her graceful act of stone-throwing to his youthful training it gives rise to Rochester's paranoiac jealousy that will ruin any possibility of their happiness. It is also implied that he and Antoinette had an affair before her removal to England.

18. See Brontë (1993 [1847]), 323.

19. It seems that many more critics read the end of the novel as a final resolution of Antoinette's divided subjectivity. Her unequivocal choice, they say, is with the Caribbean side of herself. See for instance Drake (1990), 110. Emery goes as far as to suggest that Antoinette 'transformed into the flying trickster' takes the 'flight [of] *marronage* . . . She can make this choice, not because she has consolidated her character, but because she has lost and multiplied it, become enslaved, and thus joined the history of the blacks on the island, learning from them the traditional means of resistance', Emery (1990), 59.

20. This phrase is Maurice Blanchot's from his *The Writing of Disaster*, [1980] trans. Ann Smock (Lincoln & London: University of Nebraska Press, 1995) 30.

21. See Thorunn Lonsdale, 'Literary Allusion in the Fiction of Jean Rhys', *Caribbean Women Writers: Fiction in English*, eds Mary Condé and Thorunn Lonsdale (New York: St Martin's Press (now Palgrave Macmillan), 1999, 59–66. See also Belinda Edmondson, 'Race, Privilege, and the Politics of (Re)Writing History: An Analysis of the Novels of Michelle Cliff', *Callaloo* 16:1 (1993): 180–91.
22. Caruth (1991), 423.
23. Elspeth Probyn, 'This Body Which Is Not One: Speaking the Embodied Self', *Hypatia* 6:3 (1991): 116.
24. John Frow, 'The Politics of Stolen Time', *Meanjin* 57:2 (1998): 366.

4 *Lucy*: Jamaica Kincaid's Postcolonial Echo

1. Deborah E. McDowell, *'The Changing Same': Black Women's Literature, Criticism and Theory* (Bloomington & Indianapolis: Indiana University Press, 1994) 23.
2. Leslie Garis, 'Through West Indian Eyes', *New York Times Magazine* 7 October 1990): 70.
3. Jamaica Kincaid quoted in Diane Simmons, 'Jamaica Kincaid and the Canon: In Dialogue with *Paradise Lost* and *Jane Eyre*', *Melus* 23:2 (1998): 67.
4. Helen Tiffin, 'Cold Hearts and (Foreign) Tongues: Recitation and the Reclamation of the Female Body in the Works of Erna Brodber and Jamaica Kincaid', *Callaloo* 16:3 (1993): 920, n.7.
5. Jamaica Kincaid, *Lucy* [1990] (London: Picador, 1994) 18. Henceforth, references to Kincaid's text will appear in parentheses in the main text.
6. See, for instance, Alison Donnell, 'Dreaming of Daffodils: Cultural Resistance in the Narratives of Theory', *Kunapipi* 14:2 (1992): 45–52; Helen Tiffin, ' "Flowers of Evil", Flowers of Empire: Roses and Daffodils in the Work of Jamaica Kincaid, Olive Senior and Lorna Goodison', *Span* 46 (1998): 58–71.
7. *The Complete Poems of Thomas Gray: English, Latin and Greek*, ed. H.W. Starr and J.R. Hendrickson (Oxford: Clarendon Press, 1966) 10.
8. Roger Lonsdale, *The Poems of Thomas Gray, William Collins, Oliver Goldsmith* (London: Longmans, 1969) 55. 'Prelapsarian innocence' is Lonsdale's phrase.
9. Lonsdale (1969), 55.
10. My reference to an 'imagined community' refers to Benedict Anderson's oft-cited concept which provides a means of understanding the need of people to form an identity by participating in a group whether a small and localised collectivity such as a school or the wider complications of national identity. However, Anderson's conceptualisation is masculine-dominated. I wish instead to approach the idea of both a literal and a figurative belonging that is both race and gender cognisant. Benedict Anderson, *Imagined Communities: Reflections on the Spread of Nationalism* (London: Verso, 1983).
11. Lonsdale (1969), 10. The emphasis is mine.
12. Ketu H. Katrak, 'Colonialism, Imperialism, and Imagined Homes', eds Cathy N. Davidson, Patrick O'Donnell, Valerie Smith, Christopher P. Wilson, *The Columbia History of the American Novel* (New York: Columbia University Press, 1991) 654.

13. Elleke Boehmer, *Colonial and Postcolonial Literature: Migrant Metaphors* (Oxford & New York: Oxford University Press, 1995) 51.

14. Spivak, 'The Post-Colonial Critic', Harasym (1990) 73.

15. Gauri Viswanathan, 'Milton and Education', *Milton and the Imperial Vision*, eds Balachandra Rajan and Elizabeth Sauer (Pittsburgh, PA: Duquesne University Press, 1999) 273–93.

16. *Backchat* is a word that Lucy uses to describe how her relatives back home in Antigua answer back, as opposed to the black waiters on the train whom she encounters in America, who silently and submissively go about their work (32).

17. Jamaica Kincaid quoted in Kay Bonetti, 'An Interview with Jamaica Kincaid' *Missouri Review* 15:2 (1992): 129.

18. Jamaica Kincaid quoted from an interview with Eleanor Wachtel, 'Eleanor Wachtel with Jamaica Kincaid', *The Malahat Review* 116 (Fall 1996): 66, 67.

19. Sharon Achinstein, 'Imperial Dialectic: Milton and Conquered Peoples', *Milton and the Imperial Vision*, eds Balachandra Rajan and Elizabeth Sauer (Pittsburgh, PA: Duquesne University Press, 1999) 69. The emphasis is Achinstein's.

20. Frank Birbalsingh, *Frontiers of Caribbean Literature in English* (New York: St Martin's Press – now Palgrave Macmillan, 1996) 147. Kincaid describes the enormous influence that not only *Paradise Lost*, but also the biblical books of Genesis and Revelation have had on her writing. She then goes on to state: 'Some people say I've grown up in a paradise. No one growing up in any of these islands [Kincaid was born in Antigua] ever thinks it's a paradise. Everybody who can leave, leaves. So it's not this paradise that's a big influence on me. It's not the physical Antigua. It's *the paradise of mother* in every way: the sort of benign, marvellous, innocent moment you have with the great powerful person who, you then realize, won't let go' (emphasis added).

21. This phrase is a quotation of Edward W. Said (1993), 317.

22. Jamaica Kincaid, *Annie John* (New York: Plume, 1985) 76.

23. See Lizabeth Paravisini-Gebert, *Jamaica Kincaid: A Critical Companion* (Westport, CN & London: Greenwood Press, 1999) 27, 82; Laura Niesen de Abruna, 'Jamaica Kincaid's Writing and the Maternal-Colonial Matrix', *Caribbean Women Writers: Fiction in English*, eds Mary Condé and Thorunn Lonsdale (New York: St Martin's Press – now Palgrave Macmillan, 1999) 174.

24. John Milton, *Paradise Lost* [1667], ed. Christopher Ricks (London: Penguin, 1968) Book IX, 1090–1118, 223. With regard to the importance of the articulation of shame implicit in so many of Milton's colonial references, see Paul Stevens, 'Milton and the New World: Custom, Relativism, and the Discipline of Shame', eds Rajan and Sauer (1999), 90–111.

25. See Jennifer Biddle, 'Shame', *Australian Feminist Studies* 12:26 (1997): 228.

26. See Milton (1968 [1667]), Book IV, 450–88.

27. For a psychological analysis of the connections between shame and narcissism, see Andrew P. Morrison, *Shame: The Underside of Narcissism* (Hove & London: The Analytic Press, 1989).

28. Gayatri Chakravorty Spivak, 'Echo', *The Spivak Reader: Selected Works of Gayatri Chakravorty Spivak*, eds Donna Landry and Gerald MacLean (New

York & London: Routledge, 1996) 176. Spivak contends that the impetus of this essay is to 'give woman' to Echo.

29. See *The Metamorphoses of Ovid*, trans. & ed. Mary M. Innes (London: Penguin, 1955) Book III. The myth of Narcissus and Echo is told in lines 256–510, on pages 83–7.
30. Bonetti (1992), 130.
31. Spillers (1987), 65–81.
32. Spillers (1987), 66, 67–8.
33. Spillers (1987), 68. Proverbs constitute an essential dimension of communication in Africa and the African diaspora, and creating or re-troping already exisiting Anglo-European proverbs is an important part of resistance practices inherent in Black English. See Jack L. Daniel, Geneva Smitherman-Donaldson and Milford A. Jeremiah, 'Makin' A Way Outa No Way: The Proverb Tradition in the Black Experience', *Journal of Black Studies* 17:4 (June 1987): 482–508.
34. Hortense J. Spillers, 'Interstices: A Small Drama of Words', ed. Carole Vance, *Pleasure and Danger: Exploring Female Sexuality* (Boston: Routledge & Kegan Paul, 1984) 84.
35. John Hollander, *The Figure of Echo: A Mode of Allusion in Milton and After* (Berkeley, Los Angeles & London: University of California Press, 1981) 8.
36. Ovid (1955), 84.
37. Ovid (1955), 84.
38. John Brenkman, 'Narcissus in the Text', *Georgia Review* 30 (1976): 297–8.
39. Bhabha outlines his theory of colonial mimicry most clearly in his essay, 'Of Mimicry and Man: The Ambivalence of Colonial Discourse', Bhabha (1994(b)), 85–92. The word echolalia is both a psychiatric term that describes the tendency to repeat mechanically words just spoken by another person which can occur in case of brain damage, mental retardation, and schizophrenia; or it denotes the imitation by an infant of the vocal sounds produced by (maternal) others. I use this word with a sense of irony.
40. Barbara Christian, 'Fixing Methodologies: *Beloved*', *Female Subjects in Black and White: Race, Psychoanalysis, Feminism*, eds Elizabeth Abel, Barbara Christian, Helene Moglen (Berkeley, Los Angeles & London: University of California Press, 1997) 364.
41. Cornel West, 'W.E.B. Du Bois: An Interpretation', *Africana: The Encyclopedia of the African American Experience*, eds Kwame Anthony Appiah and Henry Louis Gates Jr (New York: Basic Civitas Books, 1999) 1974.
42. Du Bois (1989 [1903]), 209.
43. Du Bois (1989 [1903]), 205, 208, 209. See Barbara E. Bowen, 'Untroubled voice: call and response in *Cane*,' *Black Literature and Literary Theory*, ed. Henry Louis Gates Jr (New York & London: Methuen, 1984) 199; Chapter 1, 'African American History and Culture, 1619–1808: The Description of the Conditions of Slavery and Oppression', *Call and Response: The Riverside Anthology of the African American Literary Tradition*, ed. Patricia Liggins Hill (Boston & New York: Houghton Mifflin, 1998) 1–68.
44. Gayl Jones, *Liberating Voices: Oral Tradition in African American Literature* (Cambridge, MA & London: Harvard University Press, 1991).
45. Bernard W. Bell, 'Voices of Double Consciousness in African American Fiction: Charles W. Chestnutt, Zora Neale Hurston, Dorothy West, and

Richard Wright', *Teaching African American Literature: Theory and Practice*, eds Maryemma Graham, Sharon Pineault-Burke and Marianna White Davis (New York & London: Routledge, 1998) 132.

46. Cheryl A. Wall, 'Review of Houston Baker Jr's *Modernism and the Harlem Renaissance* and Melvin Dixon's *Ride Out the Wilderness: Geography and Identity in Afro-American Literature*', *American Literature* 60 (1988): 680.
47. Jones (1991), 197 (emphasis added).
48. Toni Morrison, *Beloved* (London: Picador, 1988) 87–9.
49. Historian Darlene Clark Hine suggests that double-consciousness would become a great deal more complex if both gender and class were also considered important in Du Bois's dialectical model. If the Negro male was to feel his 'two-ness', then, Clarke Hine argues, 'he would have mused about how one ever feels *her* "fiveness"': Negro, American, woman, poor, black woman' (emphasis is mine). Darlene Clark Hine, '"In the Kingdom of Culture": Black Women and the Intersection of Race, Gender, and Class', *Lure and Loathing: Essays on Race, Identity, and the Ambivalence of Assimilation* ed. Gerald Early (New York & London: Penguin, 1994) 338.
50. Du Bois (1989 [1903]), 5.
51. Gates Jr (1988).
52. Jones (1991), 102.
53. Du Bois (1989 [1903]), 217. For a reading of *The Souls of Black Folk* as a classic Enlightenment text, see West (1999), 1967–8.
54. Glissant (1997), 71.

5 The Search for a Voice

1. bell hooks, *Black Looks: Race and Representation* (Boston MA: South End Press, 1992) 167.
2. For a reading of the whiteness of the Virgin Mary in Western culture, see Richard Dyer, *White* (London & New York: Routledge, 1997) 66, 68.
3. Morrison (1993a), 9–10.
4. Spillers (1987), 65.
5. William Wordsworth, 'I Wandered Lonely As A Cloud', *The Selected Poetry and Prose of Wordsworth*, ed. Geoffrey Hartman (New York: Meridian, 1980) 157.
6. Morrison (1993b), 103, 104.
7. This seems particularly pertinent when you read what Thomas Jefferson said of African slaves: 'Their griefs are transient. Those numberless afflictions, which render it doubtful whether heaven has given life to us in mercy or wrath, are less felt, and sooner forgotten with them'. Jefferson went on to explain that this lack of feeling in slaves was the reason why they produced no art or literature: 'Misery is often the parent of the most affecting touches in poetry,' he stated. 'Among blacks is misery enough, God knows, but no poetry'. It would seem that Jefferson's description would be better utilised to describe both his own lack of feeling and any sense of empathy for the traumas inflicted on others. Thomas Jefferson, *The Portable Thomas Jefferson*, ed. Merrill D. Peterson (New York: Penguin, 1977) 187–88, 189. Quoted in Atkinson (2000), 13.
8. Birbalsingh (1996), 143. Her early loving relationship with her mother and

its connection with her mother's immense pride in her precocious reading ability and her love for reading is a frequent trope in Kincaid's interviews, much of the subject matter of which always revolves around her mother. It is the subject to which she incessantly returns, even to the extent that she admits that her mother is 'the person I really write for, I suspect'. Bonetti (1992), 141.

9. Jamaica Kincaid, *My Brother* (New York: Farrar, Straus and Giroux, 1997) 132.
10. See Kristen Mahlis, 'Gender and Exile: Jamaica Kincaid's *Lucy*', *Modern Fiction Studies* 44:1 (1998): 168–9.
11. See Diane Simmons, *Jamaica Kincaid* (New York: Twayne, 1994) 1–2.
12. Quoted in Paravisini-Gebert (1999), 25.
13. Selwyn R. Cudjoe, 'Jamaica Kincaid and the Modernist Project: An Interview', *Callaloo* 12 (1989): 400 and 402.
14. See Allan Vorda, 'An Interview with Jamaica Kincaid', *Mississippi Review* 20 (1991): 12.
15. Kincaid tells an interviewer that the reason Antigua suffers from drought is 'because the English people who settled it cleared it of its rain forest and changed the ecology'. Pamela Buchanan Muirhead, 'An Interview with Jamaica Kincaid', *Clockwatch Review* 9:1–2 (1994–95): 46.
16. Morrison (1993a).
17. George Lipsitz, *The Possessive Investment in Whiteness: How White People Profit from Identity Politics* (Philadelphia, Temple University Press, 1998). Lipsitz's provocative thesis is a confrontational reading of the material effects of white privilege in America and the demonisation of non-white people. He deliberates from a clearly-argued historical perspective that the so-called 'color-blind' public policy contributes to the maintenance of racism: 'Desire for slave labor encouraged European settlers in North America to view, first, Native Americans and, later, African Americans as racially inferior people suited "by nature" for the humiliating subordination of *involuntary servitude*. The long history of the possessive investment in whiteness stems in no small measure from the fact that all subsequent immigrants to North America have come to an already racialized society. From the start, European settlers in North America established structures encouraging such a view of whiteness' (20, emphasis added).
18. hooks (1992), 167–8.
19. For a gender and race-cognisant reading of Paul Gaugin's Melanesian art and the racist discourse that structures art and art history, see Griselda Pollock, *Avant-Garde Gambits 1888–1893: Gender and the Colour of Art History* (London: Thames and Hudson, 1992).
20. For a reading of the status of *white trash* who act as the polluted border between black and white races in America, see John Hartigan, Jr, 'Unpopular Culture: The Case of "White Trash"', *Cultural Studies* 11:2 (1997): 316–43; Annalee Newitz and Matthew Wray, 'What is "White Trash"? Stereotypes and Economic Conditions of Poor Whites in the United States', *Whiteness: A Critical Reader*, ed. Mike Hill (New York & London: New York Univeristy Press, 1997) 168–84.
21. Caryl Phillips, *The European Tribe* [1987] (New York: Vintage, 2000) 2.
22. See Fran Bartkowski, 'Travelers v. Ethnics: Discourses of Displacement', *Discourse* 15:3 (Spring 1993): 169.
23. Important though de Beauvoir's work is, her philosophical destabilising is

predicated on a Eurocentric reading of *sexual* difference alone. More problematic still, is de Beauvoir's reliance on Hegel's model of the master/slave dialectic in her comparison between slavery and women's oppression and her unquestioning repetition of the racist ideology that underpinned American slavery to which she frequently refers. See Margaret A. Simons, *Beauvoir and The Second Sex: Feminism, Race, and the Origins of Existentialism* (Lanham, Maryland & Oxford: Rowman & Littlefield, 1999) 24–8.

6 'The Sea is History'

1. Derek Walcott, 'The Sea Is History', *Collected Poems 1948–1984* (New York: Farrar, Straus & Giroux, 1986) 364–7 (emphasis added). Édouard Glissant uses the title of Walcott's poem (minus the definitive article) as an epigraph to his *Poetics of Relation* (Ann Arbor: University of Michigan Press, 1997).
2. West (1999), 1974.
3. Grace Nichols, *I is a long memoried woman* (London: Caribbean Cultural International, Karnak House, 1983) 31.
4. de Abruna (1999), 178.
5. Tzvetan Todorov, *The Conquest of America* trans. Richard Howard (New York: Harper & Row, 1984) 28.
6. Todorov (1984), 28.
7. Liggins Hill (1998), 14–15. Because of the enforced illiteracy in the slave plantations and the outlawing of their own languages and religions, slaves drew images for songs and tales from biblical epic narratives of the Old Testament that they heard from itinerant preachers and missionaries. Their favourite scriptural heroes were Moses, Joshua, Samson, David who killed Goliath and especially Satan, with his propensity for lying and conjuring tales.
8. Derek Walcott, 'The Muse of History: An Essay', *Is Massa Dead? Black Moods in the Caribbean*, ed. Orde Coombs (London: Anchor Books, 1974b) 11.
9. Proverbs 26: 4–5.
10. Orlando Patterson, *Slavery and Social Death: A Comparative Study* (Cambridge, MA: Harvard University Press, 1982) 338.
11. Barbara Christian, 'The Race for Theory' [1987] rpt. in *Making Face, Making Soul Haciendo Caras: Creative and Critical Perspectives by Feminists of Color*, ed. Gloria Anzaldúa (San Francisco: Aunt Lute Books, 1990) 336.

7 'Knots of Death': Toni Morrison's *Sula*

1. Quoted in Toi Derricotte, *Tender* (Pittsburgh, PA: University of Pittsburgh Press, 1997) 5. The phrase 'knots of death' is Barbara Christian's. See Barbara Christian, *Black Women Novelists: The Development of a Tradition, 1892–1976* (Westport, CN & London: Greenwood Press, 1980b) 163.
2. Toni Morrison, *Sula* [1973] (London: Picador, 1991) 3. References to the novel will appear hereafter in parentheses in the main text.
3. Morrison (1989), 25.
4. For readings of this section, see Chikwenye Okonjo Ogunyemi, 'Sula: "A

Nigger Joke"', *Black American Literature Forum* 13 (1979): 130–3; and Madhu Dubey, *Black Women Novelists and the Nationalist Aesthetic* (Bloomington & Indianapolis: Indiana University Press, 1994) 57, 62.

5. Patricia McKee writes interestingly in relation to this scene about the embodiment of pain in relation to spaces of experience that the white man can and cannot enter. See Patricia McKee, *Producing American Races: Henry James, William Faulkner, Toni Morrison* (Durham & London: Duke University Press, 1999) 151.

6. Christian (1980b), 153.

7. Maureen T. Reddy, 'The Tripled Plot and Center of *Sula*', *Black American Literature Forum* 22:1 (Spring 1988): 29.

8. Morrison describes the importance of the cycle of seasons, of birth and death and natural signs that can be read in her fictive world this way: 'It's an animated world in which trees can be outraged and hurt, and in which the presence or absence of birds is meaningful. You have to be very still to understand these so-called signs, in addition to which they inform you about your behavior.' Charles Ruas, 'Toni Morrison', *Conversations with Toni Morrison*, ed. Danille Taylor-Guthrie (Jackson: University Press of Mississippi, 1994) 100.

9. Barbara Christian, 'Community and Nature: The Novels of Toni Morrison', *Journal of Ethnic Studies* 7:4 (1980a): 67.

10. In general, Morrison stages a harsh critique of black masculinity in *Sula*, but this is always tempered by both a sympathetic and political understanding of the historical structures that resulted in the powerless position of black men in American society.

11. Wendy Harding and Jacky Martin, *A World of Difference: An Inter-Cultural Study of Toni Morrison's Novels* (Westport, CN & London: Greenwood Press, 1994) 89–90.

12. Amanda Smith, 'Toni Morrison', *Publishers Weekly* (21 August 1987): 50. Quoted in Harding and Martin (1994), 90.

13. Geneva Smitherman, *Black Talk: Words and Phrases from the Hood to the Amen Corner* (Boston & New York: Houghton Mifflin, 1994) 68.

14. Zora Neale Hurston, 'Characteristics of Negro Expression' [1934], *African-American Literary Theory: A Reader*, ed. Winston Napier (New York & London: New York University Press, 2000) 40.

15. The entwining of black musical and artistic forms are rarely acknowledged in mainstream white American culture. See Sieglinde Lemke, *Primitivist Modernism: Black Culture and the Origins of Transatlantic Modernism* (Oxford & New York: Oxford University Press, 1998) in which she uncovers a crucial history of white and black intercultural exchange, a phenonemon until quite recently obscured by a cloak of whiteness.

16. The idea of those that can or cannot read black cultural references here is not meant as a statement of self-satisfied superiority. Until I started my research for this chapter, I had no idea what the term cakewalk represented, nor, for that matter, the meaning of a jook, or the allusion to the reading of a community called the Bottom. My intention here is to emphasise the importance of the subversive double-coding through which black Americans communicate with one another in ways that the white population cannot understand. As the whole notion of double-conscious

represents an enforced knowledge of white culture as a survival strategy, it seems to me that it is a matter of respect to other cultures for white outsiders, such as myself, to learn as much as possible about the cultural heritage of those whose literature I am interested in. But it also leaves me open, as it should, to questioning, or even a double-coded 'backchat'.

17. Quoted in Eric J. Sundquist, *To Wake the Nations: Race in the Making of American Literature* (Cambridge, MA & London: The Belknap Press of Harvard University Press, 1993) 278. The cake, Edmonds goes on to relate, would be awarded by the master to the 'couple that did the proudest movement' (278).

18. Sundquist (1993), 278.

19. Paul Gilroy, *The Black Atlantic: Modernity and Double Consciousness* (London & New York: Verso, 1993) 219.

20. Frantz Fanon, *Black Skin, White Masks* [1952] (London: Pluto, 1986) 109, 112, 113.

21. Fanon (1986 [1952]), 112 (emphasis in original).

22. Morrison (1993a), 4 (emphasis added).

23. For an interesting article on the politics of vision in Morrison's oeuvre, see Edward Guerrero, 'Tracking "The Look" in the Novels of Toni Morrison', *Black American Literature Forum* 24:4 (Winter 1990) 761–73, especially 762–4, 766–8.

24. Obioma Nnaemeka, 'Introduction: Imag(in)ing knowledge, power, and sub-version in the margins', *The Politics of (M)Othering: Womanhood, Identity, and Resistance in African Literature* ed. Obioma Nnaemeka (London & New York: Routledge, 1997) 7.

25. Nnaemeka (1997), 7.

26. Nnaemeka (1997), 9.

27. Geneva Smitherman describes the term 'African Holocaust' as '[a]n emerging term among writers, Rappers, and Black activists [which] refers to the enslavement of African people in the United States and throughout the diaspora'. Smitherman (1994), 44.

28. Morrison (1989), 16.

29. Gilroy provides an extreme example of this white 'disinterest' when he quotes Stanley Crouch whose 'acid polemic' includes this reading of *Beloved*: 'Beloved, above all else, is a blackface holocaust novel . . . [that] seems to have been written in order to enter American slavery in the big-time martyr ratings contest.' Stanley Crouch, 'Aunt Medea', in *Notes of a Hanging Judge* (New York: Oxford University Press, 1990) 205. Quoted in Gilroy (1993), 217.

30. See Sigmund Freud, 'Beyond the Pleasure Principle' [1920], *Great Books of the Western World, Vol. 54, The Major Works of Sigmund Freud,* trans. C.J.M. Hubback, ed. Robert Maynard Hutchins (Chicago, London, Toronto & Geneva: William Benton, 1952) 639–63.

31. Cathy Caruth, 'Violence and Time: Traumatic Survivals', *Assemblage: A Journal of Architecture and Design Culture* (Special Issue on Violence and Space) 20 (1993): 24. This quotation refers to Freud's concept of *Nachräglichkeit* and his formulation of the temporal logic of unconsciously enforced 'deferred action'. See Leys (2000), 20–1. This is the basis of what Caruth re-terms as the principle of 'belatedness': 'Traumatic experience, beyond the psychological dimension of suffering suggests a paradox: that

the most direct seeing of a violent event may occur as an absolute inability to know it, that immediacy, paradoxically, may take the form of belatedness. The repetitions of the traumatic event – unavailable to consciousness, but intruding repeatedly on sight – thus suggest a larger relation to the event that extends beyond what can simply be seen or what can be known, and that is inextricably tied up with the belatedness and incomprehensibility that remain at the heart of this repetitive seeing.' Cathy Caruth, 'Traumatic Awakenings', *Performativity and Performance*, ed. Andrew Parker and Eve Kosofsky Sedgwick (New York & London: Routledge, 1995b) 89.

32. Caruth (1993), 24. Caruth goes on to suggest that '[i]t is only in recognizing traumatic experience as a paradoxical relation between destructiveness and survival that we can also recognize the legacy of incomprehensibility at the heart of catastrophic experience.'

33. Caruth (1993), 24.

34. Caruth (1993), 25. I have intentionally broken the textual flow here to suggest the unsettlingness of an abrupt shift in 'linear' progression that is effected by a 'break in the mind's experience of time'.

35. Morrison (1993b), 114.

36. William Hurt Sledge, 'The Therapist's Use of Metaphor', *International Journal of Psychoanalytic Psychotherapy* 6 (1977): 128. See also, Richard Billow, 'Metaphor: A Review of the Psychological Literature', *Psychological Bulletin* 84:1 (1977): 87. Sledge sees the use of metaphor as an heuristic tool because the use of metaphor can represent a form of 'indirect discourse' that allows the person speaking to maintain the necessary distance from conscious awareness of something that may be unspeakable, and at the same time provide a safe vehicle for an unconscious off-loading of latent content (114).

37. Smitherman (1977), 70.

38. Hurston (2000 [1934]), 32.

39. Hurston (2000 [1934]), 32, 33.

40. See Daniel 1–3. See also Karen Stein, ' "I Didn't Even Know His Name": Names and Naming in Toni Morrison's *Sula*', *Names: Journal of the American Name Society* (September 1980): 228.

41. Jill Matus, *Toni Morrison* (Manchester & New York: Manchester University Press, 1998) 55–6. Matus also applies a trauma reading to *Sula* along with all Morrison's other novels. She refers to the straitjacket imagery and to the notion of Shadrack as a generic trauma case, but her focus is different from mine.

42. See Elaine Showalter, *The Female Malady: Women, Madness, and English Culture, 1830–1980* (London: Virago, 1991), Chapter 7 'Male Hysteria: W.H.R. Rivers and the Lessons of Shell Shock', 167–94. It appears that the symptoms of shell-shock took different forms in officers and regular soldiers: 'paralysis, blindness, deafness, contracture of a limb, mutism, limping – appeared primarily among the regular soldiers, while neurasthenic symptoms, such as nightmares, insomnia, heart palpitations, dizziness, depression, or disorientation, were more common among officers' (174). Mutism, the most common shell-shock symptom among regular soldiers, was very rare among officers (175). Interestingly, Shadrack suffers from limping and contracture of a limb, and to a lesser extent a form of mutism, though not

in the sense of being literally silenced, but a silencing of transmittable meaning.

43. Wilfred D. Samuels and Clenora Hudson-Weems, *Toni Morrison* (Boston, Twayne Publishers, 1990) 50. Samuels and Hudson-Weems make the very valuable point that 'he sees a self that is tied to race, the missing, tangible element that must be restored if the whole self – psychological and physical – is to emerge.'

44. *Dictionary of Americanisms: On Historical Principles,* ed. Mitford M. Mathews (Chicago, University of Chicago Press, 1951) 1504.

45. Morrison (1993(b)), 105.

8 Ambivalent Maternal Inheritances

1. Mary Helen Washington, 'Introduction', ed. Mary Helen Washington, *Memory of Kin: Stories About Family by Black Writers* (New York: Doubleday, 1991) 6–7.

2. Faith Pullin, 'Landscapes of Reality: The Fictions of Contemporary Afro-American Women', *Black Fiction: New Studies in the Afro-American Novel since 1945,* ed. A Robert Lee (London: Vision, 1980) 196.

3. Herman (1992), 51.

4. Spillers (1987), 198.

5. See Monika Hoffarth-Zelloe, 'Resolving the Paradox?: An Interlinear Reading of Toni Morrison's *Sula*', *Journal of Narrative Technique* 22:2 (1992): 114.

6. Susan Willis argues that the three-woman household is a trope that 'crops up throughout Morrison's writing to suggest an alternative and utopian possibility for redefining the space and the relationships associated with social reproduction'. Susan Willis, 'Black women writers: taking a critical perspective', *Making a Difference: Feminist Literary Criticism,* ed. Gayle Greene and Coppélia Kahn (London & New York: Routledge, 1985) 234. Of the examples she offers from *The Bluest Eye, Sula* and *Song of Solomon*, Willis believes that 7 Carpenter's Road represents the 'most fully evolved [utopian] vision'. (235).

7. Kai Erikson, 'Notes on Trauma and Community', *American Imago* 48:4 (1991): 460. Erikson differentiates between *individual trauma*, 'a blow to the psyche that breaks through one's defenses so suddenly and with such brutal force that one cannot react to it effectively'; and *collective trauma* by which he means 'a blow to the basic tissues of social life that damages the bonds attaching people together and impairs the prevailing sense of community. The collective trauma works its way slowly and even insidiously into the awareness of those who suffer from it, so it does not have the quality of suddenness normally associated with "trauma"' (459, 460).

8. Caruth (1991), 4. Caruth continues: 'The traumatized person, we might say carries an impossible history within them, or they become themselves a symptom of a history that they cannot entirely possess' (4).

9. Erikson (1991), 466. The emphasis occurs in Erikson's text.

10. Harding and Martin contend that the 'opposed family structures reflect the opposition between two different types of adaptive behaviours to the racial

conflict that is always rampant on the outskirts of the black community. While the Wright family consents to white domination (cf. the railway compartment episode), the Peace household adopts a more exploitative form of semi-independence (cf. the compensation money alleged to have been paid for Eva's amputation)'. Harding and Martin (1994), 43.

11. The allusion to the notion of the 'tragic mulatto' in connection to past maternal inheritances in nineteenth-century black literature is of interest here. See Hazel V. Carby, *Reconstructing Womanhood: The Emergence of the Afro-American Woman Novelist* (New York & Oxford: Oxford University Press, 1987) especially 88–91, 140–1; and Hortense J. Spillers, 'Notes on an alternative model – neither/nor', *The Difference Within: Feminism and Critical Theory*, eds Elizabeth Meese and Alice Parker (Amsterdam & Philadelphia: John Benjamins Publishing, 1989a) 165–87.

12. Patrick Bryce Bjork, *The Novels of Toni Morrison: The Search for Self and Place Within the Community* (New York: Peter Lang, 1992) 61.

13. The train is an ambivalent symbol for it suggests one of the most visible and quotidian sites of the racial segregation and injustice bound up in the Jim Crow laws, and also hope for liberty and a very real possibility of such freedom in the shape of the escape route known as the 'Underground Railway'. See Alonford James Robinson, Jr, 'Underground Railroad', *Africana: The Encyclopedia of the African and African American Experience*, ed. Kwame Anthony Appiah and Henry Louis Gates, Jr (New York: Basic Civitas Books, 1999) 1915–18.

14. Historically, the black church and its appropriation of white Christianity in many forms is the most protected resistant space within black communities. See, for instance, C. Eric Lincoln and Lawrence H. Mamiya, *The Black Church in the African American Experience* (Durham & London: Duke University Press, 1990).

15. Smitherman (1977), 254.

16. See Dubey (1994), 65.

17. Shame and identity formation remain in a very dynamic relation to one another, and as shame comes with an awareness of one's self as fundamentally lacking in some way, it can have a devastating effect on the construction of identity. The impact of culture on individuality, or for that matter the collective identity of a social grouping, is mediated in many ways through the affect of shame. It must therefore be remembered that as the negative views of shame are constituted by the myths and beliefs of the dominant culture in which the person lives, projections of shame can never be separated from racial, sexual and class oppression. See Halina Ablamowicz, 'Shame as Abject Communication: A Semiotic View', *American Journal of Semiotics* 11:3–4 (1994 [1998]): 155–70; Biddle (1997): 227–39.

18. See C. Lynn Munro, 'The Tattooed Heart and the Serpentine Eye: Morrison's Choice of an Epigraph for *Sula*', *Black American Literature Forum* 18 (1984): 152.

19. While the use of the French word *voir* by Helene's mother, Rochelle, is in fact a condensation of the farewell, *au revoir*, 'Voir' is also the imperative form of the French verb *voir* which in translation means to see, to behold or to inspect, and thus suggests a command to look. For a reading of the politics of the visual economy in *Sula*, see Helena Michie, *Sororophobia:*

Differences Among Women in Literature and Culture (New York & Oxford: Oxford University Press, 1992) 164–8, and for a discussion of the scene that threads around the command to look, see 159.

20. See especially passages in *Sula* on 170 and 110.

21. For a careful discussion of the double-voicing of African-American literature, and especially as it relates to Morrison, see Marc C. Conner, 'Introduction: Aesthetics and the African American Novel', *The Aesthetics of Toni Morrison: Speaking the Unspeakable*, ed. Marc C. Conner (Jackson: University of Mississippi Press, 2000) xix–xx.

22. Morrison (1987), 103.

23. Morrison (1987), 109–10.

24. Morrison (1987), 110.

25. 'Both in the old-time black Gospel song and in black street vernacular, "gittin ovuh" has to do with surviving. While the religious usage of the phrase speaks to spiritual survival in a sinister world of sin, its secular usage speaks to material survival in a white world of oppression . . . In Black America, the oral tradition has served as a fundamental vehicle for gittin ovuh.' Smitherman (1977), 73. See also Smitherman (1994), 124. She lists the term here as 'git ovah'.

26. For a reading of the notion of 'body memories' and the embodiment of traumatic memory, see Roberta Culbertson, 'Embodied Memory, Transcendence, and Telling: Recounting Trauma, Re-establishing the Self', *New Literary History* 26 (1995): 169–95.

27. In a small vignette in her essay that connects memory to writing, Morrison draws an evocative picture of how 'Hannah Peace' came to be created, which very much suggests the magnetism of the unsaid that surrounds characters like Hannah and Rochelle. See Morrison (1987), 116.

28. Here again we have another metaphoric connection between sewing, seeing and female distress.

29. J. Brooks Bouson, *Quiet As It's Kept: Shame Trauma, and Race in the Novels of Toni Morrison* (Albany: State University of New York Press, 2000) 52.

30. The position of the ambivalent narratee is a theme that I will explore in more detail in my conclusion that is a reading of Morrison's short story 'Recitatif'.

31. Brooks Bouson (2000), 62.

32. Madhu Dubey states that 'Sula's refusal of reproduction is her greatest point of difference from her community; it is what renders her evil and unnatural to the people of the Bottom'. Dubey (1994), 58. Morrison, commenting on Sula's act of placing her grandmother in a home states in an interview: 'That's more unforgivable than anything else she does, because it suggests a lack of her sense of community.' Anne Koenen, 'The One Out of Sequence', *Conversations with Toni Morrison*, ed. Danille Taylor-Guthrie (Jackson: University of Mississippi, 1994) 68.

9 The 'Gift for Metaphor'

1. Chimalum Nwankwo, '"I is": Toni Morrison, the Past, and Africa', *Of Dreams Deferred, Dead or Alive: Perspectives on African-American Writers*, ed. Femi Ojo-Ada (Westport, CN & London: Greenwood Press, 1996) 175.

2. Spillers (1987), 184.
3. Spillers (1987), 184.
4. Alice Walker, 'In Search of Our Mothers' Gardens', [1974] *In Search of Our Mothers' Gardens: Womanist Prose* (London: The Women's Press, 1992) 234, 241.
5. Renita Weems, ' "Artists Without Art Form": A Look at One Black Woman's World of Unrevered Black Women', [1979] *Home Girls: A Black Feminist Anthology*, ed. Barbara Smith (New York: Kitchen Table: Women of Color Press, 1983) 97.
6. Herman (1992), 55.
7. Robert Grant, 'Absence into Presence: The Thematics of Memory and "Missing" Subjects in Toni Morrison's *Sula*', *Critical Essays on Toni Morrison* ed. Nellie Y. McKay (Boston: G.K. Hall, 1988) 98.
8. Deborah McDowell, 'New Directions for Black Feminist Criticism' [1980], *'The Changing Same': Black Women's Literature, Criticism, and Theory* (Bloomington & Indianapolis: Indiana University Press, 1995) 13.
9. McDowell (1995 [1980]), 13.
10. McDowell (1995 [1980]), 13.
11. McKee (1999), 165.
12. This phrase is Karla Holloway's. See Holloway (1995), 103.
13. Matus (1998), 67.
14. Barbara Johnson, ' "Aesthetic" and "rapport" in Toni Morrison's *Sula*', *Textual Practice* 7:2 (1993): 168.
15. For the distinguishing features of melancholia and mourning in the economy of pain, see Sigmund Freud, 'Mourning and Melancholia', *On the History of the Psycho-Analytic Movement, Papers on Metapsychology and Other Works*, The Standard Edition of the Complete Psychological Works of Sigmund Freud, trans. James Strachey, Vol XIV (1914–16) (London, The Hogarth Press, 1957), 243–58, especially, 244.
16. Alan J. Rice, ' "It Don't Mean a Thing If It Ain't Got That Swing": Jazz's Many Uses for Toni Morrison', *Black Orpheus: Music in African American Fiction from the Harlem Renaissance to Toni Morrison*, ed. Saadi A. Simawe (New York & London: Garland, 2000) 173.
17. Alan Rice also makes this point. Rice (2000), 174.
18. Geneva Smitherman describes this colour as used as a fairly neutral term for a white person. However, the connection between grey and white comes, Smitherman believes, from the grey colour of Confederate army uniforms, and if this is the case, she says, it 'originally must have referred to white racial supremacists'. Smitherman (1994), 129.
19. Caruth (1991), 417.
20. Caruth (1991), 417.
21. I borrowed this application of Caruth's trauma theory from Linda Anderson's lucid and very succinct outline of how testimonies and the trauma theory that underlines them work in autobiographical writing. See Linda Anderson, *Autobiography* (London & New York: Routledge, 2001) 129.
22. LaCapra (1999), 725.
23. LaCapra (1999), 698.
24. Eliezer Witzum, Haim Dasberg, Abraham Bleich, 'Use of a Metaphor in the Treatment of Combat-induced Posttraumatic Stress Disorder: Case Report', *American Journal of Psychotherapy* XL:3 (1986): 458.

25. Johnson (1993), 167.
26. This phrase is Allan Young's which I have taken from his essay, 'Bodily Memory and Traumatic Memory', *Tense Past: Cultural Essays in Trauma and Memory*, eds Paul Antze and Michael Lambek (New York & London: Routledge, 1996) 97 (emphasis in original).
27. Deborah E. McDowell, ' "The Self and the Other": Reading Toni Morrison's *Sula* and the Black Female Text', *Critical Essays on Toni Morrison*, ed. Nellie Y. McKay (Boston: G.K. Hall, 1988) 85.
28. Trudier Harris, *Fiction and Folklore: The Novels of Toni Morrison*, (Knoxville: University of Tennessee Press, 1991) 1, 68, 84.
29. Smitherman describes the long and painful process of straightening 'nappy' hair with a heated iron comb and other procedures. As Smitherman goes on to stress, the 'psychic pain caused by all this black self-hatred was far worse than all the hot combing and lye in the world'. Smitherman (1977), 64–7. The quotation appears on 66. Morrison makes intermittent references to the practices of hair straightening in the novel: from the image of the community women leaning back on the sink trays in Irene's Palace of Cosmetology to have their hair lathered in Nu Nile, to Helene's enforced hot combing of Nel's hair as a child.
30. Smitherman (1994), 122.
31. See Carole Anne Taylor, *The Tragedy and Comedy of Resistance: Reading Modernity Through Black Women's Fiction* (Philadelphia: University of Pennsylvania Press, 2000) 42–3.
32. Zora Neale Hurston, *Their Eyes Are Watching God* [1937] (London: Virago, 1992) 17.
33. Toni Morrison, *The Bluest Eye* [1970] (London: Chatto & Windus, 1993c) 11.
34. Karla F.C. Holloway, *Moorings & Metaphors: Figures of Culture and Gender in Black Women's Literature* (New Brunswick, NJ: Rutgers University Press, 1992) 137.
35. Hurston (1992 [1937]), 286.

Conclusion

1. Audre Lorde, *The Marvelous Arithmetics of Distance: Poems 1987–1992* (New York & London: Norton, 1993) 7 (emphasis added).
2. Audre Lorde, 'The Transformation of Silence into Language and Action', *Sister Outsider: Essays and Speeches* (Freedom, CA: The Crossing Press, 1984) 40–4. Lorde's self-reflexive positioning suggested by the term *sister outsider* has both political and personal implications. Gloria Hull describes Lorde's choice this way: 'When Lorde names herself "sister outsider", she is *claiming the extremes of a difficult identity*. I think we tend to read the two terms with a diacritical slash between them – in an attempt to make some separate, though conjoining, space. But Lorde has placed herself on that line between either/or and both/and of "sister outsider" – and then erased her chance for rest or mediation. However, the charged field between the two energies remains strong, constantly suggested by the frequency with which edges, lines, borders, margins, boundaries, and the like appear as significant

figures in her work.' Gloria T. Hull, 'Living on the Line: Audre Lorde and *Our Dead Behind Us', Changing Our Own Words: Essays on Criticism, Theory, and Writing by Black Women,* ed. Cheryl A. Wall (London: Routledge, 1990) 154 (emphasis added).

3. There is a wonderful moment in this essay when Lorde, struggling with the knowledge that the transformation of silence into language and action is necessarily an often painful act of self-revelation, discusses it with her daughter who responds with a delightful and trusting openness that helps her to proceed. Lorde (1984), 42.

4. Lorde (1984), 41.

5. Lorde (1984), 44 (emphasis added).

6. Evelynn M. Hammonds, 'Toward a Genealogy of Black Female Sexuality: The Problematic of Silence', *Feminist Genealogies, Colonial Legacies, Democratic Futures,* eds M. Jacqui Alexander and Chandra Talpade Mohanty (New York & London: Routledge, 1997) 180.

7. *Scream* is also an important word in Toni Morrison's short story to which I refer below.

8. Gilroy (1996), 203. In the last chapter of his book, Gilroy argues that black people have not yet adequately dealt with the traumas of slavery. The 'condition of being in pain' derives from the historical conditions of slavery and its legacies but it is often an unspoken and unassimilated and therefore negative grief that carries over into contemporary black culture.

9. Smith (1987), 5.

10. The song is quoted in Angela Y. Davis, *Blues Legacies and Black Feminism: Gertrude 'Ma' Rainey, Bessie Smith and Billie Holiday* (New York: Pantheon, 1998) 181. There is an eerie undercurrent of silence to the words 'Black bodies swing . . . in the Southern breeze' (181). The imagery of silence captures the notion of haunting that is so significant to the idea of recapturing and re-engaging with memories of historical trauma.

11. Toni Morrison, 'Recitatif', *Confirmation: An Anthology of African American Women,* eds Amiri Baraka (LeRoi Jones) and Amina Baraka (New York: William Morrow, 1983) 243–61. Any further references to Morrison's short story will appear in parentheses in the main text.

12. Elizabeth Abel in her essay, 'Black Writing, White Reading: Race and the Politics of Feminist Interpretation', *Critical Inquiry* 19 (1993): 470–98 – in which she uses 'Recitatif' to open and conclude her argument – maintains that it is Twyla's and Roberta's very different assumptions about the colour of Maggie's body that provides the racial 'clues for our readings of them, readings that emanate similarly from our own cultural locations' (472). However, while Abel's article is admirable in many ways for its courageous exposition of her own race-bound ways of reading, it is also problematic. Both her fascination with attaching whiteness or blackness to Twyla or Roberta, and her methodology of juxtaposing her white reading as against her black female colleague's black reading (Abel ascertains that Twyla is white, her 'black feminist critic' friend Lula Fragd is 'equally convinced that she is black' (471)) is in fact a replication of the divisive racial politics I think Morrison is trying to undo.

13. Kalpana Seshadri-Crooks outlines the same kind of structural details, but her focus is on a Lacanian reading, while mine is more concerned with the

racialisation of the trauma narrative. See *Desiring Whiteness: A Lacanian Analysis of Race* (London & New York: Routledge, 2000) 144.

14. In an interview with Claudia Tate, Morrison implies that all her readers should actively participate in the deconstruction of the fixed meanings that demean women of color: 'My writing expects, demands participatory reading . . . It is not just about telling the story; it is about involving the reader . . . My language has to have holes and spaces so the reader can come into it . . . The we (you, the reader, and I, the author) come together to make this book, to feel the experience.' *Black Women Writers at Work*, ed. Claudia Tate (New York: Continuum, 1985) 125.

15. Seshadri-Crooks (2000), 149.

16. *Dumped* is one of the repeating words in the text that carries the symbolic weight of trauma, but its meaning changes during the course of the story. Another repeated word is *shelter*, a third, *introduce*.

17. The 'ugly green slacks' that shame Twyla is a trope that repeats throughout the story, as is Roberta's mother's oversized cross. However, the icon of clothing in which most of the ambivalent pathos in the story is invested is Maggie's hat with its long ear flaps which suggest both the longing and the need to shut out the verbal abuse to which she is constantly subjected. In Twyla's words: 'She wore this really stupid little hat – a kid's hat with ear flaps . . . A really awful little hat. Even for a mute, it was dumb – dressing like a kid and never saying anything at all' (245).

18. The concept of *abjection* is usefully theorised by Julia Kristeva in her *Powers of Horror: An Essay on Abjection* trans. Leon S. Roudiez (New York: Columbia University Press, 1982). However, it is important to note that Kristeva has been admonished for her silencing of the subaltern voice in *About Chinese Women*, [1977] trans. Anita Barrows (New York: Marion Boyars, 1986).

19. Kristeva (1982), 4, 9.

20. Rinaldo Walcott, 'Pedagogy and Trauma: The Middle Passage, Slavery, and the Problem of Creolization', *Between Hope and Despair: Pedagogy and the Remembrance of Historical Trauma*, eds Roger I. Simon, Sharon Rosenberg and Claudia Eppert (Lanham, Boulder, New York & Oxford: Rowman & Littlefield, 2000) 137.

21. Walcott (2000), 137.

22. Walcott (2000), 137. Walcott is quoting Deborah P. Britzman, *Lost Subjects, Contested Objects: Toward a Psychoanalytic Inquiry of Learning* (Albany: State University of New York Press, 1998) 133 (emphasis added).

23. See Abel, Christian and Moglen (1997), 1–2 (emphasis added).

Bibliography

Abel, Elizabeth, Christian, Barbara and Moglen, Helene. 'Introduction: The Dream of a Common Language'. *Female Subjects in Black and White: Race, Psychoanalysis, Feminism*, Abel, Elizabeth, Christian, Barbara and Moglen, Helene (eds). Berkeley, Los Angeles & London: University of California Press, 1997, 1–18.

Abel, Elizabeth. 'Black Writing, White Reading: Race and the Politics of Feminist Interpretation'. *Critical Inquiry* 19 (1993): 470–98.

Ablamowicz, Halina. 'Shame as Abject Communication: A Semiotic View'. *The American Journal of Semiotics* 11:3–4 (1994 [1998]): 155–70.

Achinstein, Sharon. 'Imperial Dialectic: Milton and Conquered Peoples'. *Milton and the Imperial Vision*, Rajan, Balachandra and Sauer, Elizabeth (eds). Pittsburgh, PA: Duquesne University Press, 1999, 67–89.

Ahmed, Sara and Stacey, Jackie. 'Testimonial Cultures: An Introduction'. *Cultural Values* 5:1 (2001): 1–6.

Ahmed, Sara. *Strange Encounters: Embodied Others in Post-coloniality*. London & New York: Routledge, 2000.

Alarcón, Norma. 'The Theoretical Subject(s) of *This Bridge Called My Back* and Anglo-American Feminism'. *Criticism in the Borderlands: Studies in Chicano Literature, Culture and Ideology*, Calderon, Héctor and Saldivar, José David (eds). Durham & London: Duke University Press, 1991, 28–39.

Alcoff, Linda Martín. 'What Should White People Do?' *Hypatia* 13:3 (1998): 6–26.

Allen, Jon G. *Coping with Trauma: A Guide to Self-Understanding*. Washington & London: American Psychiatric Press, 1995.

Anderson, Benedict. *Imagined Communities: Reflections on the Spread of Nationalism*. London: Verso, 1983.

Anderson, Linda. *Autobiography*. London & New York: Routledge, 2001.

Antze, Paul and Lambek, Michael (eds). *Tense Past: Cultural Essays in Trauma and Memory*. New York & London: Routledge, 1996.

Ashley, Clifford W. *The Ashley Book of Knots*. New York: Doubleday, 1946.

Atkinson, Yvonne. 'Language That Bears Witness: The Black English Oral Tradition in the Works of Toni Morrison'. *The Aesthetics of Toni Morrison: Speaking the Unspeakable*. Conner, Marc C. (ed.). Jackson: University of Mississippi, 2000, 12–30.

Barrett, Deirdre (ed.), 'Introduction'. *Trauma and Dreams*. Cambridge MA & London: Harvard University Press, 1996, 1–6.

Bartkowski, Fran. 'Travelers v. Ethnics: Discourses of Displacement'. *Discourse* 15:3 (1993): 158–76.

Bell, Bernard W. 'Voices of Double Consciousness in African American Fiction: Charles W. Chestnutt, Zora Neale Hurston, Dorothy West, and Richard Wright'. *Teaching African American Literature: Theory and Practice*. Graham, Maryemma, Pineault-Burke, Sharon and White Davis, Marianna (eds). New York & London: Routledge, 1998, 132–40.

Benítez-Rojo, Antonio. *The Repeating Island: The Caribbean and the Postmodern*

Perspective. Trans. Maraniss, James. Durham & London: Duke University Press, 1992.

Bennefield, Robin. 'Whiteness Studies: Deceptive or Welcome Discourse?' *Black Issues in Higher Education* 16:6 (1999): 26–7.

Bhabha, Homi K. 'Introduction: Locations of culture'. *The Location of Culture*. London & New York: Routledge, 1994a, 1–18.

Bhabha, Homi K. 'Of Mimicry and Man: The ambivalence of colonial discourse'. [1984]. *The Location of Culture*. London & New York: Routledge, 1994b, 85–92.

Bhabha, Homi K. 'The White Stuff'. *Artforum* 36:9 (1998): 21–4.

Biddle, Jennifer. 'Shame'. *Australian Feminist Studies* 12:26 (1997): 227–39.

Billow, Richard. 'Metaphor: A Review of the Psychological Literature'. *Psychological Bulletin* 84:1 (1977): 81–92.

Birbalsingh, Frank. *Frontiers of Caribbean Literature in English*. New York: St Martin's Press (now Palgrave Macmillan), 1996.

Bjork, Patrick Bryce. *The Novels of Toni Morrison: The Search for Self and Place Within the Community*. New York: Peter Lang, 1992.

Blanchot, Maurice. *The Writing of Disaster*. [1980] Trans. Smock, Ann. Lincoln & London: University of Nebraska Press, 1995.

Boehmer, Elleke. *Colonial and Postcolonial Literature: Migrant Metaphors*. Oxford & New York: Oxford University Press, 1995.

Bonetti, Kay. 'An Interview with Jamaica Kincaid'. *Missouri Review* 15:2 (1992): 123–42.

Bouson, J. Brooks. *Quiet As It's Kept: Shame Trauma, and Race in the Novels of Toni Morrison*. Albany: State University of New York Press, 2000.

Bowen, Barbara E. 'Untroubled voice: call and response in *Cane*'. *Black Literature and Literary Theory*. Gates Jr, Henry Louis (ed.). New York & London: Methuen, 1984, 187–203.

Brah, Avtar. *Cartographies of Diaspora: Contesting Identities*. London & New York: Routledge, 1996.

Braidotti, Rosi. 'The politics of ontological difference'. *Between Feminism & Psychoanalysis*. Brennan, Teresa (ed.). London & New York: Routledge, 1990, 89–105.

Brathwaite, Edward. *Contradictory Omens: Cultural Diversity and Integration in the Caribbean*. Mona: Savacou Publications, 1974.

Brenkman, John. 'Narcissus in the Text'. *Georgia Review* 30 (1976): 293–327.

Britzman, Deborah P. *Lost Subjects, Contested Objects: Toward a Psychoanalytic Inquiry of Learning*. Albany: State University of New York Press, 1998.

Brontë, Charlotte. *Jane Eyre* [1847]. Oxford & New York: Oxford University Press, 1993.

Brown, Laura S. 'Not Outside the Range: One Feminist Perspective on Psychic Trauma'. *American Imago* 48:1 (1991): 119–33.

Buchanan, Pamela Muirhead. 'An Interview with Jamaica Kincaid'. *Clockwatch Review* 9(1–2) (1994–95): 38–48.

Bullock, Alan and Trombley, Stephen (eds), *The New Fontana Dictionary of Modern Thought*. London: HarperCollins, 2000.

Campbell, Mavis C. *The Maroons of Jamaica 1655–1796: A History of Resistance, Collaboration & Betrayal*. Granby, MA: Bergin & Garvey, 1988.

Carby, Hazel V. *Reconstructing Womanhood: The Emergence of the Afro-American Woman Novelist*. New York & Oxford: Oxford University Press, 1987.

Carr, Helen. *Jean Rhys*. Plymouth, UK: Northcote House, 1996.

Caruth, Cathy. 'Introduction'. *American Imago* 48:1 (1991): 1–12 and 417–24.

Caruth, Cathy. 'Violence and Time: Traumatic Survivals'. *Assemblage: A Journal of Architecture and Design Culture* (Special Issue on Violence and Space) 20 (1993): 24–5.

Caruth, Cathy. 'Introduction'. *Trauma: Explorations in Memory*. Caruth, Cathy (ed.). Baltimore & London: Johns Hopkins University Press, 1995a, 3–12.

Caruth, Cathy. 'Traumatic Awakenings'. *Performativity and Performance*. Parker, Andrew and Kosofsky Sedgwick, Eve (eds). New York & London: Routledge, 1995b, 89–108.

Caruth, Cathy. *Unclaimed Experience: Trauma, Narrative, and History*. Baltimore & London: Johns Hopkins University Press, 1996.

Cary, Lorene. *Black Ice*. New York: Vintage, 1991.

Chambers, Iain. 'History after humanism: responding to postcolonialism'. *Postcolonial Studies* 2:1 (1999): 37–42.

Chodorow, Nancy. *The Reproduction of Mothering: Psychoanalysis and the Sociology of Gender*. Berkeley, Los Angeles & London: University of California Press, 1978.

Christian, Barbara. 'Community and Nature: The Novels of Toni Morrison'. *Journal of Ethnic Studies* 7:4 (1980a): 65–78.

Christian, Barbara. *Black Women Novelists: The Development of a Tradition, 1892–1976*. Westport, CN & London: Greenwood Press, 1980b.

Christian, Barbara. 'The Race for Theory'. [1987] rpt. in *Making Face, Making Soul Haciendo Caras: Creative and Critical Perspectives by Feminists of Color*. Anzaldúa, Gloria (ed.). San Francisco: Aunt Lute Books, 1990, 335–45.

Christian, Barbara. 'Fixing Methodologies: *Beloved*'. *Female Subjects in Black and White: Race, Psychoanalysis, Feminism*. Abel, Elizabeth, Christian, Barbara and Moglen, Helene (eds). Berkeley, Los Angeles & London: University of California Press, 1997, 363–70.

Ciolowski, Laura E. 'Navigating the *Wide Sargasso Sea*: Colonial History, English Fiction, and British Empire'. *Twentieth Century Literature* 43:3 (1997): 339–59.

Clark, Christine and O'Donnell, James (eds), *Becoming and Unbecoming White: Owning and Disowning a Racial Identity*. Westport, CN & London: Bergin & Garvey, 1999.

Clark Hine, Darlene. ' "In the Kingdom of Culture": Black Women and the Intersection of Race, Gender, and Class'. *Lure and Loathing: Essays on Race, Identity, and the Ambivalence of Assimilation*. Early, Gerald (ed.). New York & London: Penguin, 1994, 337–51.

Conner, Marc. C. 'Introduction: Aesthetics and the African American Novel'. *The Aesthetics of Toni Morrison: Speaking the Unspeakable*. Conner, Marc C. (ed.). Jackson: University of Mississippi Press, 2000, ix–xxviii.

Crouch, Stanley. 'Aunt Medea'. *Notes of a Hanging Judge*. New York: Oxford University Press, 1990, 205.

Cudjoe, Selwyn R. 'Jamaica Kincaid and the Modernist Project: An Interview'. *Callaloo* 12 (1989): 396–411.

Culbertson, Roberta. 'Embodied Memory, Transcendence, and Telling: Recounting Trauma, Re-establishing the Self'. *New Literary History* 26 (1995): 169–95.

Daniel, Jack L., Smitherman-Donaldson, Geneva and Jeremiah, Milford A. 'Makin' A Way Outa No Way: The Proverb Tradition in Black Experience'. *Journal of Black Studies* 17:4 (1987): 482–508.

David, Deirdre. *Rule Britannia: Women, Empire, and Victorian Writing*. Ithaca & London: Cornell University Press, 1995.

Davis, Angela Y. *Blues Legacies and Black Feminism: Gertrude 'Ma' Rainey, Bessie Smith and Billie Holiday*. New York: Pantheon, 1998.

de Abruna, Laura Niesen. 'Jamaica Kincaid's Writing and the Maternal-Colonial Matrix'. *Caribbean Women Writers: Fiction in English*. Condé, Mary and Lonsdale, Thorunn (eds). New York: St Martin's Press (now Palgrave Macmillan), 1999, 172–83.

de Man, Paul. 'The Epistemology of Metaphor'. *On Metaphor*. Sacks, Sheldon (ed.). Chicago and London: University of Chicago Press, 1979, 11–28.

Delgado, Richard and Stefancic, Jean (eds). *Critical White Studies: Looking Behind the Mirror*. Philadelphia: Temple University Press, 1997.

Derricotte, Toi. *Tender*. Pittsburgh, PA: University of Pittsburgh Press, 1997.

Derrida, Jacques. *The Truth in Painting*. Trans. Bennington, Geoff and McLeod, Ian. Chicago & London: University of Chicago Press, 1987.

Dimen, Muriel. 'In the Zone of Ambivalence: A Journal of Competition'. *Feminist Nightmares, Women at Odds: Feminism and the Problem of Sisterhood*. Weisser, Susan Ostrov and Fleischner, Jennifer (eds). New York & London: New York University Press, 1994, 358–91.

Donnell, Alison. 'Dreaming of Daffodils: Cultural Resistance in the Narratives of Theory'. *Kunapipi* 14:2 (1992): 45–52.

Drake, Sandra. 'All that Foolishness/That All Foolishness: Race and Caribbean Culture as Thematics of Liberation in Jean Rhys's *Wide Sargasso Sea*'. *Critica: A Journal of Critical Essays* 2:2 (1990): 97–112.

Du Bois, W.E.B. *The Souls of Black Folk* [1903]. New York & London: Penguin, 1989.

Dubey, Madhu. *Black Women Novelists and the Nationalist Aesthetic*. Bloomington & Indianapolis: Indiana University Press, 1994.

duCille, Ann. 'The Occult of True Black Womanhood: Critical Demeanor and Black Feminist Studies' [1994]. *Female Subjects in Black and White: Race, Psychoanalysis, Feminism*. Abel, Elizabeth, Christian, Barbara and Moglen, Helene (eds). Berkeley, Los Angeles & London: University of California Press, 1997, 21–56.

Dyer, Richard. *White*. London & New York: Routledge, 1997.

Edmondson, Belinda. 'Race, Privilege, and the Politics of (Re)Writing History: An Analysis of the Novels of Michelle Cliff'. *Callaloo* 16:1 (1993): 180–91.

Edwards, Bryan. *The History, Civil and Commercial, of the British Colonies in the West Indies*. Dublin: Luke White, Vol. 2, 1793.

Emery, Mary Lou. *Jean Rhys at 'World's End': Novels of Colonial and Sexual Exile*. Austin: University of Texas Press, 1990.

Erikson, Kai. 'Notes on Trauma and Community'. *American Imago* 48:4 (1991): 455–72.

Fanon, Frantz. *Black Skin, White Masks* [1952]. London: Pluto, 1986.

Farrell, Kirby. *Post-traumatic Culture: Injury and Interpretation in the Nineties*. Baltimore & London: Johns Hopkins University Press, 1998.

Felman, Shoshana and Laub, Dori. *Testimony: Crisis of Witnessing in Literature, Pyschoanalysis, and History*. New York: Routledge, 1992.

Flagg, Barbara J. ' "Was Blind, But Now I See": White Race Consciousness and the

Requirement of Discriminatory Intent'. *Michigan Law Review* 91:5 (1993): 953–1017.

Frankenberg, Ruth. *White Women, Race Matters: The Social Construction of Whiteness*. London & Minneapolis: Routledge and University of Minnesota Press, 1993.

Frankenberg, Ruth. *Displacing Whiteness: Essays in Social and Cultural Criticism.* Durham & London: Duke University Press, 1997.

Frankenberg, Ruth and Mani, Lata. 'Crosscurrents, Crosstalk: Race, "Postcoloniality" and The Politics of Location'. *Cultural Studies* 7 (1993): 292–310.

Freud, Sigmund. 'Beyond the Pleasure Principle' [1920]. *Great Books of the Western World, Vol. 54: The Major Works of Sigmund Freud.* Trans. Hubback, C.J.M. Hutchins, Robert Maynard (ed.). Chicago, London, Toronto & Geneva: William Benton, 1952, 639–63.

Freud, Sigmund. 'Mourning and Melancholia'. *On the History of the Psycho-Analytic Movement, Papers on Metapsychology and Other Works.* The Standard Edition of the Complete Psychological Works of Sigmund Freud. Trans. Strachey, James. Vol XIV (1914–16) London, The Hogarth Press, 1957, 243–58.

Frow, John. 'The Politics of Stolen Time'. *Meanjin* 57:2 (1998): 351–67.

Fuss, Diana (ed.), *Inside/Out:Lesbian Theories, Gay Theories.* New York & London, Routledge, 1991.

Garis, Leslie. 'Through West Indian Eyes'. *New York Times Magazine* 7 (October 1990): 42–4, 70, 78–80 and 91.

Gates, Henry Louis, Jr *The Signifying Monkey: A Theory of African-American Literary Criticism.* New York: Oxford University Press, 1988.

Genovese, Eugene D. *From Rebellion to Revolution: Afro-American Slave Revolts in the Making of the Modern World.* New York: Vintage, 1981.

Gilbert, Sandra M. and Gubar, Susan. *The Madwoman in the Attic: The Woman Writer and the Nineteenth-Century Literary Imagination.* New Haven & London: Yale University Press, 1979.

Gilroy, Paul. *The Black Atlantic: Modernity and Double Consciousness.* London & New York: Verso, 1996.

Glissant, Édouard. *Poetics of Relation.* Trans. Wing, Betsy. Ann Arbor: University of Michigan Press, 1997.

Grant, Robert. 'Absence into Presence: The Thematics of Memory and "Missing" Subjects in Toni Morrison's *Sula.*' *Critical Essays on Toni Morrison.* McKay, Nellie Y. (ed.) Boston: G.K. Hall, 1988, 90–103.

Grosz, Elizabeth. *Volatile Bodies: Toward A Corporeal Feminism.* St Leonards, NSW: Allen & Unwin; Bloomington: Indiana University Press, 1994.

Grubrich-Simitis, Ilse. 'From Concretism to Metaphor: Thoughts on Some Theoretical and Technical Aspects of the Psychoanalytic Work with Children of the Holocaust'. *The Psychoanalytic Study of the Child*, Vol. 39, New Haven: Yale University Press, 1984: 301–19.

Guerrero, Edward. 'Tracking "The Look" in the Novels of Toni Morrison'. *Black American Literature Forum* 24:4 (1990): 761–73.

Hammonds, Evelynn M. 'Toward a Genealogy of Black Female Sexuality: The Problematic of Silence'. *Feminist Genealogies, Colonial Legacies, Democratic Futures.* Alexander, M. Jacqui and Mohanty, Chandra Talpade (eds). New York & London: Routledge, 1997, 170–82.

Harasym, Sarah (ed.). *The Post-Colonial Critic: Interviews, Strategies, Dialogues*. New York & London: Routledge, 1990.

Harding, Wendy and Martin, Jacky. *A World of Difference: An Inter-Cultural Study of Toni Morrison's Novels*. Westport, CN & London: Greenwood Press, 1994.

Harris, Trudier. *Fiction and Folklore: The Novels of Toni Morrison*. Knoxville: University of Tennessee Press, 1991.

Harrison, Nancy R. *Jean Rhys and the Novel as Women's Text*. Chapel Hill & London: University of North Carolina Press, 1988.

Hart, Richard. *Slaves Who Abolished Slavery, Vol. I, Blacks in Bondage*. Kingston, Jamaica: Institute of Social and Economic Research, University of West Indies, 1980, *Vol. II, Blacks in Rebellion*. Kingston, Jamaica: Institute of Social and Economic Research, University of West Indies, 1985.

Hartigan, John Jr. 'Unpopular Culture: The Case of "White Trash."' *Cultural Studies* 11:2 (1997): 316–43.

Henke, Suzette A. *Shattered Subjects: Trauma and Testimony in Women's Life-Writing*. New York: St Martin's Press (now Palgrave Macmillan), 1998.

Herman, Judith Lewis. *Trauma and Recovery: From Domestic Abuse to Political Terror*. London: Pandora, 1992.

Hill Collins, Patricia. *Black Feminist Thought: Knowledge, Consciousness, and the Politics of Empowerment*. New York & London: Routledge, 1990.

Hill Collins, Patricia. 'Shifting the Center: Race, Class and Feminist Theorizing about Motherhood'. *Mothering: Ideology, Experience and Agency*. Nakana Glenn, Evelyn, Chang, Grace, and Rennie Forcey, Linda (eds). New York & London: Routledge, 1994, 45–65.

Hill, Mike (ed.). *Whiteness: A Critical Reader*. New York & London: New York University Press, 1997.

Hirsch, Marianne. *The Mother/Daughter Plot: Narrative, Psychoanalysis, Feminism*. Bloomington & Indianapolis: Indian University Press, 1989.

Hoffarth-Zelloe, Monika. 'Resolving the Paradox?: An Interlinear Reading of Toni Morrison's *Sula*'. *Journal of Narrative Technique* 22:2 (1992): 114–27.

Hollander, John. *The Figure of Echo: A Mode of Allusion in Milton and After*. Berkeley, Los Angeles & London: University of California Press, 1981.

Holloway, Karla F.C. *Moorings & Metaphors: Figures of Culture and Gender in Black Women's Literature*. New Brunswick, NJ: Rutgers University Press, 1992.

Holloway, Karla F.C. *Codes of Conduct: Race, Ethics, and the Color of Our Character*. New Brunswick, NJ: Rutgers University Press, 1995.

hooks, bell. *Talking Back: Thinking Feminist, Thinking Black*. London: Sheba, 1989.

hooks, bell. *Black Looks: Race and Representation*. Boston MA: South End Press, 1992.

Horner, Avril and Zlosnik, Sue. *Landscapes of Desire: Metaphors in Modern Women's Fiction*. New York & London: Harvester Wheatsheaf, 1990.

Hull, Gloria T. 'Living on the Line: Audre Lorde and *Our Dead Behind Us*'. *Changing Our Own Words: Essays on Criticism, Theory, and Writing by Black Women*. Wall, Cheryl A. (ed.), London: Routledge, 1990, 150–72.

Hulme, Peter and Whitehead, Neil L. (eds). *Wild Majesty: Encounters with Caribs from Colombus to the Present Day*. Oxford: Clarendon Press, New York: Oxford University Press, 1992.

Hurston, Zora Neale. *Tell My Horse: Voodoo and Life in Haiti and Jamaica* [1938]. New York: Perennial, 1990.

Hurston, Zora Neale. *Their Eyes Are Watching God* [1937]. London: Virago, 1992.

Hurston, Zora Neale. 'Characteristics of Negro Expression' [1934]. *African-American Literary Theory: A Reader*. Napier, Winston (ed.). New York & London: New York University Press, 2000, 31–44.

James, C.L.R. *The Black Jacobins: Touissant Louverture and the San Domingo Revolution*. London: Secker and Warburg, 1938.

Jefferson, Thomas. *The Portable Thomas Jefferson*, Peterson, Merrill D. (ed.). New York: Penguin, 1977.

Johnson, Barbara. '"Aesthetic" and "rapport" in Toni Morrison's *Sula*'. *Textual Practice* 7:2 (1993): 165–72.

Jones, Gayl. *Liberating Voices: Oral Tradition in African American Literature*. Cambridge, MA & London: Harvard University Press, 1991.

Jordan, June. *Naming Our Destiny: New and Selected Poems*. New York: Thunder's Mouth Press, 1989.

Katrak, Ketu H. 'Colonialism, Imperialism, and Imagined Homes'. *The Columbia History of the American Novel*. Davidson, Cathy N., O'Donnell, Patrick, Smith, Valerie and Wilson, Christopher P. (eds). New York: Columbia University Press, 1991, 649–78.

Keating, AnnLouise. 'Interrogating "Whiteness," (De)Constructing "Race"'. *College English* 57:8 (1995): 901–18.

Kincaid, Jamaica. *Annie John*. New York: Plume, 1985.

Kincaid, Jamaica. *Lucy*. [1990]. London: Picador, 1994.

Kincaid, Jamaica. *My Brother*. New York: Farrar, Straus and Giroux, 1997.

Kincaid, Jamaica. *My Garden (Book)*. New York: Farrar, Straus and Giroux, 1999.

Kincheloe, Joe L., Steinberg, Shirley R., Rodriguez, Nelson M. and Chennault, Ronald E. (eds). *White Reign: Deploying Whiteness in America*. New York: St Martin's Press (now Palgrave Macmillan), 1998.

Kincheloe, Joe L. 'The Struggle to Define and Reinvent Whiteness: A Pedagogical Analysis'. *College Literature* 26:3 (1999): 162–93.

Kirmayer, Laurence J. 'Landscapes of Memory: Trauma, Narrative, and Dissociation'. *Tense Past: Cultural Essays in Trauma and Memory*, Antze, Paul and Lambek, Michael (eds). New York & London: Routledge, 1996, 173–98.

Kleber, Rolf, Figley, Charles, Gersons, Berthold (eds). *Beyond Trauma: Cultural and Societal Dynamics*. New York & London: Plenum Press, 1995.

Kloepfer, Deborah Kelly. *The Unspeakable Mother: Forbidden Discourse in Jean Rhys and H.D.* Ithaca & London: Cornell University Press, 1989.

Koenen, Anne. 'The One Out of Sequence'. *Conversations with Toni Morrison*. Taylor-Guthrie, Danille (ed.). Jackson: University of Mississippi, 1994, 67–83.

Kristeva, Julia. *Powers of Horror: An Essay on Abjection*. Trans. Roudiez, Leon S. New York: Columbia University Press, 1982.

LaCapra, Dominick. *Representing the Holocaust: History, Theory, Trauma*. Ithaca & London: Cornell University Press, 1994.

LaCapra, Dominick. 'Trauma, Absence, Loss', *Critical Inquiry* 25:4 (1999): 696–727.

LaCapra, Dominick. *Writing History, Writing Trauma*. Baltimore & London: Johns Hopkins University Press, 2001.

Lambek, Michael and Antze, Paul. 'Introduction: Forecasting Memory'. *Tense Past: Cultural Essays in Trauma and Memory*, Antze, Paul and Lambek, Michael (eds). New York & London: Routledge, 1996, xi–xxxviii.

Laroche, Maximilien. 'The Myth of the Zombi'. *Exile and Tradition: Studies in African and Caribbean Literature.* Smith, Rowland (ed.). London: Longman & Dalhousie University Press, 1976, 44–61.

Laub, Dori amd Allard, Marjorie. 'History, Memory, and Truth: Defining The Place of the Survivor'. *The Holocaust and History: The Known, The Unknown, The Disputed, and The Reexamined.* Berenbaum, Michael and Peck, Abraham J. (eds). Bloomington & Indianapolis: Indiana University Press, 1998, 799–812.

Laub, Dori and Podell, Daniel. 'Art and Trauma'. *International Journal of Psycho-Analysis* 76 (1995): 991–1005.

Lazarre, Jane. *The Mother Knot.* New York: McGraw-Hill, 1976.

Lemke, Sieglinde. *Primitivist Modernism: Black Culture and the Origins of Transatlantic Modernism.* Oxford & New York: Oxford University Press, 1998.

Lester, Cheryl. 'Meditations on a Bird in the Hand: Ethics and Aesthetics by Toni Morrison'. *The Aesthetics of Toni Morrison: Speaking the Unspeakable.* Conner, Marc C. (ed.) Jackson: University of Mississippi, 2000, 125–38.

Leys, Ruth. *Trauma: A Genealogy.* Chicago & London: University of Chicago Press, 2000.

Lifton, Robert Jay. *The Broken Connection: On Death and the Continuity of Life.* New York: Simon and Schuster, 1979.

Lifton, Robert Jay. *Death in Life: Survivors of Hiroshima* [1968]. Chapel Hill & London: University of North Carolina Press, 1991.

Liggins Hill, Patricia (ed.) *Call and Response: The Riverside Anthology of the African American Literary Tradition.* Boston & New York: Houghton Mifflin, 1998.

Lincoln, C. Eric and Mamiya, Lawrence H. *The Black Church in the African American Experience.* Durham & London: Duke University Press, 1990.

Lipsitz, George. *The Possessive Investment in Whiteness: How White People Profit from Identity Politics.* Philadelphia: Temple University Press, 1998.

Loe, Thomas. 'Patterns of the Zombie in Jean Rhys's *Wide Sargasso Sea*'. *World Literature Written in English* 31:1 (1991): 34–42.

Lonsdale, Roger. *The Poems of Thomas Gray, William Collins, Oliver Goldsmith.* London: Longmans, 1969.

Lonsdale, Thorunn. 'Literary Allusion in the Fiction of Jean Rhys'. *Caribbean Women Writers: Fiction in English.* Condé, Mary and Lonsdale, Thorunn (eds). New York: St Martin's Press (now Palgrave Macmillan), 1999, 43–74.

Lorde, Audre. 'The Transformation of Silence into Language and Action'. *Sister Outsider: Essays and Speeches.* Freedom, CA: The Crossing Press, 1984, 40–4.

Lorde, Audre. 'Eye to Eye: Black Women, Hatred, and Anger'. *Sister Outsider: Essays and Speeches.* Freedom CA: The Crossing Press, 1984, 145–75.

Lorde, Audre. *The Marvelous Arithmetics of Distance: Poems 1987–1992.* New York & London: Norton, 1993.

Lorde, Audre. *The Black Unicorn* [1978]. New York: Norton, 1995.

Lubiano, Wahneema. 'Mapping the Interstices between Afro-American Cultural Discourse and Cultural Studies'. *Callaloo* 19:1 (1996): 68–77.

Mahlis, Kristen. 'Gender and Exile: Jamaica Kincaid's *Lucy*'. *Modern Fiction Studies* 44:1 (1998): 164–83.

Mathews, Mitford M. *Dictionary of Americanisms: On Historical Principles.* Chicago, University of Chicago Press, 1951.

Matus, Jill. *Toni Morrison.* Manchester & London: Manchester University Press, 1998.

McClintock, Anne. *Imperial Leather: Race, Gender and Sexuality in the Colonial Conquest*. New York & London: Routledge, 1995.

McDowell, Deborah E. '"The Self and the Other": Reading Toni Morrison's *Sula* and the Black Female Text'. *Critical Essays on Toni Morrison*. Nellie Y. McKay (ed.). Boston: G.K. Hall, 1988, 77–90.

McDowell, Deborah E. 'Boundaries: Or Distant Relations and Close Kin'. *Afro-American Literary Study in the 1990s*. Baker Jr, Houston A. and Redmond, Patricia (eds). Chicago & London: University of Chicago Press, 1989, 51–70.

McDowell, Deborah E. 'New Directions for Black Feminist Criticism' [1980]. *'The Changing Same': Black Women's Literature, Criticism and Theory*. Bloomington & Indianapolis: Indiana University Press, 1995.

McKee, Patricia. *Producing American Races: Henry James, William Faulkner, Toni Morrison*. Durham & London: Duke University Press, 1999.

Meyer, Susan. *Imperialism at Home: Race and Victorian Women's Fiction*. Ithaca & London: Cornell University Press, 1996.

Mezei, Kathy. '"And it Kept its Secret": Narration, Memory, and Madness in Jean Rhys's *Wide Sargasso Sea'. Critique* 28:4 (1987): 195–209.

Michaels, Walter Benn. '"You who was never there": Slavery and the New Historicism, Deconstruction and the Holocaust'. *Narrative* 4:1 (1996): 1–16.

Michie, Helena. *Sororophobia: Differences Among Women in Literature and Culture*. New York & Oxford: Oxford University Press, 1992.

Milton, John. *Paradise Lost* [1667]. Ricks, Christopher (ed.). London: Penguin, 1968.

Morgenstern, Naomi. 'Mother's Milk and Sister's Blood: Trauma and the Neo-slave Narrative'. *Differences: A Journal of Feminist Cultural Studies* 8:2 (1996): 101–26.

Morrison, Andrew P. *Shame: The Underside of Narcissism*. Hove & London: The Analytic Press, 1989.

Morrison, Toni. 'Recitatif', *Confirmation: An Anthology of African American Women*. Baraka, Amiri (LeRoi Jones) and Baraka, Amina (eds). New York: William Morrow, 1983, 243–61.

Morrison, Toni. 'Memory, Creation, and Writing'. *Thought* 59:235 (1984): 385–90.

Morrison, Toni. 'Rootedness: The Ancestor as Foundation'. *Black Women Writers: Arguments and Interviews*. Evans, Mari (ed.). London & Sydney: Pluto Press, 1985, 339–45.

Morrison, Toni. 'The Site of Memory'. *Inventing the Truth: The Art and Craft of Memoir*. Zinsser, William (ed.). Boston: Houghton Mifflin, 1987, 103–24.

Morrison, Toni. *Beloved*. [1987] London: Picador, 1988.

Morrison, Toni. 'Unspeakable Things Unspoken: The Afro-American Presence in American Literature'. *Michigan Quarterly Review* 28 (1989): 1–34.

Morrison, Toni. *Sula* [1973]. London: Picador, 1991.

Morrison, Toni. *Playing in the Dark: Whiteness and the Literary Imagination. The William E. Massey Sr. Lectures in the History of American Civilization*. London: Picador, 1993a.

Morrison, Toni. 'The Art of Fiction CXXXIV'. *The Paris Review* 128 (1993b): 82–125.

Morrison, Toni. *The Bluest Eye* [1970]. London: Chatto & Windus, 1993c.

Morrison, Toni. 'Home'. *The House That Race Built: Black Americans, U.S. Terrain*. Lubiano, Wahneema (ed.). New York: Pantheon, 1997, 3–12.

Moya, Paula M.L. 'Postmodernism, "Realism," and the Politics of Identity: Cherríe Moraga and Chicana Feminism'. *Feminist Genealogies, Colonial Legacies, Democratic Futures*. Alexander, M. Jacqui and Mohanty, Chandra Talpade (eds). New York & London: Routledge, 1997, 125–50.

Munro, C. Lynn. 'The Tattooed Heart and the Serpentine Eye: Morrison's Choice of an Epigraph for *Sula*'. *Black American Literature Forum* 18 (1984): 150–4.

Naipaul, V.S. *The Mimic Men*. London: André Deutsch, 1967.

Nasta, Susheila (ed.). *Motherlands: Black Women's Writing from Africa, the Caribbean and South Asia*. London: The Women's Press, 1991.

Newitz, Annalee and Wray, Mathew. 'What is "White Trash"? Stereotypes and Economic Conditions of Poor Whites in the United States'. *Whiteness: A Critical Reader*. Hill, Mike (ed.). New York & London: 1997, 168–84.

Nichols, Grace. *I is a long memoried woman*. London: Caribbean Cultural International, Karnak House, 1983.

Nnaemeka, Obioma. 'Introduction: Imag(in)ing knowledge, power, and subversion in the margins'. *The Politics of (M)Othering: Womanhood, Identity, and Resistance in African Literature*. Nnaemeka, Obioma (ed.). London & New York: Routledge, 1997, 1–25.

Nwankwo, Chimalum. '"I is": Toni Morrison, the Past, and Africa'. *Of Dreams Deferred, Dead or Alive: Perspectives on African-American Writers*. Ojo-Ada, Femi (ed.). Westport, CN & London: Greenwood Press, 1996, 171–80.

O'Connor, Teresa. *Jean Rhys: The West Indian Novels*. New York & London: New York University Press, 1986.

Ogunyemi, Chikwenye Okonjo. '*Sula*: "A Nigger Joke"'. *Black American Literature Forum* 13 (1979): 130–3.

Ovid. *The Metamorphoses of Ovid*. Trans. & ed. Innes, Mary M. London: Penguin, 1955.

Pajaczkowska, Claire, and Young, Lola. 'Racism, Representation, Psychoanalysis'. Donald, James and Rattansi, Ali (eds). *'Race', Culture and Difference*. London: Sage, 1992, 198–219.

Paravisini-Gebert, Lizabeth. *Jamaica Kincaid: A Critical Companion*. Westport, CN & London: Greenwood Press, 1999.

Parry, Benita. 'Problems in Current Theories of Colonial Discourse'. *Oxford Literary Review* 9 (1987): 27–58.

Patterson, Orlando. *The Sociology of Slavery: An Analysis of the Origins, Development and Structure of Negro Slave Society in Jamaica*. London: MacGibbon & Kee, 1967.

Patterson, Orlando. *Slavery and Social Death: A Comparative Study*. Cambridge, MA: Harvard University Press, 1982.

Phillips, Caryl. *The European Tribe* [1987]. New York: Vintage, 2000.

Pollock, Griselda. *Avant-Garde Gambits 1888–1893: Gender and the Colour of Art History*. London: Thames and Hudson, 1992.

Price, Richard. 'Introduction: Maroons and Their Communities'. *Maroon Societies: Rebel Slave Communities in the Americas*. Price, Richard (ed.). New York: Anchor, 1973, 1–30.

Probyn, Elspeth. 'This Body Which Is Not One: Speaking the Embodied Self'. *Hypatia* 6:3 (1991): 111–24.

Pullin, Faith. 'Landscapes of Reality: The Fictions of Contemporary Afro-

American Women'. *Black Fiction: New Studies in the Afro-American Novel since 1945*. Lee, A. Robert (ed.). London: Vision, 1980, 173–203.

Raiskin, Judith L. *Snow on the Canefields: Women's Writing and Creole Subjectivity*. Minneapolis & London, University of Minnesota Press, 1996.

Ramchand, Kenneth. *The West Indian Novel and its Background*. London: Faber & Faber, 1970.

Reddy, Maureen T. 'The Tripled Plot and Center of *Sula*'. *Black American Literature Forum* 22:1 (1988): 29–45.

Rhys, Jean. *Voyage in the Dark* [1934]. London: Penguin, 1969.

Rhys, Jean. *Smile Please: An Unfinished Autobiography*. London: Penguin, 1981.

Rhys, Jean. *Wide Sargasso Sea* [1966] London: Penguin, 1997.

Rice, Alan J. ' "It Don't Mean a Thing If It Ain't Got That Swing": Jazz's Many Uses for Toni Morrison'. *Black Orpheus: Music in African American Fiction from the Harlem Renaissance to Toni Morrison*. Simawe, Saadi A. (ed.) New York & London: Garland, 2000, 153–80.

Richardson, Alan. 'Romantic Voodoo: *Obeah* and British Culture, 1797–1807'. *Sacred Possessions: Vodou, Santería, Obeah, and the Caribbean*. Fernández Olmos, Margarite, and Paravisini-Gebert, Lizabeth (eds). New Brunswick, NJ: Rutgers University Press, 1997, 171–92.

Robinson, Jr, Alonford James. 'Underground Railroad'. *Africana: The Encyclopedia of the African and African American Experience*. Appiah, Kwame Anthony and Gates, Jr, Henry Louis (eds). New York: Basic Civitas Books, 1999, 1915–18.

Rody, Caroline. 'Burning Down the House: The Revisionary Paradigm of Jean Rhys's *Wide Sargasso Sea*'. *Famous Last Words: Changes in Gender and Narrative Closure*. Booth, Alison (ed.). Charlottesville: University Press of Virginia, 1993, 300–25.

Roman, Leslie G. 'White is a Color! White Defensiveness, Postmodernism, and Anti-Racist Pedagogy'. *Race, Identity and Representation in Education*. McCarthy, Cameron and Crichlow, Warren (eds). New York: Routledge, 1993, 71–88.

Ruas, Charles. 'Toni Morrison'. *Conversations with Toni Morrison*. Danille Taylor-Guthrie (ed.). Jackson: University Press of Mississippi, 1994, 93–118.

Ruddick, Sara. 'Maternal Thinking'. *Feminist Studies* 6 (1980): 342–67.

Sacks, Sheldon. *On Metaphor*. Chicago & London: University of Chicago Press, 1979.

Said, Edward W. *Culture and Imperialism*. New York: Knopf, 1993.

Samuels, Wilfred D. and Hudson-Weems, Clenora. *Toni Morrison*. Boston, Twayne Publishers, 1990.

Sandoval, Chela. 'The Theory and Method of Oppositional Consciousness in the Postmodern World'. *Genders* 10 (1991): 1–24.

Savory, Elaine. *Jean Rhys*. Cambridge: Cambridge University Press, 1998.

Seshadri-Crooks, Kalpana. *Desiring Whiteness: A Lacanian Analysis of Race*. London & New York: Routledge, 2000.

Showalter, Elaine. *The Female Malady: Women, Madness, and English Culture, 1830–1980*. London: Virago, 1991.

Simmons, Diane. *Jamaica Kincaid*. New York: Twayne, 1994.

Simmons, Diane. 'Jamaica Kincaid and the Canon: In Dialogue with *Paradise Lost* and *Jane Eyre*'. *Melus* 23:2 (1998): 65–85.

Simons, Margaret A. *Beauvoir and The Second Sex: Feminism, Race, and the Origins of Existentialism*. Lanham, Maryland & Oxford: Rowman & Littlefield, 1999.

Sledge, William Hurt. 'The Therapist's Use of Metaphor'. *International Journal of Psychoanalytic Psychotherapy* 6 (1977): 113–30.

Smith, Amanda. 'Toni Morrison'. *Publishers Weekly* (21 August 1987): 50.

Smith, Valerie. *Self-Discovery and Authority in Afro-American Narrative*. Cambridge, MA & London: Harvard University Press, 1987.

Smith, Valerie. 'Black Feminist Theory and the Representation of the "Other"'. *Changing Our Own Words: Essays on Criticism, Theory, and Writing by Black Women*. Wall, Cheryl A. (ed.) London: Routledge, 1990, 38–57.

Smitherman, Geneva. *Talkin and Testifyin: The Language of Black America*. Detroit: Wayne State University Press, 1977.

Smitherman, Geneva. *Black Talk: Words and Phrases from the Hood to the Amen Corner*. Boston & New York: Houghton Mifflin, 1994.

Spillers, Hortense J. 'Interstices: A Small Drama of Words'. *Pleasure and Danger: Exploring Female Sexuality*. Vance, Carole (ed.). Boston: Routledge & Kegan Paul, 1984, 73–100.

Spillers, Hortense J. 'Mama's Baby, Papa's Maybe: An American Grammar Book', *Diacritics* 17 (1987): 65–81.

Spillers, Hortense J. 'Notes on an alternative model – neither/nor'. *The Difference Within: Feminism and Critical Theory*. Meese, Elizabeth and Parker, Alice (eds). Amsterdam & Philadelphia: John Benjamins Publishing, 1989a, 165–87.

Spillers, Hortense J. 'Response'. *Afro-American Literary Study in the 1990s*. Baker Jr, Houston A. and Redmond, Patricia (eds). Chicago & London: University of Chicago Press, 1989b, 71–3.

Spivak, Gayatri Chakravorty. 'Three Women's Texts and a Critique of Imperialism'. *Critical Inquiry* 12 (1985): 243–61.

Spivak, Gayatri Chakravorty. '"Can the Subaltern Speak?"'. *Marxism and the Interpretation of Culture*. Nelson, Cary and Grossberg, Laurence (eds). Urbana & Chicago: University of Illinois Press, 1988a, 271–313.

Spivak, Gayatri Chakravorty. 'Subaltern Studies: Deconstructing Historiography'. *In Other Worlds: Essays in Cultural Politics*. New York & London: Routledge, 1988b, 197–221.

Spivak, Gayatri Chakravorty. 'Imperialism and Sexual Difference'. *Contemporary Literary Criticism: Literary and Critical Studies*. Davis, Robert Con and Schleifer, Ronald (eds). New York & London: Longman, 1989, 517–29.

Spivak, Gayatri Chakravorty. 'Questions of Multi-culturalism'. *The Post-Colonial Critic: Interviews, Strategies, Dialogues*. Harasym, Sarah (ed.). New York & London: Routledge, 1990, 59–66.

Spivak, Gayatri Chakravorty. *Outside in the Teaching Machine*. New York & London: Routledge, 1993.

Spivak, Gayatri Chakravorty. 'Echo'. *The Spivak Reader: Selected Works of Gayatri Chakravorty Spivak*. Landry, Donna and MacLean, Gerald (eds). New York & London: Routledge, 1996, 175–202.

Spurr, David. *Rhetoric of Empire: Colonial Discourse in Journalism, Travel Writing, and Imperial Administration*. Durham & London: Duke University Press, 1993.

Starr, H.W. and Hendrickson, J.R. (eds). *The Complete Poems of Thomas Gray: English, Latin and Greek*. Oxford: Clarendon Press, 1966.

Stein, Karen. ' "I Didn't Even Know His Name": Names and Naming in Toni Morrison's *Sula'. Names: Journal of the American Name Society* (1980): 226–9.

Sternlicht, Sanford. *Jean Rhys.* New York: Twayne, London: Prentice Hall, 1997.

Stevens, Paul. 'Milton and the New World: Custom, Relativism, and the Discipline of Shame'. *Milton and the Imperial Vision.* Rajan, Balachandra and Sauer, Elizabeth (eds). Pittsburgh, PA: Duquesne University Press, 1999, 90–111.

Suleiman, Susan Rubin. 'Nadja, Dora, Lol V. Stein: women, madness and narrative'. *Discourse in Psychoanalysis and Literature.* Rimmon-Kennan, Shlomith (ed.). London & New York: Methuen, 1987, 124–51.

Sundquist, Eric J. *To Wake the Nations: Race in the Making of American Literature.* Cambridge, MA & London: The Belknap Press of Harvard University Press, 1993.

Tate, Claudia (ed.). *Black Women Writers at Work.* New York: Continuum, 1985.

Taylor, Carole Anne. *The Tragedy and Comedy of Resistance: Reading Modernity Through Black Women's Fiction.* Philadelphia: University of Pennsylvania Press, 2000.

Terborg-Penn, Rosalyn. 'Black Women in Resistance: A Cross-Cultural Perspective'. *In Resistance: Studies in African, Caribbean, and Afro-American History.* Okihiro, Gary Y. (ed.) Amherst: University of Massachusetts Press, 1986, 188–209.

Thomas, Sue. *The Worlding of Jean Rhys.* Westport, CN & London: Greenwood Press, 1999.

Tiffin, Helen. 'Cold Hearts and (Foreign) Tongues: Recitation and the Reclamation of the Female Body in the Works of Erna Brodber and Jamaica Kincaid'. *Callaloo* 16:3 (1993): 909–21.

Tiffin, Helen. ' "Flowers of Evil," Flowers of Empire: Roses and Daffodils in the Work of Jamaica Kincaid, Olive Senior and Lorna Goodison'. *Span* 46 (1998): 58–71.

Todorov, Tzvetan. *The Conquest of America.* Trans. Howard, Richard. New York: Harper & Row, 1984.

Varadharajan, Asha. *Exotic Parodies: Subjectivity in Adorno, Said, and Spivak.* Minneapolis & London: University of Minnesota Press, 1995.

Viswanathan, Gauri. 'Milton and Education'. *Milton and the Imperial Vision.* Rajan, Balachandra and Sauer, Elizabeth (eds). Pittsburgh, PA: Duquesne University Press, 1999, 273–93.

Vorda, Allan. 'An Interview with Jamaica Kincaid'. *Mississippi Review* 20 (1991): 7–26.

Wachtel, Eleanor. 'Eleanor Wachtel with Jamaica Kincaid'. *The Malahat Review* 116 (1996): 55–71.

Waites, Elizabeth A. *Trauma and Survival: Post-Traumatic and Dissociative Disorders in Women.* New York & London: Norton, 1993.

Walcott, Derek. 'The Caribbean: Culture or Mimicry?' *Journal of Interamerican Studies and World Affairs* 16:1 (1974a): 3–13.

Walcott, Derek. 'The Muse of History: An Essay'. *Is Massa Dead? Black Moods in the Caribbean.* Coombs, Orde (ed.). London: Anchor Books, 1974b, 1–27.

Walcott, Derek. *Collected Poems 1948–1984.* New York: Farrar, Straus & Giroux, 1986.

Walcott, Rinaldo. 'Pedagogy and Trauma: The Middle Passage, Slavery, and the Problem of Creolization'. *Between Hope and Despair: Pedagogy and the*

Remembrance of Historical Trauma. Simon, Roger I., Rosenberg, Sharon and Eppert, Claudia (eds). Lanham, Boulder, New York & Oxford: Rowman & Littlefield, 2000, 135–51.

Walker, Alice. 'In Search of Our Mothers' Gardens,' [1974]. *In Search of Our Mothers' Gardens: Womanist Prose.* London: The Women's Press, 1992, 231–43.

Wall, Cheryl A. 'Review of Houston Baker Jr.'s *Modernism and the Harlem Renaissance* and Melvin Dixon's *Ride Out the Wilderness: Geography and Identity in Afro-American Literature'. American Literature* 60 (1988): 680–2.

Wall, Cheryl A. 'Introduction: Taking Positions and Changing Words'. *Changing Our Own Words: Essays on Criticism, Theory, and Writing by Black Women.* Wall, Cheryl A. (ed.) London, Routledge, 1990, 1–15.

Wallace, Michelle. 'Variations on Negation and the Heresy of Black Feminist Creativity'. *Invisibility Blues: From Pop to Theory.* London & New York: Verso, 1990, 213–40.

Ware, Vron. *Beyond the Pale: White Women, Racism and History.* London & New York: Verso, 1992.

Washington, Mary Helen. 'Introduction'. Washington, Mary Helen (ed.). *Memory of Kin: Stories About Family by Black Writers.* New York: Doubleday, 1991, 1–8.

Weems, Renita. '"Artists Without Art Form": A Look at One Black Woman's World of Unrevered Black Women' [1979]. *Home Girls: A Black Feminist Anthology.* Smith, Barbara (ed.). New York: Kitchen Table: Women of Color Press, 1983, 94–105.

West, Cornel. 'W.E.B. Du Bois: An Interpretation'. *Africana: The Encyclopedia of the African American Experience,* Appiah, Kwame Anthony and Gates Jr, Henry Louis (eds). New York: Basic Civitas Books, 1999, 1967–82.

Wilkerson, Abby. 'Ending at the Skin: Sexuality and Race in Feminist Theorizing'. *Hypatia* 12:3 (1997): 164–73.

Williams, Eric. *Capitalism and Slavery.* London: Andre Deutsch, 1964.

Williams, Patricia J. *Seeing a Colour-Blind Future: The Paradox of Race; The 1997 Reith Lectures.* London: Virago, 1997.

Williams, Sherley Anne. 'Some Implications of Womanist Theory'. *Reading Black, Reading Feminist: A Critical Anthology.* Gates Jr, Henry Louis (ed.). New York & London: Meridian, 1990, 68–75.

Williams, Sherley Anne. 'The Blues Roots of Contemporary Afro-American Poetry'. *Afro-American Literature: The Reconstruction of Instruction.* Fisher, Dexter and Stepto, Robert B. (eds). New York: The Modern Language Association of America, 1979, 72–87.

Willis, Susan. 'Black women writers: taking a critical perspective'. *Making a Difference: Feminist Literary Criticism.* Greene, Gayle and Kahn, Coppélia (eds). London & New York: Routledge, 1985, 211–37.

Wing, Betsy. 'Translator's Introduction', *Poetics of Relation,* Édouard Glissant, trans. Betsy Wing. Ann Arbor: University of Michigan Press, 1997.

Witzum, Eliezer, Dasberg, Haim and Bleich, Abraham. 'Use of a Metaphor in the Treatment of Combat-induced Posttraumatic Stress Disorder: Case Report'. *American Journal of Psychotherapy.* XL:3 (1986): 457–65.

Wordsworth, William. 'I Wandered Lonely As A Cloud'. *The Selected Poetry and Prose of Wordsworth,* Geoffrey Hartman (ed.), New York: Meridian, 1980.

Wyndham, Francis and Melly, Diana (eds). *Jean Rhys Letters 1931–1966.* London: Penguin, 1985.

Xie, Shaobo. 'Rethinking the Problem of Postcolonialism'. *New Literary History* 28:1 (1997): 7–19.

Young, Allan. 'Bodily Memory and Traumatic Memory'. *Tense Past: Cultural Essays in Trauma and Memory.* Antze, Paul and Lambek, Michael (eds). New York & London: Routledge, 1996, 89–102.

Young, Robert J.C. 'Neocolonial Times'. *Oxford Literary Review* 13 (1991): 2–3.

Young, Robert J.C. *Colonial Desire: Hybridity in Theory, Culture and Race.* London & New York: Routledge, 1995.

Index